SKY RIDGE HOTSHOTS
FIGHT
SLOANE ST. JAMES

Line Editing by Dee Houpt | www.DeesNotesEditingServices.com
Developmental Editing by Bri | DevEditingWithBri@gmail.com
Cover by The Whiskey Ginger | @whiskeygingergoods
Formatting by Cathryn | FormatByCC@gmail.com

1st Edition 2025

CONTENTS

🌶 One-handed reader shortcuts

GLOSSARY

Anchor point: a strategic location from which to start building a fire line, starting at a natural unburnable area, such as rock scree, creeks, or trails. The goal of an anchor point is to prevent the fire from burning around the fireline, pinning firefighters from behind.

Ash pit: a hole in the ground filled with hot ash and embers.

Backburn, backfire, or burnout: terms for intentionally putting fire on the ground and burning vegetation against an active flame front to deprive it of fuel.

Black: the area that is already burnt.

Buggy: a transportation vehicle consisting of seating with no water supply. It has a total of 8 seats allowing for a large amount of crew to be transported to the fire.

Chain: a unit of measurement, commonly used in wildland fires. Eighty chains equal one mile, so one chain is sixty-six feet long.

Control or containment line: any constructed or natural barrier used to impede a fire's progress.

Crampons: a metal plate with spikes fixed to a boot for walking on ice or rock climbing.

Crown fires: when canopies of trees light with flame. These are often the largest, hardest to contain, and fastest-moving fires. When one canopy ignites, that fire can begin jumping from tree to tree.

Division: the person who implements xan assigned portion of the Incident Action Plan (IAP) and is responsible for all operations conducted in the division/group, on wildland fire incidents.

Drip torch: a handheld tool used to set controlled fires, or prescribed burns, by intentionally igniting fires by dripping flaming fuel onto the ground.

Ember wash: a shower of hot embers, carried by the wind, often enabling the fire to "jump" over control lines and spread by creating spot fires. Embers can travel over a mile before falling.

Engine: a truck or other ground vehicle that can transport and pump water, via hoses, onto a fire.

Engine Crew: a team of up to ten firefighters attached to an engine, tasked with initial, direct engagement of a wildfire. They use a variety of tools, primarily relying on hoses and water.

Escape route: a predetermined route to allow firefighters to get to safety, should the situation become unsafe on the ground.

Fire-chasing beetles or Melanophila beetles: insects attracted to forest fires because they use freshly burnt (and sometimes still-smoldering) wood to lay their eggs. They gather near the fire and have a vicious bite, often attacking wildland firefighters while working on a fire line.

Fire line: A line of ground without vegetation that will presumably stop or direct a fire's progress. Firefighters dig line by hand, using Pulaskis and other tools.

Green: fuel-laden area that hasn't yet burned.

Hand Crew: general-purpose wildland firefighters. Hand crews are typically eighteen to twenty people and work on digging line, clearing trees and brush with chainsaws, and setting controlled burns with drip torches.

Helitack crew: a team of firefighters trained and certified to support helicopters to fight fires.

Helibucket or bucket work: a bucket that hangs from a helicopter by a cable and is used to transport and apply water or retardant directly onto a fire. Helibuckets can be dropped into a lake or river to refill with water, holding as much as 2,600 gallons.

Hotshots: an intensively trained team of wildland firefighters primarily tasked with directly engaging a fire and digging hand lines.

I-Met: the Incident meteorologist.

Incident Commander: the leader on a fire and one of as many as dozens of people managing the complex planning, safety, strategy, and operations on a conflagration.

Ladder fuels: flammable materials, like small trees or low limbs, that allow a fire to move from the forest floor up into the canopy, increasing the intensity and potential growth of a fire. When those fires grow larger and "ladder" up trees, they can ignite crown fires.

MRE: Meals Ready-to-Eat. A self-contained, lightweight ration that provides a full meal for an individual.

Nomex or Yellows: the yellow shirt worn by wildland firefighters. Nomex is a trademarked term for a flame-resistant fabric widely used for industrial applications and fire protection equipment.

Osborne Fire Finder: a type of alidade used by fire lookouts to find a directional bearing (azimuth) to smoke in order to alert fire crews to a wildland fire.

Prescribed or controlled burn: a planned fire that is intentionally set to achieve specific management goals such as reduce wildfire risk and restore natural ecosystems.

Pulaski: a tool with a head that has an ax blade on one side and an adze on the other.

Roll: a fire assignment.

Scree: a mass of small loose stones that form or cover a slope on a mountain.

Ship: a helicopter.

Snag: a dead, often fire-killed, standing tree that presents a hazard for firefighters on the ground.

Spot fire: an occurrence when embers drift across control lines, and settle on vegetation or other flammable material, igniting new flames.

Stihl: a brand of chainsaw, used by wildland firefighters to cut brush, snags, and debris.

Torching: when one or more trees go up in flames.

UTV: a Utility Terrain Vehicle. A motor vehicle designed for off-road use that's typically larger than an all-terrain vehicle (ATV) and is often used for work rather than recreation.

Volly firefighter: a volunteer [wildland] firefighter.

ORGANIZATION FLOW CHART

THERE ARE THOUSANDS OF PEOPLE FROM
VARIOUS COMMAND TEAMS INVOLVED WITH
WILDLAND FIRE OPERATIONS, BUT FOR THE
SAKE OF KEEPING IT SIMPLE, WE ARE ONLY
LISTING THE ROLES MENTIONED IN THE
SKY RIDGE HOTSHOTS SERIES.

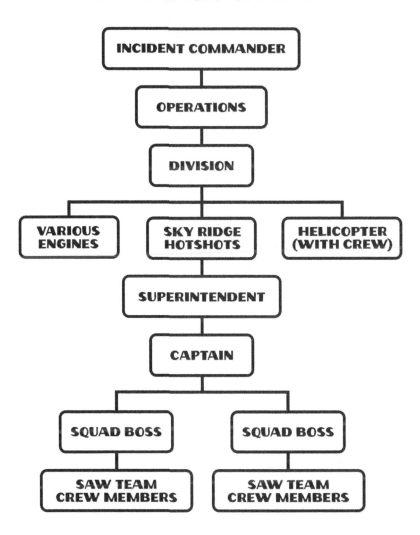

PLAYLIST

Prologue (Breaking Point (FU) - Logan Michael)
1. Pesticides - Moselle, Matt Hip
2. Bride at a Bar - Vwillz, Mike
3. Weren't For The Wind - Ella Langley
4. American Dream - Drayton Farley
5. Let it Burn - Shaboozey
6. Coal - Dylan Gossett
7. Risk - Gracie Abrams
8. Spin You Around - Morgan Wallen
9. Up In Flames - Leszewo
10. Straight and Narrow - Sam Barber
11. FMRN - Lilyisthatyou
12. Unhealthy - Anne Marie feat. Shania Twain
13. Smoke and a Light - Ole 60
14. White Mustang - Lana Del Ray
15. Ghost In My Guitar - Alana Springsteen
16. Twin Flame - Brennan Story
17. A Lot More Free - Max McNown
18. Ain't Doin' Jack - Josh Ross
19. Fuck Your Sunshine - Laszewo
20. Dead to Me - Viola
21. World on Fire - Nate Smith
22. Amnesia - Josh Abbott Band

23. Civilian - Wye Oak
24. Backroad - Lecade
25. It Is What It Is - Abe Parker
26. Good Die Young - Wetzel
27. Everything Under the Sun - Waylon Wyatt
28. The Emotion - BORNS
29. If I Were The Devil - Colby Acuff
30. Hold On - Chord Overstreet
31. Red Flags - Josh Ross
32. The Night We Met - Lord Huron
33. I'm The Sinner - Jared Benjamin
34. Everything We Need - Wilfred
35. Wine into Whiskey - Tucker Whitmore
36. Pitchin Fits - Drayton Farley
37. WOW - Zara Larsson
38. A Cigarette - Gavin Adcock
39. Burning Down - Alex Warren
40. Feathered Indians - Tyler Childers
41. Make It Out Alive - Matthew Gold
42. Maxed Out - Bayker Blankenship
43. Love is Beautifully Painful - Darkrose Ghost Duet
44. Religiously - Bailey Zimmerman
45. Beneath Oak Trees - Dylan Gossett
46. Half of Forever - Henrik
47. What He'll Never Have - Dylan Scott
48. Let It Burn - Jared Benjamin
49. Holy Smokes - Bailey Zimmerman
50. Skin and Bones - David Kushner
51. Shake the Frost - Tyler Childers

TROPES

Workplace romance, enemies to lovers, miscommunication, new girl in town, one bed, us vs. nature, strong FMC in peril, and reformed playboy

TRIGGERS

This book features abusive religious trauma, including conversion therapy and homophobia. There are also depictions of claustrophobia, natural disasters, close encounters with wildfire, C-PTSD, panic attacks, and flashbacks of witnessed death. If you are triggered by these situations, please skip this one.

CONTENT WARNING

This book contains profane language and explicit sexual scenes containing consensual breath play, use of restraints, cum play, cockwarming, spitting, mutual masturbation, praise, and light degradation.

SUPPORT WILDLAND FIREFIGHTERS

I won't call them heroes because they'd hate that, but I could not write this book without acknowledging the real wildland firefighters who perform these hazardous duties every fire season. They work long hours in treacherous conditions, facing extreme heat, smoke, and inhospitable terrain—oftentimes without receiving an adequate living wage and while sacrificing time with their loved ones. The challenges they face are beyond what most of us can imagine, taking a toll on their physical, mental, and emotional resilience. Their dedication to protect our communities, landscapes, and natural resources deserves our deepest appreciation and support.

Grassroots Wildland Firefighters advocate for proper classification, pay, benefits, and comprehensive wellbeing for federal wildland firefighters by providing solutions and support through policy reform.

If you would like to contribute monetarily, please consider donating at http://givebutter.com/GRWF

For S—
This book feels as much yours as it is mine.
Thank you for everything.

PROLOGUE

CALLAHAN

FIVE YEARS AGO

When did we start complimenting funerals, calling them *nice*? Who started that? I'd love to trip them up a flight of stairs. Comment after comment today has been admiring the service, as if it's the only small talk anyone knows how to make. Funerals are funerals. They all suck. However, this one is the worst... because I watched him die, and the fresh memory of his lifeless body plays on repeat in my thoughts. The only grace is that he went instantly.

It's a relief to leave the funeral home, but driving to Garrett's duplex seems equally, if not more, daunting. I'm not sure where they will put all these people, it's not a huge house. Along the residential street, I shift my truck into park behind many other vehicles belonging to friends and family.

Garrett Macomb was our leader, the superintendent of our hotshot crew, and the father of one of my best friends. Though many of our crew members would argue he was like a dad to all of us.

"You okay?" my fiancée, Molly, asks while flipping down the passenger visor and drawing on a fresh coat of lipstick. She's trying to be supportive, but there's an underlying tone in her voice. She's frustrated with me, and I can't blame her. Since watching Garrett die, I've been less and less present. My thoughts steal me away, and I'm constantly distracted.

With my work schedule, the time I have with Molly is short and valuable. We've been together since high school, then made a home in Sky Ridge, Washington, so I could chase my dream of fighting wildfires, and Molly found a great school to start her teaching career. In the beginning, things were great, but with each annual fire season that passes, the strain on our relationship grows. Fire assignments are fourteen days at a time, then it's only a few days at home for R&R before I'm sent somewhere new.

Occasionally, we'll have projects nearby, which gives us extra time together. She's my priority when I'm home, but she's pulling away. And lately, my mind is stuck at work. Every night when I go to sleep, that day plays on repeat in my mind. I have to get through these mental hang-ups, then I can figure out how to fix things at home and we can get back to normal again.

"Yeah," I lie. "I'll meet you inside. Just need a minute."

Sighing, she climbs out of the truck and straightens her dress, then I follow her with my eyes until she vanishes into the house. I gotta get my shit together, or I'll lose her too.

I'm struggling to gather the courage to walk through the front door of Garrett's home, where the reception is being held. Eventually, I pop the handle on my truck door and hop out. Closing it, I take a deep breath and an older woman dressed in black falls in stride next to me—Ruth Haggleberg, the town gossip. I've been so wrapped up in my thoughts I hadn't even noticed her and her casserole dish covered in tinfoil.

"Can I help you with that?" I offer.

"Why, thank you!" She passes it to me, and we stroll toward the house. Ruth beams up at me with a cheerful grin. "That was *such* a nice funeral."

Jesus Christ.

Inhaling through my nose, a stiff, tight-lipped smile is all I can offer. "Mm-hm."

She chatters about all the *nice* things said about Garrett during the eulogy, but I'm not listening. I wonder if there's any tequila left from the bottle King had earlier. We took a few pulls before the funeral service to get us through.

I tuck the casserole into my side when we reach the front steps, then open the front door for her.

"Such a gentleman!" Ruth croons.

She lightly pats the top of my hand and marches ahead of me.

"I'll bring this to the kitchen for you," I say before she disappears into the throng of guests. I enter the hall, and weave through the bodies crowding the living area, forging a path to the kitchen, where I not-so-gently deposit the pan onto the counter with a loud thunk. Not sure what the old bird made, but it's denser than lead.

Turning around, I scan the room for Molly but don't see her. A few people pass by me, and I step out of their way until I'm leaning against the wall. Then my gaze lands on Xander. I force myself to look at my best friend who I hardly recognize. Grief radiates from him; he'll never be the same.

It's as if Xander is hollow inside, gutted by the death of his father, and I was the one who held the knife. The day I had to notify my best friend that his dad died was the worst of my life. It will be a long time before I see the light in my friend again.

"Where's Molly?" King asks, startling me, then leaning against the wall at my side. He's my other best friend on the crew, and I appreciate his presence.

"She's around here somewhere…"

"Probably got cornered by ol' Ruthie."

I huff out a small laugh. "Brought in a casserole for that woman—I've swung axes that weighed less."

He shakes his head with a smirk, and we observe the masses while pinned against the wall.

"How are you feeling about the promotion?"

When I first earned my quals for a captain spot, I was ecstatic. The plan was simple. Garrett Macomb was set to retire at the end of the fire season, allowing Xander to take over as IHC Superintendent of the Sky Ridge Hotshots. I'd worked my ass off in preparation for Garrett's retirement so when Xander moved up, I could replace his role as captain. This promotion was a BFD.

It came with a much-needed pay bump and would allow me to give Molly her dream wedding. We're on year seven of our engagement; I promised her that wedding, and I'm not marrying her until I can give it to her. On top of that, the salary increase meant we could finally vacate our rental. There's a fixer-upper I've had my eye on since I moved here. The house is in rough shape, but it's within our budget and has a lot of potential. It might take time to get it there, but with some TLC, I have zero doubt.

Molly and I were thrilled the next phase of our life would start once this promotion happened. However, with Garrett's death being before the end of season, plans shifted. Now the would-be happy occasion has been marred by the death of our superintendent, and it doesn't feel like cause for celebration.

I shrug. "Wish it was under different circumstances, ya know?"

"We all do."

"It's weird being here, right? With all his stuff," I add, scanning the room.

Between the nearly wall-to-wall people are small memories of him. The recliner he watched baseball in is occupied by a stranger balancing a plate of food on their lap. I shake my head when a glob of dip spills off the side of the plate and onto the floor. It will likely be mashed into the carpet when somebody walks over it later.

Pictures of Xander and his family adorn the walls. His mom and brothers flew in from Michigan for the funeral. I've heard Xander is getting the duplex, and at some point will be going through his dad's stuff. I don't know how he's going to handle that.

From the corner of my eye, I see Jacob, another guy on our crew, enter. His twin sister, Vi, is close behind. Steady chatter hums all around. It has an overall cheerful tone, like you might hear at a wedding reception or graduation party. It's the sound of people catching up on their lives and sharing fond memories of Garrett. I've avoided reminiscing. Every time I do, the thought is quickly overshadowed by the image of him right before he died. Fuck that.

Molly says I need to find a way to move on. I'm trying, but sometimes, it feels like I'll never get over this. No matter how much I want to. I met with a therapist, but after coming home exhausted and drained, I felt no better and had no energy left for Molly, which resulted in a big argument that night, then she stayed at a friend's place. Whatever issues are piling up in my brain, I can't allow them to rip my life apart at the seams. I need to find a way to shove it deep enough that it won't surface. Or at the very least, not let it show. Nobody would understand the shift in personality. This isn't like me, I'm supposed to be the easygoing one.

"What's weird is being here with this many people," King states, standing up taller to make room for someone walking through with a bouquet of white lilies. We turn our heads to the left to avoid getting smacked in the face by the petals. He nods to the small group of county firefighters who have congregated in the corner of the room. "I'm surprised the structure monkeys haven't started kicking people out. We're definitely over capacity."

I chuckle. "At least Dave isn't here." The words are out before I can stop them.

Dave and Molly grew up next door to each other. She says he's like a brother, but I wouldn't be surprised if Dave's been crushing on her since they were kids. I find it suspicious he ended up in the same town we did. He's also been trying to make the jump from structure to wildfire. As a favor to Molly, I gave him a spot on our seasonal crew, which was a mistake. He was problematic from the get-go. On the crew, he was a cocky motherfucker, always acted above everyone, constantly questioned orders, and never looked out for the guys around him. Plus, he had a shit work ethic and dropped more chainsaws in the dirt than anyone I've ever seen.

When Garrett asked for my opinion on if we should give him a permanent spot, it was an easy "Hell no." However, being in a small town like Sky Ridge, word got back around to Dave, and he's been a dick about it ever since.

"Probably didn't want to show his face after he got rejected," King adds. He's about as big a fan of him as I am.

Xander's height makes him easy to spot as he makes his way over.

"Hey, man."

He lines up next to us along the wall. "Hey."

"Too bad nobody showed," King says, words laced with sarcasm.

"I think it's safe to say my brothers underestimated how many people would be here. Tried telling them…" His voice is empty. I hate it.

We stand like sardines between the kitchen and living area,

and I couldn't be more thankful we're shoulder to shoulder, because looking at a broken Xander is absolute torture. Being the one to give him the news was terrible. The words tasted foul as they left my lips. If I could have swallowed them down, I would have done it in a heartbeat.

The steady white noise of conversation around us fades into nothing as my mind is swept back to that day. The expression on Garrett's face just before he died... A million words passed between us. The image will be seared into my brain forever. There was nothing I could do to stop that tree from falling.

The sorrow in his features will haunt me forever. He knew he was going to die; I saw it in his eyes, and he wasn't ready.

I'm glad Xander wasn't there to see it, and I'll take that memory to my grave. I only hope I can bury it inside me so deep even I can't find it. I want to forget it's there. Unfortunately, it surfaces every time I see photos of him, which are everywhere today. As my thoughts spiral, the room suddenly feels stifling hot, the air is thick—it's like I can't get a breath. *Get a fucking grip.* I glance toward the front door, but it's blocked with people saying their goodbyes.

I need air.

"I'm gonna find a bathroom," I say, pushing off the wall. I make my way to the back hall, hoping the spare bedroom is available to lock myself inside while I get my shit together. My heart pounds with each step, and the only thing I'm able to hear is the whoosh of my pulse in my ears as my vision tunnels. *Fuck, am I having a heart attack?*

It's as if my thoughts are circling the drain, and I can't pull out of its vortex. Despite my best efforts, I can't derail them to anything else. *Inhale.* My chest is too tight to take a breath, and it feels like I'm being crushed under the enormous weight of everything that happened. My fingers shake as I work to loosen the tie around my neck; it feels more like a noose.

Finally, I reach the room and wrap my hand around the doorknob, then force it open while holding my breath and waiting for relief to hit me.

It doesn't.

I'm sucker punched by my future wife getting fucked by another man.

Looks like Dave showed up.

CHAPTER 1

Scottie

PRESENT

The fluorescent lights flicker in the dingy municipal office, but it doesn't seem to bother anyone here. It's quiet, save for the clacking of keyboards and mouse clicks coming from nearby cubicles and offices. Occasionally, the silence is broken by a ringing phone.

I straighten my pressed slacks. The dryers in the women's locker room didn't get hot enough to pull all the wrinkles out of my cotton blouse, but it got most of them. Living out of a suitcase will do that—living out of a *car* will do that.

Hopefully, my attire isn't a make-or-break factor for getting this EMT job. If I get the offer, I'll be able to put a deposit down on a small studio apartment in Sky Ridge. The landlord said I could pay with cash on a month-to-month basis. I've already agreed to take it, sight unseen. As long as it has a roof, four walls, and a bathroom, I don't care what it looks like. I've already listed it as my address on my paperwork, and so far, no one has checked.

A man steps out of one of the offices. "Hi, Prescott? I'm Noah, we spoke on the phone earlier."

I school my face into a smile and glance up into the kind eyes of a large man. He's the hiring manager of this municipal office, where they handle some openings for county resources— like the EMT position I'm hoping to land.

Rising to my feet, I eagerly take his hand. "Yes. So nice to meet you."

Gripping his palm, I maintain a firm handshake. I'm not weak. *I'm not weak.*

I have my qualifications, I've done this job before, I've completed all the paperwork. I've earned this on my own. I'm ushered into his office and take the chair across from his desk while he takes his seat on the other side.

The tan metal desk is littered with papers and calendars. I swallow as he sifts through the piles until he snatches up a manilla folder. When he opens it, I see my name.

"It appears all your quals and packets are up-to-date," he mutters, flipping through some of my application paperwork without looking at me.

I nod. "Yes, sir."

"How soon are you wanting to start?"

"As soon as possible." *Was that too quickly?* I don't want him to know how desperate I am.

"I think we can accommodate that." He flips through the papers again, searching for something. "Did you have your vaccine records faxed over?"

Shit.

"Oh, I thought I did," I lie, leaning forward for emphasis, as if I'm surprised they aren't in the file. "My apologies, would it be all right if I email a copy of them this afternoon?"

"That's fine." He closes the folder. "As you know, we have an opening for an EMT at the Sky Ridge Fire Department, it's off County Road 2, not far from here."

I've driven by it at least a dozen times, each time saying a whispered prayer to the hiring gods. With this being such a small town, the competition is down, putting the odds in my favor.

"They've got a great crew over there. I think you'll fit in well." He slides another paper from the folder. *It looks like an offer letter.* My heart gallops, and I bite back tears. "Thirty-six hours a week. Three on, four off."

Perfect. "I'm used to working twelves."

"Pays twenty-one fifty an hour."

"Great."

Please let me sign.

"Any other questions?"

"No, sir. I'd love the job."

He grabs a pen, seemingly pleased to have me out of his hair.

"Excellent. I've already drawn up the offer letter."

He hands it over for me to glance at, and I nod, resisting the urge to squeal.

"We'll hold onto it until we get your vax records. After you send that over and everything looks good, then I'll email a copy of the offer letter, just sign and email it back. That way you don't have to make another trip out here." He clears his throat. "Once that's complete, you'll be authorized to start next Tuesday. Good?"

"Great!" I smile, it's my first genuine one in a while. "That's no problem at all, I'll email a copy of them as soon as I get back. Thank you."

I got a job.

He stands and I follow suit. We shake hands, I offer one last thanks, then I'm on my way.

Exiting the office, I head to my car parked in the far corner of the lot. I can't risk anyone snooping inside and seeing evidence that my car has been doubling as my house for the last few weeks. I'm making it work.

Turns out, a monthly gym membership is a lot cheaper than a

month in a hotel, and I get all the hot showers I want, plus the same amenities. *Minus the bed.* Thankfully, the employees assume I'm a gym rat instead of a homeless woman who needs a place to shower. On the bright side, I'm in the best shape of my life.

I'm keeping myself hidden halfway across the country. It's a long way from the small town I grew up in—and the community who's hellbent on making my life miserable.

If they're smart enough to check my social security number, there's a good chance they'll call up my place of employment and cause trouble, but it's been weeks since I've left. The coffee can I hid in the back of our kitchen cupboard had been slowly filling with coins and cash for almost a year. It's gotten me all the way to Sky Ridge, Washington, which is about as far away from home as I can be—and I've never been happier.

I casually observe my surroundings before unlocking my car door and climbing inside. Pulling out of the parking lot, I drive straight to the local library to use their computers to download my vaccine records from the patient portal back home and send them to Noah.

Normally, I would have called my doctor's office to have them fax the requested documents, but once they found out where the records were being faxed to, that information would get back to the council within the hour. Maybe they don't even care that I've left, but I'm not taking my chances.

While in the library, I refresh my email again and again, waiting for the offer letter. *Chill, Prescott. They aren't going to send it immediately.* I've got a few hours to kill.

I could go back to the gym and run on the treadmill, but the repetitiveness will make me more anxious than I am now. I've never been good at running in place; I need to be outside where I can be easily distracted by my environment.

Leaving the library, I get back in my car, turn on the music,

FIGHT

and drive to one of the local trailheads. It's a gorgeous day for a hike.

The lot is empty at midmorning, not unusual for a weekday when everyone's at work. I swap my dress clothes and shoes for some hiking pants, a light jacket, and boots. The way the blue-bird sky contrasts against the evergreen panorama is stunning.

I come from hill country, but driving northwest to Washington was the first time I ever saw real mountains. So high the tops are cloaked with snow, spearing into clouds. So wide you can't see where it starts and ends.

The second my boots hit the trail, my mouth curves up in a smile. Being close to nature is where I'm happiest. The ground is painted a rich, warm sienna with fallen pine needles. I fill my lungs with the cool, damp autumn air and inhale the aroma of evergreens, letting the content feelings linger in my soul. This could be home. I could swim in these deep forests forever. After only a few short weeks, I yearn to root my life in the mountains.

After a mile or so, the forest opens to a clearing, and the sun's rays warm my face as I tilt my head to drink my water. The path isn't as visible in the open, so I follow the cairns, tall stacks of rocks set up by trail crews as a guide. There should be a lookout spot in the next couple miles. I focus on that objective rather than the phone weighing down my pocket. *It's too soon for the offer letter.*

My thoughts wander as I pick up my pace and take in the landscape, enjoying the occasional marmot that peeks from behind an outcropping of rock—like the one chirping at me now.

"Hi, buddy. Just passing through."

His hand twitches near his fuzzy yellow belly, and I smile as I pass by. Today will be a good day. I will get my job offer, then I'll follow up with the landlord and get that studio apartment. Who knows, maybe I'll even move in before the end of the week! I may not have furniture, but I've got an inflatable mattress. Honestly, the floor would probably feel better than

13

being scrunched up in the backseat of my car like I've been for the past few weeks.

Besides, there's always something listed for free on the online classifieds. I've seen the condition of the building from the outside, and if the inside of the apartment is anything like the exterior, there's a reason it has sat vacant for as long as it has. The place is a dump, but it's about to be *my* dump. Shithole sweet shithole.

Up ahead is another sign with an arrow pointing to the left for the lookout. I take the route and continue daydreaming about my future here. This is my first time on this trail, but I'm hoping for a killer view at the top of the hill.

It doesn't take me long to approach the vista. At the end of the path, a huge valley opens up to a dazzling lake, the sun's reflection sparkling along the edges. Hills and forests go on as far as the eye can see. It's spectacular.

Yeah. This could be home.

CHAPTER 2
CALLAHAN

On the far end of the main street businesses is a big neon sign that reads BAR with an arrow pointing down at the worn brick building. Mae and Jack have been owners of the corner spot since before I moved here. Only locals know this bar is named Shifty's, and only locals drink here—a majority of which are other hotshots. Not all of them live in town, but it became a local meetup of sorts years ago.

It takes a moment for my eyes to adjust from the blazing sunset outside to the dim light of the nearly windowless establishment. More neon signs decorate the interior, mostly beer advertisements. The heavy door falls shut behind me, and I'm met by the familiar musty scent and the sound of laughter from my buddies who are probably on their second round by now.

Tonight, we're celebrating the completion of our most recent fire. It was a bitch, and we're all tired, but it's an excuse to go out and throw back a few. King and Xander are toward the middle, so I pull up a barstool beside them. As I do, a frosted Coors bottle is placed in front of me on the old worn pine bartop; the wood has yellowed over the years. I lift two fingers and nod thanks to Lou, the old bartender who knows us well.

King and Xander laugh at something Bobby said, so I take a swig of beer and get caught up in the conversation taking place. "So, he's got a bunch of our guys standing in a hot-as-fuck Florida parking lot while the rest of the Washington D.C. folks had this big fancy catered lunch—because fuck us, right? They're all chowing down on seafood in the nice cool air conditioning, meanwhile the firefighters aren't even able to grab a bite to eat, on the off chance any of the bigwigs want to come out and see the trucks and crew. Like some kind of bullshit show-and-tell. So then—" Bobby chuckles. "After hours in the sun, it's all over, right? And who comes strolling up with his pockets stuffed with peel-and-eat shrimp? Wyatt fucking Bradley. This jackass looks at the boys and says something about 'It's too bad you couldn't come inside, because the food was phenomenal!' while he's standing there *still eating the pocket shrimp!*"

"No way in hell the Chief of FS was eating pocket shrimp," Xander says, shaking his head and bringing the rim of the beer bottle to his lips.

Bobby holds up his palm. "Hand to God."

I roll my eyes and smile. That story's made its way around a few times now. Though, last time it was told to me, the Chief of the Forest Service's shirt was misbuttoned and his belt buckle was upside down too.

We go back and forth trading stories and rumors, as well as the upcoming assignments headed our way. Once fire season ends, I'll have a few weeks to do whatever the hell I please before I start up with ski patrol at a local resort. It's a great gig. Free time on the slopes and all the après-ski snow bunnies I can fit in my bed. Not a bad way to earn some extra cash. My thoughts wander to all my plans for the off-season.

"They just hired a new guy. EMT, I think," Xander says, yanking me out of my thoughts.

I'm not sure what they're talking about. "Who hired a new EMT?" I ask, attempting to participate in the conversation.

"SRFD." The local structural fire department.

News spreads faster at Shifty's than it does in the local paper.

"A new *guy*... or girl? Because that's critical data," Tex interrogates. It's been years since his transfer from the Lonestar state, but the nickname stuck.

Curly stares off into the distance. "Remember that blonde chick, Abigail? *Fuck.* She was amazing."

"Dude, those blue eyes?" Dixon puffs out a breath. "Abby was awesome."

Her blowjobs certainly were. Half the guys at the bar nod, a few staring at their beer bottles longingly, reminiscing her oral prowess. *Good lord.*

Xander laughs. "Haven't met 'em yet, but with the first name Prescott, I'm guessing it's a dude."

"Damn," Tex says, then tips back the last of his beer and sets the empty bottle on the bartop with a hollow clink. Lou is already popping the cap off a new one for him.

"Even if the new guy was a chick," King interjects, "Matt's probably gonna be the medic in charge, he's almost a bigger whore than Woods here." He claps me on the back.

"Hey." I smirk. "Don't slut-shame me."

I'm not going home with someone new every night, but I'm a bachelor who travels for work and has commitment issues. After I walked in on Molly bent over in front of Dave at Garrett Macomb's funeral, I closed myself off to any future relationships. There's a ton of infidelity in this job as it is. With the time hotshots and their significant others spend separated from each other, it happens in equal amounts on both sides. Personally, I've never cheated, the idea disgusts me on a visceral level. On almost every crew I've worked on, one-third are in relationships, one-third are divorced, and one-third are having the time of their lives—*I'm in that camp.* Life is short. Sex is fun. As long as everybody's on the same page, who cares?

Occasionally, I'm hit with a bout of loneliness, especially

when I hear about some of the other guys having a woman to go home to, but the thought of discovering another affair again is enough to keep me from getting involved with anyone seriously; I've got a lot of demons to work through, and I don't need to burden anyone with that.

It's easier to have sexual encounters with no strings attached. All the fun, none of the hurt. Besides, most women I hook up with are in it for the same reason. They want a temporary fling, and I'm happy to oblige. The ones seeking relationships, who think they can be the one to "fix" me, don't have to peel back too many layers to discover the futility of their efforts. The space my heart once occupied is barren, so there's no use in trying to plant themselves there because nothing will ever grow.

I take another drink. The bar has slowly been filling with more Sky Ridge locals as the night goes on, so when I hear the door to the bar open, I think little of it until a quiet settles over the room. I turn my head to the right to see what's got everyone hushed. Probably an out-of-towner who needs directions.

I quickly clock the gorgeous woman sidling up to the bar on the opposite end. Not a townie. If she's lost, I will drive her home—and walk her to her bedroom to make sure she arrives safely.

It's hard to tell if she's a redhead or blonde with all the neon lights in here, but it falls in loose waves over her shoulders. She's fit, but has some curves, and paired with her plush lips, this woman's a knockout.

"Dibs," Caleb says, pushing off the bar. He's a rookie shot who's wrapping up his first fire season. This kid is the most gullible dude I've ever met.

"Sit down," I warn, staring straight ahead. I set my beer bottle on the bartop and keep her in my peripheral vision. Caleb's way out of his league with this one.

"Here we go," Xander mutters.

Alright, perhaps I *do* have a bit of a reputation.

I cock my head toward him, and he exchanges a raised eyebrow at me.

Holding his judgmental stare, I retract my earlier statement. "Ya know what, Caleb? I take it back. Why don't you go shoot your shot? You called dibs fair and square. I'll get the next one."

Xander breaks eye contact and chuckles into his beer before taking a drink.

Caleb narrows his eyes at me, and I shrug. He wastes no time scrambling off his barstool to introduce himself. This woman hasn't even pulled up a seat yet. As expected, she smiles politely but appears a little uncomfortable with her back to the bar as he rushes to give her his best line, which I would *love* to hear, if only to have a good laugh. I give him a minute to make an ass of himself.

"Here it comes..." Curly says.

She gives him a sympathetic look and a smile breaks out across my face. Poor kid. The woman sends him back to us like a sad puppy. The corner of my mouth turns up, and I chuckle. He should have known better, but mistakes are the best teachers. Caleb trudges back to our end of the bar, plopping onto his barstool and muttering, "Asshole" into his drink.

"Better luck next time, buddy." One of the guys gives him a hard slap on the back.

I take a drink and feel her eyes on me. When I glance over, she quickly looks away and takes a seat at the bar. The regular hum of chatter returns among the patrons. She removes her wallet from her purse, opens it in her lap, and tabs through the contents of one of the pockets. Her lips move, as if she's talking to herself. *She's counting bills.* After a couple seconds, she nods to herself, and Lou ambles over to take her drink order.

Afterward, he turns around and grabs a bottle of Jack Daniels off the shelf and an empty glass. My guess is she's either had a rough day or is celebrating. I observe the casual way she leans back on her stool and rolls her lips together. With outstretched arms, she pitter-pats her fingers on the bartop, surveys the room, and takes in the unfamiliar faces with a soft smile.

Celebrating.

When her gaze finds mine, it stays locked until Lou breaks the spell and sets the glass tumbler with a couple fingers of whiskey in front of her. She bobs her head appreciatively, and he gives her the total.

She plucks out one of the carefully counted bills.

I clear my throat. "Put it on my tab, Lou."

A disgruntled mutter comes from Caleb.

Her gaze snaps to mine again, and it earns me a smile that reaches her eyes. She holds up her glass, mouthing *Thank you.*

I nod and wink while taking a swig of the beer in front of me, then turn back to the guys to continue our conversation.

Until Dave Banner bellies up to the bar next to her.

Dave, the structural firefighter who I've never liked. Dave, who couldn't make it as a hotshot. Dave, who slept with my fiancée, Molly, got her pregnant, and then married her. *What hole did he crawl out of?* They just had their second baby a few weeks ago. He's got no business looking at this girl the way he is. My jaw tics. I never thought Molly and Dave were a match made, but apparently, I was wrong. They deserve each other. Few things rank worse than their betrayal. I'd want no one to go through what I did.

"You good?" King asks at my side.

"Fine," I state, turning away from the situation unfolding ten feet away.

Dave's standing too close for my comfort, and based on her body language, it's too close for hers as well. When Caleb tried to put moves on her, it was funny. I figured I'd get my shot in later, but now, with two guys hitting on her tonight, there's no way in hell I'm throwing my hat in the ring. Our town is already proving to be a bunch of desperate swinging dicks. She doesn't need to add anyone else to the mix.

She shakes her head at his advance, but he's not accepting the brush off the way Caleb did. I set my beer down and brace my hands on the bar to shove off, then Xander leans back and shouts behind me.

"Hey Dave!" He spins around to face us. I avert my eyes, relaxing my arms and leaning forward. I don't need that asshole to see the anger I still harbor toward him. "Say, how's the new baby? Is this you and Molly's second or third kid? Sorry, I can never remember."

Smirking, I take a sip of my beer.

"Second," Dave grinds out.

"Oh, that's right. Well, congratulations... Be sure to give the wife my best."

Dave backs off, likely to return to the table where some of the other guys from the local fire station are sitting.

"You didn't need to do that," I grumble to Xander.

"Yeah, I did." He tips back his beer and gulps, continuing, "I rather enjoy the lovely atmosphere of this shithole, and I'm not sure if Lou here"—he gestures with his bottle to the bartender, who's grinning at us—"would be so keen on letting us return to this fine establishment if you ripped Dave's head from his shoulders. I sure as shit know Mae and Jack would have a thing or two to say. Which, based on the fire in your eyes, is where we were headed." He glances back to the bartender. "Am I wrong, Lou?"

King is smart enough not to laugh, but I can feel his beaming smile radiating from the other side of Xander.

"That is correct," Lou answers with a chuckle. "Mae just replaced the bar mats."

"They just replaced the bar mats, Cal!" Xander emphasizes, gesturing to said bar mats with an open hand.

I roll my eyes at all of them and down the last of my beer.

"Another?" Lou asks me.

"Yessir."

He pops the cap and swaps it with my empty one. "This one's on the house. Don't let that guy get to you."

"What guy?" I roll my eyes. Dave didn't get to me. I don't need any special treatment.

"Beg your pardon... I believe *I* was the one that called out Dave on his bullshit. Where's my free beer, Lou?" Xander argues.

The burn of her stare creeps up my neck.

Fuck it.

While Xander and Lou bicker like old men, I slip off my stool and saunter toward the end of the bar and take the seat next to her. I look straight ahead in silence, and she does the same.

A few minutes pass.

The air between us grows thicker and thicker with anticipation as we both commit to not making the first move. It's like a game and is surprisingly entertaining. She doesn't look at me, and I don't look at her, yet I would put good money down that we're thinking about the same thing. I nearly finish my beer without uttering one word. Her drink is running low too.

Eventually, she breaks the silence.

"So, are you going to say anything, or are you just sitting there?"

I swallow the rest of my beer and tap two fingers on the bar, indicating another round.

"Definitely just sitting here."

"Ah, I see," she states.

Lou returns and collects the old beer bottle and swaps it with a cold one. "She could use a refill," I say to him. He turns to grab the bottle of whiskey and pours the amber liquid into the short glass.

"Thank you," she says to Lou when he slides the glass in front of her. I nod my thanks to him before he steps away.

"I can pay for my own drinks," she says.

"Good, 'cause I'm not paying for this one. Earlier was a one-time thing 'cause I felt bad for you."

She takes a sip. "There's that Sky Ridge hospitality I keep hearing about."

I suck my teeth. "There it is."

"What makes you think I deserve pity?" she asks.

"Honestly… I don't know if anyone's told you this…" I lean toward her and lower my voice. "But, um, you're *really* unattractive."

That makes her laugh, loud enough for Dave to hear, I'm sure, and I chuckle along with her.

"Well, I can't be that hideous if your friend over there tried to take me home before I could even sit down…"

I wince. "Sorry about that, he's a rescue."

"That might be the first honest thing you've said since sitting down."

I shrug and take a pull from my beer bottle. "I'm a habitual liar."

She takes a sip of her drink. "Oh good, I'm really attracted to liars."

"Yeah? Maybe I should give you my number, then."

"Wow," she says deadpan, and turns to face me. God, she's even more stunning up close. Her ginger hair matches the subtle freckles that dot the bridge of her nose.

I fucking love freckles… and love fucking the women who wear them.

"Hey, there are plenty of women in this town who would love getting my number."

"There're those lies again…" She gestures, fanning herself, and I laugh.

She narrows her eyes at me, and I take a sip of beer, staring back and refusing to break eye contact. I could spend all day gazing into them. Her eyes aren't the icy blue shade one would normally think of with blue eyes. They're deep and stormy, reminding me of a turbulent sea.

"Okay." She pulls out a phone, and I smile. When she hands it over, I furrow my brow. It's a flip phone. A fucking *flip phone?* I've never seen this girl in town before, I don't even know her name, and she pulled out a burner. When I open the Contacts app, and there're only two: *Boss* and *Landlord*, it's like a red flag parade. I pretend to not notice and start typing in my number while alarms blare in my head. I peer back up at her, and damn if she isn't the most beautiful thing I've ever seen. Fuck it, red might be my new favorite color. I finish typing my number in and save my contact as "Cal the Liar" before passing it back.

"Do I get a name?"
"Scottie." She holds her palm out in a handshake, and I take it in mine.

"Callahan Woods," I say. "You gonna text me, Scottie?"

"Probably not," she says, still shaking my hand and grinning.

I laugh and release her palm. "Well, it was awful meeting you."

The corner of her mouth curves up in a smile. "Likewise."

I slide off my barstool.

"Maybe I'll see you around," she adds.

"I hope not." I wink and head back to the guys, finding my spot next to Xander again.

She downs the remaining liquid in her glass and pays Lou, leaving a couple bucks on the bartop before standing and walking out the door without giving me so much as a sideways glance.

I return to my barstool next to King and Xander, and Xander shakes his head. "So, who's your new friend?" King asks.

"Scottie," I answer, stealing one more look toward the door. "Scottie the hottie."

Caleb sighs, still disappointed from his crash and burn earlier.

We spend the next couple hours knocking back beers and retelling stories from the fire we just rolled off of. With each one, our voices get a little louder and less articulate. It's gonna be a late night tearing it up. It's been a good season. A couple more assignments and we'll be wrapping up. I'm about to pay my tab when the phone in my pocket buzzes.

UNKNOWN

Thanks for the drink tonight.

A smile lights up my face, and I tap out my reply.

Anytime.

CHAPTER 3

Scottie

While adjusting the clip with my employee badge at my hip, Matthew opens a few cabinet doors at the fire station. "Here's where we keep overstock."

"Got it." I acknowledge to my new medic, who's giving me a tour of the county fire station. Is everybody in this town good-looking? Is it the water? Should I be drinking more water?

Matt is attractive the way a Ken doll is attractive. I stare at him like a scientist studying a test subject. He's just so… *pretty.* Thankfully, I'm not sexually attracted to him, and I think we're going to get along well together. He's nice, knowledgeable, and treats me as an equal, unlike other stations I've worked at where they love hazing the newbie.

The firefighters seem nice too. One of the guys, Dave, introduced himself at the bar. I think he had a few too many that night. Especially after some other patron called him out on having a wife and a couple kids at home. Truthfully, I'm not sure if he even remembers because he hasn't given me any sideways glances—for which I'm grateful.

He opens another cabinet with CPR dummies inside and some other training materials. A sealed package containing one of the Resuscitation Annie's faces falls onto the floor like one of Hannibal Lector's snacks. *Annie, are you okay?* I stuff it back in the cabinet and shut the door, then follow him through another doorway that leads to a large open room with windows spanning one of the exterior walls. The center of the room holds foosball and Ping-Pong tables. Along another wall is a mounted television and a leather couch that's seen better days.

"Rec room."

"Nice."

"Some of the fire guys take the games pretty seriously." He gestures toward the wall with two large whiteboards, one filled with a foosball bracket and the other set up with Ping-Pong scores.

"Yeah, I'm not at that level. Not anymore, at least. I could have gone pro in college, but, ya know…" I end the joke with a wistful sigh.

"Injury?" he asks, matching my bit.

"Nah, couldn't handle the pressure. The fans, the women, the money… It became too much. So naturally, I became an EMT."

"That's the logical path." Matt chuckles and I smile. At least my medic has a small sense of humor. That would not have flown at my last job. "I think you'll fit in well here. Laurel and Pete are on a call, but when they come back, I'll introduce you."

"Great, I'm looking forward to meeting them."

I spend my downtime going through the rig and bag, memorizing where supplies and gear are kept. Every station and rig are a little different, and I want to make sure I don't fuck this opportunity up.

"This is ambulance twenty-three, en route to you with a fifty-four-year-old male who fell approximately fifteen feet from a roof. GCS is normal. Left wrist deformity without active bleeding. No other injuries upon physical exam." I peek at the top of my gloved hand, where I jotted down vitals with a Sharpie. "Blood pressure 120/70, pulse 79, respirations 18, oxygen 98. C-collar in place. ETA seven minutes."

After we get the patient checked in, I give the report to the triage nurse in the emergency department. Then my phone buzzes in my pocket, delivering a small dose of excitement. I ignore it to keep from smiling while I tell the nurse about her patient's busted wrist. Few people have this number: my landlord, my work, and *Cal*.

Cal *the Liar*, as he saved himself in my phone. The man has a bit of fuckboy energy for someone who appears to be in his thirties, but his confidence and physical appearance still put butterflies in my stomach. He's handsome as hell. Scruffy beard, chiseled jaw, bright-brown eyes, and an irresistible smile that made me blush. He looks like lumberjack porn. Not to mention, he gave me my first real laugh in a long time. Conversation was easy, and for the short duration of our meeting, I forgot all about the things I ran away from. I wasn't anxious or on edge. I was just Prescott Timmons, living in the moment.

"Ready?" Matt asks after we wrap up with the emergency department.

I nod and peel off my gloves, then snap them into the trashcan on the way out. Sliding my phone from my pocket, I grin at his name on the screen.

CAL THE LIAR

Hey You.

Hi.

CAL THE LIAR

Where are you right now?

Hospital, why?

CAL THE LIAR

Is everything okay?

Yeah, just working.

We pass through the sliding doors. Matt and I return to the rig and buckle up. He grabs the radio and reports to dispatch that we're on our way back to the station. While he drives, I get to work on charting our patient. They use a software a little different than the one I'm used to, so I need the practice.

CAL THE LIAR

Oh, you work in healthcare.

I pause for a moment before I respond. Anytime I tell someone I'm an EMT, it leads to a barrage of questions, like "What's the worst thing you've ever seen?" or "Has anybody ever died on your watch?" Besides, I hardly know this guy. And technically, it *is* healthcare.

Yeah. What about you?

CAL THE LIAR

I'm a dolphin trainer.

I roll my eyes. Gotta give him credit, he knows how to commit to his nickname.

...

CAL THE LIAR

Tough crowd. I work in forestry.

That correlates with his tan lines I noticed the other night.

Lumberjack?

CAL THE LIAR

Sometimes it feels like it.

Must be having a slow day at the office then.

CAL THE LIAR

No, pretty busy actually. But I was thinking about you, so...

That another lie?

CAL THE LIAR

No, but this is...

I hope you have a terrible rest of your day, Scottie. 😏

The corner of my mouth tips up into a smile, and I shake my head.

Thanks. Hope yours sucks big time.

I snap my phone shut and stuff it back in my pocket with a conflicting feeling in my gut. I'm not at a place in my life to be involved with anyone, so I don't even know why I'm entertaining thoughts about this guy. I'm trying to start a new life for myself. He is kind of funny though... and hot. How can having a crush feel too soon yet overdue at the same time?

I have a satisfied smile when I return to my apartment after surviving my first workday with no major fuckups. It was important for me to make a good impression. I'll have plenty of days ahead to make mistakes, but I wanted my first day to go well.

I open up the nearly bare cabinets in my kitchen and figure out what I will make for dinner. Canned peaches or canned green beans? I snag the green beans and find my trusty can opener and peel back the lid. The grin on my face spreads when I drain the water; I have an actual sink! Living in your car sure makes you appreciate things like modern plumbing. No more showering at the gym. No more gas station bathrooms.

I pluck a plastic fork from the drawer and head toward the window of my studio apartment. Using my foot, I nudge the inflatable mattress against the wall, then plop down in front of the window and rest an elbow on the sill. Outside, it's not busy like Main Street, but I can still watch the town's residents walk by my building—and that's almost as good as television. I stab my fork into the green beans and stuff them into my mouth. The salty, and slightly waxy, beans taste like a five-star Michelin meal. Honestly, I'd eat this for dinner even if I wasn't broke.

I bring another forkful to my mouth but freeze halfway when I see a woman with a big orange floppy hat pushing a stroller—a cat stroller. Sure enough, a big fat tabby is propped up in the seat, bouncing along the bumpy sidewalk. I snort at the way he jiggles in his seat. This town has some characters. My phone buzzes. I set the fork in the can and rest it on the windowsill. *Another text from Cal.*

CAL THE LIAR
How was your day?

Good. You?

CAL THE LIAR
Good. Hungry. Wanna grab dinner?

I take another bite, dropping the fork back into the hollow tin can.

> Just ate, sorry.

CAL THE LIAR

Bummer. Are you free Saturday night?

The whiskey I bought the other night was a celebration after securing my offer letter. I wanted to feel like an ordinary person and be around other ordinary people. I've been so lonely since I left Arkansas, so I needed that night at the bar, but for now, the rest of my cash is reserved for emergencies only. I'm on canned dinners until my first paycheck clears.

I've only gone on dates with Jonathan. Do men still pay for their date's dinner? What if he wants to go somewhere fancy? I can't risk having to split the bill and have my bank account take the hit.

> Sorry, I've got plans this weekend. Raincheck?
> Maybe the weekend after?

CAL THE LIAR

It's a date.

What the hell am I doing? I haven't been settled in this town for more than a couple weeks and I already have a date scheduled? At thirty-two, it's been well over a decade since I've been on a first date, and I'm not sure if those even count. This is wrong, but damn, flirting felt so right. I want normalcy, and that means stepping outside my comfort zone. As much as I shouldn't entertain the idea of dating, it feels natural. What difference does it make?

"You're in over your head."

After that text, guilt has me opening Facebook. People have been leaving their condolences and offers of support for Jonathan. Some of the bolder members of the community call me names. I refuse to be a part of that life; I'm disgusted I stayed as long as I did. I warned him plenty of times that the day would come when he would wake up and I would be gone. It was the only way to escape.

Still, I worry about him. Why the hell didn't he come with me? We could have left together. Started our lives over and actually *lived* for once.

New state, new job, new people, new beginning. The slate gets no cleaner than this.

It's bizarre to go from having people constantly around to... no one. I've got three numbers in my cell phone. My landlord, my work, and some stranger I met at the bar. At first, I found peace in the silence, but lately, it feels so loud. Now is one of those times.

I need fresh air. Time to go for a run and check on my dream house. Clear my head of these anxious thoughts.

CHAPTER 4

Scottie

My worries are doused by the crisp September air when I step foot outside and suck in a restorative breath. It's chilly, but I don't give my body a chance to feel the cold before I start jogging. My feet pound the sidewalk at a steady pace while I force myself to focus on the landmarks and layout of Sky Ridge, taking the attention off my thoughts of The Fold, Jonathan, and whether I'm a complete fool.

"Hemlock Street," I mutter, passing the street sign under the orange-tinted streetlight. At each intersection, I repeat the name, hoping it will help me learn the area. I'm sure I'll know this town backward and forward after a month or so.

"Marshall…"

I jog another block. "Payne…"

Another block. "Spencer." I turn right and head down the side street. This is my favorite street in Sky Ridge. The tidy homes line each side of the street. It's Small Town, USA, right out of a Norman Rockwell painting. I admire the historic Victorian architecture, which has always fascinated me with their verandas and turrets. Most are modest folk-style versions likely built around the turn of the century. Warm light shines from the inside, and I imagine what the families are like that live here.

Almost every house has a white-painted porch with ornamental posts. Decorative planters with autumn mums and orange pumpkins dress the wooden steps. It's all so different from the rows of shotgun houses where I grew up.

There's something to like about every house on this street, but one is my favorite. I'm not sure what it is about the Victorian I love so much, but every time I see it, hope spreads in my heart. I feel a connection to it. Seeing that house makes me feel positive about my future here; it's reassuring. I like to believe that someday I could own a house like that one and make it a home. After I pass the lovely 218 Spencer, I explore the rest of the neighborhood, finding new architectural details to appreciate.

The people who live in these adorable homes probably made good decisions all their life. They were smart. They thought for themselves. They wanted something and worked hard until they got it. A strange sense of homesickness washes over me, but how can you feel homesick for something that never existed in the first place?

"Scottie!" a voice booms behind me, and I freeze. Slowly turning around, I exhale and drop my shoulders when a familiar face jogs toward me. Callahan.

I wipe the sweat from my forehead and smile. With my hair pulled into a ponytail, a breeze blows, sending goose bumps across the damp nape of my neck.

I pant out a "Hi," and lift my hand in a weak wave. He's donning sweats and a light jacket, and he wears the hell outta both. I'd say he's roughly six feet tall, which puts him about nine inches taller than me. It seems I'm not the only one who took advantage of tonight's cool air for a workout.

"Hey," he says, out of breath. "Out for a run?"

My smile widens. "How could you tell?"

"Ya know, I wasn't sure at first, but the outfit and jogging kinda gave it away. Plus, I didn't see anybody chasing you." He nods to my leggings and sneakers. I swear his gaze lingers a second longer than normal.

"Those are some deduction skills you've got." I continue my run, and he paces himself beside me.

"Thanks." We jog in silence for a few beats. "So... do you live around here?"

I bark out a laugh and slow my strides after his question. Despite my dream to someday own one of these homes, I find his timing quite amusing.

His head swivels back to me since I'm a few steps behind, then he pauses for me to catch up. "What's so funny?"

"It's kinda creepy to ask a woman if she lives nearby when she's running alone."

He shrugs. "Seems like you're already taking your chances by running at night."

I chuckle. "Yeah, it would be awful if some stranger came up and started asking me where I live..."

"Good thing I'm not a stranger then, huh?"

I glance up at him, and he winks. Damn that smile of his. Straight, perfect white teeth. It's confident. "I suppose that's true... still, I try to avoid making friends with liars."

"Even liars who jog at night? Maybe we could run together sometime, assuming I'm not on the road for work."

"Busy traveling to aquariums to train those dolphins?"

He grins. "You know it. But seriously, if you ever want to jog together, shoot me a text."

What's his endgame? I raise an eyebrow. "Are you hitting on me?"

He extends his arm in front of me, and we slow our gait, coming to a halt at the intersection of another street.

"Real talk. I'm not just giving you a line. There can be a lot of nomads in town for work. Not all of them are someone I'd want you to run into by yourself. I'd say the same thing to my sister."

I catch my breath and study his features, searching for any sign of insincerity. "I'm not a big fan of talking when I run," I state.

"We don't have to talk."

"I'm just trying to learn my way around town."

"Want a personal tour? Okay, *now* I might be hitting on you a little bit."

There's that smile again. He's determined.

"Maybe. But I should probably head home, I've got an early morning," I say, turning right at the intersection.

"It was nice running into you," he says.

I wave goodbye and take a few more steps backward. "Get home safely, I hear there's some weirdos in this town," I joke.

Cal smirks. "Consider my offer?"

"I'll think about it." Spinning around, I return to my jogging pace.

"That's not a no," he calls after me,

"It's not a yes," I shout back, turning my head to the side.

I take another right at the next intersection and return to my apartment. I smile seeing my building, gaining confidence in my newfound independence. Though, once I get inside my studio, my smile slips. After looking at all those pretty houses, it's a pathetic sight with a floor mattress and a laundry basket filled with a few of my belongings. The road to Spencer Avenue will be a long one. My apartment has a damp, musty smell, and I make a mental note to get a candle or something when I have some extra money to splurge.

In the small bathroom, I yank the sweatshirt over my head. Red splotches on my chest match the ones on my cheeks after the run in the brisk air. I turn on the water in the shower and frown at the weak water pressure. My phone buzzes in my hip pocket, and I tug it out, then peel off the leggings.

CAL THE LIAR

Checking in to make sure you got home safely.

Even locked my door to keep out the riff raff.

Callahan Woods. I go into my contact settings and change his name to just Callahan.

CALLAHAN

Smart girl.

I bite my lip as the butterflies invade my stomach again. Talking to Callahan is like getting a hit of dopamine. It's invigorating. I like flirting with him, it's fun and exciting and new. Makes me forget who I am or where I come from. After stripping from my sports bra and underwear, I step under the shower spray and drag the flimsy curtain across the rod.

"Someday..." I promise aloud, "things will be different."

This time, the silence doesn't creep in around me. Maybe it's simply the high from running, but my heart feels almost... light? I quietly hum a song I heard on the radio. Even the music is better on the outside.

CHAPTER 5

CALLAHAN

My phone dings with a new fire assignment in Oregon.

"Shit."

Not surprising with the unusually dry autumn. We're due for some rain. A wildfire can eat up those crunchy brown leaves in the blink of an eye. I get to work tidying the end-of-season paperwork I've been trying to get caught up on since we returned from the last fire. Peering down at my watch, I've got about thirty minutes to get loaded up and on the road.

Normally, I'd be thrilled. One more roll before the season closes out? Sign me the fuck up. Getting an assignment used to make my dick hard, but ever since that deadly season years ago when we lost Garrett and Jacob, there's a looming sense of dread on every mission. Every close call since has compounded into an underlying uneasiness that never goes away. It steals my sleep, my thoughts, my peace. It's hard to work through trauma when you keep getting reintroduced to it. I still love the fire; I always will, but it's just different now. I suspect Xander is going through something similar. He lost so much more than I did that day. No wonder he never goes home.

While grabbing my red bag, I realize the date night I had

lined up with Scottie will need to be rescheduled. Making plans was a surefire way to jinx myself. It's a long-standing superstition that the best way to get a roll is to make plans or buy groceries. However, things tend to settle down toward the end of a season, so I took my chances.

Not sure what's driving my attraction to Scottie, but it's the most effort I've put in for a woman in a while. Probably the prospect of something new. It's been months since I've gotten a good chase, which might contribute to Scottie's appeal. Finding a woman to hook up with, especially between assignments, has never been difficult. And while that's convenient, what fun is it if there's not a challenge? The push and pull is the best part. I fish my phone from my pocket and shoot off a text to her.

> Really sorry. I've got to head out of town for work. Going to have to cancel our dinner date for Saturday. Can we reschedule?

SCOTTIE
No worries.

Another text comes in from Xander, the superintendent.

XANDER
Heads up, I've got a buddy on the Mahonia fire, heard they're ordering the world.

> Sounds fun. Boys are getting loaded up. ETA?

XANDER
1535

> Copy

Before long, Xander rolls up, and we pack the supe rig. As the captain, I ride shotgun, Xander takes the wheel, and the rest of the guys split between the two buggies.

The sky grows hazier as the hours go by. As we approach the GPS coordinates, smoke is rising into a massive plume, mixing with dusk and making the entire sky glow orange. After three and a half hours or so of driving, we pull up to the temporary base camp.

Our phones ding with a notification from the group chat. I open it up, chuckle, and shake my head. Word slipped about all the resources on the fire, and a few guys in the other buggies are already betting on the odds of hooking up with a hot medic. I roll my eyes.

"Christ, the ambo isn't even staged yet and they're already talking about getting their dicks sucked."

Xander scoffs at me for being a hypocrite. Fair point, I've had my share of hookups on a fire. Usually, a hot helitack girl or female volly firefighter. Never a medic—well, at least not while on a fire assignment—but I know a few guys who have. It lends itself to the old stereotype: nurses and firefighters go together like tequila and poor choices. We're a match made in hell.

As far as I can tell, there doesn't even seem to be an ambulance on site, so maybe it'll stay that way. I just *love* sharing a fire camp with a bunch of rookie medics who've never been near a wildfire before. It's my favorite.

I'm guessing more resources will be showing up tomorrow or later tonight, depending on where they're coming from. Based on what Xander heard, I expected to see more of them here already, but I'm glad we can get staged first. The sky is growing dark when we climb out of the truck and stretch. The shots pile out of the buggies and everyone grabs their shit, working quickly to get settled. Xander and I find the division supervisor to check in.

By the time we're finished meeting with overhead, I'm beat. I lay out my sleeping bag on an area of the cold ground that looks soft enough and crawl inside. It's not as much soft as it is hard and unforgiving. It takes several minutes before my sleeping bag is warmed by my body heat. There's no light pollution this far out, but the stars aren't visible through the smoke, so I shut my eyes and use what time I have left to sleep. It will be an early morning.

The sun is barely up when I spot the ambulance a ways over. They must have gotten in late last night. I sit up in my sleeping bag and squint. It reads SKY RIDGE on the side. Another shot wakes up and sees the same thing.

"Hey." I nod to Xander, who's sipping coffee from a steaming tin cup. "Did you know it was a Sky Ridge resource?" My breath comes out in a fog in the early morning air.

"So much for fucking a hot medic," Tex interrupts from somewhere behind us. "That's the EMT named Preston or Prescott or some shit, right?"

I chuckle and unzip my sleeping bag, wincing as my joints pop and click when I stand. Staring out at the horizon, I take a moment to appreciate the sunrise, then turn my head toward the fire we're going after today. We've got our work cut out for us.

CHAPTER 6
CALLAHAN

The smell of wildfire is a unique yet familiar one. It's smoky, with an added layer of sweet or acrid, depending on the organic compounds released. When Ponderosas burn, they have a sweet aroma like vanilla; Aspen, on the other hand, smells bitter.

As the crew clears trees and undergrowth, the annual easterly winds during early fall continue feeding the fire and make it a real bitch to work. Occasionally, our eyes are blasted with dirt and smoke, making every blink scratch and sting.

The sawyers and crew have been clearing a line twenty feet wide through the mountainside, dropping trees and removing brush that could carry fire into the canopies. The guys scrape the vegetation and other natural debris in the fire's path, hoping to choke off its fuel supply. It's a tedious process, but lines are made one Pulaski swing at a time.

Wildfires like this one are examples of why we need more prescribed burns. Overgrowth and vegetation feed wildfires, allowing them to spread wider and faster, causing more destruction. But if we can clear the forests of the overabundant ground fuel, then it gives us a chance to contain the fire ourselves, and prevent natural fires—due to things like lightning strikes—from getting out of hand. Which is why this job is so important. We don't only manage wildfires, we also try to prevent them from happening.

Every year, less and less fire positions are filled. Less wildland firefighters equal less fire suppression and preventative measures. But hey, recruiting is a bitch when the perks include sleeping on the ground, spending time away from family for weeks or months at a time, pushing your body to the absolute limit day after day, and risking your life and safety in inhospitable terrain—all for the same base pay as a Starbucks barista.

You have to be a little bit crazy to choose this profession. Every person on this crew is here because they are passionate about the environment and care about our nation's forests. Or they love setting shit on fire. Which, to be fair, the majority of us land somewhere on the spectrum of pyromania.

Truthfully, there are some fantastic rewards. I get to work outside, help the environment, travel through some of the most gorgeous, unseen places on Earth, and have coworkers who are closer to family than colleagues. When you trust your crew with your life, you become close. Some call it a trauma bond. Whatever it is, it's forged through hard labor, sweat, and pain. Everything we do is a coordinated effort, and you give it your all. There is no work-life balance here. It's all or nothing.

We've got three burners with drip torches lighting small fires as they go, burning out any pockets of fuel on the line. It's damn near impossible to stop a raging wildfire head-on, but we can burn ahead of it, and meet it in the middle. By removing its fuel and cutting it off, we'll have a much better chance of it dying out. Or at the very least, slowing it down.

I take a drink of water and stuff the bottle back in my bag. I'm mostly serving as quality control today, but occasionally, I reach down to collect brush, or whatever organic material we've torn up behind us, to throw into the green. The wind picks up, and I straighten my spine the same time King does. Then we hear it—the telltale sizzling of a tree torching. *Shit.*

We spin in time to witness ladder fuels transforming one of the tall pines into a towering pyre, with flames soaring up the trunk and into the crowns. Pockets of sap boil and explode from the bark with loud snaps as the tree is engulfed by the blaze, and air rushes toward the fire as it sucks in fresh oxygen to fuel itself.

The wind carries a dense stretch of smoke over our line, and a wave of hot, torrid air surges through the timber, sending fiery ash and glowing embers from the fire ahead into the unburned trees like a thousand angry fireflies.

Glowing sparks land among the pine needles on one of the tall pines, and the bough slowly catches. Flames from the first tree spread to the neighboring one, which is already igniting from the raining embers. I lament as two more trees are engulfed. Other small fires quickly catch on the forest floor below.

King lets his Pulaski drop to the ground and leans on the handle. "Well, that fuckin' sucks."

While there's something alluring about massive trees turning into angry infernos, this feels like a big fuck-you from Mother Nature herself.

"Ember wash! Fifty yards!" I boom, alerting the squad leads downrange, who echo the warning to others.

I grab my radio and request Alpha and Bravo squads to help cover the area and make sure we get the spot fire put out before it gets out of control—I've seen embers cause spot fires over half a mile away. If it's not dealt with quickly, that slight shift of wind will have undone eight hours of painstaking labor.

A red-hot ember slips under my collar and down the back of my yellow Nomex shirt.

"Fuck," I grit out, slapping my hand on the scorching cinder and searing it into my skin to tamp it out. I hate when that happens. They're worse than fire-chasing beetles.

After I've asked for more guys, I contact the division to request the ship do a recon flight and some bucket work to catch any spot fires we don't have eyes on. If we can douse the nearby area, it'll slow it down, but for now, the priority is to retreat a safe distance, anchor back into our line, flank, and pinch off the fire.

Radio static interrupts the crackle and pops of burning timber, and we get confirmation on a water drop. There's a short turnaround with the nearby lake.

Less than ten minutes later, the steady thump of helicopter blades roars louder as it flies overhead, releasing a deluge of water and sending mist in all directions. On its way out, another radio broadcast comes in. *"All resources on the Mahonia fire, stand by for an incident weather update."*

The Incident Meteorologist called in over the command frequency with a division warning that a massive thunderstorm is headed our way. While we get the spot fire under control, more reports come through the radios that air traffic is being grounded. It isn't long after that we're being instructed to return to camp.

Perched on log stumps, guys huddle around a few different campfires as they eat an early dinner. It's eerily quiet with everyone shoveling food in their mouths without the usual dinner conversation and banter. Those who have finished eating have begun setting up their tents. Most of the time, we just sleep on the ground in our bags. Staff and crew around camp scramble to batten down the hatches as we prepare for what sounds like a wallop of a storm. Even the IMET says it's the largest storm cell he's seen in ten years.

As soon as I'm done scarfing down my plate of food, I head

over toward the ambulance. They should be receiving the same storm updates we are, but since it's a Sky Ridge rig, I better double-check, as a courtesy. They're parked in a grassy area, but if they stay there, they might end up with a stuck rig when this place turns into a mud pit.

I haven't heard who the paramedic leading the new guy is, but Matt is one of the medics from Sky Ridge, and we've shared a few beers in the past. He's a decent guy, so if he's on-site, I wouldn't mind saying hi anyway. I jog over to the ambulance just as Matt pops out of the side door.

"Hey, man." I grin. "Didn't know you were going to be joining us."

"Yeah, neither did I. We got a new hire—never been on a wildfire. Chief wanted to get some extra training in before the season's up and see if we can offer any support." He opens one of the exterior rig compartments and produces a couple binders with instruction materials of some kind.

"How's the training going?"

"Great!" He throws his thumb over his shoulder. "Prescott's in the back if you wanna introduce yourself."

"Sure. But, hey, I actually came over because we've got some storms coming in. You guys may want to pull onto the gravel soon so you don't get stranded in the mud later."

"Thanks for the heads-up."

Matt rounds the cab and hops in the driver's side with his papers and booklets. I knock on the side door to meet Prescott, which isn't necessary, but since he suggested it, I can't avoid it now. I step back when I hear the handle unlatch, and damn near fall over when Scottie braces herself with her hand above the door. My smile grows bigger.

She seems just as confused to see me here. "Hi?"

"Hi... I was actually looking for Prescott, but this works too."

She jabs a finger to her chest and grins. "Prescott."

The names click in my mind, and I hang my head and nod. *Fucking duh.* "Scottie... short for Prescott. Got it." *I'm a dumbass.* When I glance back up, her smile widens.

She lifts her chin, gesturing toward the smoking hills. "Forestry, huh?"

"Firefighter." I shrug. "I probably should have clarified, but anytime you say firefighter, people think of, well, *your* firefighters, and then it leads to more questions about wildfire and—"

She holds up a hand. "No need to explain. It's the same reason I didn't say EMT. I was hoping to avoid the '*What's the worst thing you've ever seen?*' interrogation."

Guess neither of us are big fans of talking about work. A silence settles between us, and Scottie's gaze darts left to right. "So, was there something you needed or..."

Already getting the shove off. *Cool.* "No, I just got done telling Matt that we've got some storms coming in, and since I was here, thought I'd introduce myself to the new guy, but it seems we've already been introduced."

Rubbing the back of my neck, I glimpse behind me and notice our crew still setting up tents. "See those guys over there?" I point. "They're a bunch of assholes. So if they give you any trouble, let me know."

"So far, you're the only one giving me trouble." She cocks her head to the side with a friendly smile.

"And I hope to keep it that way. I gotta get set up, but have a good rest of your day, *Prescott*." I turn on my heel, returning toward camp.

She chuckles. "You too." The door of the ambulance snicks closed behind me. I shake my head. *What are the fucking odds?*

On my way back, I pull out my phone and shoot off a text just as raindrops start to fall.

> Maybe we can still grab that dinner after all.

CHAPTER 7

Scottie

The fire camp looks like a ghost town, save for all the tents. Matt and I have spent the last two and a half hours getting rocked side to side as gusts of wind slam against the rig. At first, it was almost comical watching these guys try to set up their tents while getting pummeled with sheets of rain. One guy even had his rain fly ripped out of his hands. It flew up into the air, and neither of us saw it come back down. Another guy didn't have a tent, just rolled himself in a tarp. It must be miserable out there. I fan my fingers in front of the heat vents, grateful to be warm and dry.

Eventually, the crews got inside their tents, and we haven't seen a soul since. The wind and rain have eased up some, but according to radar, this thing isn't done kicking our asses yet. Until then, Matt and I have been hanging out in the cab trying to pass the time, and we're growing bored. We've done a couple training drills in the back. He tested me on where everything is located; I could do it with my eyes closed at this point.

"Lefty Lucy is gonna win. I'm tellin' ya," Matt says.

"No way. Righty Heidi is about to hit two other drops and power up. You're gonna get smoked."

We've been racing raindrops down the windshield of the

ambo since we've run out of things to keep us occupied. I've won seventeen races. He's won twelve.

"You're not gonna catch up," I tease. My drop hits the windshield wiper first. "Eighteen!"

"You cheat." He laughs, then leans forward, looking toward the camp, searching for any signs of life. When there's nothing, he sighs. "Wanna watch another movie?"

I shrug. Matt came prepared with a couple downloaded on his phone. We watched a few yesterday, but they're all starring Rob Schnieder, and there's only so much a person can take.

Radio static fills the cab with a division announcement, and we pause our conversation to listen.

"Due to flooding and heavy storms moving in, we'll be relocating crews to nearby lodging. Resources will be self-sufficient for the first few days, so make sure your crews have everything they'll need. A local summer camp has generously offered to provide dormitories. You will respect the host's property and not act like degenerates. A radio briefing will be conducted over the command channel at 1900 for crews at the new facility. For now, orders are to wait out the storm. If we don't get a break in the weather or conditions don't improve, we'll start to demob resources. Any questions?"

The corners of my mouth curve into a smile. *That means hot showers and a toilet.* I lived in my car long enough, I don't need to live out of an ambulance too.

I can only imagine the bellyaching from the hotshots who boast about being filthy and sleeping on the ground as if it'll earn them a medal—they're one of a kind. But seeing how the gravel lot is turning into a mudhole, I'm sure the forest is ten times worse. That should put them in a good mood.

The radio crackles again.

"Copy. Division, can we take the canoes over to the girls' camp for a sleepover?"

The query is not granted a response from Operations... I assume that one was from one of the hotshots.

Once we receive our orders, Matt plugs in the coordinates to our GPS, and the voice command prompts with our first direction—there's only one road in or out of this place.

We load up, secure our gear, and strap down the gurneys to prepare for the move. The camp is alive again, disassembling tents, tarps, and loading up folding tables. After a bit, a few hotshots take off in the bulky seafoam-green buggies, and headlights bounce down the gravel exit.

A couple more work trucks depart, and within a few minutes, we're on our way, rolling down the smooth mirrored-black asphalt as more sheets of rain splash across the windshield. Wipers tear back and forth, struggling to keep up with the onslaught of precipitation. Out the passenger window, plumes of smoke from the fire can still be seen hanging thick in the humid air. It's hard to wrap my mind around a job that has you running into a burning forest armed with only a shovel, axe, and the occasional chainsaw. Unreal.

After about half an hour on the highway, we're taken off the main drag to another gravel road where a large gate hangs open. Our rig slows as we clunk over the metal grate and continue down a narrow path. This one is in much better condition than the road we left behind at the previous encampment.

We round the bend and are greeted by a huge log gateway sign at least twenty feet tall. A wooden plaque hangs from the horizontal log overhead, and it reminds me of the ones I saw at ranches on my drive across the country. I lean forward and squint through the rain to make out the name: *CAMP BLUE SKY*.

A fine dose of irony.

The rig jerks as it bounces over washed-out divots, and eventually, we make our way toward a three-story building with lap siding. It's one of several like it. This is one of two with the exterior lights on. Matt ducks his head, peering at the carved sign staked out in front of the building. *Hummingbird Hall.*

"This is it."

A massive circular driveway sits in front, stretching between the matching lodges, probably used as a bus drop-off for campers. Matt finds a place to park toward the end of the row. It's not a parking lot, but it's been turned into one with all the other federal trucks and buggies.

We park a few spaces away and unlatch our seat belts, then Matt's phone buzzes in the car mount, and a text notification flashes. He plucks it from the cradle and swipes his finger across the screen. "Guys are talking about getting a poker game going in a bit," he mutters, tapping out a reply "Do you play Hold'em?"

"I think I know how to play. Are they betting?" If so, I'm out.

"Probably just snacks and stuff. I've got a bag of beef jerky and a few other things."

I've got a box of off-brand Pop-Tarts and a couple packs of Ramen noodles, but I'd rather not lose them. However, I'm willing to part with my bags of homemade caramel corn… It's cheap to make, but the last batch made so much, and I'm getting tired of eating it.

"Sure."

I throw my pack over my shoulder, grab my water bottle, and hop out at the same time Matt does. We run toward the front entry of the building, doing our best to dodge puddles. Once inside, I shake off the droplets and survey our temporary living quarters. Stale air and petrichor envelop the space. Along the wall, muddy boots are placed in rows near the vestibule, with a few bags of gear piled together.

The entrance opens into a spacious lobby of sorts with vaulted ceilings. To the right is a large staircase going up, surrounded by a couple sofas and coffee tables. Burly footfalls and voices from the floor above tell me people are getting settled into rooms.

Matt heads upstairs, and I wander the main floor since it's vacant. Opposite the staircase are propped-open double doors, and above the doorway is a small wood sign that reads MESS HALL. Inside, at least twenty circle tables have chairs flipped upside down on the surfaces.

My footsteps echo as I continue down the hall. On the left are two bathrooms. On the right is a large interior shop window that seems to be some gift shop or canteen. A child-size mannequin sits behind the glass, modeling a sweatshirt and bandana with *CAMP BLUE SKY* embroidery. A couple rustic wooden crates sit nearby, displaying other memorabilia and trinkets. There're no religious undertones, it's just… summer camp.

Around the hallway corner are a few more doors. One looks to be the entrance to the kitchen. I peek inside the lit room, observing the stainless-steel counters and commercial cooking equipment. A few silver tables sit in the center of the room for food prep. On top are brown cardboard boxes, polka-dotted with dark spots from raindrops after being transported. I recognize them as boxes of food from the staging camp, likely provided by whichever catering company offered the lowest bid to the federal government. My stomach growls, and I exit through the doorway, rounding the last section of the horseshoe-shaped hallway and heading up the stairs.

Matt calls my name from the landing above, startling me. "Sorry, didn't mean to scare you. I saved you a room at the end of the hall. Might want to put your stuff in there before someone else tries to steal it."

I nod and hoist my backpack higher on my shoulder. "Thanks!"

At the top of the stairs is a loft-style seating area open to below, and two hallways shoot off, following a similar U-shaped blueprint from the main floor.

"We're up one more."

The top floor is identical to the other. It appears most rooms contain three sets of bunk beds. Matt points to a door at the end of the hall, right across from the bathroom. "That one's yours, I'll be next door."

"Awesome. Thanks for snagging it."

I'm not sure if Matt has anybody else sharing a room with him, but I assume I'll have my own space. Not because I'm a woman, but because I'm not a hotshot. I get the impression we're sequestered toward the end here. Which makes sense. We're here for a training technicality, and so far, I haven't treated so much as a blister. These hard asses could slice off a finger and would probably duct tape it back on before coming to see us.

Unlike some of the other rooms I saw, mine has two bunk beds and one single. I drop my bag onto the single bed and flop down on one of the lower bunk cots.

I sigh, closing my eyes and thanking the universe for where I am. Hidden away.

"Cards?" I jolt upright, hitting my head on the bunk above mine.

"Shit!" I wince and rub the tender spot on my forehead. *I need to move over to the single bed.* When I crack open an eyelid, Matt is in the hallway wincing right along with me.

"Dude, you gotta lighten up. I'll try to stomp around more next time."

"Put a bell around your neck." I swing my legs over the side of the bed, ducking my head this time. "Yeah, you can deal me in. I'm just gonna put on a dry shirt first. Where is everybody playing?"

"I heard somebody say cafeteria."

I nod. "Be down in a sec."

CHAPTER 8

CALLAHAN

When I texted Matt, I hoped he would ask Scottie to join. He's not one to let the new guy sit out. However, when he enters the cafeteria alone, there's an edge of disappointment.

Matt pulls up a chair and gives a chin lift to King, Caleb, and the other guys: Opie, Bobby, and Dixon. Xander has decided to be the responsible one and get caught up on some paperwork while we have our poker game.

"About time I got to play a hand with y'all," Caleb says, leaning back in the plastic chair. "I always miss the text that goes out."

King cuts the card deck. "Funny how that happens…"

"Ever wonder if it's by design?" Opp asks.

"No, dumbfuck." He chucks an individually wrapped meat stick at him.

Opp laughs and adds it to his pile of snacks. "Keeping it as your entry fee."

Caleb furrows his brow. "Nobody else paid an entry fee!"

"No, they did not." King shakes his head and deals.

"Oh, deal a hand for Scottie. She's on her way down."

The table grows quiet.

"Scottie, the *she*? As in Scottie the hottie?" Caleb groans under his breath. "That girl could start a brush fire with a wink and a smile. Dude, one night with her and—"

"Keep that shit up and see what happens," I say a little too quickly.

"Come on, man." Matt chastens Caleb, the same time I do.

I pin him with an unamused glare. "You just earned yourself another week of veggie omelet MREs, rookie." *No amount of hot sauce can save that gastrointestinal war crime.*

"Dude, wait," Caleb pleads, holding up his palms in surrender, "but they hiss when you open them!"

Opp winces. "For anyone who's wanted to make a fart tangible..."

"Enjoy the vomlet bar." I collect my cards and blow out a breath. "Your guts are about to have a rough week, brother."

Bobby smiles. "We could switch to clam chowder?"

"No!" Caleb protests. His gaze bounces from player to player, but he won't be receiving any sympathy. "That's almost worse."

Almost.

"I don't care how many preservatives you add, no clam should be good for twenty years. Either it's not a clam, or it's not good for twenty years," Bobby states.

Dixon speaks up. "I've got a conspiracy the clam chowder MRE is actually government surplus wallpaper paste from the Truman era."

A few of us nod. It's plausible.

"Pork sausage?" Opp suggests, trying to sweet-talk him. "It comes with a free placenta."

"Still not as bad as the veggie omelet, though," King adds. "You can rat-fuck 'em for the desserts, though."

Scottie hurries through the doorway, right on schedule and thankfully, oblivious to the table talk. "Hi!"

I tuck my tongue into my cheek as King sets down the deck.

A few of the guys lift their hands in a wave as she pulls out a chair across from me and brings her cards into her chest. She's changed into jeans and a sweatshirt. Her ponytail sparks the mental image of me fisting her hair, prompting me to clear my throat and my thoughts. Like shaking a stubborn Etch-A-Sketch and watching the grainy image slowly fade. She reveals a couple bags of something from the kangaroo pouch of her sweatshirt.

"Whatcha got there, Scottie?" Dixon asks, craning his neck to take a gander at her stash.

"Caramel corn."

"Homemade?"

"Yup."

I love homemade caramel corn. I lift the corner of my two cards. Seven of hearts and four of clubs.

King lays the flop: a five, six, and a jack. I've got a chance at a straight.

We take a beat to review our hands. I throw in a small bag of Cheetos. Opp folds. Caleb throws in a Rice Krispie Treat, and Dixon adds in a fruit cup.

Bobby snatches up the fruit cup and turns it over in his hand. "The fuck is this?"

"Fruit cocktail," he replies.

"Motherfucker, this is all pears, and it went bad six months ago. Do you have anything decent? Scottie brought homemade caramel corn and you're showing up with expired poverty pears. Come on, now." His southern accent peeks out at the end, and a few of us laugh.

Dixon adds a fruit cup of peaches. "There. Bougee bitches."

Scottie folds. "I'm out."

Bobby tosses a granola bar onto the pile.

The turn is an eight of diamonds, so I toss in a half-smashed Hostess cake.

Everybody else folds, and I steal the pot of prepackaged junk food. We go a few more rounds, and Scottie folds after the flop each time. I casually slide my phone from my pocket and shoot her a text.

> You ever going to bet that caramel corn?

I keep my eyes on her as we go around the table again. I've got pocket sevens, and Dixon dropped another seven on the flop, along with a queen and a two. Scottie glances up at me, then her cheeks pinken as she texts under the table.

SCOTTIE
> If I get a decent hand.

> Life is about taking risks.

SCOTTIE
> You just want my caramel corn.

> Damn right I do.

The bet comes to her, and she smirks, tossing in her bag of gooey, buttery caramel corn.

SCOTTIE
> Come and get it.

I throw in the Rice Krispie Treat I won in the last round. Dixon gives the turn. Two of clubs. Full house. Everyone but Scottie folds. I toss in a Pearson's Nut Roll, and she throws in her second bag of popcorn. Dixon drops the river—a queen, and I rub my chin.

"What else have you got to bet?"

"I have Ramen in my bag upstairs... but I won't need it."

The corner of my mouth tips up. "Table talk from the new guy. Pretty bold of you."

Her stormy eyes flicker with mischief. She's got a wicked

streak. "Boldness with fear is courage. Boldness without fear is confidence."

I narrow my eyes at her. "So are you feeling courageous or confident?"

"Are y'all gonna fuck or play your hands? The rest of us are waiting on a new deal. Let's wrap this up."

Her cheeks heat, and I chuckle, then throw the bag of Cheetos on the pile and drop my cards to show the full house—sevens and queens.

She drops her hand. "Jacks full of queens."

"Scottie's a sniper," Caleb jokes.

I shrug and push my cards to Prescott since it's her turn to deal. She looks quite pleased with her new winnings.

> Confidence?

SCOTTIE
I'll never tell.

I peer across the table at her, and she darts her eyes away when I briefly glimpse at the two cards she dealt me. Nothing good.

> I'm stealing that caramel corn.

SCOTTIE
I'll share.

> Yeah? Picnic later?

SCOTTIE
Haha sure.

> Maybe we can get a chance to talk not over text.

This time, I feel her eyes on me, and it feels good.

SCOTTIE

"Talk" huh?

Scout's honor.

SCOTTIE

Were you a boy scout?

I'm always prepared, if that's what you mean.

SCOTTIE

Flirt.

Just with pretty EMTs.

SCOTTIE

Oh, Matt gets this treatment too?

Only until you showed up. See how
disappointed he looks?

Her gaze lifts from her phone to see Matt's furrowed brow as he double-checks his cards for the fourth time. Dude has the worst tell. She laughs across the table and tries to cover it with a cough, shoving her phone into her pocket.

Picnic tonight it is.

CHAPTER 9

Scottie

The shower slowly fills with steam. Am I really going through with this? Butterflies swarm my stomach. Maybe he wasn't even serious. It's not like we made any concrete plans. I agreed to *later*. I'm not sure what that even means. Later could mean tonight, a week from now, or on my seventy-fifth birthday.

If it is tonight, then I have a new problem to solve: *Is a picnic just a picnic?* Or is it more? If it's more, then what? Another decision.

Here's what I know: *I want to feel alive.* Desired, independent, spontaneous. Is it selfish to want those things? This is part of the new me. I can sleep with other men now. Sleep with them just for the hell of it.

"New beginnings come with growing pains."

Stepping under the shower spray, I squeeze a small amount of shampoo into my palm and massage it into my hair and recall the days of listening to endless sermons that became more and more confusing as I grew older. I would study the faces in the congregation for any sign they felt the same way I did. They didn't.

I envied every stranger on the outside, wondered what their lives were like and how desperately I wanted to trade with them. If only for a day. Everyone has their own struggles, and I understood there's no way of knowing whether the grass was greener, but the monotony was going to kill me either way, so at least I'd have a change of scenery.

One impulsive night at a fire camp could never outweigh the shame of my years spent in The Fold. So what am I afraid of?

I rinse out the shampoo and add conditioner. Then suds up my legs and get started on shaving. What is sex like when it happens organically, by choice? Doubt creeps into my mind. Perhaps I should have done this with a stranger... What if it's nothing like what I know? No, that can't be true. It's the same concept. I can follow his lead. Hell, tonight could simply be a picnic and I'm getting all keyed up over eating a damn bag of popcorn.

I roll my eyes at myself. *Stop overthinking.*

After drying off, I flip my head upside down and use the hand dryers on the wall to dry my hair while I work through some tangles. It doesn't dry completely, but it's close enough. Brushing my teeth feels amazing, but it always does when I have cold water to rinse with. Then I stand in front of the mirror and lay out my drugstore eyeshadow, blush, and mascara, then swipe on the products. My application has improved and gotten faster over the few weeks I've started wearing it.

I check my phone to see he hasn't texted me yet. *Does he still want to get together?* I shrug. I'll feel silly if I just put on makeup for nothing. We finished eating dinner about an hour ago. I sat with Matt at a different table but caught Callahan glancing at me on more than one occasion, and I like the way he looks at me.

Back in my room, I pull out my paperback and attempt to read, but every few paragraphs, I have to start over because I get distracted. There're so many people around. Even with my door shut, it's too loud.

I grab my backpack and fill it with some of my winnings from the poker game. I came out ahead, which means my junk food cache is flush with snacks. Beginner's luck. Cal kept his word and took the caramel corn. Next, I stuff my training manual and the fiction novel I was reading inside, zip it up, and throw it over my shoulder.

I knock on Matt's door.

"Come in!" he hollers.

"Hey, do you mind if I get the keys for the rig?"

He nods and rolls to his side to reach his jacket, where he feels around in the pockets until he finds them. "Something you need?"

He tosses the keys in my direction, and I catch them out of the air. "Just wanted to read a little bit. And maybe go through the handbook. In peace."

"Yeah, I hear ya. These guys can be loud as hell." His words are punctuated by some boisterous laughter below. "Did you want me to go through any of the exercises with you?"

I shake my head. "Nah, I'm good. But I'll text you if I run into any questions." I lift my hand holding the keys. "Thanks again."

"No prob." I leave, and he shouts after me. "Don't work too hard!"

"I won't!"

At first it was chilly in the ambulance, but the temperature in the back has warmed enough for me to pull off my sweatshirt and set it aside. It's been forty minutes with no messages from Callahan, but I'm not disappointed in the least. I've been savoring the solitude. Being around that many people in a small space reminds me of back home. While the hotshots have been the most entertainment I've had in a while, it's nice to have a couple hours of quiet. Thunder rolls in the distance, and raindrops spatter on the ambulance roof. It's comforting. The ambient sounds help me escape into the well-worn pages of my book.

My phone buzzes. One or two butterflies take flight in my stomach—as they tend to do when I finally get a text notification from him.

CALLAHAN
Are you awake?

Yes.

CALLAHAN
What are you doing?

Reading.

I snap a photo of the cover of my book and send it to him along with my response.

CALLAHAN
Where at? I stopped by your room.

I peer out the window, but with the interior lights on, only my reflection stares back at me.

I'm in the rig.

CALLAHAN
Want company? I've got snacks.

My stomach flips. Almost all our interactions have been through text. Any in-person contact has been in public, never one-on-one. Hidden away in the back of an ambulance while everyone else is inside the dormitory might as well be a remote cabin in the woods, though I'd prefer that scenario over this one. Remote cabins are romantic. Ambulances are... clinical.

Sure.

CALLAHAN
Be down in a couple minutes.

Exhaling, I place the gas station receipt bookmark between the pages and run my fingers over the thin paper. This receipt represents so much. It was the decision to leave the place I once called home, and even when I stopped for gas, I kept going. The date has faded, and eventually, the print will vanish, along with any evidence of who I used to be. Just another piece of paper. Just another woman.

I'm not her anymore—maybe I never was. The present has always been my destiny. I feel it in my core.

A knock on the side door drags me from my thoughts. I straighten in the gurney I've been using as a reading chair and run my fingers through my hair and over my shirt, fixing the hem. The nerves are different, more jittery than skittish. There's an underlying buzz of anticipation burning through my veins.

I open the door, and he stands there holding a blanket and a brown paper grocery bag. I back up, giving him room to enter. He climbs into the back and keeps his head ducked from hitting the ceiling. His hair is wet like he took a shower, or maybe it's from the rain. He sets the bag on the bench along the side wall and shuts the door behind him. Now that we're in close quarters, I'm enveloped in the scent of cedar and soap.

"Hi."

He takes a seat on the bench and looks around, appraising the ambulance. "Nice place you've got here."

"Thank you." I chuckle and shrug. "I like the privacy."

His eyes crinkle in the corners when he smiles. "Me too."

It's hard not to hear innuendo in his words. His gruff voice coaxes more butterflies to take flight, so I avert my gaze as a blush rises to my cheeks.

"Are you hungry?" I ask, unzipping my pack.

"Oh, no, this is my treat." He shakes open the blanket and dumps out the bag of snacks on top. "I went all out."

"I can see that. Those bags of caramel corn look a little familiar."

He laughs. "Fair point. But I brought a picnic blanket. Partial credit?"

"Where did you find the blanket?"

He turns over the corner, and it's embroidered with CAMP BLUE SKY. "Stole it from the gift shop."

"Lies *and* steals? It's so hard to find a guy that does both! Lucky me."

"They don't make 'em like me anymore," he says with a cocky smile, then gestures to the prepackaged spread before us. "You wanna get in on this?"

I move from the jump seat across from him to the bench, keeping the snacks between us.

"Okay, ground rules. Everything is up for grabs, but"—he snatches up the bags of caramel corn—"these are mine."

"You can have them."

"You don't like caramel corn?"

"I do, but I only know how to make it in huge batches. After a dozen helpings, I'm happy to share."

He drops his head down, opening the bag. "Let's see how you did." He chews thoughtfully, savoring it, and smiles. "That's heavenly."

"Thanks. I'll give you the recipe."

"Yeah, but if you make it, it gives me an excuse to see you."

A grin grows on my lips. "Why do you need an excuse?"

"I guess I don't… Does this mean I get a second date?"

66

"Is this a first date?" I ask with raised brows.

"Obviously!" He scans our surroundings. "Can't you tell by the half-empty Pringles can and the charming ambulance?"

I laugh. "Setting the bar pretty high for yourself. How will you ever top this?"

"I won't," he says, chuckling. "It's all downhill from here. You'll be looking at a future of riding go-karts and dinners with drinks. Maybe even stargazing. Poor thing." He opens a bag of cheese balls, and a couple roll onto the floor.

"Normally, I'd say five-second rule, but I don't even want to think of all the bodily fluids you have in a place like this. I don't want to catch hepatitis or something."

My hand presses to my chest. "I'm offended! My rig is totally sanitized and clean. This ambulance is spotless."

Nudging his shoulder toward the stray cheese ball on the floor. "You eat it, then." He cracks open a can of soda and takes a sip.

"Hell no. It's still an ambulance." Laughter comes easy with him, and I enjoy the effortless dynamic between us.

"Okay, see if you can catch one," he says, setting his drink to the side.

I back up on the bench, and he lobs a cheese ball in the air, but I squint and miss. "Oh no!"

"Don't close your eyes!" He laughs. "You're wasting food."

I lean forward and steal the bag from him. "It's hard! Okay, your turn." I toss one up, and he lines up his mouth with the trajectory of its fall, biting it out of the air.

He reaches for the bag, and I hand it over. "Okay, you got this, Scottie. Ready? This time, don't close your eyes."

In my second attempt, I successfully catch the flying cheese ball. My arms shoot up in victory, and I accidentally smash my knuckles on the overhead cabinet.

"Shit, are you okay?" He chuckles.

I nod, laughing harder, and tuck my throbbing hand to my chest. "Nailed it."

We go back and forth catching orange projectiles with our mouths and making small talk. We share more than a physical attraction, with a playfulness and ease that feel so... familiar. Even though I've never experienced it until now.

"So, why are you a hotshot?"

He pauses, then clears his throat. "The adventure, the camaraderie, the work we do... It's addicting. On the other hand, there's isolation from real world skills that leave us somewhat trapped. Once you're a wildland firefighter, you can't simply walk away. It's a love-hate relationship with fire. But what other job will pay you to fly into Yosemite National Park, cut hundred-year-old trees, and then light the place on fire?

"If you're lucky, your crew is tight knit. You spend years on road trips with your friends while trauma bonding, solving unique challenges, and overcoming hardships. I love the landscape I work in, and it's worth knowing I can protect its health.

"I've taken a helicopter into parts of this country that are inaccessible to most people, managed millions of dollars of air resources, rescued people on the worst days of their lives, and am paid to live in a wilderness people shell out big money just to see."

Wow.

Having only been in their presence for a handful of days, there's a nomad-like energy they all share. One I respect—and envy. It's what carried me to Washington. I work up the nerve to look him in the eye and admit something I've never said out loud. "I wasted so much of my life staying in one spot. I admire your sense of adventure."

The two seconds he holds my attention feel like two hours. The air is thick with friction, and his hungry eyes reflect the same need in mine. The sensation of being desired is something I could drown in. I never want to let go of it. There's nothing artificial or fake about his touch when he grabs me and pulls me into his lap. He's not just going through the motions with me.

"Do you kiss on the first date?" His voice is rough and gravelly. I've never loved my life as much as I do at this moment.

I nod. Cal doesn't rush, the depth of his gaze is intoxicating. It's calculated and intentional. His hands travel up my arms, and one palm threads into my hair, the touch potent. His fingers massage over my scalp as he gently grips the strands. My eyes flutter closed. It feels so good. It's firm and demanding. Passionate in ways I've never experienced. His free hand wanders to my lower back and presses me tighter to him.

My eyes open, and he pulls my locks once more. My exhale is a small moan as he brings my mouth to his lips.

It's an explosion of sexual tension and need, and my brain is filled with sizzling fireworks and exalted hallelujahs. It's every description of a kiss I'd convinced myself were lies. It *does* feel like this.

I'm paralyzed by him. He releases my hair, and with his thumb on my chin, he parts my lips and brands me with his kiss, tasting like caramelized sugar. He groans, and a heat spreads to my center. My hands drift from his shoulders to his chest, where I clutch his shirt. I never want to let go, so I draw him nearer, needing him more than my next breath.

If kissing Callahan feels this incredible, anything more might kill me. His breathy chuckle tells me he's as surprised by this kiss as I am. His tongue slides across mine, and his hands move to my waist, squeezing my sides and rolling my hips against him. I gasp and pause. Oh my god—he's hard. *For me.* The seam on my jeans pushes against my clit, and I close my eyes.

He kisses under my ear, and his teeth scrape the side of my neck. "Still with me?"

"Yeah," I whisper, out of breath.

He unbuttons and unzips my jeans, then finds the hem of my

shirt and pulls it over my head. I unhook my bra, and he slips it off my shoulders and onto the floor.

"Fuck," he mutters.

My nipples harden as his thumbs brush over them, and he plucks each one as his tongue finds mine.

"With me?" he asks again.

I hum, then he pushes me off him and works my jeans down my legs before sitting back and gazing over my body. I stare back at him and become self-conscious when he says nothing. Lowering my head, I scan over my hips and torso. *What's he looking at?*

"You're a smokeshow." He smiles bigger and stands, gripping his shirt at the nape of his neck and tugging it off. A tattoo of an eagle clutching a snake in its talons spans his chest. My eyes are lured away when he unbuckles his belt, so I toe off my shoes and kick out of my jeans. He stands and does the same, shucking his pants and boots, and the outline in his boxer briefs is more than I know what to do with. Then he peels my underwear from my legs, and I stumble backward onto the blanket-covered bench. This definitely can't go back to the camp store. He falls to his knees, and my jaw drops when he shoves my legs apart. Holy shit, he's bold.

His mouth caresses my inner thigh, then he nips. I jerk, and he grasps behind my knees, dragging me to the edge again. "Still with me?"

I've never done this before.

"Yes."

He kisses up my left thigh as his right hand slides up my other one, and the anticipation multiplies when his thumb traces my entrance. "Always," I say. *Always yes.*

He presses two fingers in, and my head falls back, then he pulls out before repeating the motion. I moan as he sucks on my inner thigh and pumps his fingers inside me, he curls them, and massages a spot I've only ever reached with a toy. Crying out, he chuckles.

"What's funny?" I can barely take a breath.

He pauses from sucking, removing his mouth, and there's a ring of bruised flesh in its place. "I like the sounds you make."

I bite my lip.

He sits back and watches while he torments me. It's so seductive. He adds another finger, and my face floods with pink as the wetness echoes through the ambulance.

"Unreal," he smiles. "All I've thought about is eating your pussy. I've been craving it all fucking night." He yanks me closer and seals his mouth over me, trailing his tongue over my clit and staring up at me from between my legs.

"Holy," I mumble, trembling. I want to scream. I take in the image of him licking between my thighs and the fire in his eyes as he does it. I get the impression he knows exactly what this is doing to me and can't get enough.

Our eyes meet and he grins. "So fucking sweet." Callahan flattens his tongue and licks up the center while staring into my eyes. His hips rock against the bench cabinet as he devours me, and I'm in awe—but I want more. "Tell me you have a condom."

No response.

"Fuck me, Cal... Please?"

He glances up and shakes his head. "I'm not done eating."

I sink a hand into his hair and relax back into the bench, tilting my head to the side and admiring how attractive he is as he brings me more pleasure than I've ever known. His fingers enter me again, and a foreign feeling grows in my core. It feels so good, but it's not fully gratifying. I grip his hair as the sensation builds and builds. *Is this...*

His lips lock onto my clit, and he sucks.

"Holy fuck. Cal... Cal!" White light explodes behind my eyes, and I'm helpless as I surrender to the euphoria.

I did it.

I came.

"That's it, baby, that's so good. Damn, you're sexy when you come."

It's the first time a man has made me come. I'm speechless.

He leans to the side and fishes his wallet from his back pocket, revealing a condom.

A smug smile grows on his lips, and I cup his chin and swipe the pad of my thumb over his scruff, clearing some of the wetness I left behind. He pulls my thumb into his mouth and sucks. The only thing I want in this entire world is to be filled up by Callahan Woods and fucked into oblivion.

He stands and shoves his boxer briefs down. His cock is thick and heavy, even in his large palm as he rolls the condom on. While sweeping the remaining snack wrappers onto the floor, he commands me to "Lay back."

I swallow and situate myself with my back on the fuzzy blanket. *Finally.* He braces one knee between me and the back of the bench and keeps his other foot planted on the floor. The bench is too shallow for anything more. His tip presses into me, and I stretch around his girth. "Oh my god... oh my god," I murmur, clasping his shoulders.

"Fuck, you're tight." He meets my gaze and lifts his chin. "Relax, Scottie."

I slowly inhale, forcing my muscles to slacken despite their objection. It's the most delicious pain. I shouldn't want more, but I do. I want all of him.

His voice is coaxing. "Eyes on me."

Cal withdraws and I exhale. *Why did he stop?* I prop up on my elbows, but any words of protest die in my throat when he spits on my entrance. "You have such a pretty pussy." He rubs the saliva around, pushing his thumb inside and stretching me before lining himself up. This time, the pain softens when he inches deeper. My body settles around him, and I relax onto the bench.

He smirks. "That's my girl."

With winded breaths, I soak up the sensation of fullness. His hand drifts up my stomach, traveling between my breasts. My nipples pebble under his touch. Gradually, his hips rock, and I feel *everything*. The blanket slides easily on the vinyl-covered bench, and I brace my arms against the cabinet behind me for resistance. "Cal... this is..."

"I know, baby," he pants, in understanding. "Me too."

I'm in over my head. It's so much all at once. I expected the physical sex being better, sure. I've visited websites that show people enjoying themselves with their partner. However, nothing could have prepared me for the emotional repercussions. *The connection.* The barrage of too-intense feelings that hit all at once. I don't know what to do with it. Passion is a powerful drug.

The attraction between us is undeniable, and this is a monumental step for me. My eyes brim with tears, so I pull him down until our chests touch. I lock my arms around his neck so he can't see the emotion rolling down my cheeks. It's happiness and joy and freedom. He wouldn't understand.

I stealthily swipe at my face and blow out a breath, gathering my composure. Then I kiss him with all that I have. His strokes become more aggressive and frantic. It's incredible. He readily accepts every whimper and sinks his teeth into my bottom lip. *Fuck.* I bury my fingernails into the flesh of his shoulders and scratch down his back. His growl is animalistic, and I can't tell if I'm the rabbit or the fox.

"Goddamn, Scottie."

Callahan is generous and demanding at the same time. He pulls out and stands, taking me with him. My mind swirls with the heady need for more. The man drops into the reclined gurney in the center of the ambulance. He turns me away from him, then guides me to walk backward. I widen my stance to straddle his thighs, and he wraps an arm around my waist, aligning my opening with the head of his cock. "Can I call you a good girl when you're being my good girl?"

I suck in a breath, and nod. *Mercy.* Directing me lower, he notches his crown inside me. The arm around my middle tethers me to his chest. He spits into his free hand, then slaps it against my clit, sending a burst of need through me.

"Ah!"

"Good girl," he praises. "Now take it all."

I'm slammed down on top of him, and my eyes roll back.

He slides his hands under my thighs and settles my legs to sit outside his, spreading his wider, putting me on display for anyone walking past the windowed doors. The risk of exposure enhances every sensation. His palm covers mine, and he positions it just above my pelvis, then presses deep. I feel the faint outline of his length, and my head falls back to rest on his shoulder. It's so hot. "Feel how full you are?"

Arousal rips through my core, and I shudder. "I need this." His other hand sweeps my hair to the side, and his lips brush over my shoulder blade.

"So tight... Keep pushing down."

I follow directions, *like a good girl.* His hand leaves mine, and I maintain the pressure against my flesh when he cups my sides and moves me up and down his cock.

"Fuck!" I cry out, and my voice grows louder.

"That's right, baby. You are such a good fuck." His chuckle is taunting.

His hand slips under my chin, and he circles my throat without applying force. "Still with me?"

I nod. "Always."

Intentional choking in the back of an ambulance... *That's new.*

With the back of my head still resting on his shoulder, I look up at the ceiling, but all I see are stars. I squirm and succumb to the urge to grind in his lap.

"I know you want to move, sweetheart, but keep your legs open for me."

Grasping the sides of his thighs is all I can do to hold on. I'm racked with involuntary shakes, and my forehead breaks out in a cold sweat as another orgasm swells. I groan with a clenched jaw. It's so hard to sit still.

My eyes find the back windows, and I stare in awe at the reflection of him pounding into me from below.

"See how stunning you are getting fucked by a fat cock? The way your eyes sparkle when you're taking it?" He slaps my clit, then impales me down on him. My mouth drops open, and his palms grip my waist again as he works me over like I'm his personal fuck toy. My moans shake as I'm bounced on top of him. It's relentless bliss. There's not a muscle in me that isn't fully engaged.

"Eyes forward."

I affix my gaze to the windows in front of us; he's so handsome. Callahan shakes his head. "Not on me—on you. Watch yourself come."

"Cal… Don't stop."

My breasts jump with each thrust. There's something strangely healing about watching myself get ravaged by this man. A smile creeps onto my face, I hardly recognize the woman staring back at me—she's uninhibited and raw and fearless. I love this. *I love sex.* How could this ever be considered a sin? It's beautiful.

"Come on, baby…" His words are deep and commanding. "Come all over me. There you go, that pussy's squeezing so tight. You're almost there."

It sends me over, and my jaw drops on a silent scream.

"Do it, Scottie!" he growls as his teeth rake against my skin, sending goose bumps across my flesh and making me shiver. My eyes pinch shut, but he shouts my name, and I open them again, witnessing myself overwhelmed with ecstasy.

"Fuck, I love the sounds you make."

I don't remember making sounds. I remember nothing at the moment. Only searing pleasure. He slowly brings me down from the high, and the sweat on his chest makes him glide against my back. "Spin around," he orders, breathless.

With wobbly legs, I stand.

"Whoa, easy." He stabilizes and pulls me back down. I can't catch my breath, but I straddle him and grunt as I'm filled with him again—this time facing each other. It's more intimate than before. He presses his forehead to mine, and I squeeze his biceps, gripping the firm muscles for support.

"We can rest for a minute, just grind."

It's exhilarating. The thrill makes my skin buzz. It's like the first time I got drunk and wondered why anyone would ever choose to be sober. Will waking up tomorrow feel like paying a debt, or will I crave it all over again? He bows his head and blows out a breath, seemingly enjoying the show of our bodies moving together.

"Beautiful," he mutters. His lips seal over my nipples, and he sucks.

His mouth on me while my hips grind against him is a different experience. My body is spent, muscles fatigued, but they don't quit. This is an indulgence like I've never known, and there's no guarantee I'll get it again.

We regard each other, and it's as if time stops, even if only briefly. His smile is magnetic. Genuine and real. He's so present, living in the moment. With his eyes on mine, our setting falls away. Callahan's gaze drops to my lips, and he cups the back of my neck, draws me closer, and kisses me. It's powerful. I roll my hips, and he moans. I love that I can affect him the way he does me. His palms rest on my waist, just above the crease of my thighs, and he leads me as I rock on his length, seeking gratification.

"Fuck, I'm not ready to come yet."

In a split second, he clutches my ass, flips me around, and drops me onto the gurney. He reclines it until it's almost flat.

"Do you like restraints?" he pants.

I glimpse down at the heavy-duty velcro straps. "I-I've never —I don't know?"

"Want to find out?"

I'm not a virgin by any means, but this is nothing like the sex I've had before. Relying on sheer untamed salacity, I respond. "Definitely."

My cheeks heat, and I scoot back toward the center. He drops one knee on the gurney, my legs fall off the sides, and he rips the velcro apart. "What do you want your safeword to be?"

"My safeword?" *I read about this. There's a stoplight thing.* "Red?"

"Red it is." He places my wrists in the strap and secures them.

"Ready?"

I nod. He lifts my legs and rests my calves against his shoulders before plunging into me. *Heaven on earth.*

I moan and he smiles. "You like it?"

I love it.

It's surrender. He could do anything to me, and there's nothing I could do but take it. My breasts angle toward him when I arch my back. "Mm-hm," I murmur.

"Okay…" he says, "I want one more from you."

Another orgasm. *Is he serious?* I'm a runner, but he's a hotshot. It's no contest who has the stronger stamina here. He's doing all the work, yet I'm the one out of breath. My chest heaves. The air feels so damn thin.

"You okay?"

"Sorry… It's like I've forgotten how to breathe."

"Shit, me too." He laughs and I join him. "Damn, I like it when you laugh while I'm fucking you." It makes me giggle harder. He groans. My laughter fades when he stares into my eyes. "Just like that."

The way this man works should be criminal. He alternates between teasingly slow, long strokes, and quick, hungry ones. Each is timed perfectly. Every push and pull notches up the tension. It's too much and never enough. I can't believe this is my life right now.

I blink up at him and hold his gaze while listening to the steady rhythm of sex as he drives inside me. This is not sex, this is something else entirely. It's far more intense and erotic. My heart drums behind my ribcage like it will beat right out of my chest.

Balling my hands into fists, I utilize every last shred of strength and flexibility I possess to meet each thrust. It's a useless exercise. Callahan doesn't compromise, he simply takes and never lets up. My inhales quickly become labored and short. *I'm so close to coming again.*

He narrows his eyes, and I shake my head adamantly. Before he has a chance to check on me, I answer.

"I'm fine. Don't stop." I'm gulping for breath. *How is he still going?*

"Time out." He slows but doesn't cease.

He pulls one of the O2 masks from the wall and places it over my face. "Slow breaths." He grins at me. "Nice and slow… Just feel."

Part of me wants to laugh at the absurdity, but the other half is so turned on by him forcing me to inhale oxygen while dragging himself in and out. I can do nothing but listen to his instruction. My body vibrates with pleasure. *Is this what it feels like to get high?* I'm floating.

"Good god… this pussy was made for me. Where did you come from?"

"Arkansas," I rasp.

He leans forward and barks out a laugh, then removes the

mask from me and places it on his face, taking a hit of O2 before dropping it aside.

"Now why don't you show me what a good girl you are and make that pretty cunt of yours milk my cock."

My eyes widen at his words, and a grin spreads across his lips. I'd do just about anything for that smile. I drop my legs from his shoulders and he presses his mouth to mine. He grips the back of the gurney for leverage and barrels into me. Every pound sends me higher. I'm so close. He adjusts his body, allowing his length to reach my G-spot.

Callahan encourages me the whole way. "Keep taking it. You can do it. Come on, one more."

My mind empties, focusing only on the carnal bliss he brings. His forehead touches mine. My brow furrows and muscles stiffen as I search his eyes.

"Show me how much you love it, Scottie. Come on this fucking cock," he demands.

His words flood my thoughts, enhancing every physical sensation with an emotional one. He massages his thumb on my clit, and his movements become more frantic. I erupt at the same time he does, and he buries himself to the hilt.

It's not as powerful as the first two, but I still come harder than any experience prior to tonight. He grunts, hammering into me with long hard thrusts. He nips at my neck, growling in my ear as he comes. I'm speechless.

"Is… is it always like that?" I ask, with winded speech.

"No." His chin drops, and he gives a headshake while we catch our breath together. When his gaze finds mine, he releases a deep exhale and smiles. "No, it's not always like that." He presses a kiss to my temple. His palms encircle my wrists, freeing the velcro and kneading the red marks where the straps dug into my skin. I never knew rough hands could be so tender.

We rest together and listen to the heavy, pelting rain patter against the roof, and our breathing returns to normal.

The moment is interrupted by a loud crack of thunder that rocks the ambulance, and the interior is filled with the brightest light I've ever seen. Callahan jolts backward, throwing himself into one of the cabinets. "Holy shit!" Adrenaline has my heart rate soaring. "Are you all right?"

He doesn't answer. He looks lost.

One of the building's exterior lights pops on. Spearing my arm through the passthrough window to the cab, I slap the patient dome light off to shroud us in darkness.

It takes a moment for my eyes to adjust, but when they do, I pick up my jeans, jump into them, and toss on my shirt, skipping over my underwear and bra. "Cal…" I reach for him, and his body trembles. *What is happening?*

"Whoa. Hey? Callahan."

"I'm fine," he snaps. "I just need a minute."

I nod and collect his clothes, setting them next to him on the bench. Sitting beside him, I thread my fingers with his. I'm not sure what he's got going on, but I want to remind him he's not alone. He grips my hand in a vise. My eyes fall to our tightly clasped hands, barely visible in the shadows.

Less than a minute later, voices can be heard near the entrance to the dorm. I lean over to peek out one of the windows, and a few guys are taking a smoke break outside. Cal releases my fingers and removes the condom, then pats the bench next to him, feeling for his clothes. He pulls his boxer briefs on, then grabs his pants.

"Don't shift too much or you'll rock the rig," I whisper.

"If the rig's a rockin', don't come a knockin'," he jokes, his voice hollow.

I've never seen someone lock up so fast. "Is there anything I can get you?"

"I'm good." He moves cautiously as he dresses. Each of us scan the area for clothes tossed on the floor earlier. I slip on my sweatshirt, then find my bra and tuck it into the pocket.

Where the hell are my... "I can't find my underwear."

"They're in my pocket," he answers. "I'm keeping them."

"Thief and a liar." I narrow my eyes and shake my head with a small smile.

"And a gambler..." he adds, sounding more like himself. "Maybe you can play me for them sometime."

"You're terrible." I chuckle and feel around on the floor for my socks. Foil wrappers from our snacks crinkle as my fingers brush over them. Thank God nobody was hurt, or this would take some explaining; what we did here was far too risky and can't happen again.

CHAPTER 10
CALLAHAN

Bobby is snoring like a fucking chainsaw two doors down. I'm about to kick his door open and force him to sleep outside. Normally, we make him sleep far away from the rest of us at camp just so we don't have to listen to all that damn racket. King is in the bunk across from me, and I can tell by his breathing he's asleep. Tonight's accommodations aren't too shabby. The cot under my back is soft and warm, but I can't get comfortable.

It took nearly two hours to clean the back of the ambo. She made it clear it's off-limits from now on. The guys will probably wonder why I smell like sanitizer in the morning, which is none of their goddamn business. I didn't mind helping her clean one bit. Scottie and I found things to laugh about. I scrub a hand down my face and flop on my side, staring into the darkness. *Fuck. Why does this feel weird?* There's a pang of *something* scratching from the inside, an emotion trying to claw out of my chest. Doubt? Regret? No. Definitely not regret.

Normally, I feel nothing after a hookup, other than release. It's not a bad thing. I don't feel like anything is lacking. Most of my escapades are no different than a fun night at the bar. I have a great time, but when it's over, it's *over*.

This doesn't feel like it's over.

I silently curse the damn thunderclap that had me all kinds of messed up. When I froze in front of her, I felt like a fucking idiot, especially right after sex. Not the best look, but I appreciate that she didn't press or try to talk about it. There's nothing to discuss. Instead, she simply sat with me and held my hand, and it was exactly what I needed in that moment.

Another minute passes by as I glimpse at the clock on my phone's lock screen. If I fall asleep right now, I can still get just over four hours of sleep.

I shut my eyes, tugging the fleece blanket from earlier over my shoulder, and the scent of her shampoo relaxes my mind. I replay the sounds she made and the way her deep-blue eyes yearned for more.

Whatever pain tomorrow brings, it was worth a night with Scottie.

CHAPTER 11

CALLAHAN

The chatter of the dining hall fades around me while I text Scottie between bites of food and bullshitting with the guys. We've been flirting all day over text. It's driving me insane. Today was brutal out there with all the mud and muck thwarting our progress. I'm fucking spent, but that doesn't mean I'm not counting down the minutes for everyone to retreat to their rooms so I can sneak into hers.

Even during dinner, we were cutting our eyes at each other like it's some fucking game.

She's so damn hypnotizing.

I want to see those lips wrapped around my dick. I want to feel the way her pussy clenches when I call her a good girl. I want to see her tits jiggle while I fuck her.

I want it all.

Half the guys have been checking her out, and I even had to yell at a couple on the line today when she became a topic of conversation. For whatever reason, I'm not willing to share this one. Scottie has planted a possessive streak in me. She's all mine. Normally, I try to avoid flirting or engaging in sex with anyone on assignment, and even if I do, it's one and done.

Keeping a firm boundary ensures everyone is set on expectations and nobody ends up disappointed or catching feelings. After a night with this woman, I'm willing to make an exception. It's not like she'll be on every assignment. It's temporary. We're just taking advantage of the situation, but, if we do this, we need to lay some ground rules so she understands this is purely physical. The sex is phenomenal, but it can become nothing more. I'm not ready to welcome commitment into my life yet, and it wouldn't be fair to lead her to believe otherwise.

> This caramel corn tastes almost as sweet as you do.

SCOTTIE
OMG

I've been taunting her through text messages most of the day. To be fair, she started it when she sent me a grainy picture of the back of the ambo.

> What?

SCOTTIE
You know what.

> Aw, come on. I said much filthier things to you last night...

I glance across the dining hall, and her cheeks burn pink as she snaps that weird ass flip phone shut. She's fun to rile.

> You're blushing.

She tries to ignore my text, but eventually, she opens her phone again.

SCOTTIE
It's an allergic reaction.

Lol

Can I come see you later?

SCOTTIE
Are you going to stop teasing me?

Please... She's the one doing all the teasing today.

I dunno, are you going to be a good girl?

SCOTTIE
You're the worst.

Never claimed to be otherwise.

Our eyes meet from across the room, and she pins me with a chastising expression. I offer a wink and a smile in return.

With all the mud, everyone has been walking around in socks, which lends itself to quiet footsteps when one is involved in clandestine activities. My knuckles rap on her door softly, and the turning knob has my mouth tipping up in a smile. Though, I'm unprepared for the sight of her in nothing but an oversized shirt when she opens the door. The stretched neck gives me a view of her bare shoulder, and the fabric nearly reaches her knees. My chest tightens. I don't like her wearing another man's shirt.

She steps aside, giving me room to enter. I run my hands down my hopefully not-too-wrinkled Henley. Hard to keep shirts pressed when you're living out of a backpack. Something tells me Scottie doesn't mind.

The room is similar to mine, except she only has two bunk beds, and the third is a single twin with a small blanket. Her things are laid out on one of the lower bunks. Everything is neat and orderly. Her zipped backpack sits upright beside clothes organized in piles. On the other end of the bed, the snacks she won at poker are arranged into groups. The groups don't make much sense, as they aren't sorted by brand or even category. It's as if she took one of each type of food and put it together, almost like she's rationing them. Whatever, to each their own.

The space smells like her, with subtle notes of jasmine and vanilla. Inhaling, a content peacefulness eases over me. It's unfamiliar, yet settling. As soon as I hear the door close behind me and the lock engage, I'm on her.

My palms find her waist, gathering the loose cotton at her sides. She raises her chin, and those lust-filled eyes turn a stormy blue. She blushes and sucks in a breath. A grin plays on my lips as I dip my head to kiss her. I like taking her breath away. She parts her lips, and I lick into her mouth while walking her backward toward the bed. Fuck, I've been waiting all day for this.

Before we get too carried away, I pull back. I've got nothing against a good fuck-and-run, but seeing as we'll be sharing a dorm for the foreseeable week, I should at least try to have a conversation first. Sure, we've been texting, but I enjoy chatting with Scottie. I haven't even said hello yet.

"Hi," I whisper, keeping my voice down.

"Hi." Her soft laugh is adorable.

She works the nape of her neck, and flinches slightly.

"Sore?"

She waves me off and nods to the bunk with all her food. "Are you hungry? I have a deck of cards if you want to try and win some of your snacks back?" I smirk and shake my head, then set her pillow aside and plop down at the head of her bed, resting my back against the wall, with my legs straight out in front of me.

Her hand finds the back of her neck again.

"Come here." I hold out my palm, and she accepts it, allowing me to thread my fingers with hers and guide her on the bed with me. "Lay on your stomach, I'll take over."

We get settled with her head in my lap, lying between my legs and resting her cheek on my left thigh, her hair fans out over my right one. She has one arm wrapped around my quad, and the other is bent near my back. The tips of her fingers brush my hip.

"Good?"

"Good," she confirms with a small smile.

Her eyes flutter closed when I cup the back of her neck, and prod until I feel the knotted muscle. "Ooh, you got a good one."

She grunts when I dig into it with my thumbs. "Too hard?"

"Nuh-uh," she purrs. "How was your day today?"

I'm not used to being asked that question. Usually, my day is the same as all the guys around me, rendering it unnecessary to ask. "Um, it was fine, I guess?" She gives me room to continue, so I do. "It's never fun working in mud, especially where the timber is dense and the sun can't permeate the ground through the thick trees."

I talk her through the events of the day with ease. It's weirdly domestic, like something a couple would do. She doesn't make it feel like small talk. She asks questions, and despite her becoming more and more relaxed as I dissolve the knot in her neck, she shows interest. I know she's paying attention when she has to ask for me to explain some of the verbiage.

"What about your day?"

She shrugs. "Kinda boring."

I huff an amused breath. I never envied EMS when they were spiked out. It's a lot of sitting around. My hand slides down the back of her shirt, drawing lines and circles as she talks. I rub her shoulders, arms, back—everywhere I can reach. With each graze, her body seems to turn to jelly. I wonder if this woman is as touch starved as I am.

Scottie moves the hand behind my back to the front of my shirt, and she slips it under my Henley. I have to fight to suck in a breath. Her feather-soft touch strokes over my stomach, causing me to shudder. She continues speaking, unaware of the effect she's having on me. Her fingers mimic mine, brushing over my abdominals in a similar pattern. *Goddamn.* It makes me hard and relaxed at the same time. I needed this more than I thought. I bury my free hand into her hair, and she groans in the middle of her story about the training exercises Matt had her working on.

I chuckle. "You like that?"

She smiles. "Mm-hm."

"I'll have to remember that." I wince as soon as the words leave my mouth. I shouldn't say shit like that; it gives the wrong impression of what this is. "I didn't mean to interrupt, you can keep going," I say, prompting her to finish her story.

She doesn't speak for a few seconds, then snickers. "What were we talking about again?"

"Training exercises…" I say, jogging her memory.

I thread my fingers through her hair near the roots, then fist them and tug gently.

She makes a small noise, something between a grunt and a moan.

"It's not important anymore. Ugh, that feels good."

I repeat the action, alternating between toying with the ends of her strands and adding tension at her scalp. Her nails dig into my muscles hard enough to flip that switch from sweet and affectionate to needing to bury my dick so deep I have to muffle her screams.

"I liked all those texts from you today," I tease, skating my fingers up her spine.

Her face pinkens, and she pulls her hand from my thigh to cover her exposed right cheek. "I'm embarrassed."

I scoff. "Why?"

"I've never done anything like that before. I've had sex, but not... like that."

It was also my first time fucking in the back of an ambo, but Scottie seemed to have an extra layer of inexperience I especially enjoyed corrupting. Seeing her face light up with pleasure like it was the first time was spectacular.

"Nah... I liked the ambulance photo you sent." The memory of her strapped down to that gurney sure helped the hours pass on the line today.

She moves to my thigh again, this time on top of my quad. "I was just messing around."

"I wasn't."

Her fingers grip a little harder onto my thigh, and when she loosens, her hand crawls up until she's palming my cock through my jeans, and I expel a breath through gritted teeth. The buildup of talking and barely-there touches has escalated into pure need.

After a beat, she confesses, "Me either." Her voice is breathy and full of sex. "But this feels so good it's hard to move."

I slip my hand from the back of her shirt and unbutton my jeans. She plants her palms on the bed, pushing off the cot to sit up.

"Nuh-uh. Don't get up."

After unzipping, I shove down the jeans and boxers, releasing my half-hard length.

"Keep your head in my lap. I'm going to play with your hair, and you're going to warm my cock between those plump lips until I say so. Understand?"

She nods with the most striking bedroom eyes, then shifts so she's straddling my right leg. I hiss when her tongue traces the underside of my length.

"Just like that," I sigh. *Perfect.*

Fucking hell. This is nice. I delve a hand back into her locks, combing through the strands with my fingers. I lift her chin up slightly so I can stare into those tempestuous eyes. My thumb skims over her soft hollowed cheek as she sucks on the crown.

"Beautiful."

My hand lets go and skims over her shoulder. I gather the back of her shirt, lifting it higher, and expose her bare ass. Damn, if I'd pulled up her shirt to rub her back, we'd probably be a lot further along right now. As tempting as that is, I like this progression better. Building anticipation is the best part.

"Goddamn. Look at you, naked underneath that shirt…" I keep my voice low. "It's almost as if you wanted me to fuck you tonight, Scottie."

My fingers sink into her hair, and she shivers. *Shit.*

"I think that's exactly what you want… So fucking needy."

She exhales through her nose, making a small sound. I'm fully hard as she lazily bobs over me.

"Do you have any idea how bad some of the guys here want you?"

She sucks harder. *Interesting.*

"I had to yell at four different guys today. Either because they were talking about how attractive you are or leering at you in ways only I get to."

She moans around me.

"I'm sure half of them were jerking their dicks to you in the showers."

She withdraws for a split second, shaking her head. "Too far."

My shoulders shake with laughter as I try to keep it down. "Yeah, you're right. I don't like thinking about that either."

A smile curls onto her lips as she takes my cock again, and my laugh dissipates while I marvel at her. Sweeping her hair behind her shoulders, I play with the strands, appreciating every inch of her.

"Good girl," I praise. "You suck so well, sweetheart. Don't stop."

Her legs press together, so I reach for my back pocket—that's now situated halfway down my thigh—and locate the condom, then set it aside.

"You talk a big game, Prescott... All those flirty texts. It drove me crazy. All I could think about was the look on your face when you came." She inhales through her nose. "The way you glow after you've been properly fucked."

She's all freckles and flushed cheeks.

"I bet you want to come right now... Remember when you came on my tongue? You tasted so sweet."

Scottie settles in, taking me deeper, and I groan.

"Fuck, that's it." With one hand in her strawberry hair, I rest the other on the back of her head. Saliva pools at the base of my cock. She's getting sloppier and I love it. "Just like that. You are such a lovely mess."

I tuck some loose strands behind her ear and continue playing with her hair, feeling triumph every time I make her quiver.

The gentle affection mixed with her lips wrapped around me is exquisite. This blowjob isn't as rough or as passionate as I usually prefer, but it's exactly what I need right now. It's intimate.

Intimate. My chest tightens. Yeah, this feels like more. With the way she's caressing me, this will turn emotional if I don't put a stop to it soon.

This is a hookup.

"Spread your legs for me."

As soon as she parts them, she's grinding against me. I can hear how fucking wet she is, and the pressure in my chest loosens. There's comfort in the familiar.

I transfer my focus to Scottie, and the way she's licking and sucking, it's almost like she's frustrated. It's amusing to watch her body seek friction where she needs it.

"Why did you send me that photo of the ambulance?"

Her hips roll, and I gather her tresses in my fist. She whimpers. I clench my jaw through the vibrations. *Jesus Christ, this girl could slurp me off the bone.*

"Come on, sweetheart, answer me."

I tug her hair, pulling her off me. Her bruised lips slide off with a wet pop, and she looks up and curses my name.

Her words come out in a breathy rush. "Because I wanted to remind you how good it felt so you'd come into my bedroom tonight and fuck me again."

Oh, hell yes. I swipe the drool from below her rose-colored lips.

"Take that fucking shirt off," I growl.

While she sits up, I stand and strip my clothes. Scottie bites her teeth into her lower lip as she watches me. It's not the first time I've been checked out by a woman, but something about the way she does it gives me an extra hit of validation. She grabs the hem of her shirt and wriggles out of it. Her body is punishing.

I drop to my knees and wrap my arms around her thighs, yanking her ass to the edge of the bed. She props herself up on her elbows, grinning like the Cheshire cat. Then spreads wider, and braces her heels on the sideboard of the bed frame.

"Still with me?" I ask.

Her head cocks to the side. "What do you think?"

I shake my head. "No guessing. I need a yes."

"Yes," she says as articulately as she can.

Then I finally let myself look at her pussy. Jesus, she's fucking glistening. I swipe my thumb over her wet clit.

"What made you so wet, Scottie?"

"You."

"You got this wet just from warming my cock in your mouth, didn't you?"

Her eyes grow big. She likes it when I talk dirty. "Mm-hm," she replies. It almost sounds like begging.

I hold her gaze while I stuff two fingers inside, then curl them up and tap that spot to bring her to the blinding edge of oblivion. She fists the blanket, and her head falls back.

Tilting my chin up, I chuckle when her thighs tremble and breathing falters. She's right on the brink, and it's *so* fucking hot.

"Can I make you come on my fingers before I finish this sentence?"

On cue, Scottie collapses, arching her back as she reaches climax. She writhes, hips rolling and toes curling. I tsk and slow my strokes, stretching out her orgasm and relishing each muscle tense and flex. "That's my good girl, I knew you could do it."

Her chest rises and falls as she catches her breath. She drops her chin, locking her stare on mine. It's a bad idea; the depths of her midnight blue eyes spear through me. It pulls at an invisible thread between us. Too much, too fast. I swallow and force myself to put that boundary back up, then avert my eyes and shut down all the communication.

Hookup.

I cup behind her knees and part her legs while wrapping my lips around the tight bundle of nerves and sucking. She slaps a palm down on my shoulder, the hypersensitivity making her body shake as she tries to scramble away. No fucking way. I flatten my tongue and slowly drag it from her cunt to her clit and once more add suction until she's unable to keep her voice down.

When it becomes obvious she's not going to stay quiet, I shove her legs to the side and nod to the bed, keeping my gaze low while I rip open the condom and roll it on.

"Still with me?" I ask.

"Yes. Always," she consents. I flip her on her stomach, facing the head of the bed. I'm relieved when she climbs to all fours and spreads her thighs for me.

"Bite the pillow." I kind of feel like a dick with the lack of words, but if I don't, I'll lose control.

As soon as she muffles her mouth, I drive inside her, and she groans, squirming for more and grinding against me. One hand massages her left cheek while my other palm inches up her spine. As gently as I can, I push her shoulders into the mattress, and she arches her back.

Scottie looks amazing bent over, she's got a fantastic ass. This girl is unbelievable.

My hands find the dip in her waist, and I use it to fuck her on me. She's so tight I can hardly see straight. At some point, I realize she's doing the work. I loosen my hold on her hips and watch her greediness take over.

"That's it, rock back on me. Show me how bad you want this, Scottie. Show me how hungry you are to get fucked by a thick cock."

Who the hell is this woman? While her pussy clamps down, I'm stunned at the ease at which she has turned my day around. Her gorgeous smiling face flashes in my mind. Those irresistible blue eyes and sexy expressions she makes when she comes. I want to see it, but I can't risk the other guys hearing her. I don't want to share the sounds she makes with anyone. They are mine and mine alone.

"I don't know how much more I can take," she whines.

I plant a palm next to her shoulder and lean forward so my lips are ghosting the shell of her ear. "You're going to take every inch fucking yourself on my cock until you come. Got it?"

She nods.

"Good girl. Every inch, Scottie. Harder."

My hand snakes around, finding her clit and rubbing small circles as I close my eyes and memorize her trembles.

I kiss her below her ear as her orgasm builds. I keep waiting for it to hit, but the wave continues to grow as she shakes, and I can't imagine the ache. She's probably in agony. Her jaw tics, and she squeezes her eyes shut. Seeing her struggle melts something inside me, so I soften my voice. "Just let go. I've got you."

"Callahan," she grits out between clenched teeth. I love my name on her lips. I get the acute sense this woman will ruin me. The way she grips me—she's so close. I love how tight she becomes as she nears her limit. She jerks, trying to keep up the movements but falters when her body is racked with pleasure as she finally crosses the finish line. It's nothing short of magnificent.

I grab her sides and take over, thrusting at the same speed. She sobs, turning her head to the side with a slack jaw and holding her breath while she clamps down. Her hands slap over mine as I pound into her, and her shaking fingers dig into my flesh.

The thrilling tension erupts, and I snap. Taking her harder than ever, as if it's a punishment for making me feel more than just physical attraction. She sucks in a breath, and I clap a hand over her mouth, muffling her cries as she moans. I growl through my teeth while spilling into the condom.

My hips slow as I release every drop, then I collapse onto the small bed next to her, both our chests heaving.

"Holy fuck," I mutter, tying off the condom and tossing it across the room, into a trashcan.

"Yeah." She bobs adamantly, catching her breath. "Yeah."

With a smile on my face, I turn my head to the side. There's that glow. Damn, this woman is breathtaking. I wrap my arms around her and pull her into me, facing her away to salvage what control I have left around her.

"You're really fun." My breath brushes her shoulder, and she nuzzles her ass into me.

"You're fun too," she says.

As much as I want to make this a regular thing, I know it's better I establish boundaries.

"Before this goes any further, I need you to understand that fun is all I'm interested in right now." She stiffens in my embrace, but I continue. "The fun we have is great, so if you're up for keeping things casual, I'd be fine with continuing this until you guys get decommissioned. Maybe even after we get back to Sky Ridge? I'll leave it up to you."

Scottie swallows and clears her throat. "Can I think about it?"

"Of course."

Shit, I probably fucked that up, but anytime I sleep with women more than a handful of times, they tend to get clingy or expect more than I'm able to give them. But damn, the sex with Scottie is so insane I don't really give a fuck. Her body responds to mine so well. It's like she's having sex for the first time, every time. Hard not to take that as an ego stroke. I may be an asshole when it comes to relationships, but at least I own it.

CHAPTER 12

Scottie

Matt hums along with the radio while the scenery whizzes by. The trees and mountains are magnificent. I'm not sure I could ever leave the Pacific Northwest even if I wanted to. We were decommissioned early, and the hotshots are heading back tomorrow morning. So far, the trip home seems to pass by faster than the initial drive out. Perhaps that's because my mind keeps replaying the week with Callahan. My stomach flips recalling his words, voice, and the way he manipulated my body. First in the ambulance, then he snuck into my room for three nights after that.

I don't know where this leaves us. It was something we wanted and let ourselves have, but now what? He said it's only fun, but I'm not sure I understand the protocol for *fun*. Still, I find myself entertaining visions of us as something more. Logically, I know these feelings are unhealthy, born from limerence and loneliness—not to mention a lack of experience. It's not smart to fall head over heels. That's putting all your eggs in one basket, which is never a good idea, but he's the first real crush I've allowed myself to have in at least a decade. *Shit, I'm broken.*

Matt is friends with him, which has to count for something.

The people Callahan surrounds himself with on the crew seem of good character. If anything, it's *my* character that's questionable. Risking my job with ambulance sex and one-night stands? What the hell.

I yawn. I've got a sleep debt to pay off.

"Don't start," Matt states, attempting to speak around his own yawn. "Besides, what are you tired for? You slept through breakfast almost every day this week. You sleep like the dead. I still can't get over that you never woke up during that thunderstorm, that was wild."

I hope my forced laugh is convincing enough. "Yeah, bummed I missed all the excitement." The story I gave Matt was that I read my book for a bit, got bored, cleaned the rig, and went to bed early... conveniently forgetting to return the keys to him. *Liar.* I had a front row seat to the excitement.

I uncross my legs and recross them again. When was the last time I acted so reckless? I can't let my judgment get cloudy after a little freedom. On the other hand, when was the last time I said fuck the consequences for no other reason than *I wanted to*? Never. Despite it not being the most intelligent move I've ever made, I don't regret one night with him. As long as I don't make a habit of behaving irresponsibly, I'll be fine.

"Normally, these tagalongs are boring and you end up sitting in the rig staring at a smoldering hill. At least we got some time to hang with the crew for a bit and change things up."

I nod and try to steer us off the topic of my sleep habits before he catches on. "It's been forever since I played poker." Again, *liar.* I'd never played poker before this week. Gambling was forbidden. I waved Matt off to the game without me so I could look up the rules. Took a few rounds of watching the others to make sure I understood them. I was too scared to make a play—until Callahan encouraged me to jump in.

It's easier to fake confidence around him. Though, sometimes, I feel like an alien trying to blend in with humans...

Thank goodness I was allowed my EMT job back home, or I'd be much worse off. Without this job, I don't think I'd ever have left. How could I? What skills would I have? Where would I have found the money? The car? Having a profession was my "reward." I should have done it sooner. It doesn't matter now. I shake it off and smile at him. "I feel bad for stealing your snacks." I chuckle.

A vibration in my pocket has me digging out my phone.

CALLAHAN

Text me when you get home.

I fight my grin and tap out a reply.

Will do! Don't get in to too much trouble tonight.

CALLAHAN

How can I when you're not around?

My smile grows, and I flip my phone closed in my lap.

"I thought for sure you were bluffing that time." He laughs. When his head cocks to the side, he's got a quizzical expression. "Hey… is there something between you and Callahan?"

I furrow my brow. "What do you mean?" I stuff my phone in my pocket and mentally chastise myself for the jumpiness.

"I dunno, I just feel like I should caution you that he's kind of a flirt."

Shit! Did he see—or worse—hear something at the dorm? Shrugging, I glance out the window and bring it back to the poker table. "He was just shit talking to win over my caramel corn."

"Yeah, maybe. Just wanted to make sure you know in case he tries anything. Not to be a creep, but you're attractive, and he's… well, he's Callahan."

He's *Callahan*? What is that supposed to mean? I'm afraid if

I ask, it'll make me appear even more guilty than I feel. Matt will see it all over my face.

"What, is he a dangerous criminal or something?" I feign boredom, inspecting my fingernails.

"No! Nothing like that. He's a good guy, just keeps himself unattached. Some women think they can fix him and end up disappointed. He's a charming guy but has a reputation. Ya feel me?"

"Gotcha." I swallow. My guts twist more than I thought they would. I want to turn back time to before he said that. Where I could simply daydream about what good things could come of this. When it was fun and exciting. Matt's version of him carves out an ugly hollow pit in my stomach.

Yet, I find myself holding onto Cal's words from the ambulance: *"No, it's not always like that."*

CHAPTER 13
CALLAHAN

It's the last night in Oregon. Between working on the Mahonia fire and sneaking around with Prescott, I had an awesome fucking week. She and Matt were already sent home to Sky Ridge this morning. Matt was itching to get back. Can't blame him; it's no fun sitting around and waiting for something to happen.

As is tradition, we're celebrating the end of our assignment by throwing back a few at the nearest establishment with a liquor license. I'm about three beers deep and feeling terrific. I can sleep on the ride home tomorrow, something I desperately need more of.

My phone buzzes, and I pull it out of my pocket. I hope it's Scottie. I've been waiting for her reply; she should have texted me back by now.

SCOTTIE

Sorry I didn't text earlier. Fell asleep.

We've had some late nights.

SCOTTIE

That we have.

It'd be a tragedy if we didn't have more.

I didn't tell her Dixon caught me slipping out of her dorm that last night when he got up to take a piss. He'll keep quiet, but he gave me a stern look to remind me I was being reckless.

He's presently sitting to my left and leans over to peek at my screen.

I roll my eyes and lock my phone. "Need something?"

He shakes his head but leans his shoulder into mine and lowers his voice. "Kinda surprised you're hooking up with her."

"What do you mean?"

Yeah, it's usually not my style to have multiple hookups with the same person. I've learned to withdraw when things start to feel too *real* because if I don't, the other person will. It's not a good quality, I'm aware, but I'm working on it...

"Just not your type."

"She's hot—that's my type." Deep down, I know she's more, but for the sake of this argument, it's not like this was the first time I've done something similar.

"She's married."

"What the fuck are you on?" I laugh and take a sip of beer. "She's not married."

"Judy over at the municipal office processed the application. She and my momma had lunch and said *Prescott Timmons* checked the box marked married on her forms. On top of that, I heard she hooked up with Dave—your favorite person."

My jaw clenches. There's no way. He's mistaken. "Nah. They're talking about the wrong girl, then." She's not married— she doesn't wear a ring, and she's not hooking up with Dave. They work at the same firehouse, but she wouldn't do that.

Doubt creeps into my thoughts. *You worked with her too.*

Still, I can't picture her doing something like that with him.

He hit on her the night we met at the bar and… She technically never turned him down. Dave was the one to walk away after Xander asked about their newborn. I shake my head. "I think you gotta check your sources, man."

"Just tellin' you what I heard."

I raise my beer bottle to my lips and take a big swig. "You heard wrong."

Fuck Dave. And fuck Dixon for spreading bullshit rumors.

"You could ask her."

I glance down at my phone, my reflection peering back at me in the black glass, then tuck the device in my pocket. It's not a matter of her sleeping with other guys, but *infidelity* is a trigger for me. The idea of her sleeping with a married man when she's a married woman, gets my hackles up, and Dave of all fuckin' people—he's the reason I'm not happily married with two and a half kids right now. I don't want to think of him being the reason I can't see Scottie again.

If there's truth to these rumors, then I'm out. My stomach sours. To even engage in the *idea* I ruined some other poor bastard's life the way Dave ruined mine, has my guts in knots.

Perhaps I *should* ask her about it… And if she comes clean? Fuck. A sweat breaks out across my forehead. Whatever, he can have her. I'm sure as hell not going to enter some fucked-up love triangle and break up two families.

I take a sip from my beer bottle. "She's smarter than that."

"How the fuck would you know?" Dixon rolls his eyes. "Just trying to watch your back. I don't wanna see you go down that road again."

CHAPTER 14

Scottie

Maybe it vibrated in my pocket and I didn't feel it. I check my phone again. Nothing. I've already deep cleaned the rig to burn off some of this nervous energy. It wouldn't be so bad if we had some damn calls to go to, but it's been dead all morning. I read the last three messages over the last three days, and they've all been from me.

> At the grocery store. Cheese balls are on sale.
>
> Hope you're having a good day.
>
> Everything okay?

It's not like he's stopped texting me altogether, but he hasn't been as talkative. Before the fire, we would text on and off throughout the day. I'm sure he's just busy, but with his job, my mind automatically goes to the worst-case scenario. I grew accustomed to having a friend. Things didn't feel so lonely in this small town.

Have I been using him as a crutch? I wince. "Goddamn it, Prescott," I curse under my breath. I'm falling back into the routine of relying on somebody else. That's not me. I'm out here because I'm on my own two feet. I angrily shove my phone back in my pocket. No more looking. Friends are everywhere. Go find them. I found the first one at the bar, that's where all the locals seemed to hang out. Maybe I could find another one there? Or perhaps a coffee shop. There appeared to be a good one in town.

Trudging into the rec room where Matt is watching television, I slump down in one of the chairs. "I'm bored."

"Whoa! Hey!" Matt shouts, darting his gaze around to check if anybody heard me. "Don't say shit like that. It'll piss off the gods, and we'll be up to our eyeballs in calls."

I roll my eyes. "The world doesn't work that way."

"The hell it doesn't."

My elbows slip from the arms of my chair, and I tip my head back, staring at the ceiling tiles. I release a frustrated sigh. "Humans just like patterns. They find comfort in coincidences that are mistaken for proof of a higher power."

Matt scoffs. "Well, aren't you a delightful little ray of sunshine today…"

My head lolls to the side, then I sit up straighter. "Sorry, just feeling really—"

"Don't say the B-word."

"Fine, fine… But seriously, what's a girl gotta do to get a patient with a dislocated shoulder or—"

Tones drop and dispatch cuts through the radio. My face lights up like it's Christmas morning, and I jump out of my chair.

"Dispatch to Medic twenty-three." The voice is half static.

Matt points a finger toward me as we head to the rig. "What did I say, huh? What did I say?"

Smiling ear to ear, I wrap my hand around the radio at my shoulder and push the button on the side. "Medic twenty-three. Go ahead."

I glance over to Matt as we climb into the ambulance cab. "I still don't believe your superstitions."

"Medic twenty-three, respond to six-four-five Wilson. Six-four-five Wilson. Nineteen-year-old male subject is claiming he was attacked by a... *pterodactyl*? Thirteen-twenty."

Matt overrides the radio.

"Dispatch, repeat last transmission."

I furrow my brow. *What the fuck*? I mouth to him. Did they say *pterodactyl*?

"You conjured it. Today is about to suck."

"Six-four-five Wilson. Nineteen-year-old male subject is complaining of a pterodactyl attack. Suspected drug use. Do you request backup?"

I nod yes. Matt presses his radio and looks me dead in the eye when he says. "Negative. Scottie's got this one. En route."

I shake my head. "I don't do pterodactyls."

"Today you do."

I fall to my knees after I walk in my apartment door and kick it shut. I'm exhausted. It started with the teenage patient who ingested approximately 600 milligrams of THC, and ended with a pissed-off Gladys Kravitz with second-degree burns. Apparently, she was so angry her neighbor's tomato plants were encroaching on her yard that she resorted to M-80s. She's lucky she didn't blow her hand clean off. This town is fucking nuts.

My phone buzzes in my pocket, and I groan. I pull myself up and fish it out with a sigh. Probably Matt giving me shit after the insane day we had.

I see Callahan's name and flip it open.

CALLAHAN

What are you up to?

Just got home from work.

CALLAHAN

Sorry it's been busy lately.

No worries. Hope everything's all right.

CALLAHAN

I think we should talk.

My stomach sinks, but I try to stay positive. I'm picking up a split shift tonight for some extra cash, which means I've got roughly six hours left for sleep before I have to be up and get ready for third shift. And I need the sleep.

Sorry, I can't tonight. Could we meet up for coffee tomorrow morning?

CALLAHAN

How about I stop by your place in the a.m.?

There's an uncomfortable lump in my stomach. I don't like the sound of this. Not one bit. I text him my address and tell him that I'll see him tomorrow.

CHAPTER 15

Scottie

Maybe I should have met with Callahan when he texted yesterday. Not only is the fear of the unknown eating at me, but by the time this shift ends, I'll be even more exhausted than I was yesterday afternoon. I snuck in a small nap halfway through. That's the only thing saving me. There's one of those giant cookie cakes wrapped up in tinfoil on the breakroom table, and it's significantly smaller than it was earlier. I cut off a slice and pick at it while watching some rerun on TV.

It's been a slow night, and I'm not complaining, but I'd be lying if I said my mind hasn't been going in circles about our upcoming "talk."

I stare at the cookie slice before stuffing the entire thing in my mouth. Which is when Dave walks in. He's wrapping up his shift too.

"Hey, haven't seen you in a while," he says, pulling up a chair to the table. "How are things going?"

"Yeah, it's going well. Thanks," I say around my bite.

"Good." He cuts his own slice off the stale, nearly brick cookie. "Making friends?"

I swallow. "Yeah, I think so."

"I heard you and Cal are getting kinda cozy."

My brow furrows. "Callahan Woods? I don't know if I would say that." I cock my head to the side. "Do you know him?"

"Oh yeah, he and I go way back."

Hmm. "Oh, you're good friends then?"

Dave sighs. "Depends on what your definition of a friend is... He's nice enough. But there's something you should probably know about him. He's the town heartbreaker. Sleeps around, never settles down."

I roll my eyes. "What makes you think I would sleep with him?"

He raises his brows. "Sorry, I didn't mean it that way. Look, I like Cal, but I wouldn't let him near my sisters."

He eyes me up and down, and I don't like the way his gaze lingers.

"Why?"

"You know how they say the value of a car drops when you drive it off the lot? Well, Callahan likes to collect cars and never take them out again."

Comparing a woman's value to a car is gross.

I'm not a fan of Dave, but unfortunately, what he says was echoed by Matt on our trek home from the fire in Oregon, and it adds to my unease.

"Well, I've got some stuff to work on. I'll see you around." Pushing out of my chair, I exit the breakroom and check the rig to see if there's anything I can restock. After that, I spend the rest of my shift finishing a training module on one of the desktops, then do a quick Google search for Arkansas news. Nothing that pertains to me. No news is good news.

When it's finally time to go home, I get in my car and catch my reflection in the rear-view mirror. I look haggard. I'll need a shower before I see Callahan. My car doesn't start immediately, and I gulp down my frustration. It turns over on the second try, so I focus on getting back to my studio apartment in time to clean up.

I turn on the radio and sing along with a monotone voice, anything to keep me awake, until I hear a noise. It's almost like a... thumping? I turn the radio off and listen. The noise is familiar, but my brain is too tired to put it together until the car starts to bounce—Shit! I've got a flat tire. I quickly pull over to the side of the country road.

I already know there's not a spare. I bought the car bare bones and paid cash. Just in case the magical tire fairy blessed me with one, I check the trunk anyway. Empty.

"Shit." I kick the shredded tire and slap the roof of the car. Closing my eyes, I lean against the frame, resting my forehead on the cold glass of the rear passenger window. I want to smash my head into it. *Deep breaths.*

Who do I call? Callahan? It's seven fifteen in the morning; he's probably not even awake yet. Ugh, this day just won't end.

A couple cars zoom by, but tires crunching on gravel—the sound of hope—has me glancing up. *Please don't be a serial killer.*

It's Dave. *I'll take it!*

I walk toward him as he steps out of his vehicle.

"Car trouble?" He slams his door shut.

"I've got a flat."

"That sucks. I'll help you change it."

I cringe. "I don't have a spare."

He scratches the scruff on his chin as he meets me near the trunk of my car. "That's gonna be a problem."

"Yeah." I wince.

"Where do you live?"

"I'm in town, an apartment building off Main."

He trudges around my car, as if to inspect it. "Okay, here's what we're going to do. I'm gonna call Carl, he owes me a favor and can get it towed to the tire shop—"

Alarm bells. I can't afford a tow. I wave my arms. "No, I can't—"

He gestures with an open palm for me to stop talking. "He owes me a favor, free of charge. You're new in town, and I'm guessing those paychecks are all going to getting settled. Am I right?"

I nod, and my cheeks heat with embarrassment. *Does everybody here know I'm broke?*

"I'll replace your tire and throw in a donut, in case you find yourself in this predicament sometime down the road, no pun intended."

I'm not in a position to argue. "I'll pay you back, I promise!"

"I know you will, I'm not worried," he says, peering down at his phone and tapping the screen. He holds it to his ear. "Hey Carl... Yeah, I wanna cash in that favor. I've got a car on County Road 2 that needs a tow to Bill's shop." He gives Carl the make and model, then chuckles at whatever the man says. "Keys will be in the visor.... Yup.... Thanks."

He wraps up the conversation, tucking his phone into his back pocket.

"Dave, I don't know how to thank you for all this. I was going out of my mind for a minute. Again, I'll pay you back, I swear. Thank you!" I beam at him. Dave just showed up and took care of these problems like it was the easiest thing in the world.

"Okay, get your stuff, I'll drive you home."

I hustle back to my car and place the keys in the visor like Dave said and reach over to collect my purse. Then I make sure the car is unlocked and shut the door. It's not like anyone is gonna steal it. Even if it didn't have a flat tire, the thieves would take one look at this heap and leave me a few bucks out of pity.

Dave's already behind the wheel when I climb in. He starts his truck and pulls out onto the road. We make small talk until we get closer to my apartment.

"It's that one on the left." I point to the small building with aged yellow bricks and paint peeling from the window trim.

"That one?" he asks. His words aren't judgmental, and I appreciate him allowing me to hold onto my dignity. The place looks decrepit. I know it does. Dave knows it does. The blind, stray dog walking past it on the sidewalk knows it does. However, it's mine, and I've really tidied up the studio. She may not be the prettiest belle of the ball, but she is the cleanest. Beggars and choosers.

He parks his truck, and I unbuckle my seat belt.

"I should get your number so I can bring you to the shop once they get the tire swapped out."

"Oh, of course!" We exchange information, and I grasp the door handle.

"I've always wondered what these apartments are like inside."

"The inside matches the outside," I reply with a chuckle.

"Do you mind if I take a peek?"

My gaze jumps between the building and Dave. "Umm..." I shrug. "Sure? I'm still getting settled, so I don't have much furniture yet." *And money is tighter than my landlord's wallet.*

He gets out of the truck. We amble to the building, and he holds the door open for me and follows me up the stairs. I get my keys out and unlock the door, and he walks in behind me.

"Not much to see," I say. He saunters in and heads toward the window, near my unmade bed. Okay, maybe it's not that tidy, but after picking up a split shift, I used every second for sleep since yesterday's calls had me dragging my feet.

He leans toward it and surveys the lookout.

My stomach rumbles, and I walk the three feet to the kitchen and locate a pan and place it on the stovetop. Then I open the fridge and pluck out my carton of eggs.

He peers back at me and throws his thumb over his shoulder. "You've got a great view of Main Street."

Nodding, I say, "I people watch sometimes."

"Hungry?" he asks, glancing at the eggs on the counter.

"Yeah, I was going to make some breakfast—or is it dinner?" I smile, and he smiles back but says nothing. Then it hits me, and I suddenly feel rude. "Oh, did you want to join me?" Shit, he just hooked me up with a tow and a new tire, it's the least I can do. I say a silent prayer that he says no. Dave is a nice guy, but I feel uneasy with a man I don't know well in such a small space. *My* space. I glimpse at my phone. This needs to be a quick breakfast since I'm hoping to get in the shower and tidy up before Callahan stops by.

"Sure, I can stay for a bit."

Damn.

My phony grin freezes on my face. "Super!"

Guess I'm making scrambled eggs for two. These eggs were expensive, damn it.

"Would you like toast?" I offer.

"I'm gluten free."

Good, that'll get you out of here sooner. I point to one of the two chairs at my table. "Have a seat." He walks toward it and pulls out a chair. "Actually, use the other one. That one's kind of wobbly."

Welcome to the Ritz.

The eggs sizzle when cracked into the pan. I use my partially melted spatula to break the yolks and whisk the eggs together, trying to hurry the process. I shake salt and pepper into the pan and continue pushing the eggs around until they thicken.

My feet shift back and forth, and I break the silence with more small talk. "So, how long have you lived in Sky Ridge?"

The coils on the electric stove burn brighter as I turn up the temperature, hoping to speed up the coagulation of these damn egg whites.

"Around twenty years."

"Oh, that's a long time. Where did you move from?"

"Small town not far from here."

Once they're done, I turn off the stove, split the eggs into two equal servings, and shovel them onto mismatched plates. From the drawer, I remove two plastic forks.

"That's cool. This is a lovely area. I can see why people like it."

He thanks me when I hand him a plate and a fork. His genuine appreciation makes me feel guilty for assuming the worst about him. Stabbing my eggs onto the tines, I ask him about his family.

"Did I hear your wife recently had a baby?" I ask, recalling the night at the bar when one of the hotshots asked how the new baby was doing.

"Yeah."

"That's exciting! Do you enjoy being a dad?"

He nods. "I love being a dad. Teaching them to take their first steps, throw a ball... it's the best."

I tilt the corner of my mouth in a half smile. In my experience, women did all the child rearing.

"It's tough being gone for a few days at a time, but that's the way it is."

"You and your wife must make a good team."

He shrugs. "Eh. The last couple years have been a bit rocky... Actually, we're separated, but with a new baby, it's easier to co-parent if we're both in the same space."

Uh-oh.

"We haven't really told anyone yet, so if you could, ya know, keep it between us."

"I'm sorry to hear that. It's no one else's business."

I finish my eggs as he swallows his last bite.

"Yeah, it sucks. But it's for the best. It's nice to be able to tell somebody, it's been weighing on me."

"Anytime." A silence pulses between us, and I check the

clock on the stove. "Wow, is it already that late? I've got so much to do today!"

"Yeah, I won't take any more of your time." He stands, and relief washes over me. "I'll send you a text later and can give you a ride to pick up your car."

"That would be awesome, thank you again," I say, walking toward the door.

He turns the knob and pulls it open. "You bet. Thanks for the eggs."

CHAPTER 16

CALLAHAN

The two Styrofoam containers of pancakes and waffles squeak in the passenger seat of my truck as I turn into the parking lot of her apartment. She asked to meet for coffee, but I insisted we meet at her place. I need to see if another man is living there. It's also why I'm early. I figure if she has a husband, I want to catch him before she shoves him out the door for work. If I'm wrong—*and I hope like hell I am*—I thought I'd surprise her with breakfast. It sounded like she had a rough day yesterday. My plan is for us to talk so she can straighten out this whole mess, and we can pick up where we left off. If things go well, maybe we can even have a repeat from Oregon; I never claimed to be a saint.

I park, grab the containers, and hop out of my truck. My keys swing around my finger when Dave walks out of the main door. *What the fuck?* Why's he here? I'm not going to jump to conclusions, but it's hard not to feel the weight of betrayal every time I see his face. I exhale slowly. These are apartments, he could be here for anybody. They work at the same place, maybe she left something at the station and he's dropping it off. *At nine in the morning?* Shit.

"You pick up a second job as a handyman?" I ask as we

amble toward each other. I nod at the property that's seen better decades. "Looks like your work."

"Are you here for Scottie?" he asks, glimpsing at the Styrofoam containers in my hands. "Hope that isn't breakfast."

I narrow my eyes. "Why?"

"We just ate." He licks his fingers and grins at me. God, I'd love to take a swing at him, but this asshole would be happy to collar me with a battery charge, and I'm not about to give him the satisfaction. "She makes some mean eggs."

I cock my head to the side. I don't want to ask, but I have to. "So, what, are you two sleeping together?" She's too good for him.

"Last night? We spent the night together, but we were definitely not sleeping." He looks behind him to her apartment building, then back to me and smirks. "She's cute though, right?"

I clench my jaw and square my shoulders. "Your wife know you're hooking up with other women? Not that it should be any surprise, considering the way you two met."

He doesn't reply, just walks past me toward his truck. He turns his head to the side but look back. "Molly isn't your concern anymore."

Despite my instinct to turn around and drive off, my feet carry me into the building and climb the stairs until I'm staring at her door. It's made of cheap, hollow wood, and the varnish is worn thin in a few places. Clearly, security is at the bottom of her landlord's to-do list. My closed palm hovers in the air, ready to knock, then I scrub a hand down my face and spin in a circle. I lift my arm a second time and freeze.

Someone once told me when you get on the wrong train, it's best to get off at the first stop because the longer you stay on, the more expensive the return trip will cost you to get home.

So why the fuck am I standing here?

CHAPTER 17

Scottie

As soon as I closed the door behind Dave, I wasted no time checking the clock before getting ready. Thankfully, I was able to shower, put on makeup, dry my hair, and get dressed.

I hurry over to my mattress and make the bed, fluffing the pillows and trying to make it appear less... pathetic. When I stand, I whirl around, looking for something to tidy. I stride into the kitchen area and straighten one of the chairs slightly. There. That's a little better. I didn't care what Dave thought of it, but Callahan? I want it to be as warm and welcoming as possible.

I check the time on my phone and frown. He should be here by now. I type out a text message.

> Are we still on for today?

CALLAHAN

> No.

Oh.

> No?

CALLAHAN

Things have run their course with us.

My depleted energy, compounded with the events of this morning, forms a hot ball in my chest. I've been hanging on by a thread, and his text message severed the last frayed strand. My face burns, eyes brimming with tears.

Rejection. My first true experience with it, mixed with exhaustion and a hefty dose of humiliation. I pocket my phone and inspect the space I spent extra time sprucing up. This isn't how I pictured the day going. I pull my phone out again and reread his message.

Getting attached too quickly was my fault, but after years of numbness, he came into my life and made me feel anything but.

I didn't have a chance in hell to keep a boundary.

Still, everyone told me this is what he does. For whatever reason, I was charmed enough to, what, hold out hope? What an idiot. I fell into the same trap as every woman who came before me. How easy it is to be replaced when relationships aren't forced upon you.

To punish myself, I scroll to our earlier messages. The ones that gave me butterflies and excitement. Even when I know it's unhealthy, I still want to feel the memory of his affection anyway. I want to read just one of those texts from him and feel the warmth I felt the first time I read it.

I scroll higher; *the words aren't real.* Any meaning I found in them were a product of my imagination. Yet I read them again because feeling pain is still better than feeling numb. This time, they are bitter with betrayal.

A tear slips down my cheek, and I swat it away angrily. No way am I crying.

"You're being foolish. If you want to live in the real world, this is part of it."

I don't have feelings for him, I convince myself. This is

simply a cocktail of mental exhaustion, rejection, and a silly crush on a boy who had no intention of taking anything further. I've weathered shit harder than this. I started a new life; I'm not getting tripped up by asinine feelings based on a few nights of sexual freedom and *fun*.

He had me in the palm of his hand and decided I wasn't worth holding onto.

Okay.

CHAPTER 18

CALLAHAN

Shifty's is busy tonight. The buzzing chatter makes it sound like my head is stuck inside a beehive.

"Do you remember that time I bet you that you couldn't eat all the carrots in Gram's garden, and then you did? You blamed it on rabbits, and then barfed orange all over her sofa?" Teddy, my sister, struggles to get out the words through a fit of giggles.

We've been talking since I walked in—no, wait... no, that was Tiffany. I was talking with Tiffany last I checked. Did I black out? I jerk my head around. When did my sister show up? *And where the fuck did Tiffany go?* I rest an elbow on the bar and squint one eye at Teddy, trying to figure out which one I should be looking at. "How long ya been 'ere, Ted?"

"A while. You texted me you were at the bar and needed to talk, 'member? It's not like every day your big brother asks for advice, so I left the kids with Logan." She snorts like it's the funniest thing she's ever heard; she's clearly as drunk as I am. "And now you're too drunk to remember."

I laugh right along with her, but then the ugly memory surfaces. I wanted to talk about Scottie.

Originally, I planned to pick someone up. The best way to get over one woman is to get under another, but Tiffany isn't here anymore, and I'm way too fuckin' sauced. Even if she was, I don't think I could get my dick up if I was sober.

I'm just so damn disappointed. This afternoon, I jumped on the internet and did a deep dive search on her. I found out Scottie is married... to Jonathan Timmons. Timmons is her married name. I saw the newspaper archive of their wedding announcement. No doubt the woman in the photo was her.

On top of that, there's the whole thing with Dave. I know the reason he's fucking Scottie is to get back at me. For what? Not letting him on the crew? He was shitty as a seasonal in his prime. Now he'd be a total slouch.

Fucking married. Unbelievable.

I have no idea what I'm supposed to do. Do I tell her husband? Do I ignore it? It's not like I knew. And if she's having an affair with Dave, I'm sure everybody will find out eventually anyway. Doesn't matter, I'm in no mental state to make a decision like that right now.

"'Ey Ma!" I call to the owner of the bar, Mae Taylor. After getting chastised a few times, she earned the nickname Ma from everyone on the crew. Usually, Lou is working, but she moonlights here every once in a while to give him a night off. "Top me off, will ya?"

I sway on my stool. This bartop feels so nice and smooth. I could rest here and close my eyes for a bit, perhaps just long enough for Mae to fill my glass. My cheek presses to the wood, and she slaps the side of my head. I sit up and laugh. My cheek is totally numb. I heard the smack more than I felt it.

"Can I call you a cab?"

"While I'm known for giving lots of rides, I'd prefer you call me by my name, Cal-uh-han."

"Very funny." She picks up the phone; it's one of those twenty-pound fuckers. Easily could kill a guy if you smashed it

123

hard enough against his skull. "Callahan Woods needs a ride home."

"Hey!" I whine. "How come I have to go home but Teddy doesn't? She's trashed too!"

Teddy cuts in. "Don't listen to him, Mae. He's a liar."

I swallow. That was the joke when Scottie and I first met—in this very bar. Funny, it was her lying the entire time, and now *I'm* the chump. I shake it off and flip my empty glass upside down, pushing it with one finger toward Mae with every ounce of coordination I have left.

"And Teddy needs a ride too," Mae says to the cab service, rolling her eyes at us. "Make sure they each end up at their houses and not at another bar."

"I'll drive her home, Mae." Xander's deep voice cuts in. "I finished my last beer an hour ago."

I snap my head around and bark out a laugh. "Where the fuck did you come from!?"

Teddy and I cackle, and it feels like we're the chatty kids in class who the teacher has to separate and send to the hall. Or in this case, be sent home.

"I've got no tolerance for alcohol since having kids," Teddy mumbles while Xander helps her off her barstool. "I'm gonna be so hungover tomorrow." She gets one arm in her jacket and bats around for the other. Xander grasps her hand and threads it through the other sleeve. She grunts, trying to free her hair out from under the jacket.

"Yes you are," he says, sweeping under her blonde hair and releasing it from beneath the collar.

"No funny business, X! She's married!" I warn.

Teddy pins me with a look.

"I'm aware," Xander says under his breath.

"Go warm up your truck or some shit," I say. "Gotta pay our tab."

"I'll pull the truck up front," he says. I mumble something

else, but he ignores my bullshit and helps zip up her coat before walking out.

My hand scrubs over my face. "Fuck, I'm tired," I groan.

"Same. I'm gonna be so hungover tomorrow," Teddy says.

I chuckle at her. "You already said that." Mae slides the receipt in front of me. I scribble a swirl at the bottom—no use in even trying to sign my name.

I'm told the cab is outside, and I hop off my seat, pausing a moment to get my footing. The room is spinning.

"Fun's over. Ready, dude?" I put an arm around Teddy's shoulder to steady us, and she leans into me. The tanked leading the tanked-er.

We take two staggered steps, inciting more laughter between us, but eventually, we make it to the exit. I yank the bulky door to the bar open and freeze in my tracks. I may be drunk, but I swear half the alcohol evaporates out of my system when I see *her* face.

Prescott Timmons. *Mrs.* Prescott Timmons.

She glances at Teddy, then back to me. Our eyes meet. Hers are shimmering, and mine are likely glazed over like a dead shark. Fuck, she's a smokeshow. And it makes perfect sense that she's married. I should have been suspicious from the start. I peek down at her hand. Still no ring. The taste in my mouth grows bitter. *How could she?*

"Here to pick up a new suitor?" I snide, ushering Teddy past her. My eyes are filled with contempt. "Good luck."

She actually has the audacity to look hurt, and I want to shout at her that she's a shitty person and an even worse wife. I want to tell her how much it hurts to find out the person you loved is fucking someone else. I want her to know how gut-wrenchingly awful it is to unknowingly *be* the other man; she made me into a villain without my permission.

But most of all, I want her to know how much this fucking sucks because we could have been awesome together.

CHAPTER 19

Scottie

Tears burn behind my eyes when I see him walk out of the bar with another woman.

Fuck him.

CHAPTER 20

Scottie

My feet hit the pavement in a steady rhythm as I jog down Spencer Avenue. When I'm not at work, I jog. When I'm not jogging, I sleep. *You need friends.* I ignore the inner criticism. I can feel myself retreating, but I don't know how to switch up my routine. It's easier this way. I tell myself this is all temporary, but without plans to make any real change in my habits, it's all bullshit.

The entire time I was with Jonathan, I felt less than. When there's an attraction between two people, you can see it in their eyes. I saw it in other couples. I saw it in Callahan; he looked at me in ways Jonathan never did. Back when it was a constant reminder that I was never enough, even when it wasn't his fault. After enough times of being gazed at with eyes longing for something else, it breaks a person. And that's exactly what I am, broken.

As I pass by the decorated autumnal porches and neatly raked piles of leaves, this put-together neighborhood is such a juxtaposition to my life. Yet I want to belong so desperately, and jogging down the sidewalk lets me pretend I'm a part of their charming world in Sky Ridge, even if it's for the brief moment it takes me to pass through.

The house I always look for—number 218, is one of the few homes left undecorated for the season, which gives me a blank slate to imagine what I'd do if I lived there. I would have pumpkins with carved faces on the porch steps and tie corn stalks around the painted posts. I'd add those fake cobwebs that the neighboring houses have. Halloween wasn't something we could celebrate, but if I lived at 218, I'd have skeletons and ghosts in every window, and the biggest bowl of candy for trick-or-treaters.

A car pulls up front, and two laughing kids barrel out of the back seat and run into the front yard. I smile as the presumed father jumps out of the driver's seat, chasing them. The mother exits the passenger side just as the dad catches the young daughter, who squeals when he tickles her belly. It's so delightfully normal. I knew a happy family must live there, and it fills my heart to see my hunch confirmed.

218 Spencer always has a way of cheering me up.

I'm distracted by the antics of the lively family across the street when I approach the intersection and turn right. My joy is short-lived when I almost plow head-on with another runner.

I put my hands up defensively and stumble over my feet, attempting to get out of the way. The man grips my biceps and steadies me. I suck in a breath, ready to apologize when I glance up to see Callahan glaring back at me.

I rip my arms from his grasp. "Stay away from me," I snap. *So much for that apology.* The words are the first thing that came to mind, and I suspect they came about not literally but as more of a generalized statement. I might even be projecting, but you won't hear me admitting that to him. The near collision was one hundred percent my fault, but I can't bring myself to say sorry. I can hardly stand to look him in the eye again. Instead, I sidestep and literally run away without another word. Like a coward.

CHAPTER 21
CALLAHAN

MID-OCTOBER

"What are you doing before you start ski patrol?" King asks.

This is our last roll of the season, and we're putting finishing touches on the containment lines when a few guys start talking about their plans for the off-season.

"Probably blow all my hazard pay at the strip club. Then maybe steal a car... cook meth... rob a bank..." I count on my fingers.

"So, the usual?"

"Everybody's got their hobbies..." I shrug. "I dunno. Probably hike Quell's or Briarburn. Hell, might just plant my ass on a barstool at Shifty's and get trashed. What about you?"

"Shifty's sounds great, I think I'll join you."

"You could always join me on a hike?" I suggest, scanning down the line. Caleb leans on his Pulaski, and his face is pale. One of the guys swiped his lunch and swapped it for another veggie omelet MRE. I thought he would barf on the spot. I chuckle, recalling my own rookie season and all the bullshit those guys put me through. It's done out of love and as insurance to make sure you can handle it.

"Why would I climb a mountain in my free time," he grunts, grabbing a large limb and tossing it in the green. "When I can just get paid to do it next year? Besides, it's too fuckin' cold for summits."

"Best time to go," I argue with a headshake. "All the tourists are gone."

King smirks. "I thought tourists were your favorite part."

"The hot and single ones," I add with a wink.

He raises a brow. "I dunno, man… we've been prepping this line for a week, and you haven't so much as flirted with one waitress when we go out to eat."

I raise my shoulders. "So?"

"So, that's unlike you. Got anything to do with Scottie?"

Talking about that woman makes my blood pressure rise. "Why the fuck would it have anything to do with her?"

"Just askin'… Xander said y'all got pretty loaded at Shifty's a couple weeks ago, and he drove your sister home, and she mentioned y'all meeting up because you were having girl trouble."

"I don't have *girl trouble*," I scoff. "Scottie and I aren't anything. Not that it matters, she's married."

He stands up straight. "What? She's married?!"

"Yeah." I huff. As if it's no big deal. As if I didn't ruin a marriage. As if I didn't sleep with another man's wife.

"Who's she married to?"

My back teeth grind. I'd love to discuss anything else right now. "Not sure." I gather a handful of brush, tossing it out of the way, not wanting to meet his eyes.

"Well, you said she was married." He throws an arm to the side. "You don't know who her husband is?"

Jesus, fuck. I find a limb and chuck it as hard as I can, then straighten my spine. "Motherfucker, I don't know!" I scoff. "I don't know shit about that woman. You wanna know who her husband is, go ask her!" I shake my head, walking up the line to check on the saw team's progress.

"Whoa, chill."

I spin on my foot. "I am chill!" I laugh for added conviction. "I just can't figure out why you're grilling me about a person I have nothing to do with."

The pause in conversation is awkwardly silent. I may have had a slight overreaction to his questions about Scottie.

He mutters to himself, "Married... that's so fuckin' weird. Sure does raise more questions than answers."

What's that supposed to mean? I shouldn't ask, but my impulse control gets the better of me. "What do you mean?"

He shrugs. "Nothin'."

Anger rises up my neck. "No, why do you think it's weird?" Now my interest is piqued. What does he know? Did he hear something? Small towns can churn out rumors all day long, but every once in a while, they get it right. If it's got to do with Scottie, I wanna know about it despite my better judgment. Apparently, I'm a glutton for punishment.

Maybe it will fuel my anger toward her. I can't seem to let go of this. I'm so pissed I'm starting to obsess over her. No one knows we slept together. Well, apart from Dixon. I'm too ashamed to even bring it up to King or Xander, and they're my brothers, for all intents and purposes, though they obviously suspect something went down between us.

"What do you care?" King taunts. "You've got nothing to do with her."

Asshole. He's right. There's no way for me to respond, so I don't.

"You're getting a little long in the tooth to be playing around," Bobby says, eavesdropping nearby. "When are you gonna settle down with someone?"

I turn away from the ridiculous question; it's about time I get back to work. "Fire's the only woman for me. She's cruel and she's hot."

"You do have a type," King adds.

I chuckle and spit into the dirt. "That I do."

CHAPTER 22

CALLAHAN

END OF OCTOBER

Finally done with fire season, and I've already gotten a decent start on the next room that needs renovation in the house. Even after a full day of manual labor and being covered in sawdust, I'm still feeling restless, so I do what I always do during those times. Run.

Brown leaves crunch underfoot as the frigid air burns my lungs. I needed this. Swinging a hammer is great for alleviating aggression, but running quiets my thoughts; it brings me peace and soothes my soul.

Or at least it does until I see her.

My pounding feet slow to a stop—no fucking way—the woman jogging toward me is the one and only Scottie Timmons. *How does this keep happening?* This woman is driving me insane.

I haven't been able to get her out of my head since the night we met, and after getting burned by her, I've tried doing anything to distract myself. It's an impossible task when we can't stop running into each other—last time, it was literal. Then she had the audacity to snap at me like *I* was in the wrong. I was too dumbfounded to even respond.

Our arrangement was casual. *It was only supposed to be fun!* So why the fuck can't I get over her?

I've switched the time of day I go running to keep us from crossing paths, but apparently, she had the same idea, because here we are. When recognition hits her, she stops. We regard each other with bitterness, our feet firmly planted and time standing still. How the hell can she look at me like *I* hurt her. I've been up front since the beginning, she's the one who lied.

Eventually, she turns around and jogs back in the direction she came.

I hold my arms out wide. "Can't you run in a different neighborhood?" I shout.

Please do me that one fucking kindness.

She holds up her middle finger and continues jogging. *Cute.*

CHAPTER 23

Scottie

I plan to make the most of my few days off before snowfall—
something I am eagerly awaiting. I've never been anywhere with
a lot of snow and am excited to experience my first winter in
Washington. Maybe I can even learn to ski or snowboard. On a
little hill… a baby hill… perhaps a fetus hill if they have one.
I'm good on my feet, but the thought of sliding down the side of
a mountain has my forehead breaking out in a cold sweat.

Tomorrow will be my first big hike in the mountains. I've
hiked parts of Arkansas, before, but the scenery is noticeably
different in the Pacific Northwest. Not only are there snow-
capped mountains, but the trees are mightier, the flora is greener,
and the forests are darker and deeper. The urge to immerse
myself in nature has never been stronger.

After all this business with Callahan, I can't rely on others to
make me happy. That was the whole point of moving away. How
long have I sacrificed my own peace so others could have theirs?
I'm *done*. If I'm going to make it in this world, I have to protect
my heart and not offer it so freely, even if it is just for *fun*.

This hike is important; it's part of finding myself. I'll never
be who I once was, and I don't want to. So it's time for me to

rebuild a version of me I can love. So that someday, someone else can love me too.

It's an undertaking that will prove I can overcome obstacles, whether they be mountains or hot men. Quell's Peak trail is one I've chosen very intentionally. It's a challenging hike but comes with the reward of captivating vistas. I don't plan on making it to the top, as the peaks have snow on them and I don't have the appropriate gear, but my objective is to reach the false summit that will serve as my finishing line.

I've done my homework. Quell's is roughly a twelve-mile hike to the summit. It's out-and-back style, no loop. However, I'll only be doing about nine of those miles. Someday, I'll do the full route, which continues on through a fairly flat section of forest that gradually rises in elevation until it opens up with rocky patches of scree to the top. However, based on trail reports, snow is covering that section.

This time of year, there may be icy patches, but they should be easy to navigate with no special equipment. The most difficult portion is the last mile, which I won't be completing anyway. I'd love to check it out another time because according to other hikers, the view from the peak is spectacular. I'll come back to conquer it next year, but tomorrow's expedition will provide me with the sense of control I'm yearning for.

I load up my backpack with water, some snacks, a first aid kit, and a jacket, and set it next to the most valuable thing I own: my boots. I double-check the weather one last time. Looks like there could be some storms rolling through in a couple days, but tomorrow is clear and perfect for hiking.

Flopping onto my bed, I plug the charger into my phone and set the alarm. I'm all set.

After the sun is up, I brush my teeth and tie my hair up into a ponytail. My fingers work a glob of sunscreen into my face and neck where my skin will be exposed. Layers are important, hence my current thin thermal base layer, which will wick moisture from my body on the hike.

After turning off the bathroom light, I return to my bed and tug my hiking pants over the leggings. They're wind resistant and have a couple small tears from previous use. Crouching on the edge of the air mattress, I drag thick socks over my feet, then wiggle my toes. Next to me lays my wool sweater, which will act as my mid-layer. I'll bring it with me in the car and put it on at the trailhead. My final outer layer is my burnt-orange puffer jacket that I've squished into a ball into my backpack. That jacket is probably the second most valuable thing I own, and I'm hoping it will get me through this hike—and all the cold and wet winter months to come.

I grab a granola bar to eat on the way to the trailhead and stuff it in the cargo pocket of my pants, then step into my hiking boots and lace them up. The right boot is too tight, so I untie, adjust, and repeat the process. Much better. With my wool sweater in one hand and my backpack over my shoulder, I snatch my keys and head out, locking the door behind me.

The skies are mostly clear when I park at the trailhead. There's one other truck here, so apparently, I'm not the only one who thought it was a good day for a hike. First, I got turned around on my way. I was looking for a road sign, but after driving around in circles, I finally stopped to ask for directions. As it turns out, the road isn't actually marked. Helpful.

Once I got that far, the drive to the parking lot was winding with occasional rocks jutting out of the narrow gravel path. Between navigational issues and travelling slower than anticipated, I'm getting started much later than I'd originally planned, but now that I've arrived, I'm eager to put some distance between this parking lot and me. I've got nine miles ahead of me and can't get behind schedule, or I'll have to turn around before reaching my destination.

I get out, pull my sweater over my head, lock my car, and stuff my keys into one of the pockets on my backpack before I hoist it over my shoulders and clip the strap over my chest. I walk toward the wooden sign carved with QUELL'S PEAK TRAIL and tighten the backpack straps at my sides.

Pulverized rock crunches under my boots. The journey starts with a gravel path from the trailhead and becomes steeper as you reach the top, winding through boulder fields and patches of forest. The landscape ahead is stunning, and I'm in awe of the wildness of it. I marvel at the herculean mountain range peppered with rock formations, emerald trees, and white snow. My smile grows as I trek ahead.

I'm not twenty minutes into my hike when I see another hiker descending. I'm assuming it's the owner of the truck I saw earlier, and a man, based on his height. I doubt he reached the top; he would have had to get here hours ago. Or maybe he's just fast and has a lot of stamina. His strides are likely much longer than mine. I keep my gaze down on the uneven path, glimpsing up occasionally, but the next time I glance up, I notice he almost looks like... *It can't be.* I straighten my pack and stand taller.

Yup. It's him. Sweaty, sexy Callahan Woods. I am unaffected by him. I'm totally not even a little bit affected by him.

Am I okay? No. But am I going to be? *Without a doubt.*

He was a lesson, a painful—but important—one I needed to learn: never invest more than you're willing to lose.

It's not like I loved him or anything, that would be ridiculous, but I really liked him before he showed his true colors. Before he gave truth to the rumors.

I want nothing more than to experience true love for myself. Now that I'm starting over, I'm in a much better position to receive it, but I still feel like I'm getting my start a decade behind my peers. From now on, I will go out more, meet new people, focus on my job, and have adventures like this one. I will live life fully and create my own happiness.

The moment he recognizes me, he does a double take. We ignore each other until we're right at the point of passing. If that furrowed brow is any indicator, he's not thrilled to see me either.

"Hey." There's mirthfulness in his voice, as if he's as perplexed as I am by the wild coincidence. We keep running into each other; Sky Ridge is one thing, but this is the mountains.

"Hi," I say without making eye contact. I may be amused by the happenstance, but there's no need to let it show. I'm over him, and I want him to know it.

Five hours later, I clear the thick copse of trees, and the path opens to the most breathtaking views. Wind whips up the side of the mountain, and the icy patches on the ground are more frequent. The higher I climb, the stronger the winds blow, which is normal, but the sky is a lot more overcast than when I began. The clouds aren't stormy and gray, though. I verified the weather before bed last night, and everything seemed fine. I consider whether I should start my descent but check my watch. Assuming I'm on the part of the trail I think I am, I'll reach the false summit in less than an hour. It's too close to give up and turn around.

I stop for a beat and extract my puffer coat from my bag and put it on, zipping it up to my chin. Much better. No such thing as bad weather, just bad clothing. Now that the wind isn't penetrating the threads on my sweater, my body heat fills the jacket, which insulates the warmth. After pulling my backpack on my shoulders again and adjusting the straps to fit over the new layer, I plod on, increasing my speed.

The boulder field I'm maneuvering through winds into switchbacks ahead that grow steeper at each turn; they're intimidating. The rocks surrounding me are enormous. Two in particular are enough to stop me in my tracks to marvel at. The colossal size of them is unearthly. Well, at least they are for someone not from the Pacific Northwest.

Before long, the trail through the boulder field meets the steep section of the mountainside. I'm almost there. The wind is louder, and I'm unable to hear my boots crunch on the path. Flakes begin to fall. *Is it snowing?* A smile stretches across my face, and I laugh. *Snow!* My first Washington snow! I want to spin in circles like I'm Julie Andrews in the Alps, but the better part of my judgment reminds me that snow means inclement weather. I'm almost there, and it's only a few light flurries. Perhaps it's just snow that's being blown off the peaks from above. I can't give up when I'm so close.

As I hurry forward, my quickened pace is quickly corrected to something slower by the high altitude. I exhale steam from my mouth and inhale fresh, cold air through my nose, my heart battling the incline and thin air.

According to my research, this is the steepest part of my hike —the switchbacks. After completing two, I have to stop for a water break. Thankfully, the pathway is wide enough so I'm not having to cling to the mountainside on the inner pass. Curiosity gets the better of me, so I slip my water bottle in my bag and move toward the outer edge. Those sixteen foot boulders from earlier don't appear so big anymore.

The call of the void. How easy it would be to just... leap. A blast of wind hits me, and I tense, pushing away from the ledge. Small rocks crumble under my hands, falling over the side and bouncing off the vertical wall to the path below. *Okay, that's enough intrusive thoughts for today.* Backing away from the edge, I choose a safer footing toward the inside wall. The gusts of wind strengthen until it's all I hear. It's a loud white noise, and the only thing that occasionally breaks through is my own panting breaths. Gazing up, I estimate there are three or four cliffside switchbacks left before the trail breaks into something more gradual—the false summit.

The patch of trees above the switchbacks mark my finish line. I'll stop to take in the view, have a short break, then head back to my car. As I ascend, sporadic flurries are whipped into a frenzy, and it's hard to tell if it's coming from above or below. More snow is sure to fall, and in a few weeks, the ground I'm standing on will be blanketed in white.

Another switchback down. Then another. The wind lashes at the exposed portions of my face and hands. Why didn't I bring gloves? I tuck my stiff fingers into the sleeves of my coat. Almost there. My eyes fix on a point in the distance, and I use it as the next marker for me to rest and drink some water. As much as I want to get out of the wind, I need a minute to catch my breath.

Another switchback. My body is shouting to turn around, that I won't have enough energy or time to make it back if I keep going, but I can't give up now. I have to finish what I started. If it was easy, it wouldn't be rewarding.

The cold batters me with every step as I climb higher. I knew this would be a difficult spot. *Keep going.* I'm almost to my rest marker when a rumble startles me. It's been constant white noise for the last twenty minutes; what could be loud enough to break through the roar of the wind?

I pause, ripping off my hood and hoping to get a better idea of where the rumbling and crunching is coming from. The hair on the back of my neck stands up, and I freeze. The noise fades as it carries the sound of popcorn popping. Another thud triggers the rolling thunder again, occasionally interrupted by more pops —like snapping toothpicks or... *trees.*

Blood drains from my face as I'm hit with a flashback from The Fold when they wanted to construct a giant cross at the top of a hill. It was a giant monument from some foundry out west. There were dangerous boulders near the top, and they used a bulldozer to roll them down the hill to ensure they wouldn't move during the construction and endanger the workers. I was there when they pushed those massive rocks down the hill. There's no mistaking it now, it's the crash of trees being mowed over as massive rocks carve new paths in the earth. This is a rockslide or a runaway boulder.

If it's a boulder, I might have a chance to dodge it, but if it's a rockslide, I'm likely already dead. The flurries disappear against the white sky when I look up, but I can't see anything. I scan the ledge above for any falling rock or dirt. Do I hug the wall? The cracking crescendos until it sounds like gunshots. My hands shake. A rock the size of a brick falls about twelve feet behind me.

Run.

I unsnap my backpack and drop it as my feet hit the trail, covering as much ground as I can. With my bag gone, I'm able to move faster and am a smaller target than I was while wearing it. The echo of snapping trees is replaced by scraping dirt and a steady thump as rocks pummel the earth behind me, chasing me higher up the mountain. Prayers I learned as a child are recited in my thoughts over and over again. My heart hammers against my ribcage as I push my legs harder than I ever have before.

Then everything is silent and the world goes dark.

CHAPTER 24

CALLAHAN

The drive home from the trailhead doesn't faze me. My thoughts are occupied with a certain five-foot-something ginger-blonde pain in the ass. I pull my truck into the detached garage behind my house, collect my pack, and hop out, slamming the door behind me. While typing the code to close the door, a few flakes fall from the sky.

She better not be trying to summit with a storm coming in. I turned around to stop her and ensure she knew about the weather, but after her less-than-thrilled "Hi," my pride got the better of me and I continued off the trail. Not to mention, her telling me to stay away from her when we bumped into each other on our run. I should have said something.

She's hiked before, she should know the rules, and she's not my responsibility anyway. *She never was.* She's got a husband to worry about her.

Where is her husband anyway?

I unlock the back door of my fixer-upper and step into the kitchen, dropping my pack with a thud. While untying my boots, my phone buzzes in my pocket, and I fish it out.

XANDER

Just saw there's some ugly shit moving in near Quell's. Text me back so I know if I gotta delete your browser history and start planning your funeral. You wanted strippers, right?

> Just got home, I got an early start.
> Yes, strippers. The good ones from Vegas.

XANDER

Darlene from Hangers said she'd do it for half the price.

> Sold.

My thoughts return to Scottie when I slide my phone back in my pocket. Is she still up there? I glance out the window, and more flurries fall. A mountain is the last place you wanna be during a storm. I check the time; she's probably already turned around and is in her car.

Probably.

I dismiss the anxious thoughts and open the fridge to gather ingredients for a sandwich. After grabbing a butter knife, I twist off the mayo cap. She doesn't know how the weather works in the Pacific Northwest mountains. I slam the knife on the counter and snatch my phone out of my pocket. Goddamn it.

> Hey. Are you off the trail?

I finish assembling my sandwich. My gaze bounces back and forth between my meal and the phone screen, waiting to see it light up with a text notification. Each time I look, I'm met by my angry expression reflected in the dark screen.

Slapping a slice of bread on top, I take my plate of food and plop into a chair at the dining table. Still nothing. I take a bite and chew while waiting for her response, but it doesn't come.

It's been almost ten minutes since I first texted her. I lick a smudge of mayo from my thumb and unlock the phone again. She should have service if she's off the mountain. Being worried about a woman I'm not responsible for is ruining my lunch. This is dumb. I tap the call icon next to her name, clearing my throat while I wait for the ring, but it goes straight to voicemail. After five seconds, I try again. Voicemail. *Shit.*

"Damn it, Scottie," I grumble. "You better not be acting stupid."

After turning the ringer on loud, I bring it with me into the bathroom and take a shower. While rinsing the shampoo out of my hair, it hits me that she might have my number blocked. Matt probably has her number. I finish getting clean and dry off, then tap his name to dial.

"Hey. This is gonna sound weird, but can you give Scottie a call and tell me if she picks up?" I pace back and forth until I find myself in the bare living room. I'm in the process of sanding down the antique wood floor and moved all the furniture into the home office last week.

He chuckles. "Is there a reason you're not doing it yourself?"

"It goes to voicemail, but she might have my number blocked." I sigh.

"Gotcha." He's disappointed. He probably assumes I did my usual fuckboy routine, but he can think whatever the hell he wants. "Yeah, gimme a sec. Call you back."

I hang up and shake my head, then lean against the wall, staring out the large front windows as my anxiety creeps in. A minute later, the screen lights up with Matt's name, and I swipe to answer before the phone has a chance to ring.

"Hey," I answer.

"Goes to voicemail," he says.

I pinch the bridge of my nose. "'K... Thanks."

Ending the call, I rub the back of my neck and groan, then throw on some sneakers and head out. My thumb is tapping the steering wheel in a steady staccato when I pull onto her street.

"Come on…. Be home. Be home. Let me see your piece of shit, rattletrap of a car sitting there so I can go home and quit this bullshit."

After seeing her vehicle this morning, I was shocked it even made the drive from Sky Ridge to the trail's entry point.

Any remaining hope plummets when the empty parking lot comes into view. I pound my fist on the steering wheel. "Fuck!"

The only way to know for sure is to go back to the trailhead and see if her car is still there. *And if it is, then what?* Do I go after her? My immediate response is a resounding *Hell yes.*

My gut instinct says she's on the mountain, which means I can't show up unprepared, and I need to move fast. She's facing a serious punishment when I get her ass back down to Sky Ridge. Can't believe she's making me go get her. There's no telling what mess lies ahead of me, but my thoughts spiral with worst-case scenarios. What if she fell? Or crossed paths with a cougar? What if she's lost and is wandering around miles off trail? I'd never find her.

My foot presses down on the accelerator. The tires on my truck squeal as I turn into my driveway and shift into park. After throwing open the back door to the house, I swap my shoes for boots and grab my pack, adding supplies for every situation I thought of on the way over. Crampons, space blanket, extra water bottles, and two handfuls of MREs. In addition, I fetch my ski patrol bag. It contains some miscellaneous survival gear, like a handwarmers, first aid kit, pocketknife, rope, and an avalanche shovel.

"Scottie, you better be in a such a fucked situation for me to be coming after you like this." I grip the steering wheel as I approach the road to the trailhead, praying I don't see her car. My neck cranes as I come around the bend, and my sight lands on her vehicle.

"Oh, fuck."

She's still up there.

CHAPTER 25

Scottie

A dull ache pulses behind my eyes. With a wrinkled brow, I wince as my lids slowly open. My right ear has a stabbing pain, and my cheeks sting like they've been slapped. I'm not sure how long it takes me to pry both eyes open, but when I do, a thin layer of white fuzz covers everything. Snow. My mouth is gritty like I ate a handful of sand, making it difficult to swallow.

My muscles and body are so fatigued it takes great effort to not close my eyes again and succumb to the drowsiness. I blink, squinting as I attempt to find my bearings. Double vision makes it nearly impossible to get a clear view of my surroundings. *This is not good.* I pause for a moment to mentally check my body for numbness or injuries, ignoring the pain in my head and focusing on the rest of my limbs. Did I fall?

How did I get here?

As soon as I get to all fours, my stomach retches, and I rotate my head in time to vomit off to the side. The pressure on my skull intensifies, and the pain has me seeing bright lights when I close my eyes.

My fingers probe my forehead and land in a section along

my hairline that's caked and sticky with dirt. I draw my hand back and notice the blood. I groan. It's not bright red, so that's a good sign.

Cautiously, I turn my neck to assess the vicinity, hoping I don't make myself throw up again. Am I on a ledge? About twenty yards behind me is a rock wall. The wall juts out over the side. It's as if I was picked up and dropped somewhere else. Did I walk here and don't remember? I've got symptoms of a concussion. Maybe if I take another rest. I could close my eyes and when I wake up, I'll remember what happened and can figure this all out, but there's a small voice in my head that's having none of it. *Get up.*

I palm the rock wall to the right of me for balance and squint, shielding my eyes with a hand as my gaze travels upward. It instantly makes me nauseous, so I keep my head down. No more looking up. Red smudges are left behind when I pull back from the wall.

Sliding to my ass, I lean against the nearly vertical rock of the mountain. My vision is delayed as I glimpse the path that ascends to the right of me. The trail is here, so I can't be on a ledge. Wait… I glance to the left again, and will my eyes to focus despite the now piercing headache. It's not a wall; it's a pile of rocks and dirt. Some the size of grapefruits, some the size of a basketball, some the size of Volkswagens. All covered in that same thin layer of snow. *Rockslide.* I shuffle backward like a crab, needing to put as much distance as I can between it and me.

Holy shit. A laugh escapes my mouth. How am I not dead? The amusement quickly turns to tears as a new problem surfaces: I have to get down this mountain, and there's no route back. The boulder and rock have blocked my exit. Not only that, but I dropped my backpack, and there's no sign of it anywhere. For all I know, it's buried under the rock pile. I brace one arm against the inner wall of the path and try to stand, testing to see if I can put weight on my legs. Nausea swarms me, so I lean against the mountain, gently lowering my body until I'm on my ass again.

I have no supplies. Wind and snow are whipping around as temperatures plummet, and I've got no way down. I curl into a ball and chuckle at the irony. All I did was trade a quick death for a slow one.

Triage. First priority is getting out of the elements. How do I get out of the wind? If I climb higher, the gusts will only get stronger. I stare at the pile of rubble... Can I climb over it? There's no way. I can barely stand, much less free solo a loose pile of boulders that could easily collapse or send me off the side of a mountain.

A gust of wind hits me, and I suck in a breath. My eyes water as they're blasted with more wind and dirt. If I stay like this, it won't be long before frost forms on my lashes. I've got a better chance with the rocks than I do the elements. I huddle up in one of the corners, giving myself a few minutes to rest in a ball. Holding up my index finger, I move it side to side and track it with my eyes. It's not as staggered as before; nystagmus is improving.

Could I shimmy down the side of the ledge somehow?

I creep toward the edge of the path on my hands and knees. My depth perception isn't one hundred percent, but peering over the side, it's gotta be twenty or thirty feet. I search for hand holds or tree roots to use to no avail. Surviving the fall is possible, but I'll be useless to move. I shake the negative image of my splattered body on the trail below.

Retreating to the rock pile, there's a smaller boulder, roughly the size of the small kitchen table in my apartment, next to the base of the larger one. I shakily hoist myself to the top and feel around the massive one blocking the path. It's no use. A slab hangs over the taller one like a roof overhang. Even if I could scramble up the almost-vertical side of the big boulder, I'd have no way to get above the slab. If I was an expert rock climber, I might have a chance, but I'm a novice with a head injury.

Can't go around it. Can't go over it.

There's a space behind the table-sized stone, like a mini cave entrance. Could I fit in there? I have no clue how stable that rock is, it could come loose and crush me. How do I die? *Let me count the ways...*

I carefully lower myself back to the ground and crouch down on all fours to inspect the tunnel created by some of the large boulders.

"Oh my God."

Splinters of daylight greet me from the other side, and there's a narrow channel between the rocks and the mountain. It doesn't even look that deep. Maybe twelve feet? Hard to tell. The passage appears to get smaller before it gets bigger, so I'd have to crawl on my belly, and even then, it would be tight. I could end up in one of those situations where I have to cut off an arm to escape. Like a fox gnawing off its own leg.

At least there's enough room for me to fit behind the smaller boulder to get out of the wind. I crane my neck to peer into the confined space again. I'm confident I could push through the rocks at the opposite end to clear an opening if I could just get to that side. I can already imagine the clack they would make as I knocked them away. I reach into the tunnel, then yank my arm back.

"Don't be an idiot, Prescott. This boulder isn't going anywhere."

Yeah, how many people said the same thing about this exact rock when it sat at the top of this mountain?

I drop to my elbows and study the passageway once more. I can see to the other side, but could I make it? It's challenging to decipher whether it's a perspective thing or an error in my depth perception. If I make it through, I should be able to descend the trail, assuming I don't run into another obstacle like this one.

If I get stuck or the shaft collapses as I'm trying to pass under... Well, then I guess I'll become the Green Boots of Quell's Peak and stay frozen until spring or until scavengers burrow through and rip my rotting limbs off. *That's pleasant.* It's not the worst way to die. I mean, how many people can say they've died between a boulder and a mountain? I suppose nobody can, they're all dead. *That's the spirit!*

It's this or die from exposure. Playing will it-won't it is a waste of time I don't have. If I don't survive this, at least I'll have tried.

Lowering to my belly, I wiggle into the gap. "Go for a hike, Scottie! Claim your independence... The world is your oyster!" I grunt, mocking myself. "How's all this freedom, babe? Feeling liberated yet?" My shoulders bunch as I duck my head and try to squeeze between two rocks. I drag myself in deeper and hear a loud tear—my coat. The wind whistles through the hole and kicks up the dust, throwing it into my eyes.

"I hate this mountain. Zero out of five stars... Boulders inconveniently placed," I groan. "Understaffed... Amenities are lacking..." I inch farther. "Gift shop sucks..." Another inch. "Save yourself the time and crawl through a ditch culvert."

It's hard to take a breath, as there's not enough room for my ribs to expand. Resting, I let my breathing regulate to something more relaxed. I know little about spelunking, but I know enough to understand panicking is bad.

Once I'm ready, I try to wiggle forward, but it's like I can't get the leverage to propel myself. With my arms tucked up like a T-Rex, there's nowhere to go, but there's also not enough room to stretch in front of me. I try to wiggle backward, but can't. *Stay calm.* You're not stuck, you just need to relax your muscles. Exhaling, I close my eyes and focus on making my body loose. But I'm freezing, and every limb feels rigid. With crawling fingers, one of my hands slides down. Bit by bit, I wiggle my other arm to stretch above my head. I have to get an arm out from under me, but it's against a sharp edge. I pause and reassess, attempting to rotate my shoulders. It doesn't work. If I get my elbow caught ahead of me, I'll have even less body heat. I'm tired.

With weakened, stiff muscles, my body is unable to move as easily as before.

It's so cold.

My hands hurt. I ball them into fists, and they throb as the impending frostbite sets in. I kick my feet, seeking purchase on anything to help squirm in any direction. It's futile. The more I fight to free myself, the less room I have. With each unsuccessful motion, the thought of dying here is easier to accept. Odds are I won't make it. Wiggling again, I try to rotate. I'm not ready to give up, but it takes so much effort to move half an inch. *Am I even moving at all?*

My eyes are heavy. Tilting my head slightly, I catch sight of the end of the narrow channel. It can't be more than six feet away, but it might as well be six miles, because this tunnel gets smaller before it gets bigger, and I'm... I'm *trapped*. Neither rock will budge. A tear rolls over my temple as a hard lump forms in my throat. My car is here. Someone will find my body.

Another tear falls and I sniffle, sucking the freezing air into my lungs. I close my eyes and blow out a narrow current of air through my lips. It's not looking good.

I'm familiar with the human body—what it's capable of and what it isn't. Freezing to death isn't the worst way to die. In fact, it's pretty favorable. My fingers and toes ache now, but eventually, I'll lose all sense of pain. After that, my heart will draw blood from hands and feet, which will create a temporary feeling of warmth. As my internal temperature plummets, I'll grow drowsy. It will be gentle, like I'm falling asleep. When I'm unconscious, my organs will fail one-by-one until I go into cardiac arrest.

It's simple, really.

This tunnel isn't my escape, it's my grave. I wrestle to turn my body inward, but the strength isn't there. I'm too tired. Tranquil acquiescence washes over me, and I rest my head on my shoulder, closing my eyes.

CHAPTER 26

CALLAHAN

This isn't how I saw today going. A rescue mission is not a wise idea. In fact, it's flat out fucking foolish, but there's a person up there who needs help. It doesn't matter that it's Scottie—though the fact that it is gives me one more reason to be pissed at her. I can't believe she'd be so foolhardy. She's a smart woman, smarter than this.

At the six-mile mark, I stop to rest. Digging my crampons out of my bag, I slip them over my hiking boots and pull ski goggles over my eyes to keep the windburn at bay. After zipping my bag, I chug some water and keep going. I'm used to pushing my body to the absolute limit during fire season, but this storm is turning ugly. At a certain point, my self-preservation will kick in and I'll need to make the decision to turn around. I've done several alpine climbs over the United States. I love traversing over the spine of a mountain and making the linkup to the next peak, but this storm is making conditions brutal.

How have I not run into her yet? What if I never do? She could have lost the trail somewhere along the way, and we could be ten miles away from each other. Is she taking shelter? I think back to earlier, and she didn't appear to have gear for an overnight trip. This route is set up for day hikes, out and back. She should be *back*.

I check my watch. It will be dark in a few hours. I'm running on pure adrenaline, which has allowed me to move at a pretty good clip. I'll give her one more hour, then I'll have to turn around. I tuck my water into my bag and keep going. I've got to cover as much ground as I can before dark, or I won't have a chance.

Whatever is keeping her up on this mountain can't be good. With each minute that passes, the likelihood of her being injured goes up, and the odds of me finding her dwindles. I shout her name into the wind and scan the landscape for any sign of her. She only had a sweater on earlier. She could be dead from exposure alone if she didn't have an outer layer.

Why wouldn't she turn around when the weather got bad? The Scottie I know wouldn't be so hellbent on a summit that she'd risk exposure, but there're a lot of things about Scottie that I had wrong.

Toward the summit, scrambling is required in one of the sections with scree. It's easy enough for hikers with experience, but the ground is less stable. Mountaintops are subject to extreme temperatures and erosion year-round. The fractured ground is loose and more dangerous than it is at lower elevations. Hikers, or even a strong gust, can trigger rockfall, depending on the conditions.

Why this woman? The only person I hate more than her right now is myself. I never should have slept with her, and now I'm risking my life for someone who lied. The ache in my knee has me wishing I'd wrapped it before attempting a second climb.

Clearing a copse of trees reveals the boulder field and switchbacks ahead. I cup my hands over my mouth and yell, "Scottie!"

I scan the open switchbacks and detect an out-of-place section. There's a rock formation that looks odd from this angle?

What the hell is that? It's almost like an optical illusion of a small overhang, but it's too high up to see.

Once I get through the boulder field, the switchbacks begin. Each spans approximately 200 to 300 feet, and I resist scaling straight up the side. My knees can't take it. After the second switchback, I'm given a vantage point of the landscape I've already hiked through. I squint through my goggles, looking for any sign of movement off the paths. Nothing.

She and I are the only ones out here, but we might as well be on opposite ends of the earth. Glancing up, I furrow my brow and wrench off my goggles to see if it helps me gain perspective, but with the bright snow swirling around and sticking to everything, it provides no further insight. Probably my eyes playing tricks on me, but any sudden change in landscape is bad.

Another switchback down and I notice a large rock in the middle of the path that's at least as high as my knees. I wouldn't have missed that earlier. My heart pounds in my chest, urging me to pick up the pace. Another rock. Then another. And another. The higher I climb, the more peppered the area is with debris of varying sizes.

I purge the image of her lifeless form from my thoughts as quickly as it appears. I can't handle another dead body. Injuries... She's injured. We won't be able to get back down in time if she's wounded. My hand finds my pocket, and I run my fingers through my key ring. *That might be my only option.*

As I round the bend, I crane my neck to look ahead and almost freeze in my tracks when I see one of the biggest boulder blockages I've ever witnessed. The dread of seeing that boulder is nothing compared to the fear that strikes me when my gaze lands on a backpack. *Scottie's backpack.*

As I get closer, my stomach lurches. The thought of her being crushed under that giant pile has me bending over and nearly throwing up. Why would her backpack be off? I look out from the ledge and cup my hands.

I shout her name as loud as I can, trudging over to her bag. Fuck. *Fuck, fuck, fuck.*

I'm panting when I hear a faint noise. It's so hard to hear over the wind. It could've been my imagination. Maybe it was nothing. I scream her name again, and this time, I hear it... It's weak, but it's there.

"Help!"

My eyes gape. "Where, Scottie? Keep yelling!"

She says she's underneath, but she can't be trapped under the boulder, or she wouldn't be alive. Even a much smaller rock could have killed her instantly. There's a small pile of rubble, so I begin pulling away the loose bits of dirt and stone.

"Here!" she shouts.

I drop my cheek down, prying my goggles off and squinting inside the opening. It's dark, but there's some daylight showing through. "Scottie?"

"Yes!" she sobs. "I tried to squeeze under."

I stumble back at the sound of her voice, my relief soaring. I swallow and drop to her level. "How do I get to you?"

"I dunno..." she chokes out. "I'm stuck. Tried to squeeze through." Her words shake like she's being racked with shivers. Even her chattering teeth can be heard over the air whistling through the narrow opening. She's been here awhile—it's a miracle she's still alive.

"I'm gonna get you out, baby. Just stay calm."

CHAPTER 27

CALLAHAN

I force myself to push aside the impending panic attack and focus on the task at hand. Time to problem solve. The barricade is at least twelve feet tall. Some areas are closer to fourteen. Thankfully, I've been rock climbing and soloing since I was a kid, which allows me to spot a few handholds, but this is not a secure rock wall. Any of these could slide, taking me with it or crushing Scottie below.

First, I pick up her backpack by one of the straps and launch it over the heap. Almost positive it cleared the other side. I'll find out in a minute, because I've got to climb over this thing to get to her.

Pulling off my gloves, I stuff them in my bag, along with the key ring in my pocket. My fists clench as I plan my route across. The wind isn't doing me any favors, and in addition to being fucking freezing, it's whipping up loose dirt in my face, so I'm grateful for the ski goggles. When I feel confident enough in the path I've chosen, I jump to seize my first handhold, instantly slip and hit the ground, stumbling backward a few steps. I try again, and on my second attempt, gain leverage.

My knuckles bloom white as I hang from the ledge and

stretch with my free hand to the next target. The rock is large but could be loose, so I'll have to act quickly. I go for it, but the boulder shifts and my fingers miss. I shoot an arm out to an opening above, and thankfully, it's got a good chunk of grit that provides me with better purchase. Glimpsing down, I place a foot on a small lip on another boulder just as the rock next to it gives out. I freeze, waiting for the next movement. This is easily the dumbest fucking thing I've ever done.

A crevice in one of the rocks allows me to clasp it with my left hand. My fingers tremble as I move to the next mark and the one after that. As I traverse across the pile, there's noticeably more gravel on this end. A little gravel is fine, but a lot can reduce friction.

My heart races. If I can get to the footing on my left, I'll be able to get a better view of the other side. This fucker better not even think about rolling on me. I transfer one hand, falter, then throw an arm up and grab onto a sharp lip of the boulder that cuts into my fingers. I roar through gritted teeth, pulling myself up. There's no choice but to grip it harder, bringing with it a pulsing pain. My foot finds a divot and pushes off while I reach for a different section. I feel around for anything, and finally, brush against something to hold onto. Then I wrap my hand around it, let go of the razor edge of the rock, and grunt as I haul my body over the top.

"Hell yeah," I huff, wiping my palm on my pants and smearing blood across them.

I creep closer to the inner wall, wanting to distance myself from any rocks with the potential to slip or cause a collapse.

My body shakes as I cling to the slab and use my right arm to brace against the mountain wall while I plan my next move. The top of the boulder pile comes to a point, and I straddle it, swinging my other leg over an angled rock that slopes away from the mountain and toward certain death.

"I will not lose my fucking footing," I mutter.

Inching across laterally allows me to make it to the other side safely. However, I'm not exactly thrilled with what I find.

There's a drop-off. A big one. The slab of rock I'm on overhangs the ground below. Something shifts below me, and the slab tilts even steeper. I'm suddenly acutely aware of what a precarious spot I'm in. I need to move—now. I've got no choice but to drop off the side. There are no more options, not from here, and with the amount of scree below, it's only a matter of time before these giants start to act like marbles. Not to mention, Scottie is underneath this mess.

Cursing the wind, I roll onto my belly and ease my legs over the side. My biceps and forearms are shaky as I battle for muscle control. I peek over my shoulder, and the drop doesn't seem so bad. I'm six feet tall, but my vertical reach is about eight feet, which means my drop is probably only around four feet once I'm suspended off the end.

I lower my torso over the side. I just need to dangle over the edge, extend my arms to bring myself as close to earth below as I can, and then... let go. Except this fucking slab veers again, so I shove off as hard as I can, turning my four-foot drop into something closer to seven. I fall into a patch of scree and shuffle back as the slab slides off the massive boulder and over the mountain ledge. The crack of it colliding with the rocky landscape echoes from below. Holy shit.

I tumble back but miraculously find traction underfoot. I feel nothing as adrenaline hammers through me. *Scottie.*

She's in what appears to be an empty shaft between the boulders and the mountainside. Peering behind an almost three-foot tall rock, my eyes catch on one of her hiking boots. I wrap a hand around the heel and shake it. "Hey. I'm with you."

"Cal." Her sob is full of renewed hope. She's a first responder, so the idea of death must have been in her thoughts for a good amount of time, and that's bound to fuck up anyone's psyche. If I hadn't gotten here when I did, she probably would have been right.

"Are you hurt?"

"I-I'm c-c-cold." Her teeth chatter and the words are stuttered. That could be from the cold or a concussion. "Really cold," she repeats.

"As soon as I get you out, we'll get you warmed up. Just sit tight."

"Mm-hm." She sounds sleepy.

"Don't go to sleep, just keep talking to me. What hurts?"

Carefully, I roll a few rocks out of the way.

"Headache. Don't feel much."

Fuck, if she doesn't feel pain, she might feel nothing. "Do you feel your legs?"

"Did before."

"Keep your eyes open, hear me?"

"Mm-hm."

How did she even get in here?

"You with me?"

"Mm-hm," she squeaks.

Moving into position, I grip her ankles. "I'm gonna pull, yell if you need me to stop. The more you can wiggle yourself out, the better off you'll be."

She rocks her hips as I tug, wriggling her body in jerky motions. She's fighting for it. *Thatta girl.*

She shouts with a hoarse voice over the wind.

"What is it?"

Nothing.

"Scott—"

"Pull!" she cuts me off.

As I do, her hips twist and she jolts, releasing a small yelp.

"More!" she yells.

I grasp her calves and continue. Soon, her knees are out, and she's able to roll to her back, scooting and wiggling side to side.

"Keep your head down! Slow!" As more of her body clears the space, I see she's bracing one arm with the other like she's injured. Her hands look like that of a corpse. What's with her shoulder? Did she dislocate it? Is that what the yelp was?

When her face emerges, a smile spreads across mine, but quickly falls. *Holy shit.* She's been out here too long, and there's a big gash on the perimeter of her hairline, but at least she's out. Her light-ginger hair is a chestnut brown, matted with blood and dirt.

"Hands too cold. Take my arm, pull it forward, and guide it back into the socket... Grab it."

I gape at her. *Okay.* "Forward like in front of you or forward like in the direction you're laying?"

"Straight in front of me."

"Shit. Ready?"

She nods. I follow her instructions, and she winces, then rolls to her good side and pushes off the ground to get to her feet. Her fingers are as white as the snow swirling around. I curl my arms around her waist and help her up, then put her hands together between mine and blow my hot breath on them a few times, rubbing them. Afterward, I snatch the gloves from my bag and fit them onto her stiff fingers. Her teeth chatter again, and I wrap my arms around her body.

"Let's move."

I want to put as much distance as I can between this pile of rock and us. She has a limp, so I glance down. "Can you walk?"

"Jus' cold. Need to c-cir-late."

I furrow my brow. Huh?

"Needa walk!"

Circulate.

"Why the hell were you out here with a storm? What the fuck!"

She glares at me, her eyes cussing me out more than her words ever could. It's the first spark of fire I've seen in her.

Good, she will need that feistiness for the trek we have ahead of us.

"Gimme my pack... First aid... Hand warmers." I'm getting better at translating her garbled words.

I drop to my knees and rifle through her backpack until I find them, then tear open the plastic wrap and shake up the pouches. There are four, but only three heat up. She leans against the mountainside while I unlace her boots and shove two of the working ones deep inside near her toes, then re-tie her back up again.

"How're we gonna get down?" she asks, bewildered.

I chuckle, zip up her backpack, and slip out the water bottle, making her drink while I find another pouch in my bag to replace the dead one.

She takes it from me. Then stuffs her water in her bag and attempts to hoist it on her back. She grimaces as she slides it over her recently dislocated shoulder. I try to take it from her, and she yanks it back, glaring.

"Scottie, give me your bag. You can't carry that with your injury."

"I've got it!"

I shake my head at her stubbornness. I'm not going to bicker with her. "We're not going down."

"Yes we are! I'm not dying up here!" She stumbles to the side and catches herself with her good arm on the mountainside. She's barely steady on her feet.

"I don't have gear to get you over this wall, and you're in no condition to do it yourself." I shout over the wind. *And I'm not climbing that fucking thing again; we've both tempted fate enough as it is.* We need every bit of luck we have left to get us to the top.

"Gotta be another way down." Her gaze scans the surroundings. "You know the mountain. Find another way." I rip off the goggles from around my neck and place them over her red eyes and tighten the strap behind her head.

"Scottie, we have to go higher. We're past getting off the mountain tonight. We need to seek shelter."

There's a tower at the top we can stay in until the storm blows over.

"Where!?" She sobs. "There's nowhere! If we go higher, we'll freeze!"

I shake my head, getting frustrated with her. We don't have time to argue. Like she said, I know this mountainside better, so if we're going to survive, I need her to follow my lead. She's starting to panic, and if she doesn't fall in line now, it'll cost both our lives.

"Even if the path wasn't blocked, we're eight miles from the parking lot... but the trail is *gone*. We can either go higher and find a new route down, which will be more than eight miles, or we can go to the summit and take shelter at the fire tower."

"The wind will blow us off the mountain!"

The storm coming in is big. It's our only shot.

"What's the rule of threes?" I ask.

"No." She frowns, and tears swell in her eyes, fogging up the goggles. I loosen them to clear the condensation. I don't know how else to make her understand the severity of this situation.

"What is it?" I demand.

"Three weeks without food. Three days without water. Three hours without shelter in extreme cold." She's still not speaking properly.

"Exactly." I put an arm under her. "Now move."

She trudges with me. "I don't know how long I've been out here. I was un—uncon—"

"Unconscious," I finish for her. "Then move faster."

She's unstable with stiff legs and struggling keep up, so I tuck an arm around her and haul her with me.

"What if I can't do it?"

"You're going to do it. Because I'm going to make you," I growl. "You did not bring my ass up this mountain just to die. There's not a ton of daylight left, so pick up your pace, Scottie, I mean it!"

"You're a dick."

If she's too scared to fight the mountain, I'll force her to fight me instead. Whatever it takes to give her the gumption to keep one foot in front of the other. I'll be an asshole all the way to the top if it keeps her moving.

"Stop talking and walk," I snap. I hate being this callous with her, but I need her to survive. Anger seems to be her only motivation. I promise to apologize and make it up to her later.

Surprisingly, she does what I ask, and we make it around to the last switchback. This one is only about one hundred and fifty feet long. As soon as we reach the top, there'll be a false summit, where we can get into the cover of trees, which will hopefully block out some of the wind. *Hopefully.* From there, we've got a mile hike to the tower. Uphill.

CHAPTER 28

Scottie

I never thought I'd be happy to see Callahan Woods again, but he saved my life. I was ready to abandon hope before he showed up and pulled me out. My stomach is churning with nerves. I have no idea what the plan is once we arrive at the fire tower, but I trust he knows what to do. It's my only option. We're not out of the woods yet, literally.

Between the brutal pain in my shoulder and the acute headache, I'm feeling pensive. So with each command Callahan barks at me, I become even more irate. I was ready to give up, but now I'll make it to the top of the mountain just to spite him.

Reactive hyperemia is setting in, and the sudden rush of blood back into my extremities is excruciating. My fingers feel like they're on fire stuffed in his gloves with the handwarmers. The sensation is like stabbing knives, almost unbearable. Gritting my teeth, I attempt to focus on anything else. Somehow warring with Cal and getting that anger out seems to make it better.

Fighting back tears of embarrassment, pain, anger, relief, and fear, I ask, "How did you know I was up here?"

He sighs. "Texted you. You didn't respond. Didn't see your car at your apartment. Just had a bad feeling."

"You drove by my apartment?"

"You weren't answering your phone!" he grumbles.

"Thanks." My voice is genuine.

He scoffs. "I didn't have a choice."

Okay, fuck you. "Oh please, you always have a choice. Just like when you..." The fact that my lips are still too frozen to form words angers me.

"What was that?"

"Nothing!" I yell, thankful he didn't hear my slip up. Every time he looks at me, his eyes flash with compassion, and it makes me angrier. *It's not real.* I fell for it last time, and now I feel myself falling for it again. It's my own fault, but it's easier to take it out on him. I know it's wrong, but I can't stop myself.

"Isn't there some other man who should be out here searching for you instead of me?" he asks.

What the hell is he talking about? "Probably! Anybody would be better than you. Surprised you even cared enough to show up."

Especially considering he didn't show up the day we were supposed to meet at my apartment. Instead, he texted he was done with me, with zero explanation. I wasn't even worth the time to say it to my face.

"You say the dumbest shit sometimes. Come on." He grabs under my arms and tugs me forward. My shoulder screams out in pain, and I smack his hand which sends the overactive nerves in my fingers into a fiery rage. I bite my tongue to keep from howling in agony, then pick up the pace as best I can. *Fuck him.*

"You should have just left me. Dying hurt less."

His jaw clenches, and he glares at me. "Move!" he shouts.

When we reach the false summit, he freezes in his tracks, staring at the path the rockfall made after mowing down a wide clearing. It looks like a power line corridor, with trees neatly folded over to the ground like a woven rug.

"You should have heard it," I say.

We exchange a quick glance, then I step forward, and he continues with me.

"If we make it to the fire tower—"

"When," he corrects.

"Whatever. Then what? We break in?"

He shakes his head. "I have a key."

"Why?"

"Wildland firefighters have yale keys to the lookouts." I don't reply, so he proceeds. "They're supplied to us when we join and only returned when we leave the agency. I keep mine on my key ring."

"Lucky us." I know I should conserve my energy and not speak, but my face feels so frozen I'm afraid what will happen if I don't.

"You can quit with the sarcasm now."

I was being sincere, but I don't blame him for mistaking it for more attitude. I'm in a lot of pain, and every word out of my mouth has a layer of sass. It's shocking he can decipher as much as he is, but I am grateful for the tower. Twenty minutes ago, I thought I would die between a rock and a hard place.

"It's not sarcasm. We get a free Airbnb, complements of the US federal government."

"Glad this is a big joke to you."

Crying would be much easier, but tears will fog up these goggles. "I'm trying to be appreciative! I owe you one, okay?"

"You have no fucking idea."

I wince at a throb behind my eyes that hasn't quit.

"Stop talking and move your ass. You're slowing us down."

"Oh, it's my fault I got rocked by half the mountain falling down? Sorry!"

He groans. "No, it's your fault because you didn't turn around sooner. You should have been keeping an eye on the sky, should have known a storm was coming through—you acted fucking stupid today."

"You're an asshole." I swallow down my emotions. He's right, I should have turned around, but I'm also right. Rockfalls are random, so it could've happened to anyone. "If you haven't noticed, I'm kinda having a shitty day, so if we could save the reprimands for later, that would be awesome."

"Yeah, because my day has been all roses, thanks to you," he seethes. *Point taken.*

I stomp through a pile of snow. "I thought I was going to die earlier!" I pause, trying to regain my composure. "I still might die before we get there," I snap.

"You better not waste my fucking time and die."

I trip over a rock, my arms shoot out to catch myself, bringing back the shoulder pain, but he's hauling me up before I hit the ground. I grunt as he puts me back on my feet.

"Jesus, would you watch where you step? Quit whining and focus on getting to the top! I'm not giving you any sympathy." He flinches at his own words, and his compassionate gaze finds mine again. *Cal the Liar.* His features shift, and he narrows his eyes. "Just, shut up, Scottie."

CHAPTER 29

CALLAHAN

I'm an asshole, but her fury will get her up the mountain faster than fear. Though, it hurts like hell to treat her so badly. I'm mad at her for lying, but I could never blame her for what happened today. That falling rock wasn't her fault, and even if I haven't expressed it, I'm so fucking thankful she's alive.

At the moment, anger is the only thing shielding my concern. Scottie's not in good shape, but good God, I need that woman to stop picking fights with me. I understand she's scared, but she's purposely plucking my nerves like a fucking banjo. We're so close. I know she can do it.

She scared the shit out of me earlier when her weight came down on her shoulder as she scrambled through the roughest section of the climb, and the noises she made told me she was in pain. We had to drop to a crawl through the loose rock and snow. I think we were both holding our breath, afraid we'd trigger another rockfall.

My adrenal gland is permanently broken thanks to my career choice, so there's not much that excites me, but playing Jenga with boulders the size of cars and strolling into a mountaintop blizzard are chipping away at my limits. I'm one more catastrophe away from a full-blown panic attack. Being up here reminds me of the time our crew was caught at the summit by a fast-approaching lightning storm.

The snow-swept trail in front of us fades away as I'm consumed by memories of that storm. Weather had been building in the distance, but we were stranded at spike camp. The ridge we were on was not the place to ride out a thunderstorm. We took shelter as best we could, but we were sitting ducks. It was a fucked-up situation. We crouched on the balls of our feet low to the ground while fire from the heavens struck the earth all around us. Every guy was waiting for the next bolt to take us out.

"Cal!" Scottie shouts over the wind, pulling me into the present.

"Huh?" *Fuck.*

"Is that it?"

Glancing up, I get eyes on the structure and nod. Nestled on the top of a rocky peak, the fire tower sits, bracing the winds that threaten to take us down. The 360-degree shutters are all closed, making it look like a solid box with a roof. It's the most welcome sight. A single short flight of stairs rises from the ground to the catwalk that wraps around the perimeter. *We did it.*

It's been a while since I've spent a night in a fire tower, and if this storm is as bad as the radar suggested, we might be here for a few days. During the season, hired lookouts live here. They're responsible for maintaining the space, gathering and splitting wood, lugging water, planting gardens, caulking windows, and maintaining the outhouse. They are self-sufficient. Thankfully, based on the condition of the structure, the last ones did a good job.

I'm really counting on the tower having leftover provisions we can use to survive. We need heat, water, and food if we're to have a fighting chance. All I care about is getting Scottie out of this fucking wind and making sure we've got shelter and warmth, because this storm won't be short-lived.

A strong gust slams into us, so we widen our stances, leaning into it, and drop lower as it pushes us backward. We brace ourselves, anchoring into the snow as we wait for it to pass. When it eases, we plod forward with more eagerness than before. Winds must be blowing close to sixty miles an hour as we approach. Snow blankets the top in drifts, giving us a means to ground ourselves. It's hard to imagine anything sticking to the ground the way the flakes are whipping up all around us.

As we approach the base of the stairs, I thrust Scottie in front of me, and the sound of our boots clomping are barely a whisper over the wind, but the break of something other than the constant blowing is a welcome one. When we reach the deck, I unclip the straps around my chest and take a knee, dropping my pack and unzipping the side pocket to locate my keys. My fingers are stiff as hell as I flip through them. I should have had another pair of backup gloves. Once I recognize it, I rise to my feet, insert the key, and turn hard to unlatch the door. When the lock pops, the door damn near flies off its hinges as the wind throws it open, and papers blow around the room.

Scottie scurries across the threshold as we're chased inside by the icy air lashing at our backs. In the tower, I lean my shoulder into the door, cutting off the wind where it tries to follow us inside. It takes some force but finally clicks shut.

"Fuck!"

The remaining daylight is quickly obscured when I shut the door, so I fish out my phone, using the flashlight to find a lantern.

As soon as it lands on one, I snatch it off the shelf next to the door and turn it on. The warm glow dimly illuminates the space. Shadows dance around the room as I walk the lantern to the Osborne Fire Finder on the table in the center of the room. Darkness settles behind every object and corner, adding to the ominous undercurrent. I smile at the pile of chopped wood resting next to the black stove.

Sonnofabitch. We might not die after all.

Now sheltered, it's quieter, but not by much. It's also the first time I've felt my body heat in over an hour without the wind instantly ripping it away. Who knows how much energy I've burned trying to keep up with it. I dig a protein bar out of my bag, throwing one at Scottie too.

"Eat that."

My icy fingers struggle to tear the wrapper, so I use my teeth. The bar is hard as a rock, like it's been kept in a freezer, but I work my jaw to scarf it down.

She pulls off my gloves and carefully works to unwrap hers. She pauses before taking a bite. "What about rationing food? Should I save some of it?"

I chug a few gulps of water and take a deep breath, shaking my head. "Eat all of it." Then I pass the water to her. Now it's time to make a decision. I'm losing daylight fast, and if we're to survive, we need more water. I can't be sure this storm won't get worse before it gets better.

Striding over to a small inlet of cabinets, I start throwing open doors and rummaging through the space. I grab a couple canteens, but it's not what I really need: a cubie. My eye catches on the flattened clear plastic, and I snatch up the collapsed five-gallon reservoir. *Bingo.*

"Hand me my goggles," I say. "I'm going to get water."

She passes me back the water bottle. "No, sweetheart, we need water that's actually going to last us more than the next twenty-four hours." I shake an open palm, gesturing for her to give me the goggles.

"Now?" The panic in her voice is evident. She tugs the goggles off her head, leaving a red ring across her forehead and over the bridge of her nose, where her freckles are camouflaged by windburn. "You need to get it now?!"

"If we want to survive, yes. Toss me your water bottle."

She finds her pack and slides it out with shaky hands, still questioning me. "Can't we just melt the snow?"

What? I cock my head to the side, then remember she's from a region that likely never received more than an inch or two at a time, if any. To her, snow is likely a novelty, something to play pretend with, simple fun instead of something you learn to live with for months on end.

"Do you know how much snow it takes to make a cup of water?"

I adjust the strap on the snow goggles and secure them over my face.

"No…"

"A fucking lot. We'll burn through all our fuel and wood trying to melt enough to drink. If we can start off with water, we'll be in a lot better shape." I take her water bottle and top it off without giving her everything I have left. That way if I don't make it back, I won't be leaving her helpless.

"Where are you going to find water?"

"There's a stream not far from here, less than a mile. I have to get to it before it freezes."

I kneel on the floor in front of my pack and toss out everything nonessential. The less weight, the better. Water is heavy enough as it is. After digging out my headlamp, I pull it over my hat, then tuck the empty canteens in the bag. I test the headlamp by turning it on. Scottie shields her eyes from the bright light, and I turn it off. If I move fast enough, I'll get there before it's dark, but I'll need light to find my way back. For added measure, I steal a flashlight off the shelf and add it to my pack for backup, along with a pack of batteries sitting next to it. I'll be blind out there without a light source. Scottie can keep the lantern.

"Will it be contaminated?"

"We'll boil it." I zip up my backpack and stand, hoisting it over my shoulder, then retrieve the gloves she borrowed and shove my hands inside. They are still toasty from the handwarmers; it's marvelous. "I'll be back in thirty. Do not leave." I point a finger at the ground. "I swear to God, Scottie, if you step foot out of this tower, I will tan your ass. That's a promise."

Her eyes gape at me. Grabbing up the cubie, I head for the door.

"Wait, but—"

"Prescott. I will be back in thirty."

I open the door and fight the wind to close it behind me. There's no time to argue.

CHAPTER 30

Scottie

The door closes and I'm left alone. Until he returns, this place will feel like a crypt. I know first aid and basic life support, but I don't have the wilderness survival skills Callahan possesses. The dull ache of my shoulder is what's to be expected after having an arm pulled out of its socket and put back again, but it's nothing in comparison to the pounding in my skull. I rifle through my bag and find the first aid kit, then dry-swallow a few ibuprofen.

The room is roughly fourteen by fourteen feet, surrounded by wall-to-wall windows. Tall awning shutters protect them from the snowstorm raging outside. It appears they've battened down the hatches for the season.

One wall is lined with the scuffed-up lower cabinets Callahan tore through while searching for the cubie he kept mumbling about. The cabinets continue halfway down the adjacent wall in an L-shape, they remind me of the ones you see in houses built in the 1940s. On the short side, there's an open base cabinet at the end, and it seems the door was removed at some point so it could be used for storing stacks of split logs.

A divider is set up, near the wood, providing a barrier for the cast iron wood stove that sits on the other side. It's small, but likely creates enough heat to easily warm the modest living quarters. There's a little windowed door on the front of the stove and a newish-looking stove pipe that rises, making a couple turns before it meets the ceiling to vent out of the roof.

On the opposite wall to the cabinets is a twin bed with a bare mattress. The bed has two drawers underneath, providing additional storage, and it's painted white to match the rest of the lookout. A crude handmade nightstand housing books on a shelf sits next to it, probably added sometime later.

The center of the room is taken up by a small island, and on top sits a large circle-shaped instrument with a topographic map. I assume it's used by the lookout to calculate the location of wildfires.

I pick up the lantern to explore.

Directly underneath the freestanding cabinet, is a passthrough space that reaches the other side, and a few notebooks and maps sit in the opening. Below, clipboards hang from hooks on the side. I glance over the papers clipped to them; they're some kind of daily logs that Callahan probably understands, but to me it reads like nonsensical jargon. Shallow shelves are built into another side of the island; a pair of binoculars, an old metal tin, field guides, writing utensils, and other miscellaneous items sit in the cubbies. A first aid kit hangs from another side, and beneath it is an old picture of Smokey Bear, who tells me that only I can prevent forest fires. The corners are peeling and the tape has yellowed with age. The remaining wall of the island has a sky chart nailed to it; it's probably been there for half a century based on how badly the images have been bleached by the sun.

I head toward the bed and open one of the drawers, pleased to find linens and blankets. Dryer sheets are tucked into the bedding, it reminds me of home where we did the same thing to keep mice out of the church's altar linens. The artificial smell of "clean cotton" permeates the musty space.

After making the bed, I get acquainted with the rest of the room. The white cabinets could use another layer of paint, but they're in better condition than the ones at my apartment. *What's in here, anyway?* With the lantern in hand, I peer inside. The first one has a few plastic rodent-proof containers stocked with cans of food and a few bags of prepackaged soups or other ready-to-eat meals.

"Whoa." That's a huge win.

Another door houses a green metal toolbox, and a broom and dustpan sit next to it. Nearby, an open cabinet showcases a folded-up camp stove and forest-green cans of propane. A set of drawers reveal a dented steel pot and other cookware. The shallow one at the top has silverware, a can opener, and a couple random cooking gadgets. I close the cabinets left open from Callahan as I investigate.

I'm cold, my body shivering, but my mind is in such a strange place right now. Everything feels out of order. *Concussion.* Thoughts flit in and out, like waves of consciousness. There's something I should be doing, but I don't know what it is. My eyes scan the room and land on the firewood.

Fire.

I have the logs, but I need matches or some kind of fire starter. I search the shelves but can't find anything. The moment I open one of the drawers, the lantern flickers and goes out, dousing the room in inky blackness. I smack the lantern. Nothing.

"Peachy! Just peachy." Now I will never find those damn matches.

Feeling around for my backpack, my fingers brush the canvas, then I navigate through the pockets to find my cell phone. I open the flip phone, but nothing happens. Then I press a button to light up the screen, but it doesn't turn on. I feel for the power button and hold it down. Nothing. Maybe it's cold? I slip it in my bra, hissing when the cold plastic touches my flesh, and continue digging for anything that might substitute a fire starter.

I open a few other compartments, feeling around with my hands, but it's no use. Even using my fingers to feel the objects, I struggle to decipher what it is I'm touching. I might have touched five lighters by now, but my brain wouldn't know the difference. I sit at the corner of the L-shaped cabinets and pull my knees to my chest. The lack of light plays tricks on my eyes, and static blinks in front of me, adding to the headache. I don't like it. I feel more claustrophobic here than when I was trapped earlier.

After a period, my sense of time has me questioning how long ago Callahan left. It must have been half an hour by now, right? If it hasn't been half an hour, it shouldn't be much longer. He'll be here any moment. The darkness makes every second feel like an hour. Counting gives me something to focus on instead of the utter dread of loneliness and abandonment.

Did something happen to him? Is he hurt?

He's right, I fucked up. I fucked up so badly. I should have turned around sooner. Goddamn it. I return to counting in sets of sixty, attempting to measure minutes. After ten, I get fidgety. Something's not right; he should have been back by now. What if he found an easy path back and left me here to get more help? I could be alone for hours. I pull my arms from the sleeves and curl them to my chest. The wind is no longer stealing my warmth, but it's still bitterly cold. There has to be a way to heat up.

The absence of light is disorienting. Crawling along the cabinets, I open two doors before I lay my hands on the large smooth rectangle. I remember this from before, what is it? Focus... *camp stove*. Next to it are the curved propane tanks. There has to be some light outside still, right? On my hands and knees, I feel my way to the door and turn the handle, it flies open sending tiny biting flakes whorling inside. It's a black void of nothingness, save for the freezing air that lashes every inch of my exposed flesh. I lean my weight into the door to close it.

This is bad. *This is really bad.*

Dropping to the floorboards, I scoot to my previous spot and feel around for the camp stove and propane tanks. Perhaps matches are inside. After several tries, I figure out how to lift the lid and run my fingers along the top, side, and every greasy crevice. No matches. I continue down the line of cabinets, searching by touch. Never in my life have I wished for a lighter so badly. I have all the tools to keep the fire going, but without that first spark, it's pointless.

With this head injury, who the fuck knows how long it's been. Maybe it's only been fifteen minutes instead of thirty? *Count again.* I count to six hundred, another round of ten minutes. Then another ten. We're definitely over the thirty-minute mark. I've counted that many at least. Right? Did I miss any numbers? I probably missed numbers.

What if he fell off a ledge? What if he needs help?

I'm so stupidly powerless! "Please, please, please…"

I drop my face into my hands and breathe slowly. There's no way I'm sleeping until he's back. What if he never comes back? What if morning comes and he's still not here? If he dies trying to keep us alive, I'll never escape the guilt. Shaking off the anxiety, I tuck loose hairs behind my ears, feeling the crusty, matted blood in the strands.

"He's going to come back. He *has* to come back."

Counting is all I know how to do. It's useless, but it keeps my spiraling thoughts occupied. When I reach 433 out of 600, the door blows open and a light explodes into the darkness I've been staring into for hell knows how long.

"Oh my God!" The release of my fear is strong enough to spin my emotions into thoughtless rage. I furrow my brow and yell at him. It makes no sense, but I'm unable to grasp logic at the moment.

"You said you would be back in thirty minutes! What the *fuck* took you so long?!"

Callahan sets the giant water cube down with a huff, shoving it to the side with his boot. Then he closes the door behind him and faces me. The light from his headlamp is blinding, so I shield my eyes and keep my gaze on the floor. I've been in darkness too long and don't want to close my eyes.

"Are you actually serious right now? Can I take off my pack before you lose your goddamn mind? Jesus Christ!" He's panting when he unclips the straps across his chest and hips and lets the bag slide off his shoulders.

He gestures to the five gallons of water with an open palm. "Do you see that? You're fucking welcome!" he shouts back at me.

"I didn't know where you were!"

"The stream was covered in snow, so I had to go farther down before I found it."

Oh.

"Good Lord, woman, you're a piece of work," he mutters, shaking his head in frustration. Cal turns around and points to the stove. "You didn't start a fire?! What the hell have you been doing since I've been gone?"

He turns off his headlamp, and we're plunged into blackness, so he turns it back on.

"I couldn't find the matches in the dark!"

"Oh, but you had time to make the bed and play house? Super! So glad you had your priorities straight." He grabs a few small pieces of wood and drops them in front of the stove, then finds a box stashed inside the corner and thrusts it in my face.

"Matches!" He reaches down and snatches up a neon-green stick lighter. "Lighter!"

I looked there… I *swear* I looked there. I just didn't know what I was touching.

He glares in my direction. He's not just mad, he *loathes* me. I can't blame him after all the shit I put him through today. My lips form a thin line, and I hold back tears as he yells.

CHAPTER 31

CALLAHAN

It's fucking freezing. I can't believe she didn't light a fire. My hands are devoid of any color when I tug my gloves off, even on the fingers cut by that rock earlier.

Her voice lowers until she's mumbling, "We're gonna freeze to death in this tower, aren't we?"

I groan. "With all your bitching, hopefully sooner than later."

"Shut up, this is serious."

Laughing without humor, I say, "You shut up!" Not my best comeback, but I can't deal with her negative attitude. The laceration on her forehead has me biting my tongue before I say anything more. She needs to take care of that. She must see me staring at it, because her fingers find the edge of the cut, then she pulls them away.

"I'll deal with it."

"I'm sure," I say, rolling my eyes.

I drop the box of matches in front of the wood stove and select the skinniest pieces of tinder. Opening the little door, I squat down on the balls of my feet and am immediately greeted by a stiff dead squirrel with no eyes.

It's at that moment she has the genius idea to instruct me on how to start a fire. Me. A hotshot. I light fires for a living, and she thinks she knows better than me? I about lose it on the spot. My blood pressure skyrockets. I cannot believe the level of frustration this woman brings, I'll stroke out before I freeze to death with her.

I remove the squirrel and drop it on the floor as she continues to tell me how to do my own damn job. Slowly, I turn my head to glower at her. "You are fuckin' brain damaged if you think I don't know how to start a fire."

"I'm just trying to help!" she shouts, crossing her arms.

"You wanna help? Here, get rid of this." I pick up the squirrel and lob it toward her like a big fat dart. The squirrel torpedoes through the air with its tail flapping and lands next to her on the ground with a soft thump.

"What the hell is that?" She brings her face closer to inspect it, then screams and scrambles backward. Turning back to the stove with a small satisfied grin, I get the kindling set up and adjust the damper so there's less wind barreling through as I try to light it. I'm pleased when the dry slivers of wood catch quickly and heat rolls off the fresh flames.

"Asshole!" Something hits my back with a thud.

"I know you didn't just chuck that squirrel at me," I say, warning in my voice.

"You threw it first."

I twist around on my heels, dropping a knee, and glance down. Sure enough, there's our flat furry friend. I clutch the squirrel and shake it at her with each declaration. "I saved your ass by pulling you out from under that rock. I practically carried you up this mountain. I gave you shelter. I fetched you water. I started this fucking fire. I gave you everything, Prescott! Everything! And it's still not enough for you!"

Holy shit, that felt good to get off my chest.

She clamps her mouth shut. I hold my breath, and we stare at each other for a solid ten seconds, barely blinking.

Finally, I break the silence. "I'm not playing catch with you, get rid of it." On the last shake, the critter's neck snaps and the head falls to the floor. I gaze down at the eyeless, shriveled rodent face with orange teeth. *Ugh.*

She's got the nerve to bite her lip and look away as she attempts to smother a grin. Does she think this is funny?

"Don't you dare laugh."

"I'm not!" she says, her lips breaking into a smile around the words. She can't even look at me with a straight face.

I fling the body back to her, and it lands at her feet. This time, she picks up both pieces of the squirrel and wisely steers for the door. I purse my lips and return to stoking the fire. It was *kind of* funny. Holding my hands up to the flames, I rub them together, willing the blood to return, and it's not long before prickles work their way to my fingertips. I hiss through my gritted teeth as the nerve pain intensifies.

She opens and closes the door quickly, evicting the dead vermin. Behind me, the sound of a zipper and rustling of her bag tells me she's rifling through it for something.

"Get over here and warm up," I growl.

A couple seconds later, she squats down next to me and offers a small bottle of sanitizer. "Here."

I take it from her and rub it on my hands. They're still rigid as the numbness takes its sweet time dissolving. "Sorry about the lantern," I say, barely above a whisper. I don't want to apologize first, but I do it anyway.

She doesn't respond, and we simply crouch shoulder-to-shoulder in front of the flames.

"Thank you for starting a fire." She unzips and shrugs out of her coat. Nodding in my direction, she encourages me to do the same. "Get down to your base layers."

"In a minute." I'm too tired to move.

"Are these boots wet?" She reaches down and unties the knots in my laces.

"How do you think I found the stream?"

My toes are numb. While she does that, I turn off my head-lamp. I don't need to see how pale they are. I sit down, and she yanks at the boot, removing it from my foot, then peeling off my wool socks. Even with the dim orange light from the stove, my feet look like they belong in a morgue. She rubs them carefully and guides me to sit closer to the crackling fire.

"Agh!" I say as my heels feel like they're getting poked with needles.

"Wimp," she mutters, pulling off her own boots and socks. Hers are equally pale, save for the delicate pink nail polish on her toes.

"It fuckin' hurts," I argue.

She ignores me, pushing down her soft-shell pants.

I raise an eyebrow. "How big of a show are you gonna give me?" I ask, mostly to piss her off. She's kinda hot when she's feisty.

"You're a dick."

I shrug. "Well, I'm a dick that's going to keep you warm tonight… You have no idea how many women would love to be on the receiving end of that sentence."

She scoffs. "I'm aware of your proclivities. You don't need to rub salt in the wound."

What's that supposed to mean? I roll my eyes and scoot back to grab the first aid kit hanging on the side of the island. "Speaking of wounds…"

I shove the box toward her. She pops the latch and digs around until she finds a sterile alcohol pad, then brings it to her forehead to wipe away the dried blood; however, without a mirror, she misses a lot of it. I watch her struggle until I can't take it anymore.

"Here, give it to me… close your eyes."

She does, and I flip my headlamp on, aiming it at her fore-head. It's the first time I'm getting a good look at the gash along her hairline. Dried blood cracks, flaking off as I clean up the crusty edges. It's a gnarly cut. She probably should have gotten stitches. I fold the pad in half and dab off the rest of the dirt on her face.

"How is it?" she asks.

"Better. You're gonna have a decent scar though."

"I don't remember how it happened."

"Still have a headache?" I mutter.

"I took some ibuprofen, it took the edge off."

"Concussion?" I ask.

"Probably."

Shit. I don't know what to do for a concussion. "So what do I have to do? Make sure you don't fall asleep or something?"

She shakes her head no. "I'm able to hold a conversation with you—"

"You're able to *argue* with me," I correct.

"Even better. Besides, if I decide to stroke out or have a seizure, there's nothing you'll be able to do about it anyway."

"So the cup's half full, then?"

CHAPTER 32

Scottie

Wind howls outside as we crouch around the crackling fire. After he cleaned up my forehead, Cal used some of our water supply to wash the matted clumps of dirt and blood from my hair, which was oddly sweet, considering his displeased demeanor toward me. I comb my fingers through the strands as an orange glow from the stove flickers on the walls. We've been sitting in silence for probably twenty minutes. He grabs his bag and locates his phone.

"You have service this high up?" I ask.

"You usually do at the top..." He walks around the small space. "I'm not getting anything in here though."

His fingers swipe across the screen.

"What are you doing?" I ask.

"Writing a text, hoping if I go out on the catwalk, I'll get a bar or two, enough for it to send."

"Did you tell anybody where you were going?"

He doesn't respond as he taps out a message, and it soon becomes apparent he's not going to. I told no one either. My gaze returns to the flames in front of me. My core temp is finally coming up, and I'll never take warmth for granted again. I don't care that I'm stranded at the top of a mountain with the man who hates me. He may have crushed my weak heart, but he's also the reason it's still beating.

With my eyes fixed on the fire, he shoves his newly heated feet back into his boots and shrugs on his coat, the snow that clung to it when he walked in is now nothing more than beads of water. He opens the door and steps out quickly. The cold air rushes in and quickly settles.

We're shrewd enough to know sharing that twin bed is the best option, but neither of us have acknowledged it yet. There's no polite *you take the bed, I'll take the floor* conversations happening; that's out of the question. We need to share body heat. We're in survival mode.

The dancing flames before me are mesmerizing, but with each blink, my eyelids grow heavier and scratchier. I'm unsure if it's due to exhaustion or actual dirt. Maybe a little of both; my body is spent. Turning my back to the fire, I allow it to heat my thermal until it's too much to bear. The room's overall temperature has gone up enough for me to back away from the stove. I stand and pull back the wool blankets on the bed, then crawl into the cold, crisp sheets. My teeth chatter, but the second my head hits the pillow, my entire body melts into the mattress.

A smile grows on my lips. "High. Cotton."

To my stiff aching muscles, the bed feels like a cloud. Closing my eyes, I don't know if I'll ever be able to peel them open again. I curl into the fetal position and use my body heat to warm myself and the blankets around me.

Callahan comes back inside, announcing, "No signal."

I pretend to be asleep, listening to him stock the stove with more wood and adjust the damper accordingly. Before long, the bed dips, and he scoots me to the edge, placing himself between me and the cold wall of windows. We lie side by side like sardines. He smells like the forest, same as when we were in Oregon together, and the scent engulfs me. I've missed it.

"Curve into me," he whispers, his breath hot against my skin. Goose bumps spread like wildfire across my body. The way he says it is so affectionate it hurts. I swallow when he wraps an arm around my waist, pulling me into his chest and hips. The warmth of him at my back feels like coming home. Which is odd, because home is supposed to be stable and constant, and he is anything but. *He is fleeting.*

This isn't cuddling, it's self-preservation and nothing more. As much as it pains me, I can't help but soften in his arms. How terrible would it be to pretend for one night... just one last time, that it's not for survival? A tear leaks from my eye. That's not unusual when one is sleepy, but this one is accompanied by an ache inside my ribs and a lump in my throat. It's something I never thought I would feel again, at least not with Callahan Woods. *He'll never be mine...* so why does he hold me like I'm his?

CHAPTER 33
CALLAHAN

DAY 2

Light pours through the shutter slats, and I lift my head off my pillow, confused why I'm waking up in a fire tower. Then I remember the events from the night prior. *Fuck.*

A soft sigh from the woman pressed against my chest has me tightening my grip on her and dragging her closer. It's stupid, but up here, she's not somebody's wife—she's Scottie. And we're back in Oregon, before she lied, before shit hit the fan and we broke whatever we had into a million pieces. Dropping my cheek back to the pillow, I close my eyes, already wishing I could take back some of the things I said.

There was some shouting last night. The pent-up anger I harbored came out in an explosion when she yelled at me after I returned with water. God, that was an expedition. My muscles are already sore from all the bushwacking I did to get to the small river stream. A couple spots had me nervous I wouldn't make it back. Then, as soon as I got in the door, she snapped—and so did I. We fought like cats and dogs. She had me fired up, and I let her know. That's not usually in my nature, as I don't care enough to fight with most women.

Then there was the whole squirrel incident. A small smile plays on my lips. She wasn't about to take an ounce of shit from me yesterday, but that was yesterday, and this is today.

First priority is keeping the fire stoked. I barely slept last night, having to get up and make sure the fire didn't go out. It's already time to add another log. Carefully, I roll her away from me and climb over her small figure.

My bare feet hit the frigid floor, and a chill shoots up my spine. Upon closer inspection, I realize there's still a small flame burning. *Interesting.* She must have gotten up during the few hours I slept and put a couple logs on the fire. I appreciate that. I add more and close the door on the stove, adjusting the damper to slow the burn and prolong our wood supply. The metal squeaks, and I wince, hoping she doesn't awaken yet. Her brain needs rest after the hit she took. As delicately as I can, I squeeze behind her again, careful to not startle her. Then I pull her into me for no other purpose than to use her body heat to warm me up. It's chilly as fuck outside of this bed.

Closing my eyes, I rest my chin on top of her head and breathe her in. There's something grounding about this woman. She's like that cozy light under the microwave after coming home to a dark house. She brings me comfort.

Normally, I'd be pacing trying to figure out our exit strategy, but I'm content to lay here and let my mind race from bed. Last night, I tried to send a text to Xander and King, letting them know where we are. It'll probably be a couple days before anyone even knows I'm missing. After all, I told Xander I had returned safely. This would be the last place he'd look. Nobody will be at the trailhead to see our vehicles because no one in their right mind would hike Quell's during a snowstorm. Hell, the park service has probably closed the gates on the entrance. It's not uncommon for people to ditch vehicles at trailhead lots, so it's not like a ranger will spot it and suspect anything other than a couple of cars left behind.

Someone will notice when Scottie doesn't show up for work —although, if this is her first day off in a stretch, it could be days before that happens.

I turned off my phone to conserve the battery. I'll try to send a message again later. Doubt I'll have any more luck with the way the wind is whipping up around the lookout. It's even louder this morning than it was last night.

We have food, water, and shelter for about a week. There are a few dead trees I spotted that look dry enough to burn, eventually we'll run out of firewood and need more for the stove. I do some mental math to figure out approximately how many logs we're burning an hour and how soon my ass needs to get outside to chop more. The lookout has two levels. The top is living quarters; the base, which is only accessible from outside, contains tool storage. I estimate we'll run out of wood by midday tomorrow.

As far as a rescue goes, it's not like I can just call in air support. It doesn't work like it does in the movies, and even if I could, there's no way they could fly in this weather. We got ourselves up here, we're set on supplies, so we just have to wait it out, then get our asses back down when this bitch of a storm blows over. Unfortunately, it doesn't sound like she's letting up anytime soon.

Scottie stirs in my arms, and I release my hold on her despite myself. She pops up from the pillow, and presses a palm to her forehead. Then lies back down again.

"Oh, man."

"How's your head?" I ask.

"No complaints yet," she says, her voice raspy with sleep. I smirk. I remember that voice from Oregon, after a night of phenomenal sex and trying to muffle her moans. The fact she's making jokes is reassuring. Unfortunately, it also makes my cock twitch, because I can confirm her statement. Our sensual night of snuggling and sex was something I'll never forget. It was exhilarating.

I clear my throat and back up against the wall before she feels my dick press into her from behind.

"Mild headache, but it's better than yesterday. Just feel hungover..."

I hum in agreement.

"Sounds like the storm is raising hell out there. Are we gonna be okay?"

I shrug. "Maybe."

"Your confidence is inspiring," she says, words oozing with irritation.

There she goes plucking my nerves again. Grumbling, I add, "What do you want? A guarantee? We're stuck on a mountain in a blizzard, the trail is blocked off, and you've got a head injury. We are barely *okay* as it is." I've been in life-threatening situations too many times, and sometimes, they don't work out. Especially considering we need to find a new path down, and the snow makes any bushwacking even more treacherous and conditions ripe for storm slab avalanches.

She rips the blanket off, bringing with it a cold draft, and swings her legs over the side to stand. "Jesus, read the room."

I wrench the covers back over me. "Who was it that was talking about strokes and seizures last night? I'm just being realistic. We need to be honest with ourselves here."

It's a fact of life. Some call it cynicism, but I'd rather expect the worst. At least then I'm not blindsided when luck goes south. That doesn't mean I won't fight like hell for our survival, but I can't handle the crippling depression of losing someone unexpectedly. Preparation is everything.

"Well, *honestly*, I have to pee. Really bad."

I roll over, facing the wall and close my eyes. "There's an

outhouse. Might need a shovel to get to it. Have fun. I'm going back to sleep." I barely slept last night.

That's nothing new. It's been years since I slept well, but this situation isn't helping the constant agitation and anxiety clinging to my thoughts. My doctor has thrown around the word complex post-traumatic stress a few times, which basically means my brain is fucked, and there's nothing I can do about it... other than avoid alcohol and drugs—which is useless advice. If my mind is busted, I'm not going to deal with it sober.

"Good. Maybe it'll fix your attitude," she says.

I crane my neck to see her wiggling into her hiking pants and tugging her thick socks on. The fire crackles in the stove, and she holds her hands up to warm them. I ball up the pillow under my head, close my eyes, and sigh. "You talk a lotta shit, you know that, Prescott?"

I wish I could blame her for putting us in this situation, but to be fair, falling rocks are the one thing you can't prepare for. You can have all the right gear, have all the right experience, but if a rock or rolling log chooses to come down in your path, there's nothing you can do but meet your maker. It's a miracle she wasn't hit by another rock when she was knocked unconscious.

Daylight pours into the room when she opens the door. Truthfully, she's lucky she's not dead. She punctuates that thought by yanking the door closed as hard as she can when she exits the lookout. The wind puts up a fight, but she gets her message across, it bears all the angst of a door slam. This is her brand of bullshit. She saunters into my life peacefully and storms out, leaving a path of destruction in her wake—in like a lamb, out like a lion. Scottie gets under my skin like no other.

After a few minutes, she comes clomping back inside. I turn over to see snow clinging to her pants, confirming it's thigh-deep on her. She carried a pile of snow in just by walking through the door.

I sit upright.

"Scottie, you brought half the fucking mountaintop in here. Keep that shit outside, yeah?"

She raises her eyebrows and blinks at me, then throws her arms out to the side. "I see your attitude is still here... It's a whiteout out there, by the way! The catwalk is covered, I knocked a bunch off the side, but it's a mess. It sticks to everything."

Sticky snow means it's wet, which means it will be an even bigger pain in the ass to hike through, and we're at a higher risk for avalanches, depending on how it's packed.

"I was so excited to experience my first real snow," she murmurs.

"Enjoy your morning stroll through winter wonderland, did you?" Her face blooms red and I close my eyes. The corner of my mouth turns up with a smug grin. She shuffles around the room, and I crack open one eyelid, watching her strip her outer layer, and the neck of the sweater stretches, revealing the edge of a bruise. "How's your shoulder?"

"Fine."

"Good."

I shut my eyes and fall asleep to the sound of her setting more logs next to the fire.

I'm back to that day. Seeing Garrett Macomb crushed and lifeless. Then Xander's expression when I had to tell him his father was dead.

Protocol is to alert authorities so they can contact next of kin, but Xander needed to hear it from someone who knew and loved his dad. Garrett was our supe, and he became like a father to me after my own dad passed.

I choke as I attempt to comfort my best friend, but he's like a statue. He doesn't react. His face is coated with dirt and soot, and clear eyes search mine for hope. Hope that I'm wrong, that I'm mistaken, that his dad is still alive. I have nothing to offer him except hurt and the worst day of his life.

Xander fades away, and the vision of Garrett takes his place.

My eyes brim with tears, and my throat tightens. The utter panic and dread threaten to drown me. I inhale, but the air doesn't reach my lungs. It tastes like ash. I'm held hostage, forced to relive the incident like it's happening for the first time. Guilt, fear, and fury battle inside me. I'm powerless, unable to breathe as I'm crushed by the overwhelming weight of utter misery. My heart thrashes in my chest, and the pounding fills my ears until it's the only sound I hear.

I'm sleeping.

Another nightmare I can't wake from. No matter how much I try to move, my arms and legs have been filled with lead, holding me down while I'm doomed to experience every second in excruciating detail. I'm trapped. Paralyzed by my broken mind.

Warmth rushes over my body, and I jerk awake. I thrust my eyes open, replacing the images of his charred flesh with the interior of the lookout. Scottie's arm is draped over my side, and she threads her fingers with mine. For the first time, I'm able to come up for air, gasping like I'm breaking the water's surface after being held under. My chest heaves, and I sense the sweat across my forehead. *Fuck.* "It's not real," she says.

I swallow, gulping in more oxygen. I wish she was right, but it *is* real. It already happened. Her cheek presses to my back, and for the second time, she helps me through a panic attack, giving me a safe space to release the tension in my muscles. Her gentle touch is soothing, keeping me in the present.

"Concentrate on your breathing. I'm still with you."

I squeeze her hand in mine, thankful to not be alone.

CHAPTER 34

Scottie

After about an hour of listening to Callahan's regulated breaths, I'm convinced he's asleep again. I sneak out from behind his body and tuck the warm covers around him so he doesn't wake. He stayed up most of the night adding more logs on the fire so we didn't freeze, so he needs the rest.

This isn't the first time he's locked up like that. It happened after our night in the ambulance when a loud clap of thunder shook the entire rig. It was startling, sure, but Callahan's reaction was more concerning, it was as if he dissociated completely.

As quietly as I can, I stoke the fire and pile on two more logs. The door on the stove creaks when I close it, but thankfully, Callahan doesn't rouse. It's nice seeing his face relaxed as he sleeps, instead of the usual scowl he reserves for me. I don't understand the contempt he holds. When he ended things with us, it was his decision, so what did I do to make him look at me with so much disgust?

Shaking my head, I come to the conclusion he's an enigma. I crouch next to the small nightstand that serves as a mini bookshelf with a *take a book, leave a book* system. My fingers skate over the spines. A few have man versus nature themes—survival fiction—I'm not in the mood to read any version of the actual predicament I'm in, so I opt for a spy novel instead.

Pulling out the wooden chair under the desk, I take a seat and stow my legs up on the edge to keep them off the cold floor, wedging my shins against the desk. There's a knot hole in one of the wood shutters outside, enough to provide ample reading light. After a few pages, my surroundings drift away and the howling winds fall silent as I'm sucked into the story. It's a nice reprieve from reality.

I'm unsure how much time passes, but eventually, the light from the hole in the shutter dims, and I'm made painfully aware of how unforgiving this chair is on my numb ass. I'm sixty pages into the book, which is probably more reading than I should have done after the hit I took yesterday. I'm supposed to be resting my brain, but sitting with my thoughts seemed worse.

The logs in the stove have mostly burned through, and there's a small flame dancing on top of the red embers. My stomach growls. Since leaving The Fold, my body has adapted to eating less food. Callahan's probably going to be hungry when he wakes up.

I close my book and place it softly on the desk. Crossing the room, I open the cabinet with the propane camp stove and set it up, paying extra attention to ensure it makes little noise. The wind battering the side of the tower covers most of the sound. Next, I locate a pot and add water from the five-gallon cubie, cringing at the way I flipped out on him yesterday after we got back. I add a little extra for drinking and washing, then place the pot on a burner and light the stove with the lighter. We need to boil the water so it's potable anyway. When it's partially warmed, I pour some into a cup, then return the pot to the stove so it can finish heating.

I turn around to make sure Callahan is still sleeping before I strip out of my base layer and wash up using some soap and a towel I found in a cupboard containing washcloths and rags. My phone clatters to the floor. I forgot I slid it into my bra last night. I snatch it up and duck behind the table in the center of the room. Peering through the passthrough slot, I observe Callahan sighing, but, thankfully, he sleeps through the interruption.

I desperately crave a shower after yesterday, and simply scrubbing warm water over my skin is enough to feel refreshed. Once I finish the world's fastest sponge bath, I tug on my hiking pants and sweater.

While waiting, I select a soup mix from the food storage container—chicken wild rice—and measure a satisfying serving we can share between us. I let the water come to a rolling boil for a bit, setting aside a portion to fill our water bottles later. Then I gradually add the premeasured soup mix and stir toward the center, preventing the spoon from clanging on the sides of the metal pot.

Once it's mostly dissolved, I cover and lower the flame on the camp stove, leaving it to continue cooking. While I wait, I try to turn on my phone with no success. I extract the battery and replace it again, then slump forward. No luck. What did I expect? I bought the cheapest prepaid phone I could find. I just needed something that could give me shitty internet and a phone number to put down on job applications. Looks like we're left relying on his phone.

I do some more snooping, taking inventory of our provisions. There are wash bins for dishes, a couple of board games, cleaning supplies, more linens, and some tools.

I stir the soup for a while, then remove two mugs from a cabinet on the left. After carefully closing the door, I'm startled by Callahan awake and studying me—I freeze. *How long has he been watching?* We stare at one another long enough for me to wonder what he's thinking. His eyes are pained when he gazes at me.

"Are you hungry?" I ask.

He clears his throat. "Yeah."

"Soup is almost done."

Callahan sits up, swings his legs over the side of the bed, and rests his elbows on his knees. His head hangs between his shoulders, but he doesn't move. Yeah... I would give my last dollar to know what thoughts were running through his mind.

I check under the lid, and a plume of hot steam escapes. The aroma has my mouth watering and stomach growling. I divide the helpings between the two mugs, and the spoons slowly sink into the thickened soup.

After handing one to him, I take a spot next to the wood stove, sitting sideways on the rug in front of it.

"Thanks for this," he says. "And for earlier."

I nod, blowing on a spoonful of the steamy sustenance. Once it's cooled off, I get my first taste and have to resist shoveling the rest into my mouth. The savory broth comforts me from the inside out, pacifying my worried thoughts and rumbling stomach. "This tastes delicious." Callahan hums in agreement upon taking a bite.

We eat in silence, letting the crackling fire, powerful winds, and scraping spoons do all the talking. Occasionally, we exchange glances, but eventually, I turn and face the fire to finish my meal.

"I found some board games," I say. "If you want to—"

His empty mug lands firmly on the top of the bookshelf, and the spoon rattles. "We need more wood for the fire."

"Oh." I spin around. "Is there anything I can do to help?"

He stands, pulling on his outer layers. "No."

"Okay," I respond. "I'll clean up."

He exits the lookout but doesn't slam the door like I tried to do earlier. I spend the next half hour cleaning up from lunch, stretching out the task to keep my hands occupied. I place the remaining wash water in a pot on the wood stove to keep it warm and pour the preboiled water into our water bottles. Then I dry the bowl and return it to its place on the shelf. Once that's done, I busy myself with tidying the space, including making the bed. What if he wants to go back to sleep? I unmake the bed and muss the covers the same as before. *What's wrong with me?* I remake the bed and ignore any other stupid idea my brain churns up.

He was right last night; he did everything. Got us shelter, water, and fire. I gotta start pulling my weight by cooking and cleaning. It's an easy role to fill, considering I was raised to serve men in whatever capacity God or the church needed me to. It was my duty, and one I was proud to perform, until I started questioning things. At first, the guilt of doubting my faith had nearly swallowed me whole. I kept to myself, fell depressed, and prayed away my thoughts, but they only grew stronger. Then I started EMT training, which exposed me to new people and new ideas, and some of those ideas made a lot of sense.

Peeking between the slats on the shutters, I observe Callahan putting together a decent heap of wood. He's splitting logs with an axe, and even half camouflaged by snow, he looks hotter than any man should doing chores. *Good Lord.* Clearing the lust-filled haze, I layer and lace up to brave the blizzard, trudging through the snow and collecting as much split wood as I can carry inside.

I pile the remaining wood logs from the cabinet next to the woodburning stove and refill it with the freshly cut ones. I'm tempted to use a blanket to help carry more pieces at once, but with the wind wreaking havoc out there, I'm too afraid it would get ripped from my fingers and blow off the side of the mountain.

Once the base cabinet is restocked, any extras are stacked on the platform outside the door for easy access. When Callahan is satisfied with the quantity, he carries the axe back to an exterior door at the base of the lookout, where he must have found it. We work in tandem without exchanging words, picking up logs from the shrinking pile and climbing stairs until wood is stacked about three feet tall. He gathers the last chopped pieces and tosses them up on the catwalk. I arrange them with the others, then we stomp the snow off our boots and pants before entering inside.

I don't need to check a mirror to know my cheeks are blotchy from the stinging cold air. His are rosy too, but his appear to be due to exertion not windburn. He strips down to his base layer and lays his pants over the chair I sat in earlier, then grabs his water bottle from the table. He inspects it, noticing it's been recently refilled, and takes a few glugs, replenishing himself after the workout. With the hem of his thermal shirt, he wipes his brow, exposing his chest and the tattoos I remember from our nights together.

I sit on the floor, quickly averting my gaze to untie my boots packed with snow from hiking back and forth. I peel off my damp socks and lay them near the fire, then sweep up the bits of bark and wood splints from the recent haul using the dustpan and push them into a small mound. We can use it as kindling later.

Gulping from my water bottle, I relax, happy to be out of the storm.

"Have you cleaned the cut on your forehead today?" he asks.

"Yeah, I washed up earlier and added some antibiotic ointment from my first aid kit. There's warm water in that pot"—I gesture to the wood stove—"in case you want to wash up. It feels nice."

He acknowledges me with a nod but doesn't do more than remove his socks and lay them next to mine to dry. We've barely spoken today, and it's wearing on me. With each unspoken word, we feed the elephant in the room, nourishing it and helping it grow.

"Did your text message go through today?" I saw him with his phone on the catwalk earlier.

"No."

"I tried to turn on my phone, but it's dead. Or broken. I don't know."

Dead air.

"Have you ever been here before?" I ask.

He gives me a blank stare.

"Well, of course you have, you're the one that got us here. Obviously, you've been here. That was a stupid question." Great, now I'm rambling.

He cocks a mirthful eyebrow at me, then turns away.

"You know, if this weren't life or death, this place would make for a cool vacation spot."

He scoffs. It's the most enthusiastic response I've received yet.

Ugh, why do you have to be such a dick?!

I'm trying to be civil, but he's giving me nothing to work with. I pick up my book. "I started reading this earlier. It's pretty good. It's about this guy who…" He's not listening. My lips roll together, and I nod at the unspoken rejection. "… 'Kay." I hang my head in defeat and resign to the other side of the lookout to read beside the window that has the most light streaming through the shutters.

A few minutes pass, and he clears his throat. "I, um, I lived in one of these towers for a bit. Years ago."

My eyebrows shoot up at the attempt of conversation.

"Yeah?"

"Mm-hm."

I let some of the tension settle before I take my turn to speak again. "What was it like?" I'm hesitant to move or say too much and scare him off like a deer.

"Unbelievable views and tons of wildlife to watch. It was a fantastic experience."

"That's really cool… Did you ever get lonely?"

He shrugs. "Nah, I knew it was temporary."

I grin. "How long were you there?"

"A few months."

It feels like the first normal conversation we've had since Oregon.

"A few months and you didn't get lonely?" I tilt my head to the side. "What about women?" I tease.

The corner of his mouth tips up, and he gives that sexy smirk that had me tripping over my words when we met that night at the bar. "Well, maybe a *little* lonely."

"Hm." I hum in agreement and offer a small smile.

I don't want to push my luck, so I wait for him to continue. After a long pause, I retreat into the pages of my book, but as soon as I pick up where I left off, he speaks up.

"What board games did you find?"

CHAPTER 35

CALLAHAN

She narrows her eyes. "B-7."

Goddamn it. "Hit."

Scottie beams proudly. "B-8."

I sigh. "You sank my patrol boat... Why are you so good at this?" She's won the last three games, and none of them have even been close.

"I cheat."

"How?!" I lean forward, seeing if she's able to view my board. Doubtful, the sun set an hour ago, and we're playing by the light of the fire. I had a hard enough time seeing my own board.

"I'm only kidding." She chuckles and shrugs. "I'm good at hiding my ships."

Once the pieces are picked up, she hands me the box, and I return it to the cupboard with a couple games and choose a new one.

"Sorry, I need to ask," she says, taking a serious tone. "Are we just talking because we're in each other's proximity? Are we friends now?"

I slide the box on top of the other games and stand. "Huh?"

"You said things have run their course. Does that mean sleeping together *and* friendship? Do we go back to not speaking to each other once we get out of here?"

I roll up my sleeves. I guess we're hashing out our shit now. So much for having a decent time.

My voice hardens. "We're for sure not sleeping together, but honestly... I don't know... I don't think I can be friends with somebody who..." I rub the back of my neck. Damn it, I'm mad at her for lying to me. "Why did you sleep with me, Scottie? Why the fuck did you do that?"

She furrows her brow. "What do you mean?"

"And why did you fuck Dave? I mean, *that* guy? Seriously? Of all people—"

She stands with her arms open wide and drops her jaw. "What are you talking about!? I never slept with Dave! He's married!"

I snap. "And so are you apparently!"

She flinches as if I slapped her, closing her mouth and letting her hands fall at her sides.

"Yeah..." I say. "I know about that."

"I didn't sleep with Dave," she says, barely above a whisper.

"I saw him leave your apartment after he spent the night? You really think I'll believe you two weren't fucking?"

She takes a giant step forward, attempting to get into my space. She's close enough that at her short stature she has to slant her chin up to face me. "He didn't spend the night!" She pokes her chest. "My car had a flat on my way home from working third shift! He picked me up and dropped me off at my house. He only was inside because he basically invited himself in!"

I level her with a glare. "But you *are* married."

She shrinks away from me, curling her arms around her stomach. "But it's not what you think."

I throw up my hands and walk to the other side of the room. "Well, I *think* you're fucking married! What else is there?!"

"It's not a real marriage."

I laugh sarcastically. "I saw the wedding announcement in your town's newspaper, darlin'. It's real."

"I'm trying to get a divorce."

Crossing my arms, I ask, "Did you serve him papers?"

"No, but—"

I scoff, and spin on my heel. What game does she think she's playing?

She stomps her foot like a toddler. "Would you just shut up and listen? It was a lavender marriage! I didn't have a choice. The only way to leave the marriage was to leave home. I left everything I had!"

When I face her, she's wearing a scowl. "A lavender what? You both looked pretty fuckin' happy in that photo."

"My husband is gay!"

I throw up my arms. "Oh, is he now?"

She continues despite my obvious doubt. "It's a fucked-up form of conversion therapy. I come from a fundamentalist community, where, when a man is found to be, or, hell, even suspected to be gay, the church intervenes. They choose a woman in the congregation to be chosen for what they refer to as a *purity bride* with the hope that the man's *evil inclination will pass*"—she gestures using finger quotes—"once they've been with an attractive woman."

Is she serious? I shake my head. "No way."

"Jonathan and I are friends, we've been friends since we were little. His parents were like my parents. We saved each other. I love him, but not in the way a wife loves her husband. I begged him to come with me, we fought about this for months. I stayed for as long as I did because I loved him, but eventually, I couldn't wait anymore. I had to leave. And so I did. Alone."

"Why would anyone agree to that?"

She covers her face with both hands, then drops them. "A few reasons. If we chose each other, then I wouldn't be given to another member of The Fold—that's what it was referred to as, like a shepherd's fold—including the elders or council members. Better the devil you know than the one you don't. The other women never spoke poorly of their husbands. The only thing they talked about were children or housework, but the girls who were given to the older men always looked dead behind the eyes."

This kind of thing doesn't really happen, right? This sounds like a cult.

"The second reason, the one I'm most ashamed of, I grew up believing something was wrong with Jonathan. I thought being with him was my calling, my purpose. Believed the reason we were best friends was because God had chosen me to *save* him. All my life I've wanted to help people, and I thought that's what I was doing. He was attractive, received attention from the other girls, though it was never reciprocated. I figured out early on that Jonathan wasn't like the other boys, but I also noticed the way he looked at them. I loved Jonathan and knew he loved me. We figured we could be a life raft for each other.

"If we faked a relationship, got engaged, and fell in love without the church having to intervene, then nobody would be the wiser, and Jonathan wouldn't have to go through any other forms of conversion therapy—and I would have a partner I knew was kind and loved me. We knew a platonic marriage was far safer than taking our chances."

I run my hands over my scalp, willing myself to listen and trying to wrap my head around what she's saying. It's almost too much information to take in.

"I went to school to become an EMT, and someone at the local firehouse was able to get me a job. It was a big deal, almost everyone worked in our small town, we were self-sufficient, save for a few resources, like fire. While I was in school, suddenly my world got a lot bigger. I met people who had different beliefs than me—but they weren't bad people like I'd always been told.

These were *good* people with *kind* hearts. The more I was exposed to the outside, the more I realized I wasn't helping anyone." She blinks away a couple tears. "I was hurting Jonathan and hurting myself. It might have been the safer option for us, but it wasn't right. I was part of the problem." She wraps her arms around her middle. "I wanted out."

I shake my head but struggle making eye contact. "This sounds fucking crazy."

"Because it is crazy! It's awful! I don't want to be part of any community who would cause others so much pain. But leaving The Fold isn't just moving, it's exile. There were stories of people escaping and being dragged back. I tried to get Jonathan to come with me, but he wouldn't." Her chin trembles as she peers down at her hands. "So I left."

Holy shit. This is the most bizarre situation—her story is almost too strange to believe. I've never heard of anything like this happening outside of the movies or true-crime documentaries.

"How do I know you're telling the truth?"

She doesn't speak as if she's making up a lie, it's as if she's finally unburdening herself. Like it's the first time she's been able to tell someone her story; she's bearing her soul.

"You have to trust me. I can't prove it. It's not meant to look like anything more than a normal marriage. We needed the church to believe Jonathan was *cured.* Though, I'm sure they're questioning both of us now that I've left. I've never seen another woman attempt to leave the community, only heard rumors of it, and none of them ended well."

I cross back over to her side of the room. "How was he supposed to be cured? Did you sleep with Jonathan?"

"Yes."

"Like, sex?"

"Yes."

"He could...? How?"

She shrugs. "After so many years, it becomes a biological attraction. Humans have needs. With enough sexual encounters, our bodies reacted the way they had to in order to achieve sexual gratification. It was almost clinical. At first, it was something we did because we thought we were doing the right thing. Later, it just became a habit."

She opens her mouth to say more but stops short.

"Once I started realizing how messed up the entire thing was, I refused to sleep with him anymore. It became a point of contention between us. He knew I was pulling away, and it scared him. It was about a year before I left when I started proposing we leave, but he was stuck in denial. I worry he's still under the impression that he needs to be saved from some kind of sinful affliction... I think he believes them."

"So, do you still have feelings for him? Are you separated? What's the deal?"

Hearing about her marriage to another man brings back all the betrayal I experienced with Molly.

Her eyes brim with tears, a wistful smile on her lips. "We're separated. My feelings for Jonathan will always run deep, but they aren't romantic. He's my best friend. We saved each other." Her voice wavers, and she sucks in a breath, holding it while she composes herself. "And I will always feel guilt over our marriage. The Fold made him believe he was broken, and I went along with it. He was never broken, *I* was.

"I told him we could start our lives over. Together but separate. He didn't understand why I had this pension for leaving the only life we'd ever known. I told him what we were doing wasn't natural, but he always told me to pray more and to stop questioning everything, but to me, I was nothing more than a pawn for a hateful God.

"I was tired of chasing unmet needs, I wanted a partner who truly desired me. I was sick of going through the motions, experiencing shallow intimacy that only existed on a platonic level. I wanted to have sex and feel truly *satisfied*. I'd been craving it my whole life but always blamed it on my own shortcomings, something that was my fault—I didn't try hard enough, didn't pray loud enough."

She shakes her head, swiping away the tears and pasting on a neutral smile, as if she can somehow minimize the years of misery she's been living in and the way she left an entire life behind to start over. I'm dumbfounded.

"I failed Jonathan twice: the first time when I married him, and the second time when I abandoned him. But one of us had to make the first move, so I did."

I'm unsure of how to respond, so I say the only thing I can think of. "I'm sorry."

"Maybe I should have divorced him before getting involved with anyone, but it wasn't going to happen. He knew the only way we'd be able to get a divorce was if we left, trying to do anything back home would have set off alarm bells. I never felt romantically obligated to him, and I wanted the taste of freedom... And then I met you."

I don't even know what I'm feeling right now. I sit on the edge of the bed hunched over, struggling to process so much information. I have so many questions. My gaze remains fixed on the floor as I rub my forehead. *Fuck.* I'm being bombarded with so many emotions. I'm devastated for her, the agony in her eyes is clear as day. She's been carrying such immense weight on her shoulders, not only for her husb—Jonathan but adjusting to a new life altogether.

Another part of me is experiencing massive relief that maybe we've got a real shot. I still feel guilt over sleeping with a married woman, but I'm no longer disgusted with myself the way I was before. And the rest of me is stunned by the entire ordeal.

"I'm sorry I kept my past from you... I'm really sorry."

I lift my chin to meet her sullen face. "I should have met you that day for breakfast. I heard rumors from some guys in town, and I've been beating myself up for weeks thinking I broke a marriage apart. I was engaged once and walked in on her having an affair at a really low time in my life. It messed with my head —bad. This whole time, I thought I did the same thing to another man."

I haven't mentioned Molly until now, but I planned to. I should have knocked on her door that day instead of walking away. We could have avoided all of this.

"I didn't tell you earlier because I'm ashamed." She clears the tears from her cheeks. "And embarrassed. From the outside looking in, it's so obvious. But when you're raised within those walls, the cracks of doubt are well hidden. What I participated in was abhorrent. I didn't want anyone to know—they wouldn't understand. What would the outside world think of me? What would *you* think of me? You said it yourself, it's crazy… But if you heard rumors, why didn't you just ask me directly?"

I bark out a laugh. "What the hell was I supposed to think? Gee, she's married, but maybe she's actually in a religious cult covering for her gay husband?"

My harsh words cause her to recoil, and I instantly want to take them back.

"I could have explained all of this back then. You never gave me the chance!"

"When I hear hoofbeats, I think of horses, not zebras."

She paces back and forth. "Well, you sure thought zebras when you saw Dave leaving my place! You're not the only one who's been hurting for weeks, you know? You've been callous and cruel with every interaction. I've been racking my brain trying to figure out what I did to upset you so much. Everyone told me you were a womanizer, that you were just using me. I defended you every chance I got and then looked like an idiot when you tossed me aside as if I were nothing." She bites down on her bottom lip to keep it from trembling and lets her hands fall to her sides. "It would have opened up a conversation."

I lean forward, bracing my forearms on my thighs and letting my head slump between my shoulders. "I didn't show up because hearing from your lips you were married would have hurt worse." *I ran.* I was fucking scared. "It would have been reliving my past. I didn't want to go there... After I found out you were someone's wife, I shut down. It's not an excuse, but it's why I did what I did."

When I look up, her expression is pained.

My brows knit together. "Then when I showed up at your apartment, Dave said some shit that insinuated he spent the night with you—"

"He *what*?!"

"It doesn't matter. I should have trusted your word over his. I should have come to you first." I scoot deeper into the bed and lean back until my shoulder blades are resting on the cold windowpane behind me.

Scottie closes the distance between us. Her eyes search mine as if she's searching for some courage to borrow. She has me holding my breath while I wait for her next move. I exhale when she plants her knee on the bed beside my thigh and straddles my lap. I sit up, and we stare at each other for a long minute.

"I'm sorry." I hear the sincerity in her voice, see it in her downhearted eyes.

My throat burns seeing her like this. She wraps her arms around my neck and rests her head on my shoulder, hugging me. We made such a mess of things.

"Me too." I slide my hands around her back and hold her the way she's holding me. And damn, it feels good. I allow myself to bask in her touch before I speak, because even though the truth is out, it doesn't change the situation. "I don't know where we go from here."

"What do you mean?" Her breath is warm against my skin.

"You're still married." I muster the courage. "Do you *want* to divorce him?"

She doesn't hesitate. "I do."

The corner of my lip turns up. *Ironic phrasing.* "We can't do anything until you file your paperwork."

She raises her head to face me. "But he knows I'm gone—"

"Would you kiss me in front of him?" She stiffens. "Would it hurt him to watch me put my arms around you?" They may not have been romantic, but they still had a relationship, so there must be *something* there on his side. I'm not going to be with her in the shadows.

"Jonathan and I have had this conversation before. We told each other that if the other one ever needed to go, we wouldn't fight it."

I can't imagine anyone willing to let go of her so casually, romantic or not. I have a better understanding of the tenacity she possesses, leaving everything and everyone behind. This situation is so fucked, and I've never felt so torn. With her ass in my lap and arms on my shoulders, all I want to do is lean in and take her.

My jaw tics. "If we do this, we need full transparency from now on. I want to know every skeleton in your closet. No more secrets."

"Okay. And I expect the same courtesy from you..." Her fingers fidget at the collar of my shirt, and she averts her gaze. "Who was the girl you left the bar with that night?"

My brows jerk to attention. I don't understand the question. *What is she talking about?*

"When?"

She pulls from my hold, and looks down at her hands. "When I saw you at the bar the other night, you were walking out with another woman, you had your arm around her about to get into a cab. Are you still sleeping with other women?"

"No." I rest my palms on her knees to restore our physical

connection. It takes me a moment to figure out who she could be talking about. I haven't been with anyone since her. Realization hits and my brow relaxes. "That was my sister, Teddy," I say, trying not to laugh. I loosen her arms and place them back on my shoulders. "I'll introduce you when we get back."

"Oh." Her face flushes as if she's embarrassed.

I glide my hands up her thighs and rest them on her waist. My fingers itch to squeeze the soft curves I've been reliving in my mind during every shower since Oregon. This woman is Kryptonite.

"You really think we're going to get back?"

"Yes," I reply with absolute confidence. Nothing will stand in the way of seeing her sign those divorce papers. I tuck a few loose strands of hair behind her ear and swallow.

We search each other's eyes for answers.

"So where does that leave us?" I ask.

"I know what I want, but it's likely there will be more challenges ahead. What do you want?"

My gaze drops to her mouth, and I lean in, then pause. The divorce proceedings haven't even begun. I said we would wait... I need to make a decision. Am I really willing to enter a physical and emotional relationship with a married woman?

For Prescott? Yes.

She meets me in the middle, and her lips ghost over mine.

"Fuck it."

With one hand pressed to her lower back, I cup the nape of her neck with the other and bring her mouth to mine.

My tongue sweeps across her bottom lip, and her small sigh spurs me on. Nails dig into my shoulders, waking up every nerve in my body. I skate my thumb over her chin, giving myself access to take her mouth like I've wanted to for weeks. She's like that first high.

With each brush of our lips, I forget why this situation is so complicated. Soft gasps and firm grasps are all I need to know she's with me. This time, it will be different. This time, we're doing it right. And *nothing* feels more right than this.

Her fingers press against my chest. "But what do you *want?*" she repeats.

"I want us to be more than fun, Prescott," I state. "I wanna make you mine."

Kissing Scottie feels as natural as breathing air. Depriving myself will only make me crave her more.

CHAPTER 36

Scottie

I silently say a prayer of thanks for this storm. I've never been so grateful to be stranded at the top of a mountain facing a merciless Mother Nature. Without this lookout, I can say with complete certainty Callahan and I would still be hiding our cards.

We wouldn't have had that kiss or be wrapped up in each other's arms in this twin bed, gripping one another like we're trying to hold onto a dream we could wake from at any moment.

With my head on his chest, he sinks his hands into my hair and runs his fingers through the strands. Like he did in Oregon, because he knows what it does to me. Callahan knows it's my favorite. He presses his lips to my temple, and my weary eyelids flutter closed.

The last thing I hear before falling asleep is his gruff, hushed voice. "God, I missed you."

CHAPTER 37
CALLAHAN

DAY 3

After we got cleaned up with the help of body wipes, washcloths, soap, and warm water, we're both feeling better having the dirt and funk knocked off us. We made a paste with some baking soda, but neither of us have a toothbrush, so we've been using small pieces of paper towel to scrub our teeth with it.

The lookout windows are fogged up thanks to our slightly damp clothes hanging from random hooks and furniture while drying. When Scottie saw I had a spare change of clothes in my bag, she insisted we launder the ones we showed up in using a bucket, our leftover "bath water", and a bit of Campsuds. I'm used to being filthy for a week or more when spiked out on a fire, a few days is nothing. Scottie? Not as much.

I'm not even a little bit mad about it, because seeing her in nothing but socks and a T-shirt—*my* fire shirt—is sexier than any lingerie. It nearly reaches her knees, and the short sleeves hit her at the elbow. I scrub a hand down my face. It's distracting as ever. A small Sky Ridge IHC logo of a bear holding a chainsaw sits over her breast, large letters read FIRE across her shoulder blades. It's about all I can do to keep my dick relaxed while I sit on the rug, leaning against the bed in only socks, boxers, and a hoodie.

Focus.

"J-3." I'm feeling good about this one.

"Miss."

Damn it. That shirt's the reason I'm losing this game of Battleship, I swear. I'm more attracted to her than ever, especially after we hashed out the reason we fell apart. She's got a fucked-up past, that's for sure, but I can understand the reasoning behind her actions now.

We haven't fully discussed details of what comes next. She's separated and will eventually have to address her unfinished business from back home, but I've made it clear I intend to pick up where we left off. Of all the women to bring me to my knees, figures it's the one who comes with the most baggage, but hey, at least we have a matching set.

She narrows her eyes at me. "E-5."

How the hell does she do that? I pluck my aircraft carrier from the board and quietly relocate it to the row below. "Miss."

Her laugh fills the space. "Bullshit!"

"What's *bullshit* is you never losing this game," I say, raising an eyebrow.

She grins. "Next time, I'll only use four boats, even out our handicap."

"You found my carrier last, so I wouldn't go talking trash, woman," I announce, moving my carrier back to the original spot and adding a red peg to the middle. Can't believe she's going to win again.

"Whatever you say."

We wrap up the game quickly. She's got a weird knack for knowing exactly where I "hide" my boats. At least I sank three and a half of hers this time, which is a new record for me. I'm getting better.

"We should be betting money," she says, smiling, satisfied with her undefeated streak.

I like where her head's at... "How about clothes?"

She laughs. "What?"

I shrug and gesture to the baggy T-shirt hiked up to her mid-thigh while she sits on the blanket on the floor. "Afraid you'll lose?" Her nipples harden under the cotton, and I resist groaning.

She narrows her eyes while considering my proposal. "No... but you have more clothes than I do. You're at an advantage."

I cock my head to the side. "Oh, I thought you wanted to even our handicap? Scared now?"

The corner of her mouth curls up. "Of you? *Please.*"

"Famous last words." I tsk. The next time she says *please,* my head will be buried between her thighs.

We set up our boards, and this time, I cluster my pieces in the corner. "B-9," I say, starting the game.

Her eyes grow wide, and she looks up at me, gaze filled with disbelief. "Hit."

"Well, well, well..." I'm very delighted with my luck. She doesn't have to remove clothing until I sink a ship, but I'm already halfway there.

"A-3," she guesses.

"Miss." I grin. "B-8."

"Miss," she echoes. "F-4."

"Miss." *Maybe she has her boat lined up vertically.* "C-9?"

She purses her lips. "Hit."

Two rounds later, I've sunk her destroyer. She peels off a single sock.

I point toward the other one. "Socks count as one. Take them both off."

"What? Since when?" She argues.

"Since always." I nod to her feet. "Both of them, Scottie."

She loses the second sock and throws it at me in a small act of rebellion. "H-6."

I smile smugly at her unsuccessful shot. "Have you ever missed this many in a row before?"

Scottie grumbles something snarky under her breath.

"What was that? I can't hear you over the wind."

"Oh my god." She tucks her tongue in her cheek and shakes her head. "You're the worst."

"G-10." I glance up when she doesn't reply.

"What the fuck?!" She covers her face with both hands and laughs, then jabs her finger in my direction. "You're cheating!"

I bark out a laugh at hitting another one of her ships. "You're kidding?"

She scoffs, and takes a red peg from the tray, placing it on her board. *This is amazing.* "J-9," she guesses.

Ooh, now she's got me. "Hit." I'm not concerned, I'll have her naked in only a couple plays anyway. "G-9."

"Hit," she relents. "I-9?"

She's struck a different ship, but I don't have to tell her that.

After two more rounds, I announce she's sank my patrol boat and remove my socks. She studies me curiously, and her eyes light up, realizing I've stacked my boats next to each other.

"G-6," I say, my final shot.

"You sunk my carrier."

Fuck yes. "Take it off."

I know for a fact she's not wearing underwear because the only pair she has is drying in front of the wood stove. She shimmies, dragging the shirt past her crossed thighs, and pulls the hem up and over her head. She sits there, attempting to cover up with the Battleship board on her lap, but nothing could hide her curves. *Amen.*

"Looks like I win," I tease, admiring her body.

Her jaw drops. "What are you talking about? I still have two ships left!"

I chuckle. "But you don't have any more to lose."

"We could bet on other things."

I raise my eyebrows. "Like what, sexual favors?" My stare trails up her body, and I smirk at her hard nipples. "Does the idea turn you on?"

Her face flushes pink.

"What did you have in mind?" I ask.

"I don't kn—"

"Yes, you do. Come on, Scottie. Tell me what it is you're thinking about."

Naked and blushing? Good god, what I would give to get in that pretty head of hers and read all those dirty thoughts.

"H-10," she says, avoiding the question.

"Hit," I reply without looking at my board. "A-2?"

"Miss." She taps her chin. "H-9?"

"Hit."

She examines her board and chuckles. "You put all your boats in the corner, didn't you?"

"Maybe."

"That's a poor strategy."

"Are you sure? Because which one of us is naked right now?" I wink at her.

She sighs. "H-8?"

"You sank my submarine." I tear off my sweatshirt and toss it on the floor. I'm growing harder by the second. "G-10?"

"Hit." She adds a red peg, shaking her head at my strategy, but then misses her next guess.

"I-4?" I ask.

Her chest rises when she sucks in a breath. "Hit."

My palm rubs the back of my neck. "You better decide what you're going to do once I sink your ship, before I decide for you."

She swallows. "G-9?"

"Hit," I answer. "I-3?"

"Hit." *Oh hell.*

I stare at her, and she squirms under my scrutiny. Is she

remembering how I made her feel in Oregon? "Come on... say it, Prescott."

"G-8?" she guesses.

"If you don't tell me what you want, I'm choosing."

Her top teeth rake over her lower lip, and lust flickers in her eyes. She *wants* me to take control. "G-8," she repeats.

"Hit." Setting the game on the bed behind me, I stand and push my boxers down. My cock bobs out, damn near slapping my stomach. She gasps, and it's one of my favorite sounds. "What do you want your safeword to be?" I ask.

Her gaze is locked on me.

"How about *destroyer*?" I suggest. "I-5?"

She doesn't reply. Her tongue darts out to wet her lips, and it sends my pulse soaring.

"I-5..." I say again.

"Hit... F-10?" She says, breathy.

"Hit," I reply happily. This is my new favorite game despite somehow losing again. "I-2."

"Hit," she rasps. "Battleship."

I hold my palm out in front of her. "Spit." Her eyes dart between mine and my hand. "*Spit*." My voice firmer this time.

She does, and I make myself comfortable on the perimeter of the bed, lazily stroking my dick while using her saliva as lube and watching her.

"Show me how you play with your pussy when you think of me."

She rolls her shoulders back, mustering the courage to set her board down at her side. I inhale through my nose, watching in awe when she pulls up her knees and parts them, showing me how wet she is.

"Fucking hell, Prescott." I lick my lips, wishing they were hers. "What's got you so turned on?"

Her hand travels down her stomach, and she brushes her middle and ring finger over her clit. "You."

"That's right." I match her speed. "Spread your thighs wider. Let me watch." Her eyes glaze over, and she plants an open palm behind her, reclining and giving me a private performance.

I groan. She's hypnotic. "That's perfect, baby. You're doing such a good job." Her brows scrunch together as she keeps her eyes fixed on mine. "A little faster," I coax.

"Come here," she pants.

I shake my head, still gripping my length. "Is there something you want?"

"Make me come."

I slide my fist up and down. "Be specific."

"Use your fingers to make me come... please." She plants both hands behind her and spreads her thighs wider for me. "I love the way you do it."

I smile at her desperation and stand, then kneel between her legs. "You need me to take over for you?" I trace my thumb over her clit, and she moans. "You like doing what I tell you?"

She nods, and her chest rises and falls with each pass.

"Good," I reply matter-of-factly. "Because I asked for a show, and you're going to give me one, aren't you?"

More hurried nodding. "Mm-hm."

"I want to see *all of you*. Don't be shy for me, we're past that now. No secrets means no secrets, you're going to practice telling me what you need. Understand?"

I slip my middle finger inside, reveling in the sound of her wetness as I pull out and push back in again. Then I add a second, and she sits up, rocking against my hand.

"Oh god."

"Understand?" I repeat.

Her breaths grow louder. "I-I understand." She writhes.

I smirk. "You're so fucking cute when I finger you..." I decide to test her. I already know how she likes to be spoken to. "How do you want me to praise—"

"Good girl."

I tilt my head, astounded by the speed of which she answers. She must notice my surprise. "You called me that before, and I loved it," she explains.

"Tonight you're going to earn that title."

I bend forward, seeking her lips, then kiss her and curl my fingers at the same time, tapping her G-spot and rubbing my thumb side to side over her clit. She mewls against my mouth.

Scottie straightens her spine, grinding against my hand. I chuckle at her sudden eagerness. Her body tightens around me, and I lean in, our foreheads almost touching. "Eyes on me, that's right. Just you and me, Prescott."

I pump my fingers faster, and she cries out. "Cal..."

"You're going to come for me, aren't you?"

Her brows knit together, and she exhales. "Mm-hm."

Her thighs tremble under me. "That's it, you can do it, baby. I've got you."

I kiss her and pull back to see her eyes filled with trust, and after everything she's been through, it's a trust I will never take for granted.

She's so close.

She moans louder and louder the higher she climbs.

"Be a good exhibitionist, and remind me how stunning you are when you come. Make that needy little pussy drip down my fingers."

Her lips part with a small gasp.

"Did you think I forgot?" I growl. "I haven't been able to get that image out of my head since Oregon. You have no idea how many times I've closed my eyes and pictured you coming for me."

I slap her swollen clit and press the pad of my thumb against the spot that makes her shake, and she jolts, lifting her hips off the floor as she comes.

"There she is... *There's my good girl*," I whisper.

Her body grips me in a way that has my cock jealous.

Feeling her drench my fingers while staring into her half-lidded, blissed-out blue eyes sends my heart racing. Her round ass drops to the blanket as she comes down from the high. "Breathe into it."

She bobs her head, holding my gaze, and slowing her bucking hips. *Incredible.*

I steal her lips, and she curls her hand around my length, making me groan.

"I'm so proud of you, baby." She's entrusted me to take care of her, and there's an observable shift between us, an openness that's unique from our previous encounters. She's vulnerable in ways she wasn't before, and so am I.

I stand, and seeing her big stormy eyes stare up at me is almost too much. I sweep her hair over her shoulder and tuck the loose strands behind her ear. Cupping her chin, I stroke her cheek with my thumb and admire how full her lips are and how badly I want them wrapped around me. "So beautiful," I murmur.

She places her palms on my knees, drifting them up my thighs. "Can you show me what you like?" she asks. The sinful smile on her face has me prisoner. I collect her hair in my fist, then urge her toward my length, watching her take me in her mouth. She gags and wraps a hand around the base, covering me with her lips and taking me a second time.

"Fuck, Prescott," I hiss. "You're my girl, aren't you? Look at me." I lean back so I can catch her gaze, relishing the feel of her tongue sliding under my dick. The sparkling mischief in her eyes has my rapt attention. "Unreal…"

She shivers and I chuckle. "Aww, do you love sucking cock, baby? Did you need this?" I cover her hand with mine, twisting it at the base of my shaft. "Just like that…"

She moans around my length as I push her deeper.

"Tell me it's just my cock you want." My words come out more distraught than intended, but I want to know that I'm the only one. It's probably my own fucked-up insecurities after Molly, but I have to hear Scottie say it.

She swirls her tongue around me as I slip from her lips. "You're the only one I want, Callahan."

Fuck.

She grips the base and teases the ridges with small licks. My brow furrows and I grumble, then take a deep inhale through my nose and blow it out slowly. "Now wrap those plush lips around my dick and take it all."

Scottie spits on the tip, and pushes the crown between her pursed lips, hollowing her cheeks, and sucking hard. Her tongue glides across the underside. The vibrations from her sultry sounds stall my breathing. I wrap a hand around my balls and tug just enough to add more pressure. She moves my hand away and replaces it, letting me manipulate her wrist to instruct how much tension I like. I bury my fingers in her hair and guide her faster. I need more, it's not enough.

I usher her off me before I lose control, and her eyes shimmer. "Thank you for making me feel wanted."

Her unprompted words have the wall in my chest crumbling a little more—*shit.*

Has she not felt wanted before? I swallow. "You should see yourself right now, how exquisite you are on your knees... I love watching you take me like that. You're so sexy, Prescott." I move to the bed and haul her with me. "Get up here."

When she straddles my thighs, I take her hip and direct her to turn. "Spin around. Head down, ass up while you suck. See how deep you can take that cock in your mouth..."

I recline back as she gets situated facing away from me, and she straddles my chest. I cup each side of her waist and yank her toward me, placing her knees on the mattress near my shoulders, bringing her even closer to my face.

"Such a sweet thing..." My eyes roll back when the tip presses down her throat, and I growl. "Oh, good *fucking* girl."

She's more than good, she's perfect for me. So goddamn perfect.

At first, I simply marvel at the view. This woman was made for me. She sucks and licks, and I want to reciprocate so bad. *My god.* I want more, but I edge myself with her body. I chuckle at the sight. Her swollen pink pussy is slick with arousal. "Your body is torture. I want to taste you."

"Mm-hm," she whines around me. "Please?"

She's wet enough that I could probably drive every inch inside her on the first thrust. When I can't take it anymore, I let myself touch. I fan my fingers open, inching my hand down and allowing my thumb to brush over her glistening clit. Her legs instantly widen, showing me more. Her eagerness is so attractive.

I want to dive between her thighs and feast on her, but I need to draw this out since I don't have any protection with me. With a feather touch, I graze my knuckles up and down her center. My other hand finds her ass, groping and filling my palm with the soft flesh. I cluck my tongue. She sucks harder, and I have to close my eyes, biting my cheek until I taste pennies, to keep from coming.

Her body is calling out to me. I outline her entrance, pushing the pad of my thumb just slightly around the perimeter. Her hips roll. I smile. "You're a mess... What was it, baby? Was it taking your clothes off for me? Was it watching me finger-fuck you until you came, crying my name? Was it sliding my cock between your lips? Was it putting your dripping cunt in front of my face and teasing me? You know how much I love eating your pussy."

She moans.

"Yeah, it makes you wet to show off for me, doesn't it? I get so fucking hard watching you, it's torture, and yet you do it anyway. Because the thought of turning me on... turns you on."

She digs her nails into my quads, and I chuckle. *Got her.*

"I'm built the same way. Nothing gets me off more than the sight of you coming. I think you enjoy driving me wild." I plunge my middle and ring fingers into her, pleased by her gasp. With my hand motionless, I enjoy the way her frantic muscles contract around me.

"Come for me, Prescott. Be my wild girl."

She sucks harder, then I pull out my fingers and push them back in, hitting the spot I remember from last time. Her back arches, and she drops her elbows, stretching out like a cat. A second later, her tongue is circling the crown before she takes every inch to the back of her throat. *Jesus Christ.*

I lose all control. Gripping her hips, I bring her pussy down to my face where I nuzzle between her thighs. She tastes so fucking delectable... My dick slips from her mouth, and she cries out. I resist smirking as I lick every inch of her weeping cunt, cleaning up the mess I made. Her small body shakes in my arms.

"Already, sweetheart?"

Her desperate voice is muffled against my skin, where her cheek is pressed as she takes the onslaught of pleasure I'm controlling her with. With a confident smile, I wrap my lips around her clit and suck. Her palm slaps the bed. "Ohgod, ohgod, ohgod..."

I suck again. Overstimulated, she tries to scramble away, but I lock my arms around her thighs and seal my lips on her, gently nibbling her clit as punishment before replacing it with suction again. "This is mine." She finishes on my tongue, tasting like the perfect candy.

"You're so wet, look how much you came," I praise, then drop an octave. "With the way I'm about to fuck you, you're going to need it."

Her chest rises and falls with anticipation.

"Callahan," she whines. She grinds against my lips, and I'm thoroughly enjoying the steady sound of ecstasy as it magnifies. Fuck, I could come just from the noises she makes. I love that

I've distracted her with my mouth, but my dick is throbbing, craving any form of friction at this point.

As if she can read my mind, she takes hold of my length and squeezes. "There you go...Feel how hard I am for you?" I growl. "There's nothing I want more than to shove my cock inside you and feel you shake."

"I need it!" She cries. "Fuck me hard. Please."

I pause for a half second and force myself to think logically. "I need a condom... I don't have one."

"Then don't come inside me."

I push her off and flip her on her back. Her freckles, plump bruised lips, and big seductive eyes are irresistible. She's a bombshell. I throw her legs open, line myself up, and press inside her. Her eyelids flutter closed, and I groan. "Goddamn it, Prescott. You take my cock like it was made for you."

"Maybe it was." When she blinks open, I briefly withdraw, and her gaze fixes on mine before darting away. I'm a goner. Her jaw drops open on a silent scream when I drive inside again. She arches her back, and I tilt my head down to wrap my lips around one of her peaked nipples.

This will be quick and dirty, not at all the way I planned to fuck her. I wanted to take my time, but it's too late for that. When she starts to quiver, I know she's close. I suck on the other nipple and sit up to watch her face when she comes apart. It's the best view on the mountain.

With one hand braced on the bed, I place the other at the base of her throat as she clamps down on me. I lower my head to look her right in the eye.

"Remember how we had to be quiet last time?" I croon. "We aren't at camp anymore. You can scream as loud as you want from this tower and nobody will hear you... The only one who can save you out here is me."

"I've already been saved, Cal. So why don't you make me scream?"

I blink. Every so often I get a glimpse into Scottie's dirty side, she's been kept in a cage for so long, but deep down she's wild and untamed. "Who are you?" I ask, chuckling.

She simpers at me. "I'm your good girl."

Goddamn.

"Then you better scream my name so loud everyone in the valley below hears how much you love being fucked—and that you belong to me."

She shatters as her orgasm plows through her. As soon as that dam breaks, she cries my name over and over. I smile, in awe of her.

"So perfect. Don't stop, baby. Keep coming."

Shit, I'm about to finish.

"I'm gonna paint these pretty tits with my cum, and then you're going to swallow it." With the last functioning brain cell I have, I pull out and straddle her stomach, pumping my cock twice and coating her breasts with me. It's as passionate as it is obscene.

Scottie excites me in ways no other woman has. We may be trapped up here, but there's nowhere else I'd rather be. She props herself on her elbows and looks down at my masterpiece, chest heaving.

"I've never—" She sighs. "It's never..." The smile on her lips grows, and she practically giggles. My fire for her doesn't burn out after I come. It consumes me, thawing the dormant heart in my chest. Cum pools between her breasts.

"It's never what?"

Dipping my head, I lap up my mess. Then I gather her hair in my fist, and tighten my grip. She instinctively parts her lips. I spit it into her mouth, then slide my tongue against hers, and she greedily takes every bit. My thumb caresses her jawline as I cup her face, sweeping up a lingering drop and tracing her lips with it.

"Go on. Be my good girl."

She swallows, devouring me.

Scottie gazes in my eyes like I'm the one who rescued her from the cage she's been kept in so many years, and it rocks me to my core. There's something powerful about this connection we share. Like it was written in the stars long ago, and we're finally at the right place at the right time—at the top of Quell's Peak, stranded in a fire tower. I press a kiss to her forehead and clutch her hair. Her thighs squeeze my hips. She's never looked so beautiful. Her cheeks have the perfect glow, one that can only be achieved through mind-blowing sex and multiple orgasms.

I'm half gone with her, and I'll do whatever's necessary to keep that glow on Scottie's face... because I'm keeping Scottie.

CHAPTER 38

CALLAHAN

I like her. Right now, the real world is miles away. We have this bubble, and I'm making the most of the time I have to repair what I ripped apart. I've got no clue how this is supposed to work, but I'll figure it out. Regardless of how her marriage was, it doesn't change the fact she's still married. We'll deal with it eventually, and I'll support her in whatever capacity she needs.

While standing in nothing but boxers and socks, I fill a pot with water and light the camp stove. We have to refuel after that. I grimace at the cubie sitting on the floor. With each day we're here, the water line falls lower. It's a stark reminder that our days in the lookout are numbered. The storm continues to rage, but for the first time, it's not worse than the day before. As soon as we get a window of clear weather, we'll have to move quickly.

I've been spending the afternoon poring over maps while we had proper light, and I think I finally found a decent route for us to follow. It'll take longer, since we have to traverse over Goat's Ridge, but it's not nearly as steep and we can follow the riverbed to meet the main trail closer to the base.

Our biggest challenge will be the snow and wind at the top,

but once we reach a lower elevation, we'll be in better shape. This is the safest way back. I'll still need to check the snow for avalanche conditions. If all goes well... then we should be good. The problem is, if we end up in trouble, anyone looking for us will be searching the trail, not Goat's Ridge or along the riverbed.

With water boiling on the stove, I stare through the slats of the shutters. I can just barely make out the shadow of a nearby mountain peak. That's a good sign. Until today, the constant snowfall has kept the visibility no farther than twenty feet or so.

Scottie snuggles under the covers, turning pages in her book while I prepare a meal for us.

"Are you feeling like chicken wild rice again or should we switch up and go with chicken noodle? Keep in mind, we are out of chicken..."

Her bright eyes find mine, and they still have that sparkle in them. Seeing her smile as if she's completely forgotten about our predicament, is enough to make me forget too.

"Hmm. Could we use the leftover foie gras as a substitute?"

"We could, but the fig confit I made just went bad yesterday," I reply, matching the bit.

"Aw, rats." She snaps her fingers.

"Nope, we're out of rats too."

"Typical." She flips a page and sighs. "These new rodent migratory patterns are getting ridiculous. I guess we'll just have to use the caviar."

"Good idea. Did you want the Beluga caviar?"

"Obviously. You know it's the only one I can eat."

"Because the other types make all your teeth fall out, right?" I ask, trying to make her break character.

She purses her lips, attempting to hide a smile. "Yes, and my dentist is already furious with me."

"Well, I think he took issue because you insisted the dentures be made out of cadaver teeth."

She sits up in a huff. "What's wrong with that?" she asks, dropping her book on the bed in faux frustration. "They look more realistic this way," she adds, baring her teeth like an animal.

"I know, but was it necessary to use a horse cadaver?"

She covers her mouth. "Are you saying you don't like my dentures?"

"Not at all. Sure, blowjobs are a little terrifying, but as long as I use an open palm..." I cough to cover a laugh. "But you've gotta quit making an enemy of the equestrian community."

Her shoulders shake with silent laughter as she covers her face with her hands. She composes herself and picks her book up, shielding herself with it. "I'm really not supposed to talk about it without my lawyer present."

I add the chicken noodle mix into the boiling water and stir. She picks up her novel again. "How's your book?"

"I lost my page when I dropped it on the bed," she says, chuckling and flipping through pages.

"I appreciate your commitment to the joke."

"Anything for the fans," she muses.

Only Scottie could keep me this relaxed while trapped in a lookout during a snowstorm. Her calm presence soothes my anxiety.

"It's good though. Could use a little more romance, but whatever."

"Yeah? Do you read a lot?" I ask.

"I do. I need to get a library card when we get back to Sky Ridge. What about you?"

Setting down the spoon, I cover the pot and brace my palms on the counter behind me, crossing my ankles. "Yeah, I usually have a book with me when I go on assignments. Or I'll listen to audiobooks. Do you have a favorite?"

She sits up on the bed with her legs crisscross. "That's a silly question. How could one ever choose a favorite book?"

"Fair. Well, do you have a favorite genre?"

"Romance," she blurts immediately.

I grin. "What do you like about it?"

"Love stories are... an escape. In Arkansas, they were my only escape." She sets her book down again, fidgeting with her hands. "My marriage was obviously complicated. I didn't even know books like that existed until a coworker, Sheila, was talking about one she'd read. Women in our community weren't allowed to read books like that."

"That blows my mind."

"At first, I would just ask Sheila about what she was currently reading. The things she said were so exciting and taboo. Then my curiosity got the better of me and I was able to get a library card in a neighboring town." My chest aches for her. She may not have had a loveless marriage, but the way she looked at me when she thanked me for making her feel wanted says a lot. In addition, I'm guessing the passion wasn't off-the-charts either.

"When I wasn't working, I would go to the library and read all the forbidden books. It was exciting and fun, and even though it was fiction, it felt more real than anything I had with Jonathan. I craved it, the way two characters wanted to tear each other's clothes off. They wanted to be together. It was passionate and wild. The woman's pleasure mattered. It was for more than reproduction... I know that's not always realistic, but I just needed to experience a piece of it." She glances down at her book and runs her fingers over the pages. "Did you know you were the first man to make me come? I experienced more passion in the back of that ambulance in Oregon than in all four-teen years of marriage. Pathetic, right?"

Holy shit. Based on the way she talks about romance, I assumed she wasn't getting a lot of orgasms in her marriage, but to be the *first?*

"I felt like I missed out on so much. I'm not sure how to explain what our relationship was like, but it wasn't the love stories I read about. The ones that made my heart hammer and my face flush. The ones that gave me butterflies." Her voice cracks. She's smiling, but her eyes are filled with tears and the longing for something real. I give her the space to continue.

"Then one day, we were called to an accident on the highway. The woman in one of the vehicles died on impact, she was the same age as me, and I realized I didn't want to die without knowing what real love felt like." She sniffs and pushes down the emotion, swiping her fingers under her eyes.

Do I know real love? At one time, I thought I did.

"Molly and I grew up together. We were high school sweethearts. She was my everything, we were engaged and waiting to save up enough to give her the wedding she always dreamed of. When I found out about the affair—which was with Dave—I didn't fight for her, I just left." Scottie and I only knew each other for a few weeks when I discovered she was married. Walking away from Scottie was harder.

Being trapped with her in a fire lookout, even on our worst day, was better than my best day with Molly.

I haven't known the woman across from me for long. When I think of how we began, the passion and excitement we shared… I have a better understanding of what those experiences must have meant to her. That was her first taste of something real, and knowing I stole it back without so much as an explanation has me hanging my head in shame.

"*Molly?* Molly was your ex?"

"Yeah."

"And Dave—"

I nod.

"Fuck Dave!" she shouts. "And he insinuated we slept together? God, no wonder you were freaked out."

"Scottie, I never should have listened to him. I'm sorry for how things ended between us." *I'm sorry they ended, period.*

"I didn't mean to hurt you—"

"I should have communicated with you better, at least confronted you. Instead, I cut and ran."

"You reacted the way anyone would, seeing Dave leave my place must have drudged up a lot of painful memories. I should have told you about Jonathan. Looking back, I understand how messed up it was to keep that a secret... I should have waited for the divorce, I know that. It's easy to say that I'm waiting to get established, but it only kicks the can further down the road. I've been avoiding it. Marriage is final in accordance with the church. It's a covenant. But I can't hide from them forever like a coward." She sweeps her fingers under her eyes and clears her throat. "Anyway, how's the caviar coming along?"

I shove off the counter, lifting the lid on the pot, and stirring the soup. "I think we're ready to eat." I still feel like shit, but I'm not about to make this about me.

She must sense my emotions, because she hops off the bed and crosses the room, wrapping her arms around me from behind while I dish out the soup for us.

Scottie rests her cheek against my back and whispers, "Are you going to feed it to me with an open palm?"

I bark out a laugh, appreciating the levity. I hand her a mug and one of the protein bars sitting out on the counter. We settle on the bed across from each other with our hot meal.

"Found a route for us to take back," I say. "The storm is slowing down, we might be hiking in two days."

She nods, swallowing a bite.

"Are you nervous?" I ask.

Her brow furrows, and she shakes her head. "No. I trust you... Besides, your life depends on me just as much as mine does on yours."

I blow on a spoonful of soup. "Why's that?"

She pauses, bringing her spoon to her mouth. "Seriously? Your face would be plastered all over the news networks, they would think you off'd me."

"You're fun."

"I know," she replies. "So, what do you want to do for the rest of the day? I don't think I can play another round of Battleship with you. No offense."

My mouth tips up in a smile. "Too boring?" I ask.

"It's not enjoyable if there's no challenge."

I push my tongue into my cheek with an amused grin. "Such a smart mouth," I mutter, tangling my legs with hers.

"Maybe you should do something about it."

I cock my head to the side and smirk, enjoying this sassier version of her. "I've got no problem training your mouth." I drop my spoon in my mug and lean forward to lift her chin and press my lips to hers. I pull back, our gazes meet, and I study her face. My hand drops, and I return to my meal, but not without first noticing the pink that fills her cheeks.

"What, um…" She wavers.

I eat while she collects her thoughts.

"What happens when we get home?"

"Well," I say on a sigh. "We gotta contact your boss. I had Matt try to call you when I couldn't get through, but I never explained why. I'm not sure if he's going to try to reach out again and worry about you. You mentioned you've got work in a couple days, right?"

She nods.

"I have a feeling you're going to be quite popular when we make it back. We'll need to get that cut on your forehead checked out too."

"Do you think I'll get fired?"

"No." I shake my head adamantly. "They're gonna be worried about you more than anything. You'll probably be getting casseroles brought to your door for the next two months."

She stirs her soup. "What about you?"

"Xander, King, and I have a pretty active group chat. I texted with them after I returned from my hike. I'm sure they're wondering why I haven't been very chatty, but fire season is over, so it's not like my job is waiting for me or anything. I doubt the boys have sent out a search party yet, but two days from now... who knows."

"And us?"

I bring the mug to my mouth and drink the rest, then place it on the windowsill beside me. Scottie's had a few bites, but she's mostly swirling her spoon around. Her brows are creased with worry. She may not be concerned about our trek back to the trailhead, but it seems she's got a few reservations once we return to Sky Ridge.

"What do you mean?"

"So, this continues back home too?"

I chuckle. "Yes."

"What about Jonathan?"

"I think you're the only one that can answer that question."

"I can't afford a lawyer yet," she says. "I wish he would have just come with me in the first place."

Grabbing behind her knees, I pull her closer. "Do you think he would fight you on the divorce?" She doesn't need a lawyer if he's in agreement.

She pauses for a second to consider the question. "Not if he knew how good it was on the other side. He's just scared to take the first step. The church will pay for his attorneys, and they'll turn hostile if he wants them to. It's not just a divorce, if he doesn't remarry, they'll likely force him into conversion therapy. If he leaves, it's exile from everything he knows."

"Do you have assets together?"

"I've already forfeit everything. Our house was on the church property."

I narrow my eyes. "Like a compound?"

"Like a *town*."

That seems a tad excessive. "A church can't own a town."

"But they can run one. All of the businesses are owned by the church. The local government is made up of members. It's not a huge municipality, but it's big enough. And it's growing."

"Is that legal?"

"Separation of church and state only exists if there's someone willing to enforce it. The church can legally own businesses as long as they generate income *for the church*. The town feeds the church, and the leaders profit, returning just enough money to the congregation to ensure no one has enough to leave and start a life somewhere else."

"How could they be growing? Who would sign up for that?"

"You're looking at it from a logical perspective. We're talking about religion. Faith can make people do terrible things in the name of God. Throw in a charismatic leader who can pander to the public and mold their beliefs, and it's not long before they are showing up every Sunday and opening their checkbooks. Everybody wants to go to heaven.

"They're great at recruiting with the promise of taking care of their flock, not to mention the religious guilt and constant threat of making sure our community stays pure and idyllic by severing ties with anyone who tries to make an exit."

"How many people have tried to leave?"

"That I know personally? Just me. I've got no clue what Jonathan's been going through. I feel awful, but I had to make myself disappear."

"So you just snuck out in the middle of the night?"

Scottie shakes her head. "Jonathan knew what my plans were. He said 'If you leave, I'll never be able to talk to you again,' and I told him that was a choice that *he* was making, but that I'd be ready to help him whenever he was ready to go."

I give her a long stare. "This sounds like a cult."

She shrugs. "Fundamentalist church? I'm not ready to call it a cult yet. It makes me feel like I've abandoned him and everybody else there. I chose myself over others. It's selfish." Her voice breaks.

"You made the right choice." I knead her thigh with my palm. "You're not selfish."

CHAPTER 39

Scottie

DAY 4

After four days in the lookout, we've fallen into a pattern. Every morning, we wake in each other's arms, get up to add wood to the fire, shovel the catwalk and stairs, make a trip to the outhouse, then crawl back into bed until there's enough light streaming through to heat water on the stove for our packets of oatmeal. Life is simple in the fire tower.

However, this morning, something is different. I can't quite place it. My mind is still drowsy, and with Cal folded around me, I'd rather close my eyes and sink back into a slumber where there are no worries about whether I have a job, no divorce papers, no shitty apartment. I must be doing awesome if my current precarious predicament of being marooned on a mountaintop is preferable to real life.

Then it hits me. It's *quieter*. I can hear the crackle of the fire from the bed. Since we arrived here, the wind has been constant and unrelenting, blowing and whistling through trees and rock. It became white noise that faded into the background.

"Cal." I rotate in his embrace, jostling him awake. "Do you hear that?"

"Mm?" he mumbles, still half asleep.

"It's quiet. I think the storm is coming to an end."

That has him blinking awake and sitting up. He squints, peering through a hole in one the slats of the shutters behind us. He climbs out of bed and not so gracefully throws on his jacket and boots. The door isn't thrown off its hinges when he opens it and steps outside. *That's new.*

He sticks his head in. "Scottie, come outside, I wanna show you something."

It's not my first choice. Blankets warm, outside cold. But I drag my butt out of bed and shuffle over to my gear, pulling on my clothes and hiking boots. I grab my jacket and draw up the hood. When I open the door, I brace for that first gust to suck the breath from my lungs, and it does. The wind may be lessened, but it's still raw and breezy enough to snatch your soul.

Squinting against the light reflecting off the snow, which has taken on a golden color, I shield my eyes, and he guides me down the catwalk. I slowly drop my hand, noticing a patch of orange through the clouds—it feels like weeks since I've seen a sunrise or sunset.

Callahan ushers me in front of him, looking out over the railing, and I gasp at the vista laid before us.

It's a mountain top. And another mountain. And another. I'm speechless. It doesn't look real. A good portion is hidden behind cloud cover, but the bits that peek through are nothing short of magnificent. The range of summits to the north are washed with pink and orange where the sun reaches their snowy caps, and every shadow and ridge is painted in a cool blue. It's living art.

"Great, huh?" His voice is rough with sleep.

"Wow." It's the only word I can think of, and it's not enough. There's no use in taking a photo, the pictures will never do it justice. There's no use in talking about it either. I'll never be able to describe it. It's something that has to be experienced firsthand and will only ever be understood by the person at your side.

My hair blows in the wind. I'm freezing, but nothing could steal me from this spot as we watch the sun rise from the top of the world. It's unbelievable. The most breathtaking place on the planet as far as I'm concerned.

This is one of those experiences that alters one's brain chemistry. Nothing matters. Blinking back tears, I realize every problem I was facing is so insignificant in comparison to the untamed landscape before me. The past few years have challenged my faith, but if there is a God, he's not at The Fold. He's here.

Cal wraps his arms around me from behind, rubbing my shoulders to keep me warm. We stand in silence until the sun passes over the mountains to the east. A break in the clouds has us blinded by the bright light, so I close my eyes, and for a moment, when the wind dies down, I feel the warmth of the sun's rays on my cheeks.

We hurry back inside. "We're leaving tomorrow," he announces.

"Really?"

"Yeah. Early. The snow's stopped. I'm going to check avalanche conditions, and if it looks good, I'll make tracks today. I've only got one headlamp, so it'll get us a good start and give us something to follow until the sun rises. I'll make them close together so they're easier to follow. There's going to be some deep spots."

"I know." I've been trudging through it multiple times a day when I take a trip to the outhouse. Prior to Washington, I'd only seen snow a handful of times, and each time, it wasn't more than a dusting or a couple inches at most. When I was young, there was a year we had eight inches, but I barely remember it.

I thought deep piles of snow were equivalent to walking through foam. It's not. Snow is dense and unforgiving. It packs hard like soil and ices over into bricks. Since being at the top of this mountain, I've learned just how ferocious Mother Nature can be. When she whips those pretty little flakes around in a negative windchill, they might as well be throwing stars.

"No, Scottie, there are drifts that could be above your chest in certain spots. And we have no equipment. No snowshoes, skis, or sleds."

My eyebrows shoot to my forehead. "What?"

He nods. "I'm gonna try to text the guys and see if I can get something through, now that the snow stopped and there's more visibility, we might be able to get a signal to the tower. I'll let them know what route we're taking so they can meet us halfway or at the very least be watching for us." He grabs his phone off the table, and a sense of urgency settles over me. Obviously, I knew we weren't staying up here, but now that things are being set in motion, I need to do something. One second we're watching sunrises, the next we're making plans. I spin around to find a way to make myself useful. Heat water.

"Shit," he mutters.

"What?"

He pinches his brow. "I forgot to turn the phone off yester-day. Can't believe I did that. I've only got four percent left."

"It'll be okay." I'm assuring him as much as I am myself. "We have an exit strategy. You know these mountains and—"

"Holy…" He runs his hand through his hair. "I think it might go through!"

I hurry over to him. "Really?"

"Yeah, look—" He tilts the screen toward me just as it goes black. "Shit! It still might have gone through… I think."

He tucks the dead phone in his pack and scrubs a palm down his face.

I wrap my arms around him. "Let's hope for the best. What would you like for breakfast? We've got a prime rib carving station and one hell of an omelet bar," I suggest, trying to cheer him up.

He humors me with a smile. "Prime rib sounds great."

"Coming right up," I reply, tearing open the packet of brown-sugar flavored oatmeal.

Callahan is gone for several hours while he makes a path. It's a lot easier to wait for him to return in the daylight. I'm laying out every combined piece of clothing we have when I hear footsteps climbing the lookout stairs. I smile and rush to the door, opening it when I hear him stomping the snow off his boots.

"Thanks," he says with a puff of air, entering the room with rosy cheeks and sweat dripping down his face.

"So? How did it go?"

"Good, I got us through the tough spots. A couple loose areas leading to Goat's Ridge, but I think we'll do fine if we stay on the south face, that's the windward side, and snow isn't as deep there anyway. The sun should be up by then."

Nodding, I turn on the stove, heating up water for lunch. We've got about two gallons left, which will give us enough for lunch, dinner, and tomorrow's water supply.

His clothes are soaked with sweat as he strips them off. They need to dry by tomorrow. He places the chair in front of the fire and drapes the clothes over the back. After, he returns to his pack and locates those shower wipes he had before. He stretches out in front of the wood stove, washing up. It's hard to keep my eyes off him. He's just so damn rugged and... *hot*.

"You checking me out, Prescott?"

"Obviously." I turn away, and finishing up our packing.

He chuckles, then I feel his palms cup my shoulders and slide down my arms. My face heats at his proximity, touch, and how few clothes he's wearing. He's close enough for me to pick up notes of the shower wipes he was using. I don't know what's in them, but they smell divine. It's some masculine scent that I will miss when we leave here.

I spin in his arms. "What are you looking forward to most when we get back?" I ask.

"Brushing my teeth," he replies, running his tongue over his teeth. We've been getting by with baking soda and this mastic chewing gum stuff he has, which helps, but it doesn't satisfy the way a toothbrush would. Like Cal, I'm hoping to deep clean my mouth when I return. He scratches the four-day-old scruff that's filled in. "I'm trimming this for sure."

I fake a pout. "Just don't shave it off."

"Hell no. I've grown too accustomed to the way it roughs up your thighs." His wicked grin has heat rushing to my face. "I'm not giving that up so easily."

I'm not sure what it is about his response that warms my chest, but it does. It's clear he enjoys making me blush too. His gaze lands on my flushed cheeks, and he gives me a nudge. "What are you looking forward to?" he asks.

"I want to get the dirt out of my scalp, but I'm not sure the water pressure at my apartment is gonna cut it. I'll probably take a shower at the station... Most importantly, though, I want to make sure I still have a job. I'm supposed to go to work tomorrow."

"They'll take one look at that nasty cut on your forehead and give you a week off, babe. You can take a vacation."

I can't afford a week off, or a vacation for that matter. I can't afford to lose this job. I stir the soup mix into the boiling water. My stomach churns with nerves. I don't know what I'll do if I end up unemployed. It's something I've been pushing from my thoughts since the night we arrived because I've been in survival mode, but now that there's a timeline on our return, I keep circling the drain with worry. "Vacation, huh? I've heard there's a great inn at the top of Quell's Peak," I joke.

"You can take a shower at my place."

"Oh yeah?"

"I've got some great water pressure," he adds with a wink.

"I don't believe you. You're going to have to prove it."

He retreats toward the stove to finish cleaning himself up.

"Happily."

I hum in agreement and continue stirring. After a couple minutes, I divide it between our two mugs and pass one to him, toasting, "To toothbrushes and water pressure."

"Toothbrushes and water pressure," he echoes, and we clink our mugs in cheers. He blows on a steaming spoonful. "Oh, I have some good news too."

"What's that?" I stir the soup in my mug, waiting for it to cool.

"I found some length of chain with the tools out there, with a bit of paracord, I think I can put together some crampons for your boots."

"Really?" That would be fantastic! It'll improve my mobility in the snow, especially in any icy sections.

"Yeah, when we finish eating, I'll get you rigged up. For once, those stupid emergency paracord bracelets are coming in handy."

I chuckle.

"I'm also looking forward to eating anything but soup," he says, taking a bite.

"Same." But the wild rice soup was good, a lot better than the same Ramen noodles or instant potatoes I've been living off of back home.

"Do I still get to take you out to eat?"

"Yeah." I smile, imagining what I'd order. A salad—something crisp, crunchy, and fresh... and a mean-ass cheeseburger stacked with pickles. My mouth waters thinking about it. I'm sick of soft food.

"It'll be nice to be back."

I hum in agreement. "I bet you're excited to sleep in your own bed again."

He shrugs. Silence stretches between us. "Do you think it'll be weird to not sleep next to each other?"

Tilting my head, I purse my lips, giving the illusion I'm considering the question even though I already know the answer. *Yes, it will be weird. Yes, I'll miss it.*

"Yeah."

"I noticed, that, uh…" He stirs his soup a few times and clears his throat. I examine his apprehensive expression, curious where he's going with this. "I notice that I sleep better here."

I nod. "I once read an article that explained how sleeping outdoors can improve quality and length of sleep. Plus, the fresh air had a bunch of other benefits like increased concentration, more creativity—"

He gives a headshake. "It's not the outdoors."

We exchange a glance briefly before we return to eating.

Yeah, I'm gonna miss this.

CHAPTER 40

CALLAHAN

Fire flickers on the wall. We've spent most of tonight wrapped up in each other and talking about our pasts and presents. Mostly simple things. Favorite foods, TV shows, et cetera. But deeper stuff too: her thoughts about religion and politics and how she's been navigating her feelings since leaving. We've discussed our families. Both of our parents have passed. I told her all about Teddy and my brother-in-law, Logan, and my niece, Penny, and nephew, Dalton.

I've never experienced conversation flow so easily before. Molly and I never had anything like this. We kept things from each other. Some of those things were big, but it was smaller shit too: what we wanted to eat for dinner or gossip about friends. It was all surface-level communication, perhaps for fear of judgment or opinion from the other.

I told her all about Molly and Dave. How walking in on them may have been what prompted our split, but our relationship died a lukewarm death long before the affair. Once we became engaged, things changed. We sacrificed the passion we shared for things that were stable and more mature. It was what we were supposed to do. We were growing up, but we were also growing apart. I wasn't thrilled with the way things were going, but it didn't seem like there was anything I could do about it, so I made the best of the situation. I settled.

With Scottie, everything is richer. We say what we think. We share deeper ideas. I've never had conversations like this with another woman. Maybe it's the honeymoon phase, but our connection feels... *different.*

With our clothes scattered all around us, we lie naked under the covers. On our sides, we chat face-to-face with our heads propped up. I've learned so much about her already, and my attraction grows with each joke, laugh, and story. She's the furthest thing from selfish, and it angers me that anyone could make her feel otherwise.

I drape her thigh over mine and move my leg between hers, drawing us closer. She snakes her free hand behind me, lightly scratching my back, and damn, it feels good. I love the physical touch. The way she links our fingers when my mind spins out of control, that she's not afraid to be the big spoon, how she runs her nails down my back and arms. The way she shows affection is beautiful.

"You mentioned you have a group chat with Xander and King—I met King at the poker game in Oregon. I don't think I met Xander though?"

"No, Xander is the superintendent. He tends to keep a low profile when we decide to act like delinquents. You've probably seen him though, bright-blue eyes, can't miss him."

"I think I remember seeing you with him a few times."

"Everyone on the crew is tight, we have to be, but those two are the closest I'll ever get to real brothers."

She tucks her head against my chest and breathes deep. "Tell me about them."

"Where do I start?" I chuckle. "We've been through every-thing together, walked through fire together. King—his actual name is Rowan Kingsley, he grew up in Sky Ridge. He was involved with rugby in high school, played varsity, and is really connected with the town."

"Did you play any sports?"

"Nah, I was more of an outdoor junkie. I spent my summers fishing the lakes, rafting the rivers, and hiking in the mountains. In the winter, I was on the slopes skiing or snowboarding. But King and I came up as rookies together when we joined the shots."

"What about Xander? When did you guys meet?"

"Xander is from Michigan, so he moved out here to be a shot. He's got a great sense of humor and a good heart. His dad was also a hotshot."

"Wait, with the same hotshot crew?"

"Yeah." My throat clears. "His dad, Garrett, was our superintendent up until five years ago when he died on the job."

She nuzzles into me. "I'm sorry."

"It was bad, really bad. Garrett died in the middle of the season, and then we lost Jacob toward the end of it. Fuck, that was an ugly year... Jacob was basically our brother, and Garrett was like a dad to a lot of us, his death was a huge loss for everyone, but Xander took the biggest hit losing his father. He carries it every day. It's horrible to watch someone you care about hurting without a way to fix it." I pause to collect my thoughts. It's not something I talk about with people who don't understand, but after hearing about Scottie's upbringing, I want to open up to her about my life too. And it's something she needs to know about if we're going to move forward.

"Xander was never the same after his dad died. I blame myself for a lot of that. Logically, I understand it doesn't make sense, but that's just the way it is."

She doesn't interrupt or try to convince me otherwise, she just lets me speak.

"This job is hard. There are pieces of me that are broken, and they can't be repaired. Sometimes it feels like my life's been split into all these fragments. The hazardous work and dangerous terrain… falling back into safety zones, always being a couple bad decisions away from the worst, the near misses and close calls, watching friends die."

Her soft scratches turn to gentle caresses as she listens.

"My head is constantly on a swivel. There's an underlying agitation that follows me around. Sometimes, I have panic attacks, or get lost in my thoughts, or appear distracted. It's not intentional, it just happens. Loud noises, trees falling when I don't expect it, that sort of thing tend to set me off."

She squeezes me tight. "Well, it's a good thing you don't have a job where you're around any of those things."

I chuckle. "Right?"

She doesn't laugh with me. "Really, though, have you ever thought about talking to someone about it?"

I shrug. "Yeah, I've received a diagnosis for C-PTSD, complex post-traumatic stress disorder, but it's one of those things that won't ever go away, so it's hard to justify the cost and time."

She nods against my chest. "But you don't think it would be worth it to try? It affects your quality of life, Cal."

"There are some things I'll never be able to let go of, no matter how much I want to, so dredging them up is exhausting. Not only for me, but the people around me. I tried before, and it wasn't long after that Molly and I started having major problems. I've been hesitant to get involved with anyone seriously since then, until you… I don't want to put you through that."

She retreats and tilts her head up to look at me. "Don't you think that's a decision you should let me make?"

I pull her closer. "Of course, but people don't always know how to react when I lose myself or freeze up… There are days when it feels like there's no one inside my body."

She has no idea how difficult it is for me to even discuss this with her. I'm in uncharted territory. My mind is screaming to lock it all down and enjoy the night, return to light conversation topics like music and books, the easy stuff—*like I did with Molly*. I take a deep breath.

"And you're right, this is your decision... It's a big ask, but I'm still asking."

Her fingers pause, and she stares up at me, searching my eyes. "What are you asking me?"

"I'm asking you to stay anyway."

The silence between us is heavy, and my lungs burn with a trapped breath while I wait for her response.

"I want to..."

Not a fan of the way her voice trails off, I swallow. "But?"

"But we are two damaged people. If we're going to make this work, we need to ensure we're in a position to take care of ourselves before we can take care of someone else. How can we expect to have a healthy relationship if we aren't confronting our own issues?"

Except that everything feels effortless between us. We had a rocky start, but once we came clean about our pasts, it was obvious we have something good here. Shit, this is not how I thought this would go, and I didn't anticipate it would hurt this much.

"From where I stand, we've got potential for a future. Don't you think that's still worth exploring? Even if we're imperfect?" I ask.

"You yourself said it's horrible to watch someone else hurt without being able to fix it. Don't ask me to do that. What you have going on may not be one hundred percent curable, but you still have to process it. If you don't, it will fester and eat you alive. Sometimes, the only way to do that is to cut into the pain and let it bleed out so you can heal."

"It's not that easy—"

"No, it's not. It's fucking *hard*! I walked away from everything I've ever known for a chance at happiness, meaningful relationships, and finding myself. That was not *easy*. I still have a lot to work through, but I'm determined to do it." She takes a deep breath. "It wasn't my plan to meet someone like you so soon. I'm not sure I'm ready for it, considering I have zero experience, but the way you make me feel, the things you do to me..." An exhale escapes her lips. "You're like nothing I've ever experienced. I'm *alive* with you. Callahan, I like you. A lot. And I like who I am with you, but..."

Her palm is scorching through my shirt, and she finds a way to nuzzle deeper into my shoulder. Five minutes ago, it would have been comforting, but now it feels like pity. The twinge of rejection is hot in my chest while I wait for her to continue.

"We're facing our own battles. I won't stand by and watch you lose yours because you decided it isn't worth the energy. I need to know you'll fight for yourself. If you want to do this, I promise you won't do it alone. I'll be at your side the whole time, even when it gets ugly."

Hope blooms in my chest for us, *it's not a no...*

She tips her chin up and kisses me before adding, "If I stay, I need to know you won't leave once I'm there."

Her words are like a balm, soothing my frustration and dousing the flames of rejection licking at my skin. My hand plunges into her hair, and my mouth claims hers deeper than before. This is a new beginning.

"I'm not leaving," I say against her lips.

She jabs her fingers to my chest and pushes me away far enough to pause our kiss.

"If we do this, then we're doing it. I want you to find somebody who can help you manage your symptoms. Don't make empty promises you can't keep. I've got my own issues, I'll be finding someone too."

"Okay." I agree. "And when that can of worms is opened and things get hard?"

"When things get hard, don't pull away from me. Stay and fight, Callahan."

Pressing a kiss to her temple, I roll on my back, hauling her with me so she's laying on my chest. The way her warm, soft skin feels against mine is pure bliss. "Thank you."

"For what?"

For taking a chance on us. For giving me something to work toward. For making me feel safe for the first time in a long time.

"For giving a damn."

The reflection of fire in the wood stove window flickers and dances on the walls while I bring her to my mouth and take her lips. The acute realization that she may be the last woman I ever kiss hits me... It's strange how you can have your heart locked up for years, then out of nowhere the right person comes along and it's like they know the exact combination to open up everything about you and make you want something *more*.

Her small gasps and sighs while I kiss her make me feral. My palms bracket her waist as she straddles me. I would move mountains to keep us like this, but I can't help but have some doubt.

What if I'm unable to get my problems under control? If I don't improve, will I still be enough for her? The last time I had a therapy session, it had Molly and I yelling at each other by the end of the night. I don't want to experience that with Scottie. Not after we've gotten this close and come this far. Heat rushes up my neck, and my arms tense, panic clawing at me. It's stifling, my whooshing pulse echoes in my ears while I fight with everything I have to stay in the moment with her.

I can't believe this is happening again. Fuck! It's like the vulnerability of opening up to her is unlocking all this other shit too. I can't keep up. This is exactly what I was worried about. My shoulders stiffen, and our kiss comes to a halt. I inhale slowly, trying to stave off another panic attack. The more I tell myself to stop thinking negative thoughts, the more I focus on them. It's like tunnel vision. Scottie straightens, looking down on me.

Fuck, she's stunning. *She deserves better. Someone who can give her more.*

Her hands find mine, and she brings them to her breasts, kneading my fingers. "It's okay, Cal... Just watch, okay? Focus on my voice."

I repeat her words in my mind until I'm able to really hear them. *Focus on her voice.*

"Squeeze my nipples." Her hands lead mine. She rolls her hips. "Do you feel how wet I am?" Her bare pussy glides over my cock, slick and warm.

"Yeah." I nod. *She's trying to ground me.*

"No, *feel* me." She guides my wrist between her thighs, then rises to her knees and uses my fingers to part her lips. She's soaked. I swallow and feel the chaos subsiding.

"Play with your nipples," I say, directing her back to her breasts. Then I return to toy with her clit. I grip my cock at the base and press it to her entrance, pausing and glancing up at her for permission.

She gives it to me by saying, "I'm with you," then lowering herself inch by inch until I'm fit snug inside. Her soft moans call out to me, bringing me into the present with her. *Fuck.*

The destructive thoughts dissipate, worries settle into a calm pool, and anxiety is replaced by need. She dampens all the noise in my head. The air is no longer hot and suffocating, it's cool and restorative.

This woman may have the capacity to drive me crazy, but she also holds the power to make me sane.

"You're breathtaking, baby."

A smile spreads across her lips, and she relaxes ever so slightly. Every part of her is incredible, but at this moment, her heart is what has me in awe. She's more than her jaw-dropping looks and captivating personality, she's good and decent to her core. Scottie cares about others in ways that are selfless and genuine.

She gyrates her hips, pushing me deeper, and I cup her waist, as she uses her body to rescue me.

The feelings I have for Scottie aren't love, but they're *something*.

She says she hasn't experienced the real thing yet, and maybe I haven't either. But there's zero doubt in my mind we could find it together. Because one thing is certain, sooner or later, I *will* love her.

CHAPTER 41

Scottie

DAY 5 - THE DESCENT

We packed up the night before, knowing we'd need to be ready to go before the sun came up. My fingers tremble. I'm scared to leave, of what might happen, not just on our hike, but for what the future holds for us. Our relationship has only ever existed in fire towers and dorms. Forced proximity. Can we exist in the real world too? Merging this dreamlike version with reality makes me uneasy, but I've spent a lot of my life scared, and that's no way to live. I have to trust us to make it work.

I'm adjusting my warmed socks over my ankles while Callahan spreads out the embers in the wood stove. Watching him gives me goose bumps. It's the first time we've woken in the morning to put out the fire rather than feed it. My stomach churns. I have total confidence in him to get us safely down the mountain, but it doesn't erase the trepidation of our endeavor.

After proudly rigging up my hiking boots with chain and paracord, he set my DIY-crampon'd boots near the wood stove last night so they'd be toasty when we start our journey home.

"Still with me?" he asks without looking over his shoulder.

I pull my lips into a tight smile. "Mm-hm."

"It's gonna be okay."

"I know."

He turns and squeezes my toes and hands me two plastic bags to wrap them in. "Did you eat?" he asks, referring to the energy bars we laid out for breakfast. If I eat it now, I might throw up. I'm afraid to walk away from the safety of the lookout, but we can't stay here. We're out of water, and there's an opening in the weather, so we absolutely have to leave, but with each step, I'll be closer to the things I've been running from.

"It's in my pocket." I push my bagged feet into the heated boots, lacing them up on the rug. I stand, the chains underneath feeling unfamiliar. "Are you nervous?"

"Nope. It's going to be slow moving through the snow in the beginning, but as we descend, things will get easier. We're just taking a morning hike, that's all this is."

It's just a hike.

We're bundled up using extra clothes. Cal is making me take the gloves, but he's got a couple pairs of wool socks on his hands as mittens. Ridiculous, but there's no use in arguing with him. Shadows dance around the room as we gear up. I hoist my pack over my shoulders, and he tucks my water in the side pocket.

I pull up my hood, he slides the headlamp over his hat, and our eyes meet. He tilts my chin up and slants his head to kiss me.

"Let's go home," he says with a smile.

I nod. "Home."

Callahan was right. We're hiking in total darkness through deep snow reaching the top of my thighs. This is hard, but it would have been a hell of a lot harder if he hadn't scouted it yesterday, making tracks for us to follow. Being shorter than him makes it more difficult, and I do my best to keep up, but I find myself wanting to stop and stare at the sky. I forgot how deep the universe is, the astronomical abyss goes on forever. Without cloud cover or landscapes, the stars appear closer than ever. It's otherworldly. The Milky Way is as bright as I've ever seen it.

The wind still has me squinting, but it's nothing like it was when we first arrived. The snowy terrain twinkles like glitter in my peripheral when Cal's headlamp or my flashlight—that we stole, *sorry*—catches the light. It's like staring into static, which confuses my depth perception when the sky is sparkling just as much. It's impossible to see where the heavens and earth meet. The lack of horizon makes this expedition incredibly disorienting.

"Need a break?" he asks.

My mouth is dry. "I'm good."

While ignoring the glittering void around us, it's best to keep my head down to ensure I'm staying in his footprints. Footprints is the wrong description, with snow this deep, they're more like boreholes. The ones he made yesterday all by himself. Being five-foot-three, I have to lift my legs a lot higher than he does to step into them, and I'm panting after an hour. The only savior for me in the waist-deep drifts is that we're hiking downhill, giving me an advantage. It feels like we aren't getting any closer since I have no point of reference to compare our position to. My fingers and toes are freezing, but I keep wiggling them as much as possible.

We reach a section of the woods that has us breaking off to trek toward the river bed, and occasionally, Cal pauses to hold a tree branch out of the way so it doesn't rear back and slap me in the face. *It's the little things that mean the most.* While hiking through the small forest sections takes longer, I find them preferable to the clearings where there's no protection from the wind.

"I can't believe you did all this yesterday by yourself... Thank you."

"Of course."

I'm incredibly impressed by his prowess in nature. Even carving out this path during the daytime, he had no trail to go off of. I don't mistake that he's made the tracks closer together than he would on his own. That was for me. It must have been painstakingly slow checking each step before making it, but based on how many we've taken, he must have been moving at a pretty good clip. I'm not ashamed to say it's sexy as hell. There's something about a man who can navigate his way through snowy mountains. Callahan's a beast.

Unfortunately, when we reach the end of his path from yesterday, we're slowed down significantly. Coyotes yelp in the distance, but they're far enough away to not cause concern. Eventually, he's tired out from making fresh tracks, so we break for water. I take the opportunity to eat the protein bar I was supposed to eat before we left. I'm just barely able to make out the horizon for the first time. "It's almost dawn," I comment, pointing toward the slightly lighter sky. His headlamp beam shakes with a nod.

We continue our route, and before long, the sky is a soft purple and we're gradually able to see our surroundings. After another hour, the sun's rays are warm on our face, and with the lower elevation, the wind isn't nearly as chilling. The snow is finally below my knees, and it's a blessing because a stair climber doesn't have shit on the snow at Quell's Peak. Boulders and rocks jut from the white landscape, and I'm not sure I'll ever see them the same again. By the same token, any sign of less snow is a welcome sight.

We duct taped the tears in my soft-shell pants, but it's not long before the weak waterproofing of the fabric gives into the snow. I do my best to ignore the penetrating chill as my base layer becomes the final barrier between my flesh and the elements.

We pause to rest and enjoy the rays hitting the mountain and the sunrise painting the sparkling snow a rich pink hue. It's dazzling. A couple times I find myself believing we really are on a "morning hike" instead of a survival descent.

Callahan leans to the side and points up ahead. It takes my eyes a moment to spot what he's showing me, then I make out two dark horns against the white snow about sixty feet away. There's a woolly mountain goat curled up in the snow, casually watching us.

"Amazing," I whisper.

His hand slowly drifts to the left. "There's another one." His voice is soft.

"I take it we've made it to Goat's Ridge?"

He chuckles. "We have."

"Do we need to be worried about them at all?"

"Normally, no. But since it's mating season, we're going to keep some extra distance…"

I gape in response. "What?"

"It'll be fine. These guys don't seem to care that we're here." *Cool. Cool, cool, cool.*

We march for another two hours along the ridge, and before long, the snow is down to my ankles, some areas even less. With each step, I feel the push back of rock under the chains strapped to the bottom of my boots. Callahan glimpses down, noticing how damp my pants are from the snow.

"How are your legs doing?"

"Fine," I lie. We need to keep moving.

"My knees are fuckin' killing me," he huffs. I'm feeling it in mine too. "Let's take a short break."

We pull out our water bottles for a drink.

"Your headlamp's still on," I say, out of breath after swallowing a gulp. I'm surprised our waters didn't freeze while we were battling all that snow earlier.

"Whoops," he says, flicking it off.

Callahan has me sit on the edge of a large rock as he crouches at my feet and unhooks the homemade crampons. They aren't necessary anymore. I shove my water bottle into my bag while he stuffs the paracord and chains in his pack, and we're on our way again.

Downhill sucks. I've never traversed such a steep descent for such a long period of time. About three-quarters down to the valley of Goat's Ridge, my right knee is throbbing, but I keep moving because we have ground to cover, and I don't want to be the one slowing us down.

"How are you doing?"

"Fine," I grunt.

He stops, locking his hands on my shoulders, and levels me with a stare. "Let's try this again. How are you doing?"

"I'm tired."

"Then we stop. We're out of the snow, sun is up, we're almost to the valley and making great time."

I take a drink of water. "How much farther?"

"Five miles, give or take. Mostly flat though."

I smile. "I can do five miles of—"

Cal's head snaps to the left. Did he see something? I immediately scan the area for mountain goats.

"Do you hear that?" he asks.

I fold back my hood. There's a humming. The faint purr of something mechanical. Shooting to my feet, we hurry toward the sound. It's getting louder, we're heading in the right direction, but why can't we see it yet?

The noise crescendos until the source emerges, a red and black side by side UTV comes barreling around the bend. Callahan and I stop in our tracks.

"Holy shit," he says, laughing. We continue moving, slower this time. Our five miles to safety may have just turned into fifty yards. The off-road vehicle looks out of place in the remote landscape.

Callahan grins, sticking his thumb out as if we're a couple of hitchhikers in the middle of nowhere.

As they approach, the driver and passenger are beaming. "Is that…?"

"Xander and King." His smile is ear to ear.

"Are you my Uber?" Callahan shouts over the motor as they roll up.

"Yeah, I heard somebody missed their curfew," King—*Rowan*—says, killing the engine and pressing on the emergency brake. I remember playing poker with him in Oregon, which makes the other one Xander. Callahan was right, he does have *really* blue eyes.

Xander steps out and grabs my pack, slipping it from my shoulders. Cal shrugs his off and tosses it in the back.

King lifts his chin to Callahan. "How was your hike, sunshine?"

"Lovely… Xander, King, you remember Scottie." Callahan introduces us.

"Hi." I offer a small wave, pushing down the emotion rising in my throat as relief sweeps through me. We made it. "It's really nice to see you guys."

King lifts a radio to speak into. "Found them. Subjects alive… Scottie's got a decent cut on her forehead, but it appears to be healing."

The radio crackles. "Great news. Any other injuries?" The voice is familiar.

"Is that Matt?" I ask.

He nods, and I want to die of embarrassment. The last thing I want is to have inconvenienced him and caused a problem at my place of work. It's bad enough I didn't show up at the station today.

"She dislocated her shoulder a few days ago," Cal adds. King relays it to my coworker.

We're ushered into the back seat of the side by side, and just like that, we're on our way, bouncing toward the trailhead. I shiver as my sweat cools. Cal wraps an arm around me and pulls me close.

"So my text went through?" He calls over the engine.

Xander turns his head to the side. "Yup."

King spins around in his seat. "We didn't even know you were missing until we found out Scottie was, then we put two and two together when we couldn't get ahold of you."

My brows draw together, and King faces forward again. *They knew I was missing?*

"Me? How did you find out I was out here before him?" I stick my thumb in Callahan's direction. "I wasn't due to report back at work until this morning... I don't know enough people for someone to report me missing."

Xander and King exchange a glance, but neither answer. My gaze oscillates between them, waiting for a response. King adjusts one of the mirrors, and Xander looks off to the distance. *What aren't they saying?*

"Hey!" Cal snaps, leaning forward to make sure the guys hear him. "How did you know Scottie was missing?"

"We didn't know," King spits out. "Her husband did."

CHAPTER 42
CALLAHAN

Suddenly, I wish we hadn't been rescued by the guys. Our bubble has officially exploded, and our time is running out with each mile back to the trailhead. She's been silent since she found out Jonathan's in town. We made plans on the mountain, but now that her husband has shown up, will she still hold true to them? What if he convinces her not to file for divorce?

When the parking lot comes into view, I can already pick him out. He's acting the same way I probably would if Scottie went missing. His fingers are threaded on top of his head as he paces back and forth, but as soon as he spots our off-road vehicle, he stops in his tracks, then bolts toward us.

I retract my arm from behind her back despite my body's instinctive protest. That's when I notice my sister in the parking lot, standing near one of two ambulances. "Can't believe you called Teddy." I can thank the guys for that. Great, this day just got even better. She'll probably chew my ass out.

When we pull up, Scottie climbs out and is instantly wrapped up in a hug by the man I presume to be *him*. My sister has her arms around me for a hot second before rearing back and slapping me on the back of the head.

"Glad you're alive, you fucking idiot." Her nostrils flare, and she throws her arms around me a second time.

Peeking over Teddy's shoulder, I witness Jonathan and Scottie in a tender embrace. Even after everything she's told me about their relationship, jealousy burns hot in my chest. Her eyes find mine, and she offers a sympathetic smile. How did he find her, and what does he want? It better not be to take her back home. They may still be married, but I won't give her up without a fight.

Teddy angles away. "You need a shower, dude."

"I wanna introduce you to someone," I say, ignoring my sister's gripes, unable to take my gaze off Scottie. I'm calling out to her before I realize it. "Scottie."

She withdraws from his hold and steps toward us. Jonathan follows. When she stands before me, the whole thing feels surreal. Fuck, it's like I've already lost her. I hate it.

"Scottie, this is my sister Teddy. Teddy, this is Scottie."

Jonathan shows up at her side and shakes my hand. "Thank you so much for keeping her safe. I don't know what I'd do if I lost her."

Obviously not much, took you long enough to chase after her.

My jaw tenses. "I don't know what I'd do either," I say, meeting her eyes.

Scottie's cheeks flush and an awkward silence stretches between us.

"Well, I appreciate you keeping my wife alive and getting her back to me."

Ouch.

I open my mouth to respond when Matthew hops out of one of the ambulances and interrupts our friendly little conversation. "Prescott, playing hooky already?"

Her face drains of color, and she winces. "I'm so, so sorry. I —How much trouble am I in for missing work?"

He laughs. "Nobody is mad at you, but I need to check your

shoulder and that cut on your forehead. Mind jumping in the rig for a sec?"

She shakes her head. "Sure."

Matthew asks her a few questions about the injury on their way over, and Jonathan stays right on her heels.

I waive care and quickly fill out the refusal form, then turn back to my sister, who's looking at me with raised eyebrows. She gives an exaggerated glance toward the ambulance Scottie's in and back to me. "So, you wanna tell me what that's all about?" Her lips are pursed, matching the judgmental expression on her face.

I tilt my head, scratching my overgrown facial hair. "Not really."

"Dude, after Molly—"

"It's not like Molly, okay? It's just complicated. Look, I gotta get home. I'm beat. Can I call you later? I promise I'll explain, but for now I just wanna go home and get a shower."

She inhales. "Okay. Yeah." Her arms drop to her sides.

"Give the kids a hug for me," I tell her.

From the corner of my peripheral, I spot the side by side carrying Xander and King creeping toward us. "Hey Teddy," Xander says with a smirk aimed at my sister. She waves.

"Hey, you good?" King asks me, pulling my focus.

"Yeah. Need any help loading up the UTV?"

"Nah, just take care of yourself. Text us later," Xander says.

My palm finds the back of my neck. "Will do. Thank you for saving our asses out on that mountain." I mean it sincerely.

"Whatever, you could have made it back without us," King adds. "But the guys are gonna have a heyday next fire season after word gets around."

Oh good, I can't wait to hear their version of it.

My sister laughs. "Alright, I'm going back. Call me later," she says, pointing at me. She nods goodbye to everyone and continues on her way.

"Good to see you, Teddy," Xander calls after her, his eyes lingering on the back of her head a little too long. My gaze bounces between Xander and my sister—my very *married-with-two-kids* sister. She casually lifts her hand in a wave, then looks down to her phone as she walks to her car. If Xander sees something in her, he missed his chance a long time ago. She and Logan were high school sweethearts and live a very happy life.

I shake it off. "All the same, I appreciate it."

The guys drive the UTV toward the alternate access road that leads to the main base, where they likely parked the trailer, and we part ways.

"Thank you for making sure I didn't die," I yell out to my sister, walking backward toward my truck.

She opens her car door, yelling back, "What are baby sisters for?"

I fish my car keys out of my pack and hop in my truck, turning the ignition, but I can't bring myself to leave. I remind myself she's in good care with Matthew and the other EMT.

And Jonathan.

Shaking my head, I shift the truck in reverse. It's time to go home, but as I back out of the parking spot, I can't help but feel like I've left something behind.

Back home, I push aside one of the hanging tarps that blocks off the dining room from sawdust. This place has been in a constant state of construction for nearly five years, but there's been a lot of progress made too. My footsteps echo through the unfinished space toward the stairs. The house sounds hollow.

Upstairs, I lumber to my bedroom, one of the first rooms I remodeled after I bought the place, and drop my pack in the closet. Next, I plug in my phone, and it lights up with a charging battery symbol. I leave it to power up on the nightstand while I turn on the shower in the en-suite bathroom. I brush my teeth while I wait for the water to warm. As soon as those bristles hit my gums with that cool, minty toothpaste, I moan. "Oh, baby, I've missed you." My words are muffled around the toothbrush.

I probably brush for a good five minutes straight, even scrubbing the inside of my cheeks. Then I floss. Then swish mouthwash around and delight in the brisk sensation. After stripping off my filthy hiking gear, I stand under the hot shower spray and release another groan of pleasure. I scrub my body with the same detail as my mouth and step out feeling fresher than ever. The whore baths at the lookout certainly helped, but there's no substitute for the real thing. My thoughts wander to Scottie. Has she gotten home yet? Has she had her shower? Did she get the dirt out of her hair like she wanted?

With a towel wrapped around my waist, I exit the bathroom and sit on the edge of my bed. I pick up my partially charged phone, hoping to see a message from her, but instead, it's a barrage of texts that have loaded from the last few days. Most from my group chat with Xander and King. The most recent one.

> **XANDER**
>
> Hey asshole, are you coming out with us or not?

> **KING**
>
> You better not be dead.

> **XANDER**
>
> He said he made it back from Quell... probably balls deep in home remodeling.

> **KING**
>
> Or pussy.

> **XANDER**
>
> Did he mention going out of town?

KING

Not to me.

XANDER

I'm gonna reach out to Teddy. She might know.

KING

Word is Scottie's gone missing... think they're together?

XANDER

Maybe?

Scottie and I are at the fire tower on Quell's waiting out the storm. Trail is blocked with a rockfall, both of us are fine. We have water and supplies. We're going to take Goat's Ridge to get back as soon as the weather breaks.

Not sure if my last message went through, battery low, but the storm is easing up, we're starting our descent early 11/12.

XANDER

Holy shit.

KING

Thought I told you I didn't want to go on one of your damn hikes during my off-season!

Goddamn it. I'll get the UTV on the trailer.

XANDER

I'll spread the word.

It takes real effort to resist texting Scottie, but I open the text thread with her name anyway and frown. I hate the last texts I sent to her. They're cold and callous.

Things have run their course with us.

SCOTTIE

Okay.

Hey. Are you off the trail?

I tap a message across the screen.

You don't need to respond to this, but I don't want you to open our texts later and have the last message you see from me be that. So instead, you're getting this one, where I tell you that I miss you. That it was really hard to drive away from you today. That I can't stop thinking about you. That I wish you were with me right now. I can't help but feel like a part of me is still at the top of Quell's and I hope like hell there's a piece of you there too, because I'm not ready to let go of that version of us. The rest of me is here, only a few blocks away, waiting for you. I'll be here as long as it takes, but you should know I'm keeping my word: I'm not walking away without a fight.

After I hit send, I leave the phone plugged in, and finish getting dressed. There are no new notifications. Scottie needs time to work through things with Jonathan, and it's important I give her that space. For now, there's nothing more I can do.

I flop on the bed and close my eyes, knowing this nap won't leave me feeling as rested as it is when her body is wrapped around mine.

CHAPTER 43

Scottie

Brushing my teeth was a lot more satisfying than my shower. I knew the water pressure wouldn't be strong enough to clear the dirt from my scalp. I miss the showers from that gym I had a membership at when I first moved to Sky Ridge. I stand in front of the mirror in my tiny bathroom, combing my fingers through the gritty strands trapped with filth. Everything feels sandy and wet. Not at all clean the way I wanted to feel when I got out of the shower. I try a hairbrush, but all it does is transfer the dirt. I slam it down on the sink.

"Goddamn it!" I shout.

Closing my eyes, I take four slow, deep breaths.

"Scottie?" Jonathan lightly raps on the door.

"I'm fine!" I bark. I bow my head before staring back at my reflection. "Sorry... I'm fine. I just need a minute. It's been a weird four days."

Abandoning my hair, I put on a fresh pair of underwear, jeans, and a T-shirt. At least my clothes are clean.

Jonathan is sitting in the busted kitchen chair when I exit the bathroom. One of his arms rests on the small table. We observe each other, but it's unfamiliar. We haven't spoken in roughly two months, and now he's here, in my new life.

"So. How have you been?" I ask.

"Been better."

I sit across from him in the other seat. None of these things are surprising to me, as I saw the writing on the walls years ago, but it took me a long time to gain the courage and earn enough money to leave. If only he'd come with me, we could be going through this journey together.

"How are your parents? I miss your mom's fried chicken." I give a half-hearted laugh. "I still can't believe she gave me the recipe, one of these days I'm going to master it." This week, I'm buying a full load of groceries, including produce and protein.

"You're the only one she gave the recipe to." He chuckles, then sobers. "She misses you… feels like she's lost a daughter."

I swallow, looking down at my hands. I miss her too. Jonathan had a kind family. They never knew how our marriage was. "Feels like I lost a mother too."

"She wants you to come home."

With a tight smile, I fuss with the loose thread on the hem of my shirt. He knows I can't do that. "We both know that's not my home anymore."

"Maybe it is."

My eyes plead with his. "Jonathan…"

"You have to come home, Scottie."

I shake my head and point down. "This is my home."

He stands from his chair, opening his arms and spinning in a circle. "You say this is a home?! You hardly have any food, you're sleeping on the floor, your walls are literally crumbling! I was the only one who discovered you were missing. You have *no one* here!"

My bottom lip trembles as tears burn the back of my eyes. "Maybe. But I'd bet every last cent I have that I'm happier in this deteriorating apartment than you'll ever be in The Fold."

He pinches the bridge of his nose and sucks in a breath. I exhale, releasing my nerves. It occurs to me that I haven't asked him how he even found me to begin with.

I narrow my gaze. "How did you know I was here?"

"I didn't. The council did."

"What?" The hair on the back of my neck stands up.

He sighs. "I'm here to bring you home. To The Fold, where you belong."

I wish he'd stop calling it home. Home is where you feel safe and secure. Home is with Callahan. "I don't want to go back to Arkansas."

"You made a vow to me," he argues.

"It's been weeks. We're separated. Do you remember our promise to let the other one go? What about that?"

"Scottie, they know!"

My lids shoot open. "What are you talking about?" This is a nightmare coming true. They always assumed that our marriage "fixed" him. If they realize he's still gay, he's not safe. I lower back into my chair and fix my eyes on a dent in the linoleum floor.

"They questioned me after you left, it was awful."

"Why did you even tell them—"

"Don't! *You* left *me*, remember? You have no idea what it's been like since you left."

I shake my head. "I'm sorry, I'm sorry. I didn't mean it like that. You're right, I don't know what you've been going through."

"I've been going through hell—all alone. You left me no way to contact you! I understand you're trying something new, but you need to come back now. They're going to expose everything if you don't return. You know what that means for me."

Any color in my face quickly melts away as I imagine what could happen to him. I don't want to go back there. I worked too hard. But Jonathan is facing a worse fate. It was my decision to leave, but he's being punished for it. I always said I'd protect him. My presence was his only shield, and I took it with me when I left.

"My career, my family, my medical license, our home." His voice breaks. "My life will be over."

But mine has just begun. A hard lump forms in my throat. He sits across from me, but my glare is stuck to the floor while he goes on.

"I promise, it's not forever, okay?" I wish myself back in the fire tower with Callahan. I wish he was with me right now. I'd rather digest the news with him nearby. Jonathan continues, "I swear, I'll get on board, but if we leave, we have to do it right... Let's just go back, lay low until this all dies down. I told them you would come back with me, and that we'd work harder this time."

I meet his gaze, but it feels like I'm looking through him.

"I mean, did you really think you could just sneak away in the middle of the night without tying up any loose ends? It's not that easy."

Why does everyone think what I did was easy? Did he think me leaving him was easy? Being homeless was easy? Hell, I'm still clawing my way out.

I had plans for my future. Plans for Callahan, plans for my career, plans for exploring the Pacific Northwest, I even had plans for that fucking house on Spencer Avenue. Sure, some were more far-fetched, but others were so close I could hold them—I held those plans for four nights, but now they're slipping through my fingers.

"Luke 15:3-4," he says.

Angry blood surges through my veins at his mention of the scripture. I raise my chin to meet his sympathetic eyes. My throat burns, and I swallow down the bile. I want to scream, berate Jonathan for not leaving, for being such a coward.

What man of you, having a hundred sheep, if he loses one of them, does not leave the ninety-nine in the wilderness, and go after the one which is lost until he finds it?

"The Fold doesn't represent the word of God," I spit.

He stares at me blankly.

Swollen tears blur my vision. "And how will you rejoice when you return with their lost sheep?"

"I won't rejoice in this."

After a few breaths, I settle some of the fury inside. I have to remember this isn't Jonathan's fault. This is The Fold's doing. He's been facing a persecution I've never known. In the end, he needs protection more than I do, and I couldn't live with myself if I was responsible for something happening to him.

"Why can't you just stay? Places like The Fold are considered cults by the outside world. Did you know that? People say it's a *cult*."

He rolls his eyes. "Christianity isn't a cult, Scottie."

"Maybe not, but The Fold is," I argue.

"I can't just up and leave my life like you can. Why couldn't you just wait until we were both ready?"

"Because what if you never left!? We've talked about this, multiple times! You never showed an inkling toward wanting to leave. Was I supposed to just wait forever? One of us had to make the first move."

"This time I'll leave. I promise."

My face falls into my hands. I've never despised The Fold as much as I do right now. I clear emotion from my throat. *It's not Jonathan's fault.* "You said we could just lay low until we tie up loose ends... How long?"

"A few years."

I shake my head and scoff. "Absolutely not," I disclaim. "One."

"They might—"

"One, Jonathan. And your clock starts now. *One*. Not a day later."

"Okay." He concedes, holding up his hands in surrender. "I'm sorry, Scottie."

My head bobs in understanding. It's all I can do to keep from falling apart. Maybe I should have waited until we were both ready, at least then I wouldn't know what I was giving up. "After that year, we are going to file for divorce," I say, my voice shaking at the end.

He drops his gaze to his lap. He must have known it was coming, but that doesn't mean it wasn't any less painful to say aloud. A minute of silence passes between us.

"I promise, Jonathan, there is happiness beyond where we came from." My hand covers his. "You and I both know this isn't the life we imagined for ourselves. The Fold doesn't get to decide who we love. The reason we didn't work out isn't because we didn't pray loud enough. It wasn't because we didn't dedicate enough of our time to God or spread enough of the gospel. It's because of the way we were created. And we were created perfect in His image. You are perfect the way you are, and I am perfect the way I am. But that doesn't mean we're perfect together."

It sickens me he was taught to hate himself from such a young age, and I stood by and watched, participated even. I thought I could help him, as if he needed it in the first place. "I am so sorry for going along with something that was damaging to you. I love you, Jonathan, and I loved having you as a partner, but we both know in our hearts this isn't about love."

He nods. It's not the first time we've had this argument, but it's the first time I've said it without him lashing out at me.

"We are two people with a broken upbringing, but that doesn't mean we're broken, it just means we're not like them— and praise God for that, because that is *not* love."

He sniffs. "I know. But I still don't want to lose you."

"You could never lose me," I promise. But after staring death in the face, I know life is too short. "But you can't start a new life if you never walk away from the old one."

With tears in our eyes, we regard each other, seeing ourselves independently for maybe the first time ever.

"So, in a year... we just... walk away?" He sounds so despondent.

Watching him go through the realization I experienced over a year ago brings a new kind of pain. Until recently, he was the only man I ever loved. He's my best friend. We were all we had.

"The love we have for each other will never go away, but our love isn't the kind made for a marriage. It's not romantic. I'm not what you need. We aren't enough for each other."

He bows his head in agreement, sniffling.

"You deserve happiness, you deserve affection from a partner who can give it to you the way that I never will... We have to live the lives we were meant to live. Love the people we were meant to love."

His lip trembles. "Callahan?" he asks.

It catches me off guard. Do I love Callahan? Yeah... I do. *I love Callahan.* I stare back at Jonathan, still taking in the realization.

"I saw the way you looked at him."

My tears spill over, and I push them aside. "I'm sorry."

Jonathan shakes his head and sniffs again. "I knew we were done when you left. But seeing the way you looked at that guy today, and the way he looked at you... I guess it's real, huh? We're really going to end it."

"We have to," I say. "I promise, life is so much better on the other side." My mouth tips up in a sad smile.

He chuckles, glancing at the water-stain covered walls. "Yeah, you're living the dream... When we come back in a year, we'll find you a better apartment."

I shrug. It may not be glamorous, but it's worth more than

gold. I look forward to the day of his deliverance, so he can feel the weight lift and understand the peace that comes with it.

He studies me thoughtfully. "I'm sorry, Scottie."

One year, one year.

"But I will have to give notice at work. I can't drop everything and go back to Arkansas immediately." I plan to return to this town. If I'm to get my old job back next year, a graceful exit is necessary.

"How much time do you need?"

"Two to three weeks. I need to figure it out with them." My gaze drops to my hands. "I also have to talk to Callahan."

He nods. "I, uh, I'm staying at a local hotel." He grabs a notepad and pen from the counter and jots down the name and room number. "If you need a break from this... or need to talk. Come find me."

"Okay." This apartment may not be as nice as the house we had back in Arkansas, but it's part of my journey. Someday, I will look back and see how far I've come.

"I love you, Scottie. I hope you know I don't take for granted the sacrifice you're making. You're saving me, for the second time," he says.

"You're my best friend." He squeezes my hand and sweeps the back of his fingers across my cheek. "I want some time to sit with this, and process everything. I don't know how I'm going to explain it to Callahan."

"You're worth the wait. If he cares for you, he'll wait a year... This isn't goodbye."

Emotion swells in my throat, forming a lump too big to swallow. *Then why does it feel like it?*

Freeing my hand, we stand, and I hug him. He rests his head on top of mine. I breathe him in, squeezing tight around his midsection. After realizing my feelings for Callahan, the difference between the two men I love is like night and day. Jonathan showed me what love is, but Callahan let me experience it.

He stuffs his hands in his pockets and gives a half-hearted laugh. "Yeah... I'll be in touch."

"It's good to see you again." We hug one more time, and he leaves.

Closing the door behind him, I wrap my arms around my stomach, then collapse into my half-deflated bed. Crumpled in a ball, I release one gut-wrenching sob after another.

I don't want to say goodbye.

I wake up just as the sun is setting. I fell asleep crying. Lying motionless, my body has sunk so far into the deflated mattress that I'm grazing the floor. My stomach growls. I roll over, and it's as if all my muscles have tightened up.

"Oh God," I groan. I'm starting to feel that hike down the mountain.

Disconnecting my phone from the charger, I spy a text message notification. Thankfully, my phone didn't break, it just lost charge; the cold temperature probably drained the battery.

I flip open the phone. It's from Cal.

I read the text. Then I read it again. And again.

I never thought I'd experience a love like this. The kind that swarms my stomach with butterflies and excitement. The kind from my romance books. The kind where I spend four days trapped at the top of a mountain with someone and miss them after less than twenty-four hours of being apart. The kind where leaving him feels like losing a part of myself.

Hi.

My phone dings almost immediately after sending the text.

CALLAHAN
Hey.

How was brushing your teeth?

CALLAHAN
Better than I could have imagined. How was
your shower?

Sufficient-ish? Have you eaten?

CALLAHAN
I could eat again.

We need to talk. I want to see him. Hug him. Apologize and sob all over again.

Do you want to meet up at that burger place
nearby?

CALLAHAN
Yes. Will there be anyone else joining us? It's
okay if there is.

It's his way of asking if Jonathan is still here, and I appreciate his understanding.

Just me.

CALLAHAN
I'll pick you up in 5.

Smiling, I type out a response.

It's only a couple blocks away.

CALLAHAN
If your knees feel anything like mine, we've
done enough walking for today. I'll pick you up
in 5.

I laugh because I don't have any tears left to cry.

I'll wait for you outside. I'll be the one limping.

CHAPTER 44

CALLAHAN

The breath in my lungs finally releases when I see her standing outside her building. That woman is a gorgeous sight with her glossy ginger-blonde hair, face fresh, and all those freckles I love on display. She's wearing a sweater and jeans, like it's any other night, which is a bit dreamlike. *Was it really just this morning we got off the mountain?* Time is bizarre.

I exit the truck to open her door, rounding the front, and help her up into the passenger seat. After closing the door, I can't help but let my eyes stray to the faulty structure she lives in. If the outside is dilapidated, what the hell does the inside look like?

We pull away from the curb in silence. Thankfully, the burger joint isn't too busy on a Tuesday night, and we get a perfect parking spot right in front. She groans, taking my hand as she climbs out of the cab.

Inside, the diner is mostly empty, and we find an open booth, both of us moving slower than usual. As soon as we sit, the server is handing us a couple of menus.

"The soup today is chicken and rice," the server announces with a soft expression.

Scottie and I stare at each other.

After a beat, I gape at her in mock surprise. "Did you hear that, honey? *Soup.* Chicken and rice, your *favorite.*"

"Would you like me to put an order—"

"No thank you!" She practically shouts, then bites into her bottom lip to keep from laughing.

The server glances between us suspiciously. "I'll… give you a minute to look over the menu."

"Thank you," Scottie replies with a smile, then aims a glare in my direction.

Opening the menu, I mutter, "Well, I know what I'm *not* getting."

"I want a cheeseburger with extra pickles."

Atta girl.

"And a garden salad…"

I smirk at her over the top of my menu.

"And a cookies n' cream milkshake."

"That's what I'm talking about." I fold up my menu and set it on the table. "I'll get the same."

She places her menu on top of mine and folds her hands in her lap.

"So…"

"So…" she echoes. The smile slips from her face. "Jonathan and I spoke this afternoon…"

My breath stalls while I wait for her to continue.

"We talked for a long while. About our relationship. About what we need from each other."

"And what did you need?"

She focuses on the rolled silverware in front of her, straightening it so it's perpendicular to the table, then folds her hands in her lap.

"I asked for a divorce."

I exhale. My head bows briefly before I slump back against the vinyl upholstered booth. *Thank Christ.* She shudders a breath, and I reach for her. Her palm nestles in my open one, and

I squeeze.

"How did he react?" It's taking everything in me not to pepper her with all the questions flooding my thoughts since I left her in that parking lot this morning.

She shrugs. "About as expected, but how do you tell the person you care about that you want a divorce without hurting them? It's not that he couldn't see it coming. I made it pretty clear by leaving. However, I think it hit him today that we're really done and we have to part ways in order to live our own lives." Her sad smile makes me want to wrap her up in my arms.

The server interrupts and takes our orders, jotting down the burgers, salads, and shakes. "Coffee?"

"Please," Scottie says.

I hold up two fingers, adding "Thank you."

The server tucks her notepad into her apron pocket and shuffles to the kitchen.

On our table, two upside-down ceramic mugs rest on saucers, so we each turn them upright. She selects a couple creamers and a sugar from the dish, and I make a mental note of how she takes her coffee. She pries the sealed foil tops from the creamers and pours them into the empty cup, then rips the sugar packet and does the same.

We wait for the server to reappear with coffee before we continue the conversation. Thankfully, she returns quickly, but it feels like an eternity passes while we watch her fill our mugs with coffee. Scottie's swirls into a light creamy tan color. Mine remains black enough to see my reflection.

Nodding our appreciation, the server departs, and I wait for Scottie to speak. She sighs, centering her mug in front of her and using it to warm her hands.

"I have to go back," she says.

I furrow my brow. "To your apartment?"

"To The Fold."

What? I shake my head. Absolutely not happening. "I don't understand."

"The church found out about him. He needs me to go back so we can get his life sorted, and then we can leave at the same time."

"What do you mean *'found out'*? Weren't they the ones to facilitate your whole relationship?"

"They assumed he was straight after me, but they discovered nothing has changed, they're going to submit him to more conversion therapy. He could lose his job, his family, everything. He's not ready to leave."

Ready or not, he's gonna have to figure that out without her. Scottie may not be ready to admit it, but I've heard enough about that place to not trust it. The leaders control the congregation with fear and intimidation. It's a cult.

My jaw tics. "And when does he think he'll be ready?"

Despite the itching need to fidget, I remain calm on the outside and muster all the patience I possess. It took over a month of her being gone before he even came after her. If that were me, I'd have been out of my goddamned mind.

He had time to leave and didn't.

"I told him a year, but I'm going to get us out before then."

A fucking year? I meant what I said about waiting. She's worth it, but *this* isn't that.

I trust Scottie that her soon-to-be ex-husband isn't a bad guy, it's obvious she cares for him deeply, but at the end of the day, I don't know this guy. I don't want her to suffer through a long, drawn-out divorce, especially if that fucked-up church she came from tries to get involved.

She recounts the conversation between them this afternoon, shedding a few tears. I hate hearing about the pain she went through. That said, she's not going anywhere.

"I promise I'm coming back," she says.

"You're not coming back, because you're not leaving."

"Callahan—"

"Prescott." I give a headshake. "I'm sorry, but no."

Her gaze falls to her mug. "Don't worry, it's not like I'm packing up my bags tonight. I'll have a couple weeks to deal with my job and apartment stuff. I still have to give notice—"

"Please. Just give me a week to figure something out. Don't turn in your resignation yet."

Scottie lifts her chin, and the weak smile breaks my heart. The whites of her eyes are red; I had let it pass as windburn earlier, but now I know it's because she's been crying.

"It's less than a year." Her voice sounds so small.

She doesn't know that. Any place that entertains conversion therapy probably isn't too keen on women's rights either. She's risking her own safety by going back, and that's not happening.

"I told you when things got hard, I wouldn't cut and run. I need you to uphold the same promise," I tell her.

She sweeps fingers across her wet cheeks. "But this is different. I'm not choosing to leave, I have to go back. It's going to be okay. God never closes a door without opening a window."

Bullshit.

I scoff. "So you have something to jump out of?" I shake my head. "No. We're going to open the fucking door again. That's how doors work, Prescott."

Her shoulders sag. "He needs me."

I brush my thumb over her knuckles. She's blind to how dangerous this situation is—for both of them. "Listen to me, you can't save everyone. Sometimes, you can only save one person, and it's okay if that person is yourself."

Scottie gapes at me, like she's been waiting for someone to give her permission to choose herself all her life. The hope in her eyes will have me backing up every single one of my words. I will not let her down.

"Let me deal with this," I state just before the server clunks heavy plates in front of us, and I let go of her hand to make room. I should have insisted on taking Scottie back to my house and had dinner delivered so we could avoid any interruptions.

She's still staring at me. I lift my chin, gesturing to her plate. "Eat your food, baby."

She nods. The steaming meal has my mouth watering, but my appetite is dwindling. She unrolls her silverware, places the paper napkin in her lap, and picks up the cheeseburger with both hands before sinking her teeth into it.

"Ohmuhgud," she whispers around a mouthful of food. She hovers a palm over her lips, chewing. I follow her lead, taking a bite, and it's pretty damn good. This place makes a mean burger.

We sacrifice conversation for food until I catch Scottie staring across the room at the parents with three young kids being seated. It's chaotic as the family gets settled. They find a high chair for the youngest, arranging it at the end of their booth. By the time that's done, the server at their table is passing out menus and crayons. The older two children are already asking their parents if they can order chocolate milk instead of white before the crayons get unwrapped.

I set down my burger, swallowing. "Do you want kids someday?"

She sighs. "Honestly? Not really. I like kids, but I never had the desire to have my own—not after growing up in The Fold. Even now that I'm out, being a parent isn't something I need to feel fulfilled."

It was a long time ago that I gave up the idea of having children, but I love being an uncle. After a couple french fries, my appetite is back.

"What about you?"

I shake my head. "I have the winters off, but during the fire season, I'm gone for weeks at a time. It doesn't exactly lend itself to convenient parenting. I'm not saying we couldn't make it work, but it would be more challenging."

"*We*?" She smiles around a bite.

Shit, did I say we?

"I mean… whoever my partner is." I clear my throat and add on, "Teddy and her husband, Logan, have two kids, Penny and Dalton. I love being an uncle. It's the best of both worlds."

"That's really sweet. If you didn't have the job you do, would you want a family?"

"Maybe?" I shrug. "Hard to say." I'm not sure if I would or not. It's not something that I've been dreaming about my whole life or anything. "I'm happy with the direction my life is going right now." Which includes a future with Scottie.

After days of soft, overprocessed food, this meal is hitting the spot. She must have the same thought, because the next words out of her mouth are, "It's so nice to eat something crunchy!"

As soon as we finish dinner, I'm making small talk about plans for this week, hoping it helps assure her nothing is changing. She's not leaving.

I'm not concerned, and she shouldn't be either.

She mentions she's working tomorrow, and I give her a questioning look. Scottie quickly makes me aware that any protests against her decision to return to work so soon are useless. The cut on her forehead has barely healed and she's ready to clock in. However, she says she won't be going out on calls for a couple weeks until her shoulder is healed. That's gonna drive her nuts.

We pay the bill and return to the truck. Within minutes, we're already back at her front door. She insists she doesn't need me to escort her inside, and for the second time today, I drive away from her.

Instant regret.

I make it a block before I realize I didn't even kiss her good night.

"Fuck this."

I whip the truck around and hit the accelerator. As soon as I park next to her building, I jump out. The last time I was here, I was seeing red, but now I'm able to take in more details. There's a cheap storm door with vertical metal bars and ornamental scrollwork that probably looked new in the sixties. Its metal used to be painted white, but now it's mostly rust, and large chips of paint flake off when I open the door with a god-awful screech, like nails on a chalkboard. Blue painter's tape is holding together the cracked glass on the other side.

I'm taken aback when the door behind the rusty one has a broken lock. *How did I not see that before?* Anybody could just meander in here. I remember her apartment number from when she gave me her address, and I locate her name on one of the interior mailboxes to confirm I'm right. Again, *anybody* could do it. I head upstairs and stand outside her door like I did once before. This time I knock.

As soon as she opens the door, I step over the threshold, crushing my lips against hers. My hands cup the sides of her neck, and she grips my forearms. Walking her backward into the space, I kick the door shut and groan as she responds to my kiss with equal fervor. I'm lost in her.

She slides a palm to my nape, raking her nails down my scalp and sending chills down my arms. *I love it when she does that.* I slip one of my hands into her back pocket, letting my fingers grasp the globe of her ass. Blood is rushing south. Despite every instinct coursing through me, I release her. I have to think clearly, or I will end up fucking her right where we stand. Though, I've had worse ideas.

I press my forehead to hers, and we chuckle through panting breaths.

"You forgot to kiss me good night," she says.

"I'm a fucking idiot."

Sudden movement in my peripheral draws my gaze through the rest of her apartment… well, her studio. My lips part, and I turn in a circle, regarding her living conditions.

On top of being small, the walls are painted with so many

water stains it almost looks intentional. They extend to the carpet, which was probably beige when it was first installed. To her credit, she's done everything possible to make it homey, but there's only so much lipstick you can put on a pig. I've stayed at some shady places before, slept wrapped up in a tarp under the stars, lived in a camper for a bit, and I'd take any of those over this. I don't think twice about asking her to stay with me.

I need to find a delicate way to propose she move in with me without being insulting or pushy. *Be delicate. Be delicate...*

"This place is a dump," I blurt. *Well, I tried.*

She shoves my shoulder and laughs. "Beggars can't be choosers."

"Well, I'm begging you to stay with me instead."

The smile drops off her face. "Why? I live here."

I shake my head.

"Not anymore. You can't live in a place like this. It's not safe." I plead with her.

"Cal, it's not that bad. I make due. The rent is cheap, and I can pay month to month…"

"Yeah, no shit." Out of the corner of my eye, something scurries across the floor, and this time, I spot it. My eyes track the small brown rat as it runs along the side of her half-deflated air mattress that sits on the floor behind her. *Oh, hell no.*

"What's your pet's name?" I give a chin lift in its direction.

Her brow knits in confusion. "I don't have a pet."

I point behind her, and she turns, scrambling backward and bumping into me. I catch her so she doesn't trip. "Looks like you do now."

"Ugh!" She shudders. "I hate rats."

"That's what I thought. Pack a bag. We'll come back for the rest of your stuff tomorrow."

She nods, still backing away from the unwelcome rodent. "Okay… Okay, yup." Keeping it in her sights, she picks up her backpack, the one I'm all too familiar with. She stuffs it with a few necessary things like her phone charger, some toiletries, a sweatshirt, socks, underwear, and her EMT uniform. "Wait, I work tomorrow. I can follow you in my car to your house."

"I'll take care of it. We can pick up your car in the morning." I'm done spending any more time here. We already know we can get along in close quarters. *Mostly.* It doesn't have to be forever, but I like the idea of her at my place where I know she'll be safe.

CHAPTER 45

Scottie

My skin feels like it's crawling after seeing that thing. Rats give me the heebs. Only a few hours earlier I was sleeping on the mattress while it was tiptoeing around my apartment. It was an easy decision.

"I don't even know where you live." The man owns my heart, and I have no idea what his home is like. I shake off the feeling. It's not like our situation is conventional. Not by a long shot. There's already a chasm of loss forming in my chest, but for now, I'll pretend and enjoy what few weeks I have left with Callahan. There's no use in moping through them.

"It's not far. But you should know the living room is currently under construction."

"Rats?" I ask.

"Happy to say my place is rat free."

"Marvelous."

He turns onto Spencer Avenue, and I squirm in my seat. This is the street my house is on. My lips part slightly as we approach the modest Victorian. I hope we drive far enough down so I can point it out to him. When it comes into view, a smile spreads across my face.

"There's a house I wanna show you," I tell him, straightening my spine and leaning forward.

"Okay." He chuckles. "Where?"

Just as I'm about to point it out, he flips on his blinker and slows, turning into the driveway that runs parallel to the house. *My* house. My jaw drops.

He cranes his neck to look around, then his eyes find mine again. "What house is it?"

"You live here?" I point out the window, like an idiot. "Th-th-this house?"

His head cocks to the side. "Yesss?"

I clap a hand over my mouth. "I run by this house! Like all the time!" Leaning forward, I peer through the windshield to get a better view. I can't take my eyes off it.

He matches my excitement. "No way! So do I!"

Shaking my head, I cup his bicep. "No, you don't understand. This is *my* house. I mean, it's *your* house, but… but it's also my house."

He slides the back of his hand over my forehead. "Are you sure Matt gave you the all-clear this morning?"

I'm still staring out the window, dumbstruck. It's dark, but I can make out enough of it thanks to a couple streetlights and the ones brightly glowing on the exterior of the house.

"No, I'm fine. I just, I love this house. That's why I was always running here. I would go by it on purpose because I love it so much. It's my dream house."

He laughs. "Seriously?"

"Yes!" I say with a huge smile. "I've always wondered what the inside looks like, who lived here, and what their life was like. I thought it was a family of four. One time I came by, there was a couple and they had two ki—Oh! I bet that was your sister's family!"

"They drop in every now and then, check on the house if I'm away for an especially long assignment."

My eyes get misty. "I just—I just can't believe you live *here*. I—Can I see the inside?"

His house has been a tangible goal that I've been working toward since arriving to Sky Ridge and I never knew it.

Cal winces. "Oooh, I had plans for us to camp out tonight. I hear fresh air is really good for you," he replies with a smirk, then opens the driver's door. "Come on, I'll give you the grand tour."

Bounding out of the truck, I hurry behind him toward the front door. It's even more charming up close. Following him up the steps, my eyes trace every ornamental bracket and floorboard on the wraparound porch. Unbelievable.

He unlocks the door and holds it open for me to enter. I want to pinch myself.

The first room has been stripped down, plastic sheeting covers the doorways, so I'm unable to see through, but these are the original floorboards, and they lead to the most elegant wooden staircase I've ever seen. "Like I said, the living room and parlor, and this whole area is still under construction."

"Wow."

He leads me through a large slice in the heavy-duty plastic. "This is the dining room that I never use unless Teddy, Logan, and the kids come over."

The walls have been painted a dusty blue, and the white crown molding along the perimeter is carved with delicate details.

We continue to the kitchen, also finished. It has a modern twist to the original design with updated appliances and a kitchen island, and butcher block countertops throughout. "You have remarkable talent."

"Thanks." He takes the compliment easily. His skill and craftsmanship are evident by the work he's done. He knows it looks good but downplays the pride. It leaves me smiling; he's kind of adorable when he's not being a cocky bastard.

"What?"

"Nothing. You've done a marvelous job. I'm thoroughly impressed by your handiwork."

We make our way around the rest of the first floor, which includes the laundry room, den, and an unfinished "gathering room" with a stunning fireplace. He briefly tells me his plans for these rooms over the winter, and I hang on his every word. For now, those spaces are stuffed with furniture that's been relocated due to construction in other areas of the house.

"The second floor was finally completed last year." I follow him up the curved stairs, biting my lip in anticipation as my fingers trail smoothly along the rich wood banister. We reach the upstairs hallway. He points to an open doorway immediately to our left. "Guest bedroom without a bed." Then the door across from it. "Bathroom." I sneak a glance into the spacious open bedroom. It's painted a soft green.

I follow him down the hall. "Guest bedroom *with a bed*," he says, pointing into another bedroom with a queen-size bed and a dresser. At the end of the hall are two doors. He opens the one to the left. The turret. I grin ear to ear and step through the doorway. I've always wanted to see inside one of these. The octagonal-shaped room is surrounded by tall windows, making the slight vault in the ceiling appear domed. A set of bunk beds stick out from one of the walls.

"My niece and nephew stay in this room. They like to pretend it's a castle."

Oh, my heart. The corners of my mouth turn downward, and my eyes grow big at the kindness of his soul. He chuckles at my pout. I'm completely charmed by him. This room is a piece of that soft side he hides, and it's another facet of him to love.

"I can see why."

"Come on, sap." He takes my hand, leading me out of the turret and to the last room. "This one is mine." Callahan stands back, gesturing for me to enter before him.

Crossing the threshold, I would know it's Cal's room without him saying anything. The smoky, cedar aroma is strongest here. Deep jade-colored walls foster a moody, intimate vibe. It's a juxtaposition from the other bright and airy bedrooms. It's by far the largest, with a king-size bed in the center. Between the scent, wood accents, and moose antler sheds, his bedroom reminds me of the thick Pacific Northwest rainforests. Cal belongs in nature; the outdoors are his home as much as this house is. He strides through one of the doorways and flicks on a light.

"The closet and bathroom are through here."

I take another minute to appreciate the subtle masculine details and view the street in front of the house. The sidewalk, where I ran how many times? On one of the walls are a few pictures in various sizes, framed and matted. Photos from wildfires. "Did you take these?"

"Huh?" Callahan peeks his head back into the bedroom. "Oh. Yeah."

"I like them." I turn to see him shirtless. "What are you doing?"

"Waiting on you," he says, disappearing again through the doorway.

I take the bait and walk through the closet and into the ensuite bathroom just as he turns on the water in the massive clawfoot tub.

My hand slaps over my mouth. "Is that original?"

He nods. "I can't get rid of it."

"God, no. It's far too beautiful!"

"No, I mean I *physically* can't get rid of it. It's like four hundred pounds."

I laugh, and he strips out of his boxers, pushing them down and stepping out. Damn, he's fine. He climbs into the tub and braces his arms on the sides, lowering into it and reclining back. He lifts his chin toward me. "Take off your clothes, and get in here. Come on, it'll feel good."

CHAPTER 46

CALLAHAN

While kissing Scottie in her apartment, my fingers threaded in her hair, and I felt some of the dirt she so desperately hoped to remove in the shower. I remembered her saying she had terrible water pressure at her apartment, so it makes for a great excuse to get her in the tub with me. Plus a few other bonuses: relieve sore muscles, see her naked, et cetera.

Watching her strip down to nothing heals the part of me that fractured earlier when I had to drive away from her. She came back to me, and my world is right again. Not sure what it is about this woman, but I have an overwhelming need to keep her close. After everything we've been through, seeing her in my space feels right. This is how it's meant to be. And discovering she's been dreaming about *this house* all this time? That can't be a coincidence.

She takes my hand, stepping in front of me into the tub, giving me a great view of her ass. Submerging into the soothing water, she groans.

I chuckle. "See?"

Scottie blows out a breath. "So good."

As soon as she's seated between my thighs, I wrap my arms

around her, sealing her back to my front. I lean back, bringing her with me. Laying skin to skin with Scottie might be my new happy place. My lids close, and we sigh at the same time. A small laugh escapes her. Our relaxation is perfectly synchronized.

"I could get used to this," she murmurs.

"Me too." I press a kiss to her hair. "You want me to get that dirt out?"

Her palms grip the sides of the tub, and she sits up. "Could you? I tried earlier but couldn't get it all."

"Of course."

I lift the copper handheld showerhead from its cradle and test the water temperature, that should do the trick. I bring it to her scalp, and she tilts her chin higher to give me more access. I jostle the saturated strands, raking through them with my fingers. I'm pleased to see the tiny black specs of dirt and sand peppering the bathwater.

"It's coming out now," I reassure her, then smile. "You look hot like this. Clutching the tub and arching your back... I like that."

"Glad you're enjoying yourself," she says through a small giggle.

"I'd enjoy it more if you turned around," I tease.

"If you get the dirt out, I'll do whatever you want."

"Oh yeah? Anything?"

"Anything."

"I like the sound of that."

"Me too."

I work through each section of her hair. I have to open the drain on the tub at some point because the water is getting too high. After twenty minutes of combing through her locks, I give her the all-clear. I'll be damned if there's a spec of sand remaining. I drop the showerhead back into the water and adjust the knob to re-warm the bath.

She moans, adding to the partial erection I'm sporting. Wringing out her tresses, she twists it up and relaxes against my chest. "Thank you."

"Anytime."

Her head rests on my shoulder. Holding the handheld showerhead underwater, I use the high pressure to massage our thighs and knees. "You're going to spoil me."

My hand slides between her breasts. I brace an open palm at the base of her throat, stroking my thumb back and forth over her soft skin. "You've earned some spoiling."

Bringing the water back to her tired legs I creep higher and higher. She sucks in a breath.

"Just relax," I croon. A lot of shit has gone down today, and I want to see her unwind.

Scottie melts into me on an exhale.

My hand slips under the water and travels down her stomach. "Still with me?"

"Yeah." Her voice is soft and seductive. "Don't stop."

My middle finger parts her lips, grazing her clit, and she opens her legs wider for me.

Targeting the spray between her thighs has her back arching again. "Relax your muscles, just feel. Ride it out."

Slumping against me, I bring the pressure to her clit. She startles, then softens her muscles like I've instructed. "That's my girl." She makes a small O with her lips and takes a slow breath, as if she's meditating. It's perfect.

"Whoa," she murmurs.

The pleasure painted on her face has my cock fully hardened. She's stunning like this.

Except for the powerful surge of water hidden under the surface, we remain as still as possible to keep water from sloshing over the side and onto the floor. She weeps as the pressure turns into a pulsing flutter with the push of a button. "You're doing great."

"Mm-hm." It's almost a whine.

"I like that you've been fantasizing about my house," I whisper against her wet hair.

She nods, blowing out another breath.

"I'm going to make you come in every single room until you call it home."

Her gasp puts a smug grin on my face. Directing the pulse to where she needs it most, I use my free hand to pinch her nipples, and her rose-colored lips part, a hint of a smile lingers. "*There*," she squeaks. Fingers dig into my thighs, and she arches against me. Shallow waves roll on the surface of the bathwater as she comes with a sweet sigh, rocking her hips. *Fucking hell.*

"Ride it out. Keep coming just like that," I growl. The sounds she makes getting off punch right through me. It spurs a primal need to shove my cock deep inside her.

She must read my mind.

"Callahan?"

"Yeah, baby?"

"I need you. Please." Those sexy whimpers have a sweat breaking out across my brow. "Take me to bed and fuck me."

The words administer a kick of adrenaline, and I stand, stepping out. Her hand trembles when she reaches for me, arousal still buzzing through her veins. I grab a towel, gliding it over the remaining droplets trickling off her body.

I kneel through the pain in my knees and blot her legs one at a time. Afterward, I dry myself off and cup her chin, admiring her blown pupils and the radiant flush on her cheeks after she comes. It's my favorite version of her. Soft and blissed-out eyes stare back at me with just enough spark to tell me she's begging for it.

I bite my bottom lip, imagining all the ways I want to take her. "You're the most gorgeous thing I've ever seen."

She rises to her tiptoes and kisses me. I love this girl.

Fuck. I love her.

As soon as she's in my bed, I'm bracing my elbows over her and lining myself up. We regard each other the same way, as if three words are passing between us. Scottie's fingers press into my biceps as she prepares to be stretched around me. Usually, I'm impatient, rushed, eager to satisfy a need. This time is different. I sink inside her slowly. She inhales but keeps her gaze locked on mine. Her ocean eyes shimmer, and I take her mouth in an equally unhurried kiss, every stroke of my tongue deliberate, and spill every emotion I have onto her lips.

When she's adjusted to my size, I begin moving, and every thrust is steadfast and intentional. *No way in hell I'm letting this go.* She cups my face with her hands, and I seal my mouth over hers again. I trace the seam of her lips, and she opens for me. We lick and tease, consumed by each other. I fill her pussy, and she moans against me. *So fucking perfect.*

Her fingertips skate over my scalp, and chills ricochet down my spine. No one has ever touched me the way she does, made me *feel* the way she does—in every adaptation.

I need her to know how I feel; my words are out before I can stop them.

"I love you."

Her lips part. It's been over five years since I've spoken those words, and even then they didn't hold the fire they do now. I swallow, and it's as if she's reading the thoughts in my head, and for a split second, I wonder if she's feeling the same way.

"Still with me?" I ask. *It was too much. I should have waited.* She smiles. "I love you too."

I swear every molecule of air leaves my lungs. "Yeah?"

"Just because we figured it out early doesn't make it any less real."

My lips find hers again. This confession of love delivers a burst of energy to me, and I snap my hips with a newfound vigor. She fists my hair at the roughness and arches beneath me, squeezing her eyelids shut. "Oh my god, Cal. More."

"I'll give you anything you want, Prescott. I'll give you the fucking world, but I wanna see you look me in the eyes when you ask."

She gifts me with her stunning blue irises. "Fuck me harder, Callahan. I want all of you."

I smirk. "Atta girl. I love it when you use your words."

Sitting up on my heels, I yank her closer, pulling her ass into my lap while I pound into her. Each thrust hammers, causing Scottie to press her fingers against the wood behind her to keep from getting thrown into the headboard. My palms rest on her bent knees, parting them so I can marvel her exquisite body as I devour it. One hand slides down her soft thigh until I'm massaging figure-eights over her clit, the way I watched her do it in the fire tower.

"Is this how you like being taken?"

"Yes," she cries.

"Show me, Prescott. Come on this fucking cock."

Her raptured cries spur me on. *How did I get so lucky?* Muscles tighten around my length, and I smile as her impending orgasm amplifies. "That's my girl."

With that, she begins fucking me back.

"Goddamn," I growl. "That's right, take what you deserve. It's all yours. I'm yours." She owns me like no one ever has or ever will. "Make me come, just for you."

Her mouth drops open, and her abs ripple as she bends forward, slapping her trembling hands against my forearms to squeeze them with all her might while she holds on to the euphoria coursing through her. "That's my girl, just like that, baby."

"Who do you belong to, baby?" I gruff, panting, stuffing her tight pussy over and over. Her words are mumbled, then she stops speaking altogether. I feel the second she's toppled over by the wave of her orgasm. Fuck. "Tell me, Prescott."

"You. Only you," she says between sobs. "Don't pull out." As if she needs to tell me.

Two strokes later, I'm coming. This time it doesn't feel like an explosion, it feels like being put back together. Like finding that missing piece. Like being made whole again.

I bracket my elbows on each side of her when I collapse. "I love you so fucking much." I crush my mouth to hers, and she circles her arms around my shoulders, her fingernails trailing over my skin and sending me into a deep relaxed state, in a cadence that's ours alone.

She moves her lips with mine. It's real love. I can taste it in her kiss, feel it in her touch, and see it in the sparkling blue eyes I adore so much.

CHAPTER 47

CALLAHAN

I curse the alarm on her phone when it goes off at 5:30 a.m. and wrap my arm tightly around her middle, not ready to let her go. I gotta remind myself she'll be back after her shift, but after hearing about her conversation with Jonathan yesterday, I worry. I barely slept last night, but it had nothing to do with my memories and everything to do with him asking her to go back. There's no way I'm subjecting her to that life. I saw the defeat in her eyes. I won't let anyone steal the peace she's found here.

Scottie is my home, the same way Sky Ridge is hers.

She belongs in whatever place makes her happy, where she can live fearlessly and thrive. If that was back in Arkansas, I wouldn't stop her, but she's sacrificing herself when she's already sacrificed enough.

The thought of Scottie returning to the people who broke her is enough for me to steal her away to the top of Quell's again. We can stay in our lookout, putting logs on the fire, and spending afternoons in each other's arms.

She stretches in my embrace and groans. "I feel like we just went to bed."

"Me too." I press my lips to her neck. Scottie's sleep was as restless as mine, but even in the short intervals of rest, her body sought mine out in the sheets every time we strayed too far from each other. There's a comfort in using up the same amount of space we had in the fire tower. But, as much as I want her to stay here all day, I have a lot I need to accomplish in the next twelve hours.

My grip loosens. "Time to get up, baby."

She hums, and flutters her lashes, pulling away from me. I ignore the empty feeling of her absence. *She's coming back.*

Her hand slaps the bedside table until she feels her phone. Squinting, she checks the time. "Shoot," she mutters. "I'm gonna be late."

I sit up and scrub a palm down my face. "You want coffee?"

She shakes her head. "I'll grab some at the station."

I swing my legs over the side of the bed and stretch, my joints popping and clicking like I've added forty years onto my age.

She snatches up her navy EMT uniform and hops around as she clumsily wrangles her foot into the pant leg. In the bathroom, she's brushing her teeth with one hand and awkwardly buttoning her shirt with the other. I stand behind her, resting my chin on her shoulder, then push her fingers aside and finish the rest of the buttons.

"'Hank yew," she says around her toothbrush.

"Hey, last night? We didn't use protection."

Her brow furrows, and she extracts her toothbrush, tilting her head up to keep the frothy toothpaste from dribbling out. "I'm on birth control."

"What?" I nearly shout. "Since when?"

"I said I didn't want kids, remember? My injection is good for another year."

"And you're just *now* telling me?"

She shrugs and continues brushing her teeth, then spits into the sink. "Sorry, I just thought you wanted to use condoms as an extra precaution." She rinses her mouth with water.

"No... God, no! Nobody *wants* to use condoms."

"Oh, well, then we can stop using them." She grins, showing off her pearly smile.

Shaking my head, I chuckle. "I'm gonna go warm up the truck," I say, kissing her cheek.

I throw on a pair of jeans and a long-sleeve tee and grab my keys. Within five minutes, she's climbing into the cab of my truck with a fresh face and her hair in a tight bun. I'm impressed with the short amount of time it took us to go from bed to vehicle. Must have been less than ten minutes.

"Got your car keys?" I ask. I make a mental reminder to add my house key to her keyring.

She nods, and we're pulling up to that piece of shit apartment in no time. "Can I have your apartment key? I'm going to take care of a few things today. I'll lock up on my way out."

"Oh," she says with raised eyebrows. "Sure. But don't feel like you have to do anything. I can take care of it after work."

The corner of my mouth curves up, and I hold out an open hand while she wiggles the brass key off the ring. It's not like she has a ton of stuff. I'll be shocked if it takes more than one trip once I get everything loaded up in boxes.

As soon as she presses it to my palm, I wrap my fingers around hers and grasp her chin with my other hand to give her a kiss. "I'll see you tonight," I say. It's a promise.

"Yeah." Her eyes have a shine to them when she swallows. "I'll see you tonight."

My throat burns hearing the doubt in her voice, as if we only have a few *see you tonights* before our time runs out.

"It's going to be okay."

Scottie weakly hums in agreement, but there's no conviction

in it. She pops the handle on her door and hops out. I watch her get into her car and back out of the parking lot.

Time to get to work.

I'm halfway through packing up the things in her apartment when my gaze lands on a piece of paper with the name of a local hotel and a room number. *Jackpot.* That saves me time having to call around to find where Jonathan is staying. I rip the piece of paper off the notepad and shove it in my pocket, then drop the blank pad of paper into the box next to the single pot and pan she owns. I clock a rat in the corner of the room, not sure if it's the same one from yesterday or his buddy.

"Ya know, usually I'm not a big fan of rats," I tell him, "but you were a great wingman yesterday, so I'm gonna let it slide. Looks like you'll live to see another day."

It only takes me an hour to pack up her belongings. We will have to deep clean all this shit thanks to the rodent roommates she acquired while she was absent.

Once everything is loaded in the truck and I've locked up her studio, I find the rental office. Naturally, there's a security buzzer on his door but not the other apartments.

I hit the speaker button. "Dropping off keys."

The door clicks as it's unlocked, and I enter the office without a courtesy knock and stand at his desk. He seems startled to see me. "Does Prescott Timmons owe you anything for rent?" I'll pay any outstanding debt she has to get her out of this place.

"Well, I'll have to look..." He turns to his computer.

He clicks around, scrolling his mouse a few times, but at last shakes his head. "No, she's up-to-date." *Of course she is.*

"Great. Here's her key." I drop it on his desk and steal a Post-it Note and pen, scribbling down my address. "She's moved out—"

"Now wait, she needs to give a written sixty-day vacancy notice," he argues with a smirk.

I laugh, impressed he has the balls to ask for a sixty-day notice on that rat sanctuary. "Yeah, she's not doing that."

I slap the sticky note in front of him. "Here's the address you can send her security deposit to." I glare at him until I get a reluctant nod. I'll be watching for that check in the mail. The fact he even took on a tenant in that studio is upsetting, knowing it was Scottie? Now, that straight-up pisses me off. He took advantage of her situation.

I drop the pen on the desk and walk out. "You've got rats, by the way," I call out as soon as I reach the exterior door, loud enough for the renters checking their mailboxes down the hall to hear.

I swing through a drive-through and scarf down some fast food while I sit in my truck outside the hotel. I'm not sure how long this visit will last. I've practiced what I want to say at least a dozen times since Scottie told me how their conversation went. If it ends up being anything close to that, it will be a long one. I play it over in my mind once more, then take another sip of my soda before I hop out.

Automatic doors part from the center, and I stroll through the lobby toward the elevators.

I extract the piece of paper in my pocket after pressing the up arrow and wait. Room 415. After a loud ding, I step inside, selecting the button for his floor. My reflection glares back at me in the silver doors. I look the same as I did a week ago, but I couldn't be further from the old me. As soon as the elevator climbs to the fourth floor and I exit, I'm hit with the smell of bleached towels and carpet deodorizer. I reach his hotel door and stand outside, taking one last cleansing breath, then knock twice.

Footsteps fall on the other side of the door, then the chain slides across the track. One turn of the knob later, I'm standing face-to-face with the man who's trying to take Scottie away from me. This guy is her friend, but he's not mine.

"Hey."

The moment he recognizes me, his face falls ever so slightly. Something tells me I took a big shit on his day. We regard each other in silence before he eventually moves aside.

"Come in," he offers.

I'm hoping we can remain civil, but there's no way to get through this conversation without at least some disagreement. I stuff my fists into my pockets and stride past him. He takes a seat on the edge of one of the queen-size beds and leans forward, scrubbing a palm down his face before straightening his spine and resting his hands on his thighs. I lean against the desk across from him, crossing my ankles. "Not sure if you remember me—"

"Callahan, right?"

"Yes."

He nods, an understanding of who I am to Scottie passes between us.

I clear my throat. "I don't know you. You don't know me. But we have something in common, we both love Scottie. I'm not sure what your plans are for heading back home, but there's something we have to discuss... I think you know why I'm here and what I'm about to tell you."

His chest expands as he takes in a breath. He must have known this was coming.

"If you care about that woman in any way, I need you to divorce her."

"I will, as soon as—"

"No. Divorce her now. Let her go."

His eyes turn glassy. "I can't."

I cross my arms. *"You can."*

"How much did Scottie tell you about where we come from?"

Sighing, I bow my head. I don't care if they escaped from a state penitentiary, Scottie is not going back there. "She's told me enough."

"She must not have," he argues. "I assume she at least told you about our arrangement. Here's the thing, I'm being black-mailed. They are threatening to out me to our community—"

"*Your* community. Scottie doesn't belong to them anymore."

He opens his mouth in rebuttal but then thinks better of that decision. "I'll be exiled, I will lose my job, my medical license, my home, my friends, my family, my safety—everything. If I don't return with Scottie, I will lose *everything*."

"And what will Scottie lose by returning? What about her life?"

His expression turns sympathetic as tears swell. He can't even look at me right now. He knows this is wrong. "I love her."

"If you love Scottie half as much as you say you do, you'll do this for her. She's covered for you her whole life, this is your chance to return the favor."

He stands and crosses his arms. "What do you want me to do?"

I throw my hands out to the side. "Call their bluff! Look, you are obviously important to her, which means you're important to me." *And he's lucky as hell that's the case, or we'd be meeting under very different circumstances.* "We will do everything we can to help you, but you have to take the first step. Who you choose to love is nothing to be ashamed of or fear. Staying in that *community* is far more damaging than leaving it."

He shakes his head.

"Scottie has always cared for you as you are, that doesn't change. From where I stand, she's your real family, so what are you really going back to?"

He draws in a breath, releasing it before speaking. "I understand our relationship is hard for most people to understand, but I just need to get her back until things calm down. After that, we can leave together—"

"No." My tone is sharp. "She gave you that opportunity months ago, you didn't take it. You may not like the sound of this, but Scottie is not leaving Sky Ridge. She's not safe with The Fold. She may be too fucking selfless to guard the home she's found here, but I'm not."

He scoffs, dropping his arms and looking away.

"Scottie lives in Sky Ridge, and Scottie's all you have. You deserve a life as much as she does, so maybe it's time to come to her. We will support you while you make your separation from the church and help you get established out here, but you can't expect her to do all the work. It's going to take effort from you too. She's fought too hard to get to where she is."

"I would be risking everything if I left."

"She'd be risking everything if she went back. You have the chance at a real start here. *Take it.*"

Jonathan stands and paces as he runs his hands through his hair. He pauses, glaring at me.

I shrug. "Aren't you tired of feeling trapped? I'm not telling you to come out, that's on your own time, but I am asking you to at least honor her request for a divorce before you leave town."

"I don't understand what the rush is—"

"Because I can't marry her until you divorce her," I spit out, jabbing a finger to my chest. The words catch me off guard, but now that they're out in the open, I don't regret them. It's the truth.

"She's still *my* wife, this is a discussion she and I should be having privately. Our faith doesn't concern you."

I bark out a laugh. He can't be serious. When her faith becomes something she needs to be protected from, it's of my concern. And referring to Scottie as his wife triggers something inside me, so I raise my voice. "And what's in the best interest of your *wife*, huh? What about what *she* wants? What about *her* safety? If you want to play the husband card, then act like one! Stop being a coward and protect *her*, because from where I stand, I'm doing a better job than you are."

He doesn't deserve her.

I exhale some of my anger and calm my demeanor. "Do what's best for her," I plead. "Let her go."

The silence between us is deafening while we stare each other down, and his jaw tics.

He crosses his arms in front of his chest. "I need to think about it."

I speak my next words clearly. "Here's what you need to think about: I'm offering you a chance to start over, and that offer has an expiration. I don't want to make an enemy out of you, it's obvious you're an important person to the woman I love, but I will bring hell to your doorstep if you fight me on this."

He smirks. "Is that a threat?"

"It's a promise." I straighten. "You will not be leaving with Scottie. She's staying in Sky Ridge."

My anger has reduced to a simmer by the time I'm walking down the aisles of the grocery store with my sister. I had to get some of this shit off my chest, but I also had to restock my fridge and pantry. Since I never got around to calling her yesterday, I figured I could make it up to her now. It's been a lot to catch up on. She's still reeling from the whole thing with Jonathan when I drop another bomb on her.

She grabs the side of my cart, stopping it in the middle of the aisle. "You told her you loved her?!"

"Yeah."

Her eyes widen, and she grips my arm. "Did she say it back?"

A small grin creeps onto my face. "She did."

Teddy slaps my shoulder. "Oh my God. This is like serious-serious. And now she's staying with you? Do you think it's too fast?"

I shake my head. "I know how it looks from the outside, but it doesn't feel rushed."

Her smile grows. "That's really great. I'm happy for you, Cal. You needed this."

I needed *her.* "Thanks," I say, pushing the cart forward again. "I'm thinking of making her that garlic chicken thing we used to have."

"Nice. I just made it last week for Logan and the kids."

"How are the kiddos?"

We exit the aisle, and move toward the poultry section while Teddy regales me with Dalton's latest funny story. I'm deciding on a pack of chicken when we're interrupted by the last guy I should be seeing when I'm in a mood.

"Hey Cal. Good to see you and Scottie made it back down safely," Dave says, stepping up next to me. "Sounds like you had quite the adventure."

I swear the universe is testing me.

"Yup." I clench my jaw.

"It's been nice to have her back at the station." He's baiting me.

"She missed a day, not a week," I remind him.

His smarmy smile grates on my nerves. "Well, when you're used to having her around, one day can feel like a lot."

Teddy sighs. "Shit."

We spin to look at her, and she holds up her spread fingers. "I'm just here for the violence… and—and… this turkey." She smiles innocently, wrestling a sixteen-pound bird from the refrigerated bay next to us and dropping it in my cart.

Great.

I roll my eyes at her and turn back to face Dave, briefly checking our surroundings before I continue.

Leaning toward him, I lower my voice. "I didn't fight you when you slept with Molly, I hope she's happy with you, truly. But if I find out you try to interfere with *my* Scottie, or spend extra time with her, or make her feel uncomfortable, I will feed you your fucking teeth."

I flip the chicken over in the skillet as it sizzles, and the scent of garlic is mouthwatering. Scottie should be home any minute. Overall, I think I made some progress today. I moved Scottie into my house, gave her notice at her apartment, had a nice chat with her future ex-husband, and even made an appointment with a therapist. Which, after leaving the hotel and grocery store today, I'm going to need.

Jonathan and I remained civil during our discussion, but unfortunately, I didn't walk away with a solid answer from him. Regardless of what he decides, Scottie isn't going anywhere.

Her car pulls into the driveway just as I glance out the window. My shoulders relax at the sight of her. I should be concerned with how fast I've adjusted to the idea of moving her in here, but it feels normal. There's a peacefulness about her. She has a soothing presence whenever she's near. It's been like that since the beginning, even when I wasn't ready to receive it.

I meet her at the back door, opening it up.

"Don't hug me yet, I gotta take a shower. Had a pretty messy call today." She toes off her shoes at the door.

"Thought you weren't going on calls?"

"I'm not, but I still cleaned the rig afterward."

I wince, baring my teeth. "Do I wanna know?"

"Nope," she exclaims, popping the P.

She drops her bag at the door, then steers past me. "I don't know what you're making, but it smells amazing!" she yells as she sprints up the stairs. Less than a minute later, I hear the shower turn on.

On the way to the stove, I grab tongs and click them twice before removing the chicken breasts from the pan and setting them aside. Then I pour in some chicken broth and heavy cream, stirring it around. This might not be the healthiest thing in the world, but damn is it delicious. And after a season of eating prepackaged food, I'm ready for something homemade. While the sauce thickens in the pan, I remove the salad I made earlier from the fridge and set out a few plates.

I pause at my actions. "Holy shit. This doesn't even feel weird," I mutter, then laugh, amused at the entire ordeal. "Why doesn't this feel weird?"

Scottie returned to my house after work—we practically had a *Honey, I'm home!* moment, I'm making dinner, we're going to eat in the dining room, then probably watch a movie, and go to bed. She lives here now. There's a good chance I've been running off instinct since I went after her on Quell's. We were in survival mode. Now, it's all hitting at once. The interesting part is that I'm fine with it. All of it. Maybe keeping Scottie close is part of my survival.

When the shower turns off, I pluck a couple wine glasses from the rack, pour us each a glass, and place them on the dining room table. She meets me in the kitchen with wet hair, snaking her hands around me from behind as I plate the food. Spinning in her arms, I grab under her thighs and lift her up. She instinctively wraps her legs around my waist, and I steal her lips with mine. Her delicate fingers skim over the scruff on my cheeks, and she brushes her thumbs over my temples. Scottie pulls away, and we stare at each other. She's drinking all of me in, like she's memorizing every feature.

"What are you thinking?"

Her eyes shine, and she cocks her head to the side with a reluctant smile. "That I'm going to miss this."

"It's going to be okay." I press my forehead to hers. "I promised I wouldn't let you go. I'm keeping that promise."

CHAPTER 48

Scottie

Yawning, I slog through the parking lot of the fire station to my car after my last shift of the week. My resignation letter greets me in the passenger seat. My mind wanders as I drive to Callahan's place from the station. I've chosen to turn the letter in tomorrow. I couldn't bring myself to do it during the work week and deal with the questions and judgment of quitting a job after only a few weeks. God, I hope they let me return.

When Callahan said he met with Jonathan, my jaw practically hit the floor. I immediately peppered him with questions on what they discussed. Callahan raised his shoulders and said, "*I dunno, I just asked him to reconsider, that's all.*" He spoke as innocently as if he had bumped into a college buddy and asked what they've been up to. Like it was no big deal. I don't buy any of it, but Jonathan hasn't been returning my calls either.

My biggest concern is Callahan. I worry he's not taking this seriously. When we talk, it's as if he's in complete denial. He doesn't even pretend to be upset, which is maybe what hurts the most. It takes everything in me to paste a smile on my face when we're together. Every hour that passes is one more lost. Time is eating me alive. I can't even bring myself to look at clocks when I'm at home.

However, Jonathan's safety is a bigger concern. He says it's only a year, but I'm already making plans to have that cut in half. I will have us out of there in six months. I won't stay. I can't.

When I arrive at the house, the door is locked. He must not be home yet from his first therapy appointment. I was grateful that he found someone specialized for first responders with complex trauma. I couldn't be more proud of him for taking care of himself and keeping his word, but I'm also hurting for him. The road ahead will be arduous, and I won't be here to support him. The thought of him returning to an empty house when he's depleted after a difficult session leaves a lump in my throat. I don't want him to be alone.

I was on a waiting list for someone with a focus in religious trauma. Apparently, there's a lot of that going around in the Pacific Northwest. I'm not canceling it. They offer remote sessions, and if I can get out of Arkansas in six months, like I plan to, then I'll already be established. I'll be paying out of pocket since it's out of network, but I'd do it anyway because The Fold can't find out. *Why have therapy when you can pray about it instead?*

Toeing off my shoes, I run upstairs to fit a shower in before he gets home. It's the fastest shower I've ever taken. I'm pulling on leggings and a sweatshirt when I hear his steps downstairs. Another sound I will miss. Even his footsteps bring my soul peace. I run a brush through my damp hair and fly downstairs.

He's sifting through today's mail on the dining room table when I pass through the slit in the thick plastic sheeting.

"Hey!" I say. "How was it?"

The smile when he notices me melts my heart. He draws me into his chest and wraps his arms around me. I do the same. Callahan presses a kiss to my hair and rests his chin on the top of my head.

"It was good. Just a get-to-know-you thing, but I like him. I think it'll be a good fit. He thinks I might be a good candidate for EMDR—it's this eye-movement thing. Seems interesting, I said I'd give it a try."

With my ear against him, half of the words reverberate through his chest wall. I close my eyes and memorize the familiarity. Since we've returned from Quell's Peak, I've been in his bed every night. Our nightly conversations while cuddling have become one of my favorite rituals. I'm soaking up every moment with him, savoring my time, trying to be present despite my thoughts reminding me that in only a couple weeks I'll be halfway across the country, sharing my bed with a man who isn't mine. Even though I care deeply for Jonathan, the idea tastes bitter in my mouth. I belong next to Callahan. Especially when he's working so hard on himself.

"I'm so proud of you."

He chuckles. "Weird, you haven't mentioned it!" His words are dripping with sarcasm. I've probably been a little bit repetitive lately, but facing your demons takes a lot of courage. I have no idea what'll happen once I start my therapy journey, but I know it will be necessary. There are a lot of beliefs I struggle to let go of, and my relationship with God is confusing. I'll always have my faith, but it's been a struggle to find out what that means or where I belong. I still harbor a lot of fear and guilt over leaving. And anger at The Fold. I'd like to find a new church eventually, but I'm not ready yet.

I press my fingers to his chest for balance as I rise on my toes to kiss him. His lips curve into a smile against mine, and he picks me up with one arm, sweeps the mail to the side with the other, and deposits me on the end of the dining room table. He slips his hands under the hem of my baggy sweatshirt and pushes it higher around my ribcage, skating his thumbs along the underside of my breasts.

"I've been thinking I should start making progress on that list

SLOANE ST. JAMES

of rooms to fuck you in," he says, with a mischievous grin. "What do you think?"

My legs part for him to stand between. "I think we should get started right away."

"Me too," he says through a laugh, giving me a chin lift. "Lay back, baby."

I'm reclining back just as there's a knock at the door, and we groan in unison at the interruption.

"Don't move," he warns.

I fist his shirt and pull him close. "If you take too long, I'm going to get started without you." I give him a soft shove, and he stumbles back a step.

He backs away slowly, still facing me. "You start without me, you're going to pay for it later."

"Promise?"

He shakes his head and turns, disappearing through the heavy plastic to answer the front door. I hear his voice briefly before a second set of footsteps echo in the room.

Next, I hear Callahan, taking a solemn tone. "I'll get her."

He peeks his head in the dining room, all the mischief has slid off his face. "Scottie, there's somebody here to see you."

I furrow my brow and scoot off the end of the table.

"I'm going to give you some privacy, if you need me, I'll be upstairs." Then he's gone.

I run my hands over my hair and straighten my sweatshirt. *What the hell is going on?* When I squeeze through the slit in the tarp, I see Jonathan at the door and almost trip over my feet. It wasn't the way I'd planned to tell him I moved in with Callahan. What he must be thinking right now...

Jonathan clears his throat, and my focus returns. With his hands behind his back, he peers around the room, taking in the bare floors, tools, and random boards lying around. "I like your upgrade."

"Hi... I meant to tell you, I just—"

His smile is almost shy as he stares down at his feet. It's like we're strangers. My heart breaks a little; I don't want him to hurt. He lightly scuffs one of his shoes over the floor. "It is what it is, right?"

My lips roll together, and I nod, mirroring his posture.

"I, um, I have something for you." His voice is somber. I look up, and he raises his gaze to mine again. He reveals the papers he's been holding behind him and hands them to me. My vision blurs when I see the words at the top. "I picked up a divorce packet from the courthouse today. I, uh, I've filled out my portion. There's still more forms before we can file, but it's a start."

My eyes swim with tears. I can't believe he did this. My jaw drops, and I throw my arms around him. "Thank you." We hold each other for a moment in silence before he pulls away.

"I'm sure Callahan told you he paid me a visit the other day."

"He didn't say much about it."

"Well, he had plenty to say to me." Jonathan chuckles, raising his eyebrows. "I sat with it for a couple days. Thought about what he said, but it was mostly what you said... This is the longest I've been away from The Fold."

The corner of my mouth tips up. "Feels good, huh?"

"It's a little scary, but there's more air here."

I remember that feeling. Like you've been breathing your whole life with a bag over your head, then suddenly someone takes it off and you realize how easy it is to drink in the air. It's effortless.

"Anyway, he set up a room for me a couple towns over. There's an organization that's willing to provide housing as I make the transition from The Fold. They even provide assistance for employment and transportation, as well as legal help for these sorts of situations. It's just to get me on my feet."

I look back to the stairs where Callahan retreated to, pressing a hand to my chest, my heart swelling. Cal saved Jonathan. He saved *me*.

"Have you contacted anyone at The Fold?" I turn back toward Jonathan.

He puffs out a sigh. "Not yet. There are a few things I have to get in order, banking and whatnot, before that happens. I told them about the three-week notice you needed for work, it's buying me some extra time. At the end of that three weeks..." He raises one shoulder. "We'll burn that bridge when we get to it."

He's taking a huge leap. I wrap my hand around his and squeeze.

"I don't know what will happen. Mom and Dad—" His voice cracks, and he meets my gaze. "You're the truest family I've ever had, you're the only person who has ever seen who I am and shown me love the way it's described in scripture. Love is patient, kind, and never ends. Your love has always been unconditional."

As he lifts the burden off my shoulders, it feels like I'm floating. The only thing keeping me on the ground is the knowledge that he's about to go through all the mixed emotions I felt leaving. I drove across the country, the temptation to turn around was strong, but I forced myself to keep going. It's not easy.

"There is so much good here." I set the papers on the floor and hug my arms around him again. "I promise you will find it, and until then, you'll have Cal and me. You're not alone."

He hugs me back. "I'm really glad you have Callahan. It's obvious he loves you." And that has never been more apparent, seeing as he moved a few mountains to keep me here. "It's powerful to witness."

His words have me tearing up, because I feel the same about him.

Jonathan chuckles. "And he's very protective over you."

"You have so much love to give, and I can't wait for you to find someone to give it to. It's indescribable."

"Yeah?"

"I mean, you gotta go through a survival exercise at the top of a mountain first... but yeah." I grin up at him and drop my arms to my sides. "Would you like to stay for dinner?" I ask.

He shakes his head. "I'm not sure if I'm ready for that yet."

The rejection stings a little, but I respect it. He's still processing our split. He's got a big journey ahead of him.

"I understand." I've already turned his world upside down with the divorce, I don't need to flip it inside out too.

"I think I'm gonna go back to the hotel. I just have to work through this alone for a bit."

My brows knit, and I lift a half smile. His request is familiar, and there's comfort in it. Whenever we had arguments at home, he always processed things by himself.

"Of course. I've got a few days off, do you want to grab lunch?"

"Maybe—oh, hey. I have a new email. I'll be sending some documents to you for, you know, everything." *The D-word.*

I give him one more hug. "I want to know you're okay."

He kisses my cheek. "I will be," he replies, and I sense he believes it. "It's a big adjustment, but you and Callahan? I couldn't be happier for you both. You deserve someone who deserves you... *For I know the plans I have for you,* right?"

"Plans to prosper you and not to harm you, plans to give you a hope and a future," I finish the passage.

"Bye, Prescott."

He lifts a hand, and I lean my head against the doorframe as he walks away. Deep in my soul, I know this is a step in the right direction for both of us, but it doesn't ease the ache of finality any less.

CHAPTER 49

CALLAHAN

Peering from our bedroom window, Jonathan climbs into the back of the cab he had waiting outside. I hold my breath as I leave the room, unsure of what condition Scottie will be in. Padding down the stairs, she's still at the door, watching the car drive away.

Standing behind her, I wait patiently. "He agreed to the divorce," she whispers. I cup her bicep, turning her into my chest and wrapping my arms around her in a bear hug.

"It's still hard, ya know?" she snivels.

I nod. "I know, baby."

"And you—you did all that for him. To keep me here. I don't even know how to process that. How do I thank you?" She's blubbering. I give her the time she needs to get it out, rubbing her back and standing in the bare entryway with her. After a minute, she sucks in a restoring breath, releasing it with a shudder.

"Is—is that what you talked to him about the other day?" She steps back, sweeping her palms over her face to clear her tear-stained cheeks.

I shove my hands in my pockets and shrug. "I did a little

research and found a program that I thought might help. I wasn't willing to let you go but knew that you would only be happy if Jonathan was safe. So I did what I needed to do. We may have briefly touched on the topic of divorce."

"Briefly?" She sniffles.

"I had to talk to him man-to-man. Both of us care about you, and... I wanted to make him understand my intentions."

"You have intentions?"

"I do."

Even with rosy cheeks from all the crying, she flushes a darker pink as she blushes.

"I'm not saying now," I clarify. "We're going to build some stability first. Better ourselves like we talked about. Obviously, things have escalated, but yeah, after that... when the time is right..." A small grin curves on her lips. "I'm coming for you, Prescott."

Her smile grows. "I'd like that."

I thread our fingers, guiding her toward the stairs. "Know what I'd like?"

She chuckles, following me up the steps. "I'll bet I can guess..."

Leading her to the bedroom, I drop her hand and find my pack in the closet, unzipping it and bringing forth the item I hope will cheer her up.

When I spin around, she is tugging her sweatshirt over her head. It drops to the floor in a heap, and her gaze catches on the gray plastic Battleship game in my grasp, causing her to break into laughter. It's the best sound after witnessing her fall apart downstairs.

"Wait! Is that—" She struggles to speak through the giggles.

I take in her topless body. I'll never get over how irresistible she is.

"Stripping down before we even begin, babe? I like your enthusiasm."

She points at the game boards. "You stole the game?"

I shrug. "Wanted a souvenir."

Her smile grows. "I'll never let you win."

Tossing the boards on the bed, I say, "Then let's save time and get down to business."

Her laughter is cut off by the doorbell. I hate the way her body stiffens, but when she looks toward the window and sees the pizza delivery car idling at the curb, her shoulders relax.

"Figured tonight called for an easy dinner." I plant a kiss on her cheek.

"I like the way you think," she says, bending over to grab her sweatshirt off the floor. *Damn.* My impulsive thoughts win, and I swat her ass as I slip out the door. "I'll meet you in the dining room."

We've been interrupted twice tonight, both for good reasons: divorce papers and pizza. However, now that we're no longer expecting visitors, I'm disconnecting that damn doorbell.

CHAPTER 50

Scottie

After dinner, Cal is finally able to get started on his goal of having sex in every room. It's been an emotional day, but I can't think of a better way to end it than on this dining room table. He sets me on the edge and presses his forehead to mine. His hands cup my neck as he holds me. When his lips graze mine, it's like falling for him all over again. This man has done so much for me and put me first. It's more than friendship, more than lovers, it's so much deeper than I ever knew love could be.

"What am I gonna do with you?" He gruffs.

"Make me yours," I whisper.

He lowers his hands, gripping behind my knees and yanking me closer. I rip my sweatshirt over my head, and it's not long before we're tearing off our clothes and tossing them on the floor, just like I've always wanted.

"So sweet," he comments on my damp underwear, then gathers them in his fist, dragging them upward until they're nestled tight over my clit. I deliver a squeak when the material bites into me as he jerks it taut.

"You're going to be my good girl, aren't you?"

"Mm-hm." His voice grounds me when the pleasure is overwhelming. It keeps me in the moment with him.

I squirm, and he strips the underwear off my legs, then spreads me open and drops to his knees, blowing a stream of cool air over my center and sending a chill up my spine. It conflicts with the hot pinch of fabric on my clit earlier. I'm dripping for him. His middle finger slips inside me, and my lashes flutter closed. God, this feels so good. He adds another, and I lower my back to the table. The cold wood heightens the sensation. I love feeling on display for him, because the way he looks at me with hunger in his eyes is something I've never experienced before him.

"Jesus, you have a pretty pussy."

He pumps in and out, and I drape my forearm over my mouth, trying to control my breaths. He curls his fingers inside me. Our eyes meet, and he chuckles when my body twitches, as if he takes pride in each muffled sound he pulls from my lungs.

"That's right, baby. Give me all your whimpers," he growls, leaning in and licking across my clit. My back arches, and I hold my breath, trying to stay quiet. He lifts his head and draws back his hand.

"Open your mouth, Prescott."

I sit up, part my lips, and he buries his fingers inside, spreading my arousal over my tongue.

"Suck until I say stop."

The second my mouth wraps around his two fingers, he groans, then drops his face between my thighs again and sucks my clit. My legs tremble against his jaw, and I moan. Heat rushes to my core, fanning out from the intense pleasure like aftershocks. It's so much all at once. The gleam in his eyes is wicked. He loves it when he has me coming apart at the seams.

My abs strain, right on the threshold of my climax when he stands, and I whine in frustration.

"The first time you come tonight will be on my cock."

I hardly recognize the desperate sounds I make, but they vibrate against his hand. He simply watches as I'm perched naked, quivering, and needy while I suck. My eyes are lost in the hazelnut color of his. Until I hear his belt buckle release.

I eagerly look down, waiting to see him. He replaces his fingers with his tongue, kissing me until I'm delirious from the taste and touch he provides. I'm lost in everything when I feel his crown at my entrance, then spread my thighs wider. He pushes inside, folding himself over me, and I whimper with relief.

Locking my legs around his waist, my heels press into his ass, and he takes it as a signal to rock his hips, driving inside me again and again. He wraps one arm around my lower back, and the other one fists my hair and tugs, lifting my chin to him. His mouth drops to the spot where my shoulder and neck meet. He grazes the tip of his nose up the column of my throat until he's kissing along my jawline again. I arch into him, loving the feel of his chest brushing against my nipples.

"I love you," I say on a sigh. I love him so much.

His lips smile against mine before he kisses me. "I love you too."

With his mouth on mine, the thrusts strengthen and my breath catches. Sensual Callahan is lovely, but when he's rough with me, I've never felt more wanted. There's nothing like being at his mercy when he loses control. His passion completely untamed. It's so undeniably sexy.

"Harder, Cal," I whisper, wanting to bring him to the brink. His rough hands dig into my soft curves as he snaps his hips, taking me without hesitation. "So good," I mumble.

That pressure from my almost-orgasm earlier returns, and I relish the sensation of pleasure building.

He peers down, and my gaze follows as he observes himself pumping in and out. "You're doing so well, Scottie." He slows, withdrawing completely, then filling me to the hilt, forcing every thick inch inside. "Look at the way you take it all… so fucking perfect."

I weep at the fullness. Every part of me feels complete with him. We still have a lot of work to do, but when we're connected like this, it feels like we could take on the world together. Our love will only grow stronger. My thighs squeeze against him as I pull his body closer.

"That's my pretty girl. You're doing so good, almost there. Come on," he urges. My pussy grows tighter around him. "This time, you're going to fall over the edge with me, understand?"

I nod eagerly against his chest, needing the release. *Oh god.* Bliss surges through me until white flashes behind my eyes, and the tension snaps. I come harder than I have before. My pulse pounds in my ears as he burrows deep, spilling inside me.

As soon as our bodies slow and our panting eases, he sinks his hands into my hair. I've never felt like I belong so much as I do right here. My nails scrape across the nape of his neck, and he shivers.

This is home. This is true love. This is *living.*

"Thank you."

He chuckles. "For what?"

"For fighting for me."

EPILOGUE
CALLAHAN

ONE YEAR LATER

The weather is exactly what I was hoping for. Quell's Peak is still chilly in the early morning hours before the sun's come up, but there's no freak storm that has us trapped this time. In fact, it's been abnormally warm this season. Scottie and I hiked in yesterday, together this time, through the new pass the park service made. After people saw the result of the rockslide, Scottie became somewhat of a local celebrity as the hiker who survived.

As we lie in bed, she spins in my arms so she's facing me. I'm almost positive she's still asleep. I brush my thumb over the scar along her hairline. Her ginger-blonde locks are still mussed from last night when I took her on that bed like I have so many times before. I had her ride me until she got herself off. Glancing over, I grin at the memory.

I wanted to celebrate how far we've come after a year together, and what better place to do it than where it all started. It's a surreal feeling being back here under such different circumstances. It even looks different. This time around, we can keep the shutters open on the catwalk, allowing us to take in the gorgeous 360-degree view from inside the tower while being warm and toasty in front of the woodburning stove.

I press a kiss to her forehead and slip out of bed to add another log to the stove and get started on making us some coffee. The movement rouses her, and she blinks a few times, then simpers at me from across the room as I set up the camp stove.

"I love you," she says from bed.

She makes me smile with more contentment than I've ever known.

Our love story was a twisted trail. We had to fight to get here, but we made it—and the view is worth every step.

"I love you too."

Scottie

While he waits for the water to heat, Cal crawls back in bed behind me and curves his body around mine. It's not long before the water is hot enough to mix in the bitter instant coffee we brought with us. He sits up, and I push him back down again. "I've got it."

Swinging my legs over the side of the bed, I stand and stretch in front of the flames of the wood stove. Their warmth is welcome now that I'm outside the cozy covers. I pour a couple mugs of coffee and set them aside, gazing outside and admiring the pink rays that slowly creep over the mountain tops.

"The sun is just coming over the peaks. I'm gonna watch it from outside," I say, shoving my feet into my cold hiking boots. I should have left them by the fire last night. "Wanna watch it with me?"

I shrug on my coat and zip it up, then clutch my steaming mug of coffee to keep me warm.

"In a little bit." He snuggles deeper in the covers. "I'm too cozy to move."

I chuckle and open the door to the morning chill, hurrying to close it behind me so I don't let in too much cold air. Stepping onto the catwalk, I quickly appreciate how nice it is to hear the hollow sound of my boots rather than the crunch of snow from last year.

A year ago, it wasn't nearly as clear as it is today, and I've been looking forward to the sunrise more than anything... well, almost. Last night, Callahan pulled out all the romantic stops and even brought our beloved Battleship game along, which led to many other fun activities. For a moment, I thought he might even propose, but it's okay that he didn't. Things have been going so well, there's no rush. I never could have imagined life to be *this* wonderful. It's not always easy, but it's always good. There's no rush for us to take the next leap; we're going at our own speed.

The cherry on top was meeting Jonathan's boyfriend last week. I looked like a nutjob when I bawled, but seeing the happiness and *pride* in his eyes as he introduced Oscar to us had my heart bursting. I breathe in the fresh morning air and quietly recite my daily affirmations.

"Wow," Callahan says, stepping outside in his coat and boots.

"Isn't it beautiful?"

"It sure is." He wraps his arms around my torso, tucking me into his body. I set my coffee on the railing and lean into his warmth as the rays climb over the top of the mountain and paint the landscape in pinks and oranges. The rising sun setting the sky on fire.

I'm in awe of the landscape before us. It's hard to believe it's this majestic on a daily basis. I silently say a small prayer of thanks for Callahan and the beauty of this moment with him. I gasp when he holds out a box in front of me, and I freeze, wide-eyed.

Ohmygod.

He opens the box to a stunning pear-shaped diamond ring that shoots off a million blazing sparkles in the light of the sunrise.

"True love isn't the same as love at first sight. It's not your first love. It's the one you can stand with in a storm. It's having them see everything you lack and hearing you're worthy. It's fighting for them when they don't know how. It's the one who lights the darkest parts of your soul on fire so life can bloom again. It's hearing those three words and truly understanding their meaning."

I spin in his arms and clasp his broad shoulders. Tears swell with all the love I have for this man.

"Still with me?" he asks.

Standing on my tiptoes, I press my lips to his, then offer him my left hand.

This is the real thing. This is what I've been seeking all my life, and I found it with Callahan, at the top of a mountain.

"Always."

ACKNOWLEDGMENTS

Mark, my dear husband, you survived another book. A more patient and encouraging man doesn't exist. Thank you for the sacrifices, dinners, and words of support along the way. I couldn't chase this dream without you by my side. I love you.

Paisley and Dani, can you believe we did it? How did this happen so fast? We wrote these bad boys in record time (at least I did). It's an honor to share this series with you. It's been amazing getting to work together, collaborate, and intertwine our characters into the beautiful small town of Sky Ridge! Without you, I'm not sure when I would have sat down to write this story that's been in my heart for years.

Bri, our developmental editor. Thank you for editing all three books to make sure we didn't have any major issues when it came to weaving our stories and timelines together. As usual, you knocked it out of the park. I'm so happy to have you as not only my editor, but as a close friend and confidant. I love you lots!

My line and copy editor, and dear friend, Dee. I know I say it all the time, but I'm so happy to have found you early on and am grateful to have someone who can not only find my mistakes, but help me improve as a writer. I'm sure you're pleased as hell I didn't make anybody "chew thoughtfully" this time around. Biggest hugs!

Cathryn, our formatter who made these babies as pretty on the inside as they are on the outside and coordinated all of our interiors—thank you!

The Whiskey Ginger, Loni. My god, woman. You sure know how to make one hell of a cover. When I had the idea for this series, I never thought I'd have a cover to do the story justice. But here I am hoping the story does justice to the cover. You're a beautiful person, inside and out, and it's been an awesome experience getting to know you. The Cape was amazing. We'll always have oysters.

My content team: Catie (graphics), Rachel (street team manager), Shannon (PA and reader group manager), and Kenz (TikTok/reels), who kept this train on the tracks, despite dealing with three authors who attempted to derail it on several occasions! This launch would not have happened without you. Thank you for your endless diligence, hard work, and unbelievable organization.

The series beta readers: Jess, Kara, Katie, Mel, Rose, and Trish. Y'all are rockstars for beta reading three books in a row! I'm not sure how you did it, but we're incredibly grateful for your feedback! Our books wouldn't be this good without you. For sure Callahan would have been a bigger asshole.

My team beta readers: Catie, Emma, Kailey, Kenz, Lorelei, Nicole, and Shannon. Y'all did it again. Thank you for always finding new ways to make my stories better and sex dirtier! I am so grateful to have you as friends, even if I'm not in the Discord as often as I'd like to be. Love always, Beefer Sutherland.

Our fantastic team of ARC readers who somehow managed to read all three books in a short amount of time—not to mention, the holidays shoved somewhere in there. You accomplished a near impossible feat, and we are forever grateful for your reviews that help make our release day so much fun! We hope you love it!

The Sloane St. James Street Team—y'all rocked this one, thank you so much for spreading the word about this awesome series! I am forever grateful and honored that you are willing to share my content with your audiences and followers.

Big love to my Good Girl Book Club! It warms my heart that a group of 1500+ readers found each other through the Lakes Hockey Series. Here's to hopefully even more readers in the new year!

Victoria Wilder, my beautiful friend, thank you for helping me fix my blurb and make it amazing. What would I do without you?

Lesley and her husband, my ambulance experts. Thank you so much for proofing that scene and making sure it was as accurate as fucking in the back of an ambulance could be.

S—I could not have written this book without you. Your knowledge, guidance, and infinite patience helped me understand wildland firefighters and the immense challenges they face. More importantly, your humor, vulnerability, and friendship helped me understand Callahan. Thank you for breathing life into my character and sharing such a personal and meaningful piece of yourself. I apologize for making him less of an asshole than you would have preferred. Blame the beta readers.

C—thank you for answering my questions, and sharing tons of valuable information and reports! Hopefully your girlfriend appreciates the shoutout!

r/wildfire. This community is the most lovable group of straight-up assholes I've ever had the joy of interacting with. Thank you for allowing me into your space to ask questions and work through scenarios. I cannot tell you how much I've enjoyed learning about the work you do and listening to your stories. Y'all are fucking disgusting. Never change.

SERIES ORDER

Volume 1
FIGHT by Sloane St. James

Volume 2
PROTECT by Paisley Hope

Volume 3
HONOR by Danielle Baker

MORE BOOKS BY SLOANE ST. JAMES

Lakes Hockey Series

Before We Came
Strong and Wild
In The Game
Stand and Defend

Rogues Hockey Series

Coach Sully

WELCOME TO
THE SLOANE ZONE

Thank you so much for reading Fight!
If you enjoyed it, please help spread the word by leaving a
review on Amazon, Goodreads, Bookbub, Facebook Reader
Groups, Booktok, Bookstagram, or wherever you talk about
romance. If you already have, you have my endless gratitude. I
hope you sleep well knowing that you are making some
woman's mid-life crisis dreams come true!

I love to connect with my readers!
SloaneStJamesWrites@gmail.com
Instagram / TikTok @SloaneStJames

Facebook Reader Group:
Sloane's Good Girl Book Club

Interested in my future signing events, other books, and merch?
SloaneStJames.com

Made in the USA
Coppell, TX
27 February 2025

46457572R00215